DARK EDEN BOOK ONE

# GARDEN OF ECHOES AND ASH

## J. EMBER HINTZ

*To Debra*
*for inspiring me to calculate the probabilities*
*in this life, and the next*

# Chapter One

# RENAE

A SIGN DEPICTING THE goddess Pele's fierce face warned traversing the active volcano was dangerous. Her sun-faded sneer, however, didn't stop me from ducking beneath the barrier and sneaking into the national park each morning before dawn.

Shards of moonlight pierced the cloud cover, illuminating what remained of the old Hawaiian road and the fingers of black rock that stretched across it like claws claiming their victim. My feet thudded against the ground until the pavement disappeared, and all signs of civilization vanished. Buried beneath a blanket of basalt.

I needed to run—to feel my lungs cleave and my calves cramp as I pushed my husk beyond its engineered limits. The resulting pain from ripped hamstrings and torn ligaments sharpened my focus and temporarily obliterated everything else inside my head. Running was the only therapy I needed, despite my handler's insistence to the contrary, and the low slope of the volcano offered the perfect training ground. Wide open spaces and no human witnesses.

Coarse rock crunched beneath my sneakers as I traversed Kilauea's restricted eastern rift zone. Everything that once thrived here had inch-by-inch and day-by-day been consumed by the slow grip of death. Yet there, between the cracks, rooted in ash, dozens of wind-weary bushes flowered, despite the insurmountable odds. Pink needle-like blossoms turned their faces upward toward the rain with defiant smiles.

The clouds converged and swallowed the moon. A steady drizzle soaked through my clothes as I surveyed the lava flats for the tell-tale orange glow of dangerous hot spots. I mapped a safe trail in my head and set the timer on my watch. All the pent-up energy inside me uncoiled like a spring, and I sped forward across the cracked earth. The rush of cool air over my wet skin sent a charge of static prickling down my spine. Pleasure and pain took turns dominating my sensory receptors. I couldn't tell which was worse, the friction rubbing my thighs raw or the violent impact of each footfall. Rain bit my cheeks like thousands of stinging needles, reminding me what it meant to be alive.

Sulfur-laced air stung my lungs as the black rock shifted beneath me. The thick charcoal crust gave way, releasing a wave of lung-searing gas. I lunged forward. The world became a blur as my feet flew, almost weightless, over the forsaken ground, leaving a putrid trail of melted rubber in my wake.

I didn't stop running until I crashed through the barricade at the edge of the closed road. It toppled over, and I slid across the pavement on my hands and knees. Each breath was like fire in my lungs as I rolled onto my back in the middle of the street and checked my watch.

Three minutes. My fastest time yet. A notification popped up on the watch's square screen. A new message from my handler. I loosened a sigh from my lungs. The shredded flesh on my palms and knees burned as it knit together, the explosion of power well worth the temporary pain and lecture sure to follow.

I stood and opened Ziggy's message. *We talked about this.* Gods help me. I could almost hear her chastising tone.

I sent her a voice to text message. "Took a minor spill on my run. Not a big deal."

Her response was immediate. *Not a big deal? Your pain vectors spiked off the chart.*

I rubbed the tender new flesh on my palms and spoke into my wrist again. "Already healed. Your *asset* is still in one piece, but thanks for checking up on me."

*This conversation is not over.*

I bit back a scowl as I reset the barricade and headed toward the sallow light creeping across the island from Hilo. Another day in paradise.

My empty stomach twisted as I stepped into my musty apartment. The running shoes, melted beyond repair, went into the trash like the others that had come before them. Sacrifices to my obsession. I opened the fridge and ripped the lid off a family-size container of mac salad, shoveling the tangy, mayonnaise-laden noodles into my mouth by the spoonful. When it was empty, I poured a glass of ice-cold milk and stirred in the chalky powder—a concoction of vitamins, nutrients, and gods knows what else to keep my husk operating at peak condition. The chocolate flavor did little to hide the awful metallic tang as I choked it down. The oily film clung to my teeth, tongue, and throat as I checked on my roommates.

Thirty-seven plants in various stages of death filled every available space. Test subjects rescued from neglected front porches, dumpsters, or curbside piles of trash. My personal plant hospice program. Unsanctioned training on humans or any other animal wasn't allowed until a burgeoning healer could successfully transfer energy from one living organism to another without killing the donor. The desiccated remains of my horticultural donors were stacked in empty pots on the kitchen balcony.

The ability to heal without harm could take decades to hone. Interfering with the life force of a human without a direct order was prohibited and grounds for immediate termination. My plant hospice ward was a hobby, a stone to sharpen my fledgling gift against to keep it from atrophying while I worked my way through the ranks of the Corps.

I washed the volcano's sulfuric stink from my hair and pulled on the blue dress. An impulse buy my first day on the island. The same vivid color as the ocean, bright and full of life. The low-cut halter stood out in stark contrast against the rest of my practical wardrobe. It complemented my pale complexion and auburn hair and I didn't hate the way it hid my thick thighs and gave the illusion of cleavage. The dress was my only true personal possession. The one thing I owned that hadn't been calculated or contrived to support the role I was here to play. I wore it to every meeting with my handler. Ziggy couldn't see it, of course, my avatar being clad in the Corps' white uniform during our virtual sessions, but I wore the blue dress, nonetheless.

I dropped onto the stiff couch with a grunt and pried the bean-shaped neural-lace activators from their molded foam box before placing them in my ears. It was mid-afternoon for her in New York. A tickling sensation crawled through my ear canal as I waited for the pods to connect with the neural-lace mesh embedded in my brain. A haze clouded my vision as my consciousness was transported to the virtual meeting space.

Ziggy sat behind a white glass desk in one of the Nursery's above-ground offices. Sunlight filtered through the trees, casting elongated shadows across the frozen lake and training fields beyond the remote compound.

"Punctual as usual," Ziggy said as she scrolled through a report on the desktop that doubled as a monitor. Her avatar took the form of a middle-aged woman with dark circles under tired gray eyes and the hint of a French accent—an intentional resemblance to my human mother, dead eighty years, and an overt attempt to manipulate my trust. Nothing was as it seemed with the Corps. Ziggy could be a bald man in a Nebraska basement or one of the Corps' new AI programs for all I knew. I'd never actually met her in person. All of our sessions, even during my training at the Nursery, had been virtual. I'd been assigned to her the day I'd taken my husk. She'd overseen my progress in the trials and was my only avenue to promotion and ticket off this infernal island.

"Your bio-log shows a decline in benzodiazepine levels. You stopped taking the pills." Not a question. The tracker at the base of my skull connected to the neural-lace embedded in my brain and monitored everything—blood chemistry, brain activity, heart rate. Even my location. It probably told her what I ate for breakfast.

"The pills dull my senses and make everything taste like ash." I reached out to touch the striped leaf of a plant by the window. It flickered as my fingers passed through the simulation.

"Are you still having the nightmares?"

I focused on each breath in and out, keeping my heart rate even as I lied. "No."

My chest tightened as Ziggy let loose a sigh, so much like my dead mother's—a sigh that carried the frustration of being burdened with a broken child.

I shoved the unwanted memory back into the tomb where I'd buried it and stared out the window to the footpath across the frozen lake. A shortcut I'd taken a hundred times between the Nursery and compound where my trainers and fellow recruits had tried to kill me on a daily basis. "I don't need the sleeping pills, not on days when I can run," I said.

"You need to find an alternate coping mechanism. These runs of yours are too dangerous."

I plastered a plastic smile on my face. "It was only a minor injury. I need to stay in shape and maintain peak performance for my first mission."

Her eyes narrowed. "You need to keep that husk of yours in one piece." Ziggy flung a hand toward the window and the untamed wilderness beyond. "Or have you forgotten why you're here?"

Three years of intense training at the Nursery followed by two monotonous months of probation working my boring cover job at the telescope facility had me itching for an active mission. I willed casual indifference into my voice as I inspected my sharp nails and resisted the urge to clench my fists. "How long before I'm assigned a real mission?"

"Protecting the secrets of the dead is a *real* mission." Ziggy leaned back in her chair and locked her gray eyes on my face. "If you don't believe that, you shouldn't be here."

All that training and honing of my primary gift just to sit on the sidelines and babysit a bunch of bobblehead astronomers was not what I signed up for. "The Corps trained me to track down wayward souls, not to waste my reaper gift in a support role."

Ziggy folded her arms over her chest the way she did before launching into a lecture. "Hacking NASA's observational data to prevent humans from discovering the entrance to Almega is not a support role. You take far too many risks, like these volcano runs. One misstep, and you'll find yourself back in the city of the dead, explaining your negligence to the Nūkiri. Trust me, we do not want to draw their attention or their wrath." She swiped her hand over her desk and closed the report. "You're to cease all visits to Kilauea, effective immediately."

The corners of my perception blurred as my syphons unfurled from my back—six oil-black appendages, invisible to the naked eye. My daily run was the only thing keeping the nightmares at bay.

"I'll be more careful, I promise." How I managed to keep my voice steady despite the bile burning at the back of my throat was beyond me.

Ziggy's eyes darted to the inky black shape that pulsed and twisted on her screen. A metric from my tracker. "I'm sorry, Renae. It's not worth the risk. You're an asset I cannot afford to lose right now. If you want to pass your probation, you'll keep taking the pills. They may dampen your senses, but they'll make it easier to cope with your past life trauma."

I forced my shoulders to slump in feigned defeat. Ziggy was my only avenue to promotion, and like it or not, I needed to comply with her orders.

"When you're ready, we can try talking about the nightmares, look for patterns to determine your triggers, and discuss ways to cope with them. That's what these sessions are for, to help you adjust to the side effects of living in human skin again."

My preferred coping mechanism was avoidance—staying away from enclosed spaces, motorcycles, and men in uniform. But it was impossible to avoid the unexpected catalysts that could send me into a downward spiral: a child's shrill scream, the noxious scent of gasoline, or the claustrophobic press of warm bodies against mine in a crowd.

Ziggy's face softened as she clasped her hands and rested her forearms on the desk. "There's no hurry, Renae. Some trainees take years to acclimate. Be patient and be careful with your husk. Its self-healing properties have their limits. Your body belongs to the Corps, and if they can't trust you to take care of it, you'll be deactivated and sent back to Almega. Do you understand?"

I bit down on my tongue and silenced the response that would do me no favors. I had no interest in getting kicked out of the Corps and returning to the sensory deprived hell that was the afterlife.

"Good. Now, let's discuss your socialization training. Despite what they drill into you at the Nursery, maintaining your cover is the most important tenet." Ziggy brought her index fingers and thumbs together over her sternum. A four pointed eye representing the Watcher Corps' creed. Destiny. Loyalty. Anonymity. Eternity.

The symbol was stamped on everything the Corps touched. A reminder that the dead were always watching.

"I want you to engage with the humans. Get to know your neighbors, strike up a conversation with someone at a coffee shop. If you really want to impress me, make some friends. Better yet, get laid."

"You know I don't like *people* and have trouble reining in my gift with skin-to-skin contact."

"Establishing a relationship without compromising your cover will go a long way toward proving your readiness for an unsupervised mission. It doesn't need to be sexual, but two birds, one stone." The corner of Ziggy's thin lips twitched up as if shoving me out of my comfort zone amused her. "This is your next test."

❧

Blood trickled from my ear as I ripped out the pods and hurled them across the room. The burrowing filaments hissed as they reeled back inside the bean-shaped devices bouncing across the tile floor.

The Corps encouraged operatives to get intimate with their marks. My current mark was a government database, and we were already very well acquainted. My job at the observatory, however, located atop the tallest peak on Earth if you measured from the sea floor, required limited interpersonal interaction. As much as I hated to admit it, Ziggy was right. To earn my rank, I needed to prove I could live among humans without blowing my cover.

After twisting my damp hair into a tight knot, I slipped on a pair of sandals and grabbed a shopping tote on my way out the door. Since my daily volcano run was no longer an option, I planned to focus on my second favorite distraction—gorging myself on all the flavors and textures I could shove into my mouth.

While I preferred to walk, most days, I took the bus, which provided ample opportunity to exercise my primary gift. The one that had gotten me recruited into the Corps. Physical contact amplified my reaper abilities, translating a soul's energy into flavors and textures in my mouth along with other intense physical sensations. I avoided touching people in general, but unfortunately, my gift had a will of its own.

At the bus stop, I watched a woman with two small children. The older child, a young boy, played with his mother's umbrella. He pressed the release button and erupted into an effervescent froth of laughter when the red shield popped open in front of him and sent a spray of wet drops in every direction. Several bystanders stepped back in irritation.

"Taka! Give me that!" his mother yelled and adjusted the infant in her lap as she reached for the umbrella. The boy moved out of arm's reach. An impish grin broke across his round face as he collapsed the spines, pointed it at her, and pressed the release button again. I bit back a smile as the water freckled her face.

"Boy, you wanna smack?" Her eyes widened as she glared at him with pursed lips.

His shoulders drooped, and I allowed my syphons to unfurl and latch on to him. Children were an easy read. Pure, unadulterated energy. No muddled flavors. The delicate filaments of my gift extended from the mouths of my syphons and swept through his subconscious, tasting his emotions. Sourness bloomed on my tongue as the woman returned her gaze to the little girl in her lap. I bit my lip until it bled and resisted the urge to scoop the boy up in my arms and tell him I understood his need to be seen.

I focused on the metallic tang in my mouth and throbbing lip as I reeled in all but one of my syphons. Pain was a powerful anchor. Any inconspicuous torment worked: snapping the elastic hair band I wore on my wrist, pinching the loose skin between my thumb and forefinger, or digging my pointed nails into my palm. Pain allowed me to ground myself in my own skin while I treaded through someone else's subconscious energy.

As the fresh wound on my lip healed, I pressed my thumbnail against the knuckle of my middle finger and continued to watch the boy and his mother. He plopped down next to her in a huff. She put her arm around his shoulders and kissed the top of his head.

"Mahalo, Taka," she said into his coal-black hair.

A fizzy lemon-lime sweetness bubbled at the back of my tongue and climbed into my nose as he rested his cheek against his mother's chest. Love. Untainted by fear, need, desire, or any of the other emotions adults often confused it with. I sucked it in and fed on its pureness, careful not to take too much and contaminate myself. I focused on the pain in my hand and released my syphon, ending my intrusion into the intimate moment between mother and child as the bus ambled up to the curb and stopped with a hiss of foul air.

My empty stomach grumbled as I plopped into a hard seat and pulled out a bag of Skittles to stave off the low blood sugar side effects of exercising my power. Used in small doses, it caused hypoglycemia, dilated pupils, and fatigue. Excessive sweating, a racing heart, and blurred vision were sure signs that I'd used too much. The key to avoiding total burnout was to eat constantly, sugar, carbs, anything to keep my blood sugar levels from dropping me into an involuntary hibernation.

My syphons shifted beneath my skin toward a bleached blonde with greasy dark roots sitting across the aisle. She could have been thirty or sixty. Her gaunt, ragged body made it impossible to guess. My gift hummed with the urge to read her, and holding it back consumed as much energy as unleashing it. I let my syphons loose, and they immediately burrowed into her.

A sharp burning sensation climbed my throat as her debilitating need gripped me. I ground my nails into my thigh. Addicts were a dangerous read. If I lingered too long, that need could infect one or all of my syphons, then spread through my system like poison, corrupting everything it touched. The effect could last hours or days.

However, if I could sift through her memories and find the right thread, one tainted with the same acidic burn as her addiction, and pluck it out, it might lessen her burden and offer temporary relief, even if it couldn't cure her disease.

I braced my hand against the seat in front of me as I burrowed deeper into her spectrum. The woman, oblivious to the psychic intrusion, shifted in her seat. Acid ate away at my sternum as I followed the thread of guilt through her subconscious. It wound around everything like a tourniquet. I couldn't remove it without taking it all, every single memory. Gods, I didn't have the stomach for that—stripping a lifetime of memories without consent. I yanked my gift back before pulling my water bottle from my bag and sucking it down to wash her taste from my mouth.

The bus lurched forward. I'd missed my stop and had to backtrack several blocks to the farmers market. My steps quickened when I caught the whiff of sweet fried dough. Gorging myself was both a hobby and necessity driven by my unyielding metabolism, and I took immense pleasure in the pursuit of my gluttony. After devouring a double order of andagi, I threw away the grease-stained bag and made my way to the flower stalls to purchase a new donor plant from my favorite vendor.

His booth was packed with blooming orchids of every color, along with an assortment of philodendrons and other plants I didn't know the names of. The old man's dark eyes lit up and I let the warm embrace of his energy cocoon around me. Even in their dormant human forms, isolators—souls blessed with the protective gift—could draw you in and hold you under their spell.

"Ah, Miss Renae. I thought we might see you today," he said as he gestured toward the dripping tarps that covered most of the outdoor market stalls. The skin around his eyes crinkled when he smiled. His weathered face a wrinkled road map and testament to the long journey of his life. "You only shop when it rains. Fewer customers; better deals for you."

*And no crowds.* Already, patrons were beginning to cramp the aisles. I ran my fingers over the leaves of several of the smaller potted plants, assessing their suitability as donors for my horticultural hospice program.

"Another orchid for you, perhaps?" He tugged on his ear as he gestured to a display of blooming plants.

"I need something sturdy and hard to kill. What do you recommend?"

A low chuckle floated from behind the lush foliage. Mr. Ito nodded to a young man who sat partially hidden by the towering display. "My grandson would be delighted to help you select a suitable specimen."

The younger man glanced up from his tablet, and I couldn't look away. He was the perfect likeness to the old man. The same tousled black hair and sparkling eyes, yet unravaged by time. Not a single line or freckle marred his smooth skin.

"You should try one of our Forever Fresh preserved plants. They don't need sunlight or water and can last for several years if kept indoors. It's technically already dead, so you can't kill it."

"I think I'd prefer something of the mortal variety," I said.

"Then you should go with the devil's ivy." He picked up a vine-like plant and handed it to me. "It's hardy, not too fussy, and easy to propagate in water." Feathered lashes fanned his cheeks as he fingered through the leaves. "See all these root nodes? Multiple clones can be duplicated from this single plant in a matter of weeks. If you kill this one, you'll have plenty of backups."

"Perfect." I held out a crumpled bill, damp from my sweaty palm, and took possession of my next victim.

Mr. Ito hoisted himself up on a bamboo cane. His grandson fumbled beneath the table and pulled out a cooler, as if responding to some unspoken command between them. "I have something else for you, my dear." The old man's eyes sparkled as he took the cooler and pulled out a black blossom that resembled a spider with six curling legs and reminded me of my syphons.

"A rare bloom for a rare soul," Mr. Ito said. He bowed and presented the flower on reverent palms.

The expression on the younger man's face warned declining the gift would be a great offense.

"Thank you, it's lovely," I said as I took the flower, surprised it wasn't nearly as delicate as it appeared. "Should I put it in water?"

"No, you must wear it, my dear." Mr. Ito placed a shaky hand on the table to steady himself and nodded to his grandson.

The younger man stepped out of the stall with a box of pins. "Wear it behind your left ear to symbolize that you already belong to someone, or on the right to indicate your interest in finding a lover." His golden skin flushed as he pulled a hairpin out of the acrylic box and leaned closer, lowering his voice. "And it would please my grandfather very much." He held up a bobby pin and nodded to the odd blossom resting in my palm.

I released my syphons and probed his spectrum. He tasted herbal and astringent, like a too-strong cologne used to cover something else. Careful not to graze his fingers, I took the pin and secured the flower to my bun, centered at the top so the ruffled petals cascaded down both sides. I didn't know what that symbolized, but it had to be better than advertising that I was owned, or worse, hoping to be owned by someone.

"Thank you, Mr. Ito," I said to the older man. "I'm honored by your kindness."

"A flower need not thank the wind for singing its name. Tell me, Jason, what do you think of our little blossom now?"

"Exquisite." An unabashed grin tugged at the corners of the younger man's heart-shaped lips. "I'm Jason, by the way." He thrust a palm toward me.

I reined in my gift before extending a tentative hand, planning to grasp only the tips of his fingers and let go quickly to diminish the impact of physical contact. Jason's hand shot forward and enveloped mine, holding it hostage as his essence exploded across all five of my senses. Shady green spaces, hands plunging into cool soil, the aroma of moss and dirt, a warm blanket of sunbaked earth tucked tight around me. When the whirling sensations stopped, I realized I was clutching his hand with both of mine.

"Renae," I said, more than a little breathless as I pulled back and snapped the elastic band at my wrist.

"The girl who runs in the rain."

Every muscle in my body tensed. Had he seen me? I'd been so careful on my daily pre-dawn runs. My eyes darted behind him, searching for the nearest exit.

"I'm not a stalker, I promise." He raised his arms in innocence before stooping to pick up his tablet and sliding it into a messenger bag that he slung over his head in one smooth motion.

"We're neighbors. I'm 17A, the unit below yours. You run, every day, rain or shine." Jason glanced at the elder Mr. Ito, who sat and began cleaning his glasses. "I've seen you come in a few times on my way to work." He took a step forward and spoke so only I could hear. "I think my grandfather has a crush on you."

Heat crept up my cheeks as I stepped back, putting space between us. "He's a welcoming old soul," I said. Mr. Ito was nearly the age I might have been had my first human life not been ripped from me too soon. "He was the first person I met when I arrived in Hilo."

"Let me guess," Jason said, tugging on his ear just as his grandfather had done. An inherited nervous tick. "You moved to paradise to escape a miserable climate, only to realize that it rains here every single day."

"I transferred here for work."

"What do you do?"

"I'm in IT." Technically, not a lie.

"Vague title. What do you actually do?" he asked.

"I'm a systems engineer at one of the observatories on Mauna Kea. I spend most of my time keeping otherwise intelligent people from breaking stuff and ruining everything."

Jason laughed.

I wasn't joking.

"What kind of job gets you up before dawn to spy on your neighbors?"

"I help my grandfather manage the nursery." He gripped the strap of his bag and rocked back on his heels. "Are you into plants?"

"You could say that."

"We're looking for a part-time preservation assistant." He flinched as a fat drop of water fell from the leaking roof and landed in the middle of his forehead. "If you're interested, I'd be happy to give you a tour of the greenhouse."

Gods, working in a greenhouse would be a dream. And a great way to blow my cover when I accidentally wiped out their entire inventory with my pitiful healing gift.

"I already have a job."

Jason trailed behind me as I moved toward the exit. "Do you like coffee? DaGrindz is right around the corner. We can grab something to drink, and I can tell you how to propagate the pothos." He nodded to the plant in my hand.

"Maybe another time." I glanced at my watch. "I still have some shopping to do before work."

"I'd be happy to walk with you; help you haggle with the vendors like a local." He flashed me a toothy grin. Gods, the man was annoyingly persistent.

"Fine." I bit back a scowl and let him lead me through the market stalls. He pointed out which vendors I could negotiate with and the ones who had different prices for tourists and locals. I bought a pineapple and two papayas but passed on the mangos he assured me weren't in season yet and had probably been imported. We passed racks of bright sarongs and floral shirts, tables laden with produce, homemade soaps, carved trinkets, and handmade jewelry.

"I'm relieved we could meet this way," he said, twisting to walk backward. "It saves me the indignity of lurking around the parking lot, waiting for the opportunity to bump into you."

"That was your plan?" I stopped to pick up an avocado from a produce stall.

"I worried you might carry mace, and I wasn't sure how that would turn out for me."

"Badly," I said. As a reaper, I could render a man unconscious or suck out a soul with my syphons. I had nothing to fear from humans. Not anymore.

As we approached the exit, a table covered with dried flowers and an assortment of shells caught my attention.

"Are these edible?" I asked as I leaned forward to inspect a basket of desiccated berries that smelled faintly like a tomato vine.

Jason shrugged. "This booth belongs to Aunty Cici. She specializes in homeopathic tinctures and remedies. The old-timers swear by her concoctions, and her predictions."

A robust woman in a floral skirt and matching blouse sauntered toward us. A ring of glossy leaves crowned her nest of salt and pepper curls. "May I help you find something?" The left side of her round face was beautiful. The other half sagged, lifeless—the result of a stroke, perhaps. I released my syphons and attempted to latch on to her spectrum.

The woman's mahogany eyes narrowed as I tried to read her. Each time I attempted to latch on, my gift recoiled.

"Come, child, give me your hand. I'll read your fortune. No charge for the first time."

I glanced at Jason. His amused shrug was no help. "I... I should be going." If the woman truly possessed the gift of sight, I needed to stay as far away from her as possible. Before I could move, her hands shot out and she grasped my forearm.

"Watch your step *ānela*. The road ahead is dark and covered in broken glass." A chill crept down my spine as her absent expression vanished, replaced by a crooked smile.

# CHAPTER TWO

# LIAM

RAIN-SLICK ASPHALT MADE THE island's wicked curves even more treacherous.

Logan was gonna be bent about me being late for another AA meeting. He'd taken me under his wing three years ago when I stumbled into his physics class still drunk from the night before. As my sponsor and friend, he was supportive as hell. As my boss and PhD advisor, he had zero chill and zero patience for my bullshit excuses.

I accelerated on the last straightaway before town. My skin crawled as a feminine electronic voice sounded inside my helmet. It had been a hell of a lot easier to silence the phantom voices before I'd gotten sober. Fortunately, this one was an alert from my cell phone. "Incoming call from Connor Riley."

Five thousand miles between us, and my older brother still checked up on me once a week, right before my meeting. "Accept Call. Hey Connor. What's up?"

"I've got good news. I'm headed your way next month for a conference. Think you can finagle a few days off to entertain me?"

I backed off the throttle and sat up straighter. The last time I saw my brother was in the hospital the day before our father died. The old man refused to see me, and I didn't stick around for the funeral or fake grief.

"Yea, I think I can swing that."

He rattled off the dates and his flight information. "I can text you the info as well."

"No, I got it." My sharp memory for anything with numbers had gotten me through a double master's in physics and astronomy.

"How's everything there? You good?"

We both knew he was referring to my sobriety. Connor meant well, but I could hear his silent suspicions all the way from fucking Brooklyn. "I start my six-week rotation tonight at the university's telescope facility. I should have all the data I need to defend my thesis by the end of the semester."

"That's great. Patrick and I will fly out to see you walk across that stage."

I downshifted into a curve. "That's not necessary."

"The fuck it isn't. I'm proud of you, Lee. We'll be there. Look, I gotta run. I have to scrub in for surgery. Are you sure you don't need me to send you my flight info?"

My cheeks pressed into the helmet padding as I grinned. "I'm sure."

As soon as he hung up, I hit the throttle and sped toward Hilo.

The electronic voice sounded again as I approached the outskirts of town. "Incoming call from Monika Komahaya."

"Ignore."

The voice chimed again. "Incoming call from Monika Komahaya."

"Ignore."

"Incoming call from Monika Komahaya."

*Jesus Christ.* "Accept call." I downshifted as I approached the yellow light, hoping to zip through before it changed. The asshole in front of me slammed on his brakes. I skidded to a stop six inches from his bumper.

"Hey, Mons, what's up?"

"We need to talk."

My jaw clenched. "I'm on my way to a meeting."

"Can you stop by the café after?"

"I can swing by around three, after class. Everything okay?" The light changed. No one moved.

"Yeah, of course. I'll make you a triple-shot and we can chat." It wasn't like Monika to be cryptic.

The light cycled through a second time.

"Sounds good." I glanced over my shoulder as I switched lanes and almost got sideswiped by the guy behind me who'd pulled out and tried to pass me on the outside. I laid on the throttle and shot ahead of him, then slammed on the brakes again as the turn lane came to a screeching halt. "Goddamn tourists," I muttered under my breath.

"Did you seriously try to drive through downtown on a Wednesday?"

"Yup." The light cycled a third time as the cars ahead of me waited for the hoard of pedestrians to cross Mamo Avenue. After five days of heavy rain, people were crawling out of the dirt like worms, wriggling their way to the overpriced and over-hyped farmers market.

A set of bells clanked in the background. "I got a customer. See ya at three?" Her voice pitched up at the end as if she half expected me to bail. It was a reasonable assumption.

"Yeah, I'll be there."

The muscles in my shoulders tightened as I revved the engine. Waianuenue Avenue was moving again. A chorus of angry horns greeted me as I zipped back into the straight lane. One more intersection, and it was a clean shot to the church. I squeezed the throttle, and my bike responded at once, gunning for the next green light.

A girl stepped out in front of me.

Time slowed, and I was acutely aware of everything.

The body my motorcycle was about to plow through.

Oncoming traffic.

The damp road.

Time raced forward as I laid on the brakes. The back tire locked up as I swerved to avoid the witless chick. My bike went into a sideways skid.

*Shit.*

The rear wheel swung out and nailed her with an audible crunch and blur of blue fabric that made my stomach heave. I eased up on the brake and fought to stay upright as my tire regained traction. But the road was too wet, and gravity was a bitch.

Metal gouged across pavement as my bike dragged me into oncoming traffic. Flesh peeled away from bone and a searing pain shot up my leg. Brakes screeched, and I heard a hard crack as my helmet slammed into something solid.

❧

Pale stars spiraled above me against a darkening sky. Blood-red grass as tall as my chest swayed as I took in the surroundings. The thick golden haze made it impossible to get any sort of bearing. There were others. Next to me. Behind me. Close. Something or someone compelled my body forward. I took one wobbling step, then another, despite not being able to feel my legs, or any other part of my body, for that matter.

A haunting, musical voice echoed through my head. More song than actual words. It wanted me to follow. I flung my arms out in search of my invisible companion. Iridescent gnat-like bugs swarmed around me, expelling a shimmering dust.

"What the fuck?" I stumbled back, trying to shake them off. My entire hand disintegrated into a cloud of hissing insects with every violent flick of my wrist, only to congeal again as the swarm reconsolidated.

"Do not be afraid," the voice said in an eerie melodic tone, coming from nowhere and everywhere. "Once the nymphites have established a colony around your energy, your transition will be complete."

I'd taken some whack trips down the rabbit hole before. This… this was something else. Somewhere else. "What the hell is this place?" I spun around, trying to figure out which direction I'd come from. It all looked the same, like a goddamned sea of blood.

"It's time to let go. Follow the sound of my—"

*Schgrack*. A crackle of static feedback split the air, followed by a loud hum in my chest where those bug things vibrated, flashing and changing colors frantically.

Another voice screamed in my ear. "Do not cross that field." The urgency in her words sent a sharp pain through my skull.

I fell to my knees and grasped my head. Swirling clouds of gold dust created a mirage of fleeting shapes and faceless strangers. They moved past me toward the other side of the field, where they disappeared through a massive black gate. Wherever they were headed, it had to be better than here with these fucking bugs trying to get under my skin. I managed to stand and stumbled forward a few steps before something exploded through my chest, knocking me flat on my ass and sending the hissing bugs sailing away from me.

Above me, the stars spiraled faster and faster in an unfamiliar sky. No, not stars, memories. My brother and I comparing purple tongues after getting hyped up on Monster Slurpees. The night our father demolished the Christmas tree in a drunken rage. Monika's competitive smile the day we met scratching it out at Pine Trees rocky reef break. The memories faded as they spun away.

"Don't let go." The soft words echoed through my head the same way those phantom voices had plagued me my entire life whenever I got upset. Voices I'd attempted to drown with drugs and alcohol.

A demon with a half-charred body and haunting gray eyes appeared above me. She wasn't like the other ghostly shapes moving across the field. Her burned form was solid and surrounded by looping flares of golden light and I wasn't afraid. I grasped her hand, and our bodies shot up, away from the field. Stars and galaxies blurred, speeding past us as we hurtled toward a familiar blue sphere. She released my hand, and I crashed through memories, stacked one on top of the other like panes of glass as the ground rushed up to meet me.

*

Pain pounded in my helmet as people spoke in muffled tones. Someone crouched next to me. A woman. I lifted my head. The movement sent the world spinning as the weight of my helmet dropped back to the pavement with a thud, setting off a wave of nausea and skull-cleaving fire.

"Please, try not to move," the woman said. Her voice quaked as she spoke. "You've been in an accident. The paramedics are on the way."

I squinted against the sun. My vision blurred as I tried to focus on her face and fought to keep my eyes open.

"Where am I?" The words sounded strange, miles away.

"The intersection of Keawe and... Haili, I think."

It all came rushing back. The accident. The blur of blue fabric. My stomach lurched. "There was a girl," I said. "I need to help her." Sweat pooled at my temples, fogging the inside of my helmet as I tried to sit up again.

"You *need* to stay put." The woman placed her hands on my shoulders, pinning me to the ground with a firm grip. "You could exacerbate your injuries."

"I hit someone. Please, you have to help her!" My head spun with images of the girl's panicked face and the sickening crunching noise her body made when I hit her.

"Try to relax. You don't need to worry about the girl. She's fine."

Sparklers popped behind my right eye. No way anyone would be fine after taking a hit like that. This woman was lying, trying to pacify me.

Someone needed to check on the damn girl. The pounding in my head threatened to put me under again.

"Sir, I need you to stay calm," the woman said as she tightened her grip on my shoulders. My skin tingled beneath the slow static shock of her touch.

There were several other muffled voices nearby. They asked if I was alive.

"Very much so," the woman said with a sarcastic grunt.

This wasn't a fucking joke. I reached up and fumbled with my chin strap. I needed to see the girl for myself. I'd never been the religious type, but I prayed she wasn't dead.

"He has a concussion, and his leg looks broken," the chick said to someone.

I wiggled my toes and rolled my left ankle from side to side. It hurt like a bitch. I shoved her hands away from my shoulders, sat up, and pulled off my helmet.

That was a mistake.

My stomach lurched as the two cans of Red Bull I'd chugged for breakfast came back up. I heaved over and hurled into the street between my knees. The woman grabbed my backpack and kept me from falling forward into a pile of my own vomit.

*Stubborn human. If I lose my job for this, I will come back and haunt you.* Her unspoken words drifted through my mind.

This woman was insufferable. I twisted, ready to rip into her, and came face to face with the girl in the blue dress. She was kneeling next to me with a fucking smug smile on her full lips. Auburn hair hung in clumps around her face, knocked loose from the messy knot at the back of her head. The street and buildings blurred as my peripheral vision narrowed. The only thing left in focus were her flaring nostrils. Yup, I definitely had a concussion.

"Now that I have your attention, I'd appreciate it if you'd remain immobile until the paramedics arrive. You could have internal injuries, and I'd prefer you not die again on my watch."

Why was she talking so loud?

The girl flinched when I grabbed her arm for stability. "Why are you yelling?" I whispered, trying to appease the pressure inside my head.

"Why are you still sitting up?" she said through gritted teeth.

As my vision came back into focus, I gave her a once-over. A nasty impact abrasion was visible on her right hip, where the blue fabric hung in shreds around her thigh. The bruise bloomed against her pale skin, yellow and black at the center, surrounded by purple rings. It usually took a good week for road rash to look that nasty. Aside from the bruise, she seemed intact, a little too intact for someone who'd been in a head-on collision with a motorcycle. The chick was solid, with the muscular definition of someone who had a serious addiction to the gym and a healthy appetite.

"How the hell are you not dead?" I asked.

Her pinched gaze dropped to where my fingers bit into her forearm. "Sorry to disappoint, but you really should lie down. The paramedics will be here any minute."

I let go. "Shit, what time is it?"

She glanced at her watch. "Ten thirty-seven."

"Fuck." I grasped my skull with both hands to keep it from exploding. "Logan's gonna skin my balls for missing another meeting."

Her whiskey eyes flared. "A meeting? That's why you were speeding?" She ripped into me with a surprising flash of fury. "Typical human entitlement. Putting everyone else's lives in danger because the world only revolves around you." A deep red flush crept up her chest and neck as she ranted. It was sexy as hell. "Sit up, lie down, I don't care. My work here is done." She stood in a huff.

Looking up, all I could see was her thick, creamy thigh. "While I appreciate the view, I'm gonna need you to take a step back before I hurl on your feet." The street was spinning again. I braced my palm against the pavement to keep from tipping sideways.

"You need to show some respect, brah, and listen da wahine. You all kine kapakahi." This came from the guy standing behind blue dress chick.

"Real helpful stepping into oncoming traffic like a damn tourist," I said.

"I'm *not* a tourist. You were the one doing twice the posted speed limit." Her knuckles blanched over clenched fists as she glared at me.

"I had the green light, chica. You were jaywalking."

Her exposed hip jutted out as she folded her arms over her chest. "I believe pedestrians have the right of way in Hawaii."

"And that wouldn't matter for shit if a three-thousand-pound truck had splattered your brains on the pavement." I took several slow, deep breaths, trying to push back against the darkness closing in around me.

"You didn't hit me. I fell jumping out of the way. My dress must have gotten caught in your wheel. I suppose confusion is to be expected with a concussion."

"I'm not confused." I recalled the crunching noise her body had made. A sound I'd never forget. Despite the fog creeping into my brain, I was sure about one thing. I had, without a doubt, hit her. "I heard your bones snap," I said. Vertigo won, and I tipped sideways. The girl shot forward on her knees and caught me before I hit the ground, cradling my head in her lap, her fingers stroking my damp curls. My vision tunneled in on her red wine lips, and I had to be all kinds of fucked up because all I could think about was tasting that full mouth.

The shrill cry of an ambulance assaulted my skull as it crawled toward us, followed by the unmistakable flashing blue lights of a police cruiser.

*Can't you just be thankful?* The words echoed through my head, and I wasn't entirely sure if she'd spoken them out loud as I faded out of consciousness.

I watched from somewhere above my body as the paramedics poked and prodded at me.

"He's going under," an EMT said as I floated away, following the girl. She limped backward through the throng of gawking pedestrians and slammed right into a cop. This chick seriously needed to look where she was going.

"Excuse me, miss. I understand you witnessed the accident." The cop flipped open a small notebook and pulled a pen from his chest pocket. "I need to ask you a few questions, if you don't mind."

I hovered behind her, close enough to see a drop of blood drip from her clenched fist.

Her spine went rigid. "If you must." Fire danced across her golden eyes.

"Can you walk me through what happened?"

She took a deep breath and glanced at the paramedics, who were busy strapping my body to a backboard.

I studied my hands and feet and wondered how the hell I could be in two places at once.

"The motorcycle appeared out of nowhere. Fortunately, I jumped out of the way just in time." She fisted the torn fabric at her hip, her eyes darting all over the place like a damn tweaker, as if she were trying to look anywhere other than at the cop. The evidence was right in front of his face. Did he not see the shredded dress or the way she limped and refused to put pressure on her right leg? She was in pain. Why would she try to hide that? This chick was squirrely as all hell.

She flung out a trembling hand toward my bike lying on its side, the front tire wedged under the bumper of an SUV. "He collided with the parked car." Her face paled. "When he woke, he was delirious and confused. He doesn't remember what happened. Not accurately."

"Sir, can you hear me?" I was on my back again, a bright light assaulting my eyes. "Can you tell me your name and address?" a paramedic asked.

"Liam Riley, 4108 Kihapai Road."

"Okay, Liam. We're going to lift you now. On three. One. Two..."

My body floated up toward the sky, and I was with her again, the girl in the blue dress.

"Another witness said you performed CPR," the cop said.

The wilted flower tucked into her hair flapped as she shook her head. "I just sat with him and kept him calm until the paramedics arrived."

The cop flipped back through his notes. "Another witness described you leaning over him, with both hands on his chest. Is that not an accurate statement?"

"No... I mean, yes, sort of." Sweat beaded on her brow.

"Which is it, miss?"

"I never administered CPR. When he regained consciousness, I tried to restrict his movement. I worried he might have a spinal injury."

"To your knowledge, did the driver have anything to drink when he came to?"

There were two DUIs on my record. If he pulled my plate, he knew that already.

"No, nothing," she replied with a confused expression. "May I retrieve my belongings?" I followed her gaze to a shopping bag lying in the street next to a dead plant and a split pineapple bleeding its juice all over the pavement. It could easily have been her head.

# Chapter Three

# RENAE

Sweat slicked my skin as the ambulance lumbered away from the scene. I glanced at the traffic camera and cursed myself for wearing the bright blue dress. With my red hair and pale skin, I stood out like a beacon.

My phone vibrated with an incoming call. Ziggy must have gotten an alert from my tracker, and given our earlier conversation regarding my negligence when it came to my husk, I knew I was in for another tongue lashing.

"I'm fine," I said, keeping my tone loose, despite the pain radiating from my fractured pelvis.

"Did you kill him?" Her clipped voice set my spine rigid. "I swear to the gods, Renae, if he's dead—"

Killing humans without a direct order was generally frowned upon. "He's alive." I took a controlled breath, in and out through my mouth, bypassing the cloying stench of gasoline that clung to my nostrils.

"What the hell happened? Your levels are all over the place."

I considered telling her the truth. That my gift exploded when he hit me. How it sucked every ounce of energy from the plant in my hands and had me up on my feet and racing after him while the accident was still unfolding, despite the pain and potential witnesses. How my stomach twisted with nauseating intensity when I couldn't find a pulse. Or how my syphons struck his chest and poured all my energy into him when I tried to perform CPR. How a white-hot electrical current circled my wrists like shackles, searing my flesh. How it took every bit of my strength to hold down all that taut muscle and sinew as his body convulsed. How I could still taste the sweet milky heat of his energy on my tongue even after my syphons had released him. How I couldn't break the connection, no matter how many times I gouged my fist into my hip.

No. I couldn't tell her any of that. While killing a human was frowned upon, resurrecting one was forbidden. To do so was sacrilege. A slap in the face of the gods. I couldn't tell Ziggy the truth. Not until I figured out how I'd done it, and more importantly, why my gift refused to let go of the arrogant man with sun-kissed curls and denim eyes.

"An entitled hot-head on a motorcycle ran me over," I said. "The impact must have damaged my tracker." It was a long shot, one that might buy me time to figure out how to regain control of my gift.

"That tech can take a direct lightning strike and keep working," Ziggy said. "I'm looking at the satellite footage now."

"The Corps has a satellite?" My heart skidded, then leapt forward.

"We have eyes everywhere. It looks like you stepped right in front of him. That impact would have killed a human, Renae. Did the driver see your injuries before they healed?"

The man had passed through the Void and had been violently ripped back. It should have left his conscious mind scrambled. He didn't seem scrambled. He didn't seem the least bit confused. "I... I don't know."

"Drag your husk to the hospital and make sure. Use your reaper gift to suck out whatever memory he has of the accident. Do you understand?"

I tipped my eyes to the storm-darkened sky and nodded.

# Chapter Four

# LIAM

An entire fucking trauma team greeted me at the ER, and all I could think about was how much their concierge service was gonna cost me. Maxed out on student loans and living on the university's insulting TA stipend and a handful of credit cards, I couldn't afford another damn medical bill or whatever legal action *blue dress chick* decided to take against me for running her over.

My heart thudded in my chest as the nurse swabbed the inside of my elbow with an alcohol wipe.

"I need to start you on saline." She kneaded my flesh with gloved fingers. "Your veins like to roll."

"You'll have better luck in my hand."

"Found it." She pulled my skin taut and slapped the bulging blue vein.

"That one's gonna blow out as soon as you stick it. You're gonna need a twenty-two gauge or smaller."

"You have medical training?" she asked.

"Recovering junkie." I didn't try to hide my past, not from anyone, even if it earned me a scrunched nose from the nurse. Better her disdain than her pity. I didn't give a shit if people judged me. I'd made my choices and accepted the consequences. Their snap assumptions were their problems, not mine.

The nurse moved the tourniquet to my forearm, and my body thrummed with anticipation. Clean seven years, and I still had a thing for needles. The phantom thrill of release spread through my body as it slid beneath my skin. My father's last words to me floated through my mind. *A gods damned abomination.*

After a CT scan, they stuck me in a room to wait. The nurse didn't deserve any of the wrath I unloaded on her when she came to check my vitals for the third time in an hour, my skull still pounding like a piston.

"Can I get some fucking naproxen already?"

She pursed her lips and shot me a side-eye as she lifted the melted ice pack from my ankle.

"Sorry," I said. "My head's killing me. I just want to get the hell out of here. How long is this gonna take?"

"They'll keep you overnight, at least."

Time to call Monika before she hunted me down. "Can I use my phone in here? I need to text my... girlfriend, I guess." Girlfriend wasn't the right word, but calling her my best friend who I sometimes fucked didn't seem like the right choice either. I had a semi-rigid rule about not banging my friends. I also had a love-hate relationship with rules and issues with impulse control. One thing had led to another, and eighteen months into our friends-with-occasional-benefits vibe, we had divergent views on where this was going. Mons had her ten-year life and career plans already mapped out. That level of personal commitment impressed me when we first met. Now, it just felt like pressure. Still, the best thing about Mons was she didn't hold back. Whatever was in her head came out of her mouth. She didn't have an internal monologue. Not one that I'd ever been able to hear.

"She's gonna freak the hell out."

The nurse patted my knee. "I'll go find you another ice pack."

Logan had responded to my text immediately. A quick one-liner about keeping him posted, but I decided not to call Monika until I knew more. She'd march in and boss everyone around and I didn't have the bandwidth for her helicopter routine. I just wanted to sleep.

When I closed my eyes, I saw the blood-red field and those hissing insects shitting gold dust into the air. It was impossible to rest with carts rolling up and down the hall and the incessant beeping monitors above my head. The noise ground through my skull like coarse sandpaper.

One voice rose above it all, blurring the chaos like a shot of bourbon. My head went foggy, and I sank into the sound of that silken cadence and let it pull me under as I imagined her full lips moving with every word. *Dammit.* My eyes flew open as I adjusted my junk. This concussion had my wires seriously crossed. I shifted and tugged at my jeans to take the pressure off my crotch and ended up grinding my bandaged ankle against the damn bed rail. Tunnel vision closed in, and I was with the girl again. She was in the hospital chatting it up with my nurse.

"I'm looking for my boyfriend." She lifted the phone in her right hand. "He said I could come see him now. Can you tell me what room he's in?"

Conniving little bitch.

"Oh good," the nurse replied, "he's been waiting for you."

I bobbed along behind them like a goddamned balloon tethered to the chick's wrist. This out-of-body experience shit wasn't a good sign.

The girl thanked the nurse and slipped into my room. I floated to the head of the bed and poked my cheek. My finger passed through it like smoke.

She crept toward me as she whispered, "Hello?"

When my sleeping form didn't respond, she exhaled softly and checked my hospital bracelet.

"Liam Riley." She dropped my hand as if the contact disgusted her. Her face pinched as she stared at the blood-soaked gauze at my ankle. "If I could take your pain as well as your memory, I would."

Her whiskey eyes made a slow burning sweep up my body. They stopped at the exposed strip of skin at my waist, and she let out a little grunt, half appreciative, half annoyed as hell. Her fingers twitched, and I swear I could feel invisible hands ghosting over every inch of me.

Her assessing gaze continued up my torso to the tattooed arm propped behind my head, then stilled on my face. She stared at the scar that ran from the left side of my forehead to the bridge of my nose.

"Gods, I should have left you for dead and let you cross the field," she whispered.

"What?" I was on my back again in the hospital bed. By the time I pushed through the fire in my skull and opened my eyes, the girl was gone.

# CHAPTER FIVE
# RENAE

I LIMPED AWAY FROM the hospital on too-heavy feet toward the bus stop.

The man's spectrum contained deep veins of power. Of course he was arrogant. Gods, he was probably an ancient forecaster or mimic, maybe even a reaper, bound in a reincarnation cycle. But his aura didn't have the patina of an old soul. Unlike Mr. Ito and his grandson, this man's energy tasted too new, too loud, too bright.

His spectrum was fascinating and deafening all at once, and like his rugged face and piercing blue eyes, it was hard to turn away from. My own gifts mere sparks in comparison to whatever was leashed inside him. None of that explained why I couldn't sever the connection. I'd spent my first decade in the afterlife working the harvest fields outside Almega, latching on to millions of souls and pulling them through the Void. I'd never gotten stuck inside someone else's spectrum. Not once.

Numbness crept up my legs as I angled toward the bus stop. Despite her motherly approach to handling me, Ziggy wouldn't hesitate to terminate my husk if she found out I'd lost complete control of my gift. It wasn't even lunchtime, and I'd already violated five of the Corps' covenants. Follow orders. Don't blow your cover. Don't wield healing on human marks without a license. Don't resurrect the dead. Don't break your husk.

Pins and needles pricked my feet. I stomped the sidewalk as I'd done so many times in my previous life trying to wake my dying nerves while leaning on crutches. If I lost control of my husk along with my gift, I'd be as useless as I'd been as a human. But I wasn't that broken child anymore. I was an engineered machine that shouldn't be losing sensation in my extremities. Something was wrong and I had a sinking suspicion that it had everything to do with the annoyingly attractive stranger sprawled across the too small hospital bed.

When I'd touched him briefly to read his ID bracelet, I'd felt his pain as if it were my own. Even now, the man's energy churned through my system, pulling at me like a violent storm, threatening to capsize me from one moment to the next—phantom physical sensations, sudden explosions of flavor on my tongue.

I shoved down the panic drilling a hole through my stomach and forced a steadying breath into my lungs. I had to find a way to silence the transmission. I needed a significant source of pain. Something potent enough to override the connection and allow me to break free before his energy contaminated me completely.

Sunlight glinted off the remnants of a broken beer bottle by the curb. It took several attempts to convince my numb fingers to comply and pick up the shard. I turned it over in my palm and ran my thumb over its razor-sharp edge. An awful plan took shape. I glanced at the bus stop. Too many witnesses.

With the chunk of glass clasped tight in my fist, I ambled toward the banyan park behind the medical center. Arial roots stretched to the ground from thick branches like bony fingers digging into the earth. The dense maze contained a network of shadowy nooks where many desperate souls had taken refuge before me, if the litter and ramshackle shelters tucked between the trees were any indication. I grasped the sinuous bark and pulled myself deeper into the grove. The numbness spreading through my limbs was so much like having Charcot's disease again, I wanted to scream.

I collapsed onto a concrete bench. I was alone—physically alone, anyway. He was still with me, like an electrical storm crackling through my consciousness, frying my nerves. I dragged the dead weight of my left foot into my lap and took a deep breath, the glass still clenched in my sweaty palm.

Exhausted and out of options, I slipped off my sandal and gritted my teeth as I pressed my impromptu scalpel against the soft skin on the bottom of my foot. A bead of crimson bubbled up around the glass tip. No pain registered. I needed to go deeper.

I held my breath and gouged the glass across the ball of my foot from the base of my middle toe to the arch, slicing deep into the flesh and stifling a scream as the nerves jolted to life. A glorious white-hot throbbing sensation pulsed up my leg. Warm blood seeped from the wound and soaked my dress. I loosened a heavy sigh from my lungs. The pain pushed Liam's energy to the periphery of my perception, and I could finally feel the boundary between our spectrums. I pulled my gift back, trying to untangle myself from his energy. Every time I tugged against it, my gift tightened its grip, refusing to let him go.

The pain receded as my skin knit together. The numbness returned, and the line between our energies blurred.

Tears stung my eyes as I sliced through flesh, tendon, and muscle until I hit bone. My vision went fuzzy as the trees twisted and bent around me. While the pain was at its peak, I yanked my gift back with every ounce of strength I possessed. My traitorous gift thrashed against me in response, refusing to heel to my command. The more I pulled and twisted against the cord connecting me to the man's virile energy, the more it tightened like a noose around my neck.

Option one. Tell Ziggy the truth. She'd deactivate my husk and order me back to Almega, where I'd witness before the Nūkiri and be sentenced for violating the Corps' covenants. They wouldn't throw me into the Void—a punishment reserved for fallen gods and monstrous souls. No. They'd offer me redemption, strip me of my power and memory, and send me on my way.

Option two. Lie. My husk was as much Ziggy's responsibility as it was mine. Terminating me wouldn't be good for her bottom line. If I went to her with an altered version of the truth, I might be able to convince her to send me back to the Nursery for reconditioning. But without a functioning gift, I'd be undeployable. I'd be demoted to a support detail and spend the remainder of this life processing new recruits, establishing an electronic trail, and building cover identities for other Watchers until my husk expired.

Option three: Figure out how to fix this myself.

Liam's energy rose to the forefront of my perception as the incision on my foot zippered shut. White sparks flashed behind my eyes as I pressed my thumb into the wound. Why wasn't it working? Why was my gift holding on to this man? I hurled the makeshift scalpel against the ground, and it shattered against a rock. My bloody hands trembled as I stared at the shards.

*Be careful where you step. The road ahead is covered in broken glass.* A crazed, near hysterical laugh twisted out of me as the fortune-teller's uncanny prediction floated through my head.

Temporary discomfort wasn't enough to keep his overwhelming presence at bay. I needed a more permanent solution. A constant source of unrelenting pain.

I bent over and picked up a handful of the larger pieces of glass and fished around in my bag until I found my nail file. An unnatural sound, part gurgle, part scream, tore from my throat as I gouged my foot open with the blunt metal. I pushed as many of the glass shards as I could into the laceration before I passed out from the pain.

A homeless woman was rifling through my bag when I awoke. She must have assumed me for dead because she shrieked and fell back on her derriere when I jumped up and ripped my tote from her hands.

I hobbled a few steps and immediately regretted what I'd done. Excruciating pain shot through the sole of my left foot and up my leg.

"Gods, I should have left him in Almega," I said as I stumbled toward the river, leaving my sandals and the confused woman behind. The sun disappeared behind a black cloud that matched Liam's abysmal mood.

His energy was still there, following me like a phantom, but the neuropathy in my extremities faded by the time I reached the narrow river that wound through the heart of the banyan forest. Mud squelched between my toes as I waded into the silt pools above the fall line.

I washed the blood from my hands and smoothed my hair. My fingers met the waxy petals at the nape of my neck. I unpinned the wilted flower and inhaled the light scent of nutmeg and vanilla before setting it on the water's dark surface. The orchid eddied with the current, slipping around rocks as it twisted toward the falls. An odd apprehension washed through me as it disappeared over the edge.

# CHAPTER SIX

# RENAE

Icy wind bit my cheeks, and I dipped my chin deeper into the collar of my parka as I hiked up the hill toward the concrete block building that had become my refuge in the six weeks since the accident. The climate at the summit of Mauna Kea hovered just below freezing most nights. The view more than made up for the bone-chilling cold. Cotton clouds stretched below the barren summit in every direction, giving the sacred peak the appearance of an island floating on a sea of foam. At fourteen thousand feet above sea level, it was also the farthest I could get away from the man who haunted my every waking moment.

His energy drew my attention like a compass and created static interference every time I unfurled my gift. It took an entire week to sift through one of my human coworker's emotional hot buttons to isolate the right thread and amplify it with a little added energy of my own to manipulate her into a blowup that ended with her sudden and convenient resignation.

I immediately volunteered to take on her workload and convinced Marcus, the facility manager, to secure me a permanent hotel room at the summit lodge—a privilege typically reserved for visiting astronomers. Without the commute back and forth to Hilo, I was able to cover all the gaps in the night observation schedule. Ziggy was thrilled with my newfound dedication to the job and scaled back on the frequency of our required check-ins to an as-needed basis.

I'd settled into a livable routine, working at night when Liam's energy was less chaotic, allowing me to focus on my mission. The intensity of the connection ebbed and flowed with his moods. The stronger the mood, the more it drew my attention and tugged at my chest. I attempted to rest during the day while the swells of his emotions were at their peak, tossing and turning in the stiff hotel bed. The irregular sleep cycles left me drained. Dark shadows took up residence in the hollows beneath my eyes.

The only upside to not sleeping was the lack of nightmares. Thank the gods, because my current state of soul-deep exhaustion left little strength to rebury the unwanted memories they unearthed.

Still, being stuck inside his head was the worst kind of cure, replacing one affliction with another. My only rest came with help from the little blue pills Ziggy prescribed. Two taken at the end of my shift helped me fall asleep before the surges of Liam's energy peaked.

Ziggy no longer questioned my broken tracker excuse. I let her think she was getting somewhere by probing me about my past life. We spent every session discussing my relationship with my sisters and parents and my disability. I still wasn't ready to open the vault and address my role in their deaths, and Ziggy didn't push the issue.

Volcano runs were still out of the question, so I walked, ran, and hiked the steep, six-mile trail between the hotel and the summit at dusk and dawn every day. The thin air and uphill climb helped maintain my endurance, and the pain that shot across my left foot with each step kept Liam's energy and moods from completely contaminating my spectrum.

Inside the building, I headed to the staff lounge. Half the room served as a makeshift kitchen, complete with refrigerator, old microwave that hadn't been cleaned in over a decade, toaster oven, and three coffee makers. A wobbly wooden table filled the space between the kitchen and a bank of pale green lockers that occupied the remainder of the room.

My locker was along the back wall, out of public view. I exchanged my parka and hiking boots for a pair of heels, a recent addition to my wardrobe—one that kept pressure on the glass embedded in my foot.

Wherever I went, Liam followed. My only reprieve came at night while he slept—*before* he started dreaming. His dreams brought waves of desire and spikes of fear, both of which had very real physical effects on me. I broke out into a cold sweat every time he had a nightmare. When he was aroused, which seemed like a near constant state, I drank gallons of water to clear the sweet spice from my tongue and paced the halls, grinding my feet into the floor until the sensations ran their course.

"Marcus called for you," Ernie, my one remaining telescope operator, said as he stepped into the break room, an empty mug in hand.

I opened a box of donuts, hoping there was at least one left and let out a little whimper when two pillowy masterpieces stared back at me. "What did he want?"

"To talk to you." Ernie scratched his head as he glanced around the room. "Why did I come in here?" he murmured to himself.

My stomach knotted with guilt. I'd plucked so many memories from his brain it was beginning to leak like a sieve.

"Coffee," I said, pointing to his mug. Hacking the data right under his nose had been a challenge until I found his weakness. He drank six ounces of black coffee every hour on the hour. When I wanted to manipulate his ability to focus, I switched out his regular grounds for decaf. After a few hours without the constant influx of caffeine, Ernie got sloppy. He didn't notice my data manipulations, and I didn't have to syphon him as frequently.

I left him to his ritual and headed to the control room with my donuts. Three workstations sat in a triangle at the center of the observation lab. Filing cabinets, filled with old data long since digitized, lined the perimeter. I pulled up the evening's observation schedule. Marcus squeezed an extra set of coordinates into the end of our shift. A little thrill buzzed through me. Just a quick pass over Epsilon Eridani, a small star in the Eridanus constellation, but it meant I finally had a bit of *real* work to do. It also meant I needed to switch out Ernie's regular brew for decaf sooner than later.

There were things in the Eridanus quadrant humans weren't ready to find, and it was my job to ensure they remained hidden. I hacked into the telescope's passive cooling system and activated a bug. It would bump up the temperature near the end of our shift. Ernie might not notice the temps creeping up in his caffeine-deprived state, and the heat radiation inside the camera would warp the images, rendering them inconclusive.

I nearly jumped out of my skin when my desk phone rang. The caller ID told me it was Marcus Logan—the acting faculty liaison between NASA and the University of Hawaii, and my boss.

"Hey, Renae, happy Friday. Did you get my email?" Marcus asked.

"I haven't checked yet. Ernie said you called."

"You've been indispensable these past few weeks, picking up the slack. I have some good news. I hired a part-time telescope operator to help ease your workload."

I coiled the phone cord around my fingers. "That's not necessary," I said. "Ernie and I have everything covered up here." The last thing I needed was another mark to manipulate.

"While I appreciate your dedication, I can't afford to burn out my best people, and I don't have any money left in the budget to keep paying for your room at the lodge. The newbie starts tonight. Give him the grand tour and get him set up in the system. I'd like him to shadow you exclusively. I've adjusted the shifts to get you back on a normal schedule. Ernie will cover this weekend so you can finally move back to Hilo. It shouldn't take you long to bring the new TO up to speed."

"Great," I said, strangling my fingers with the phone cord until they turned purple.

"Text me and let me know how it goes. And enjoy your long weekend. You've certainly earned it. Oh, and Renae, be careful heading home. They're calling for snow in the upper elevations." He hung up, and I slapped the receiver back in its cradle. He'd neglected to mention when my new protégé would arrive.

Ernie walked into the lab, sipping from his steaming mug. "What was that about?"

"Marcus hired a new telescope operator."

"About time. When do they start?"

I plastered a plastic smile on my face. "Tonight."

After straightening the empty workstation next to mine, I headed to the break room to switch out Ernie's coffee while I had the chance. I poured a cup from the carafe Ernie had just made and dumped the rest down the drain before starting a fresh pot of decaf, minus six ounces. While I waited for it to brew, I sat at the table for what might be my last few moments alone, sipping my coffee and wishing I had more donuts.

Liam's energy jumped to the forefront of my consciousness. Although I resented the connection, I'd gotten accustomed to his rhythms. Despite having the surface intensity of a squall, there was a quiet calm beneath the storm where the push and pull was more like the tide—gentle and full of power. I didn't dare let myself sink too deep for fear of drowning.

The coffee maker hissed and sputtered at the end of its cycle. I groaned as I stood on sore feet, unsure of how well I'd be able to assess my new employee with Liam's energy clouding my perception. Pain shot up my shin as I walked to my locker to retrieve a set of headphones and turned up the volume on my favorite nemesis-smothering playlist. The effect was instantaneous and muffled the phantom presence hovering at the edge of my perception. I rounded the bank of lockers and slammed headlong into a solid wall of muscle.

The cell phone flew from my hand as my ankle twisted and I collapsed sideways. The music stopped, and a firm arm snaked around my waist. My syphons twisted beneath my skin as visions exploded through my senses—sheets of lightning illuminating the black sky, salt on my tongue, sweat, skin and the scent of ether, the upswell of an ocean rising beneath me, the sensation of floating outside myself, listless, adrift.

I couldn't make it stop. Not with his hands on me. Not while every nerve in my body was focused on the fingers gripping my waist.

"Good grief, woman, do you ever look where you're going?" Apparently, the memory wipe hadn't been as thorough as I'd hoped. I'd sucked out his memories of my injury, but they'd been so entangled with everything else, I had to syphon bits and pieces instead of entire threads and couldn't be certain of what I'd taken and how much I'd left behind.

"Do you ever keep your hands to yourself?" I asked. The words came out too sharp.

He glanced down at his chest with a smug grin. "You wanna let go of my shirt?"

Heat crept up my neck as I unfisted the thin cotton fabric and retracted the syphons I didn't remember releasing.

Pain shot up my shin as I pressed up on the balls of my feet and shoved away from him. He released me, and I fell against the bank of cold lockers.

I straightened my blouse. "What are you doing here?"

He thrust an open palm in my direction. The inked green and black tail of a scaled beast coiled around his bicep and disappeared under the sleeve of his gray T-shirt. "Lee Riley, your new assistant telescope operator." Unkempt honey curls tumbled over his forehead, hiding the jagged scar. Patchy stubble softened the hard line of his jaw and gave him the too lazy to shave but not committed enough to grow a real beard look. "And I'm assuming you're Renae Martin?" His dark brow cocked in amusement.

Ignoring his outstretched hand, I skirted past him to retrieve my phone.

"I thought your name was Liam."

"My friends call me Lee."

I grabbed my coffee from the table and ground my weight down on the ball of my left foot. "Follow me, *Liam*. I'll show you to the lab."

With forced civility, I introduced him to Ernie, got him set up at the empty workstation next to mine, and gave him the required spiel about the hazards of altitude sickness. Denim eyes followed me with a quiet intensity that made my traitorous gift thrum beneath my skin as I rambled on about schedules. It was almost too much to be in the same room with him. Gods, I needed air.

I dropped the staff handbook on the desk in front of him with a thud. "Here, read over this stuff. I need to go... check on something."

Sequestered in the bathroom, I pulled the elastic band from my wrist and twisted my hair into a loose knot before splashing cold water on my flushed cheeks. I needed to settle my nerves before calling Marcus and telling him exactly what I thought of his new hire. How could I explain my vehement dislike for Liam Riley without sounding irrational? My fingers blanched as I grasped the edge of the sink and forced myself to exhale slowly before taking several measured breaths.

*Be smart about this, Renae.* I couldn't afford to jeopardize my cover by giving Marcus a reason to doubt my judgment or professionalism. If he wanted Liam on the team, I was in no position to argue. I'd already made one person quit. If I did the same to Liam, it might look like a pattern. I needed a different approach. I needed to find a way to get Liam Riley fired. I bit back a smile and returned to the lab with a plan.

Ernie, not one to waste time, was giving Liam an overview of the remote teams we'd be working with for the night.

"Yeah, that last observation over Epsilon Eridani is mine," Liam said.

My head snapped up.

"I missed my spot in the rotation at the university's telescope a few weeks back due to an accident." His denim eyes met mine. "Logan... Dr. Logan, got me this gig and fit my observation requests into the schedule so I can complete the research for my dissertation."

So that was it. He was Marcus Logan's pet protégé. I slipped a mask of disinterest over my features and handed him a yellow sticky note with his passwords. It changed nothing. He was just another mark, and I already had a plan.

Our fingers brushed as he took the paper. "This should give you access to the controls, main database, and batching system."

His dark brow creased, deepening the scar between his eyes. "I know I didn't make a fantastic first impression when I ran you over with my bike," Ernie's head swiveled in our direction as Liam continued, "but I don't want this to be awkward, and right now, it feels awkward as hell."

This time, I extended my hand to him. "You can call me Renae." My gift flared when he grasped my palm, sending a jolt of electricity up my arm. The visions didn't come a second time. I was, however, acutely aware of his physical sensations; the ankle that throbbed under his full weight, the headache behind his right eye, the softness of my hand in his.

I let go and clenched my palm, squeezing against the lingering static. "I suppose I should give you the grand tour." I nodded to the black jacket he'd slung over the back of his chair. "Grab your coat. It's brisk under the dome when the shutter is open."

A lazy smile clung to the corner of his mouth as I led him through the lounge, engineering office, and chilled server room. The cramped space intensified the push and pull of his energy against mine. My armpits went damp with sweat. The man failed to grasp the concept of personal space and was never more than a step behind me.

A welcome rush of frigid air hit me as we entered the dome. "I saved the best for last," I said, gesturing toward the massive instrument towering above us, a beast with a belly of electronic panels and wires.

Liam tipped his head back with a giddy, childlike grin. "Can we take a closer look?" He nodded to the perforated steel staircase that led to the dome's narrow catwalk.

The thought of navigating yet another tight space with him made my gift shift beneath my skin. But keeping him close was part of the plan. I forced a coy smile. "Of course."

"After you." He stepped aside and let me ascend the ladder ahead of him. At the top, I had trouble disengaging the safety latch with my sweaty palms. Liam climbed up behind me, grasped the handle, and released the lock. His scent, cedar and salt, engulfed my senses. Heat radiated from his unzipped jacket, inches from my back.

Air stole from my lungs at the sudden intrusive memory of too many warm bodies pressed around me. *Just breathe,* I told myself. *Don't lose it.*

"There's a trick," Liam said. "Squeeze, then lift, or it sticks."

I managed to twist and glare at him. He stepped down a rung. "Yes, I'm aware. How do *you* know about that?"

"I did an internship here as an undergrad."

"You might have mentioned that *before* I wasted the last half hour giving you a tour." The words came out too tight as I stepped onto the catwalk and circled to the opposite side of the platform.

"You were being so thorough. I didn't want to interrupt." He threw me a lazy smile before lifting his eyes to the cobalt sky. The near constant storm on the surface of his spectrum stilled. "Damn."

Peppermint bloomed on my tongue and in my nose, making my eyes water. The effects of his emotions on my senses were so much stronger when we shared the same space. I shifted my weight to my left foot, ignoring the sudden urge to explore that ocean of power at his core. "What's the focus of your dissertation? Let me guess. You're hunting exoplanets with the potential to support alien life?" Just like every other starry-eyed astronomer. Predictable.

"I'm not interested in aliens." He inched toward me; eyes glued to the glittering stars above. "I'm researching the origins of the Eridanus Supervoid. The massive region of empty space in our universe."

Okay, not so predictable. I pressed myself into the curved dome wall, the cold metal a welcome shock against my too-hot skin. "What's your hypothesis?" I asked, curious about what I was up against with this man.

My gift buzzed beneath my skin as Liam moved closer, eyes still skyward. If he took one more step, I'd be forced to make a decision—retreat to the opposite side of the catwalk or let him attempt to squeeze past me with those annoyingly broad shoulders.

"Quantum entanglement with a parallel universe."

My heart raced. "That's an ambitious theory to chase." I hugged my arms around my body, more to hold back my gift than stave off the chill.

"What can I say? I like a challenge." Liam's piercing blue eyes dropped to mine as he leaned against the safety rail opposite me, stretching his long legs across the platform, blocking my exit to the ladder. "What's your take on the Mercer-Howland Multiverse theory?" he asked.

"The astrophysicists who claim the missing cosmic radiation is being siphoned away by a sister universe?" Their research would forever remain in the realm of theoretical physics. Not because they were wrong. I would have given anything to be assigned to the team watching them.

Liam's toothy grin told me two things. He was impressed that I actually knew who Janet Howland and Allison Mercer were. And if he was in the Howland-Mercer camp, that meant he had no qualms about pushing boundaries. I bit back a smile, my earlier plan still in motion.

"Theoretical physics isn't really my area of expertise," I lied and glanced up at him through my lashes. "Do you have any questions about the observational equipment? Is there anything else you'd like to see?" I let my syphons uncoil and rove over him.

"I do have one question." He folded his arms over his chest. "You wanna elaborate on what you said to me in the hospital? The thing about the field?"

My heart tripped over its galloping beat. He'd been asleep. How did he know I visited the hospital? The nurse must have told him. That still didn't explain how he knew about the field. Unless he remembered his brief trip to the afterlife. Gods, I should have wiped the entire accident from his mind.

I pressed away from the wall with a huff. "I have no idea what you're talking about."

Liam stood, blocking my path. "You almost killed me. I deserve some sort of explanation."

"I don't owe *you* anything." I stepped forward until we were toe to toe, intentionally shrinking the space between us.

He glared down at me, refusing to retreat. "Stalking me, lying to nurses, sneaking into my room, apologizing for not being able to take away my pain? Any of this ring a bell?"

"The concussion must have muddled your memory." I held my ground against the intensity of those denim eyes. "I wasn't there, and this conversation is finished. Are we clear?"

"Crystal." His knuckles blanched as he gripped the railing. "But I still hold you responsible for destroying my bike."

I grunted. "Well, I guess that makes us even." What were a wrecked motorcycle and a few stitches compared to the jeopardy our connection posed to my gift and my future in the Corps? "You have no idea how much that accident cost me."

He leaned forward, close enough for his sweet, warm breath to cascade over my face. "You can't be serious. I've been trying to put my life back together for weeks. What did it cost you?"

Flames crept up my cheeks. "You ruined my *favorite* dress."

He took a step back. "Are you fucking serious?"

I reeled in my gift. This was not how the conversation was supposed to go.

"You wouldn't understand." I moved to circle around the dome in the opposite direction.

Liam caught my wrist. "I *want* to understand."

My eyes dropped to the spot where his fingers bit into my flesh. The tomb at my core flung open as the memories exploded through my perception—the whizzing of wire off a reel, the crush of warm bodies against mine, gunshots, and the scent of gasoline.

Nausea swelled in my stomach as I glanced behind him at the exit. Gods, why was it so far? Could I make it, or would my wobbling legs betray me again? I twisted my wrist from his grip and flattened my body against the curved dome wall for support. The shock of cold metal brought me back to the present. *Get it together, Renae. You're not a helpless human. Not anymore.*

"At least have the courtesy to look at me when you lie." His voice tightened as acid bloomed on my tongue.

I clenched my fists and shoved the memories of my previous life back into the grave where they belonged. Where they couldn't cripple me with guilt and regret. I ignored the intensity of those denim eyes and focused on the plan to get him fired. I just needed to tease out the right emotion and tug on the thread, get him to overreact. Anger or lust. Whichever came first.

"Now you're calling me a liar?" Milky sweet spice slicked my tongue and coated my throat as I let my syphons burrow deep into his core. Oh, gods, definitely not anger. I isolated the thread and amplified the emotion, all too aware of the physical effect it would have on him.

"Just calling it as I see it. Most people have at least one tell." Liam stepped forward and braced his palms against the wall next to my shoulders, leaning in to study my eyes up close. "Those frying pan pupils are a dead giveaway." His gaze dipped to my mouth. "And you keep fidgeting with your bottom lip, sucking at it like you're trying to palate something unpleasant."

Heat curled low in my abdomen as his physical sensations washed through me—the cool metal beneath his palms, the growing pressure in his groin. My traitorous gift hummed at the thought of slipping my freezing fingers inside his jacket to seek the warmth of all that taut muscle.

His brow furrowed as he leaned in, inches from my parted lips. And suddenly my plan was back on track.

Gods, help me, I *wanted* him to kiss me. I shifted my weight to the ball of my left foot—the glass embedded there cut deep, sending a streak of pain across the arch. "Whoa, what are you doing?" I said, forcing my body to shrink back as his lips grazed mine.

He shoved away from the wall. "Shit, sorry. I... I'm not sure what just happened." He reached up and ran a hand through his dirty-blond curls.

"You just pinned me against the wall and tried to kiss me," I said, hoping my flaming cheeks conveyed fury rather than the truth.

"I totally misread that."

He hadn't misread anything.

"You're an employee under my direct supervision. I have—"

"A boyfriend? Of course you do. Fuck. I'm sorry."

I opened my mouth to correct him and thought better of it.

"I'm not technically an employee," he said. "I'm an intern."

"A distinction I don't think Marcus will care about." I pushed past him and headed for the ladder as I bit back a smile.

# Chapter Seven

# LIAM

Snow fell in fat flakes as I leaned against the hood of my truck. Just enough to coat the ground and quiet the world. Our shift ended an hour ago, and she was still inside. Most likely emailing Logan to let him know what a degenerate asshole I was. She kept that fucking fake smile on her face the entire night, a smile betrayed by the flame in those whiskey eyes. She was under no obligation to listen, but I had to apologize. Not to save my own ass. It was too late for that. I'd screwed any chance of keeping this job when I lost my damn mind and tried to kiss her. I just needed her to know I wasn't *that* guy.

Renae didn't seem surprised to see me when she finally stepped out of the building at 5:00 a.m. in a parka and hiking boots.

"Why are you still here?" Anger and disgust I could deal with—not this polite indifference.

I glanced around the empty parking lot. We were the only two souls left on the summit. "I thought you might need a ride."

Flurries collected in her red hair like melting stars. "I'm perfectly capable of finding my own way down the mountain." She grasped the straps of her backpack and headed for the road.

"You can't be serious. It's forty miles back to town."

"Good night, Liam."

Shit, she was serious.

I pushed off the hood. "I remember the blood-red field," I said.

Renae halted at the edge of the parking lot.

"I haven't been able to stop thinking about it since the accident. Then you were here, and I felt this vibe, and I don't know what I was thinking. I made a mistake. I'm sorry."

Gravel crunched beneath her feet as she walked away without a word or glance back.

Major dick move—waiting to accost her in the parking lot and forcing her to listen to my apology. I got in the truck and started the engine. Just because I dreamed about her and that bloody field every damn night didn't excuse what I'd done.

Fuck. I was *that* guy.

I massaged the scar on my forehead. What the hell was wrong with me?

My heart jolted at the hard knock of her knuckles on my driver's side window. Renae waited as I cranked it down.

A scowl had replaced her god-awful plastic smile. "I still haven't decided what I'm going to tell Marcus. But it's freezing and I'm exhausted. I've decided to take you up on the ride, as long as you promise to do the speed limit."

"Jeez, you run over one person, and suddenly no one trusts you behind the wheel," I said, half joking.

She crossed her arms and glared at me, sparks flaring in those whiskey eyes.

I held up my hands in defeat. "Fine. I promise not to speed. Now get in before you freeze your ass off."

Renae braced her hands against the dash as we bounced along the unpaved access road, not letting any part of her body shift or sway in my direction. Off the summit, the road smoothed out, and she kept throwing me side-eye and swallowing hard, like she wanted to say something.

I didn't need to hear her thoughts. It was obvious. "I'm in no danger of falling asleep at the wheel." Not with her sitting this close. "Relax and try to get some rest. You look like you haven't slept in a week."

Renae rolled her eyes and tucked her hands beneath her armpits for warmth. I turned up the heat, and she leaned against the door with a yawn. No conversation, then. Message received. Breathy little snores followed.

She didn't respond to my gentle nudges as we approached town. If she wanted me to take her home, she needed to wake up and give me some damn directions. After several attempts to rouse her, I pulled into a gas station and did everything short of slapping her to bring her around. No one slept that soundly without being drugged. My gut tightened.

I opened her backpack and searched for a wallet, anything with an address. Her only form of identification was an employee badge. I dug deeper and didn't find anything other than food. She ate like a damn junkie. I pulled out protein bars, mini packs of Skittles, a bag of pastel mini marshmallows, and a bottle of vitamin gummies. The bottle rattled when I shook it. I popped the lid and fished out one of the little blue pills. Definitely not vitamins.

"What the hell are you doing with tranks, chica?"

I pressed two fingers to her throat. Her pulse was strong and steady, and her breathing was even. I pried one of her eyes open. A frying pan pupil rimmed in a gold halo stared back at me. She was fucking wasted.

The squirrely behavior. The lies she piled one on top of the other. She must have been high the day of the accident. That's why she lied to the cop. It was the same thing I would have done to hide my habit. There was a time when every word that had fallen out of my mouth was a lie. I'd lied to my family, to myself. Everyone. Detoxing from that habit was just as hard as kicking heroin.

I considered calling Logan and ran through that conversation in my head. "Thanks for the job, and by the way, my new boss roofied herself. Text me her address so I can dump her ass on the curb."

Negative. I would never, ever out an addict to their employer.

"What am I supposed to do with you?" I sure as hell wasn't going to sit here in the 76 Station parking lot and wait for her to sober the fuck up. She didn't need a hospital. She needed a damn bed. The sun would be up soon, and I needed some sleep before my afternoon lab.

Gravel crunched under my tires as I pulled into my driveway. Auburn hair tumbled across her face as I unbuckled Renae and laid her down on the bench seat.

I brushed the silky strands away from her cheek. "Sleep it off, chica, because you and I, we're gonna have a real honest conversation when you're sober." I knew better than most you couldn't force a person to want help. She'd backpedal and lie. That was a given. It might even get ugly. But this chick needed someone to hold up a brutal mirror. Someone to tell her she wasn't in control, no matter how well she thought she was hiding it.

Renae mumbled something as she tucked her hands between her thighs and wet her lips in a way that had me thinking things I shouldn't. Trying to kiss her had been a colossal fucking mistake—one I would *not* make again. I needed to block out that line of thinking altogether. Getting involved with someone who was actively using was dangerous. Like spraying gasoline on a smoldering fire kind of danger. We shouldn't even be friends. If I was smart, I'd stay the hell away from her.

⁓

An ear-splitting shriek cleaved through my skull. I bolted from my bed through the one room bungalow before my eyes had a chance to adjust to the light and took a header onto the coffee table. Streaks of white exploded behind my right eye as I scrambled to my feet and stumbled outside. The warmth dripping down the side of my face barely registered as her scream made the hairs stand on the back of my neck.

She clawed at the window like a caged animal, crying out in a language that sounded like French.

Renae swiped at me with those fucking talon-like nails when I yanked the door open and tackled her, pinning her flailing arms to her sides. Her head bucked forward and cracked into my nose. I managed to trap her legs between my thighs and stepped in closer, hugging her against my chest as she did her best to wake the damn dead.

I tucked into the hollow between her neck and shoulder to avoid another violent blow, inhaling her sweet scent—pears and vanilla. "You're okay. I got you." I repeated it over and over, rubbing my hands up and down her back until the screaming stopped and she shuddered against me.

The woman was still out cold. I couldn't leave her out here alone. It took everything I had to scoop her up and carry her across the lawn. Renae fisted my T-shirt, strangling me by the collar. I almost dropped her twice as I climbed the porch steps and pried the screen door open with my foot.

The couch, piled high with dirty laundry and books, wasn't an option.

The collar of my shirt lost its battle with her unholy grip when I dumped her on the bed. Renae immediately curled into a ball and whimpered in French. Whatever this chick's damage was, it ran deep.

"Hey," I patted her cheek, "wake up." Her flesh burned beneath my palm. I'd heard of users spiking a fever on a coke overdose, but not tranks. What the hell else had she taken? I needed to get her body temperature down—fast.

Renae groaned as I peeled off her coat and fleece, stripping her to the tank top beneath. I darted to the bathroom in search of a clean towel or washcloth—anything I could use to cool her down. I hadn't done laundry in two weeks and couldn't find anything clean. I yanked off my ruined shirt and soaked it under the tap.

Her eyes popped open, and she sucked air like a guppy as I mopped the dripping rag across her face.

"Shit. I'm sorry." I bent over and propped her up so she could breathe.

Renae reached up and clutched my shoulders. A tingling static sensation spread over my skin as if multiple sets of featherlight fingers roved over me.

"Gods, you taste amazing," she groaned.

Still fucking high.

She dug her claws into my flesh when I tried to pull away. "Please, I need you," she murmured, her voice sultry and thick with sleep.

I dropped my head against the pillow next to her, exhausted. This woman was gonna be the death of me.

# CHAPTER EIGHT
# RENAE

I WOKE TO THE weight of an arm draped across my hip and warm flesh pressed to my cheek.

*Just breathe.* I repeated the mantra as I focused on slowing my galloping heart. His scent—salt and cedar—clung to my nostrils as the metallic tang of blood bloomed on my tongue. Real blood. Not a phantom sensation.

Why was I in his bed? Gods, where were my clothes? The last time I closed my eyes, we were in his truck.

Air lodged in my throat as I lifted his arm and slowly melted out of the bed to the floor. My heart stopped when I peeked over the edge of the mattress. Were we in an accident? It was the only explanation that made sense. There was so much blood. On the pillows, on the sheets and the headboard. My hands shot to my face. Whatever injuries I'd sustained had already healed. The nasty gash above Liam's eyebrow, however, still oozed. I reached up and brushed aside his messy curls.

Oh gods. Was that bone?

My fingers hovered above his split flesh. A zap of static arced from his brow to my hand. I stopped breathing when he stirred, my lungs straining against my ribs.

He settled, and I let my finger graze the wound. A white-hot electrical shock pulsed up my arm, burning a forked, vein-like pattern into my skin. It was the same searing pain I'd felt the day we met and I'd restarted his heart.

I yanked my hand away and watched his wound zipper shut. I'd healed him. Twice. My mind raced with the possibilities, the missions I'd be qualified for as a fully fledged healer.

Liam flopped onto his back, and my gaze landed on the wet spot of drool I'd left on his chest, right on the face of that green dragon tattoo. Its yellow eyes watched me with an eerily familiar intensity.

My syphons shot out of their own accord and licked over the dips and planes of his chiseled abs like a pet showing affection for its master. I reeled them in before they drifted lower. My traitorous gift strained against its leash, refusing to dig into Liam's subconscious and pluck out the memory of whatever had happened after we left the summit. I bit back a curse and looked for my clothes. I needed to escape before he woke and demanded answers. He'd have questions about our miraculous recoveries, and I was fresh out of lies.

I tiptoed out of his bungalow and went still with every groan and complaint made by the wide planked floor. The screen door squawked as I inched it open and slipped out onto the deck. The entire house seemed to protest my departure. His front steps grumbled under my weight, as if to say, "Go back to bed where you belong."

Liam's truck didn't appear to be damaged. No sign of an accident other than a few smears of blood on the inside of the windows and on the dash.

I fished around in my backpack for my phone. Everything was out of place, as if someone had gone through it. My cell was missing. I glanced back at the bungalow. Had I taken it into the house? Why couldn't I remember? I hadn't even taken any of Ziggy's blue pills.

Nausea twisted my empty stomach. When was the last time I'd eaten?

The donuts. Twelve hours earlier. I'd been so focused on keeping my gift leashed, I'd forgotten to eat. My system had gone into full shutdown. An involuntary hibernation. Another careless mistake Ziggy would never let me hear the end of.

I shoved a handful of mini marshmallows in my mouth as my syphons strained toward the house. Toward him. I reined my gift and focused on putting one foot in front of the other. The sun climbing the sky to the northeast and the volcanic fog hugging the ground told me I was somewhere between Hilo and Kilauea's eastern rift zone. Of course he lived on an active volcano.

I shook my head and let that kernel of knowledge digest along with what I'd learned of him already. Arrogant, intelligent, not afraid to take risks. There was no way I'd be able to get him fired now. Not after I'd spent the night in his bed.

He'd be a challenge to manipulate. Unlike Ernie, Liam's memories were harder to unravel. The threads resisted my manipulations, frayed and broke, leaving fragments behind. And there was the other problem—the way my ravenous gift constantly reached for him and refused to let go. Even as I put distance between us, the connection tugged at my chest, making it difficult to breathe. Pain arced across the ball of my left foot, and my resentment for the man grew with each step.

❧

Floor-to-ceiling windows bathed Ziggy's empty office in a silvery blue light. My avatar's feet paced invisible circles in the thick carpet as I waited for her to arrive.

"I'm a healer," I said as soon as she materialized. "I want a new assignment. Somewhere far away from this claustrophobic island."

Her brow furrowed as she perched on the edge of her desk. "When the recruiters tested you at the Nursery, your healing ability was too far below the Corps' minimum standard for training."

"I've been practicing."

She twisted with a sigh and tapped the desktop. A three-dimensional orb of inky black strings slithering around one another appeared above the opaque glass table.

"This report is the result of your initial assessment." Ziggy stuck her hand inside the orb and tugged out one of the thick noodles. "These elastic loops represent your reaper gift. You have dozens of them." She fished around and plucked out a thin, translucent green thread. "This single strand is your healing gift. No matter how many poor plants you experiment on, it will never be enough to qualify you as a healer."

My jaw clenched. How did she know about the plants? *We have eyes everywhere.*

Ziggy twisted toward the desktop and pulled up my tracking log. "You didn't sleep at the summit or at home last night. I'm assuming the massive endorphin spike you experienced means you've finally taken my advice about fraternizing with the locals. I hope it was as cathartic as the report suggests."

I fought to keep my heart rate steady. Her assumption that I'd taken a lover was better than the truth—that I'd lost all control of my traitorous gift. That Liam's dormant energy called to mine like a magnet, distracting me from my mission. "That is none of your business."

"Everything you do with that husk is my business, especially when you allow yourself to fall into an involuntary hibernation in the presence of a human. I don't care who you have sex with, Renae, but you can't risk blowing your cover like that again."

Heat crept up my neck. Gods, I did not need any help imagining that scenario. Not after waking up with my mouth pressed to his flesh. I shoved the image from my mind and plopped into one of the translucent chairs across from her desk.

Ziggy pulled up a file on Liam. She was worse than a snooping mother. Her access and control over every aspect of my life made my skin crawl.

"Why him?" she asked.

I picked at my nails. "Two birds, one stone. He's researching the Void. I needed a way to manipulate him."

"Seduce and distract?"

My throat went dry. "That was the plan," I said.

"Excellent. I like the initiative you've shown these last few weeks. As a reaper, you'll need to do whatever it takes to get close enough to your marks to extract memories and information. The next time you're... intimate with him, you'll need to take better precautions so you don't fall into an involuntary hibernation." Ziggy pushed the wiggling loops back together. The oily black strands twisted around the translucent green thread, choking it.

"I healed him this morning. It was just a cut—"

Ziggy's eye narrowed. "Excuse me?"

"I didn't intend to. It just happened. He had a deep gash on his forehead. When I touched it, the wound sealed beneath my fingertips."

She stood and paced the thick carpet in front of me. "Of all the... Please tell me you plucked out the memory of that little miracle from his mind."

"I didn't need to; he was asleep."

She pinched the bridge of her nose.

"My gift is evolving," I said. "I want to be re-assessed as a healer."

"No. Your reaper ability is more valuable to the Corps."

"I need to get out of that windowless lab. If you don't call in a recruiter to reassess my healing ability, I'll sacrifice this husk to the gods' damned volcano."

"Are you threatening me?"

"I'm taking initiative."

Ziggy's thin lips curled into a smile. "Now there's the spark of passion I've been waiting for. If you'd shown that kind of enthusiasm sooner, I'd have promoted you to active-duty weeks ago. When I first took you on as an asset, I had high hopes for you, but you lack motivation. This job requires drive and a sense of purpose. There is no room for apathy in the Corps."

She glanced at the undulating orb with a sigh. "As much as it will pain me to see you waste your greatest gift, I'm going to call in another asset to reassess your healing ability. If it meets the minimum threshold, I'll recommend a transfer back to the Nursery for you to train as a healer."

I did my best to bite back a smile. No more claustrophobic labs. No more Liam Riley.

"Of course, you'll have to go through the trials again and be assigned to a new handler."

"What? I barely passed the trials the first time."

"I'm sure you'll do fine. As a healer initiate, you won't have to consume any souls to pass the final test. It may take a few days to set up the assessment. In the meantime, maintain your current orders and try to enjoy what may be your last few days in paradise."

I reached for the neural-lace pod in my ear.

"Oh, and Renae, there isn't any room for insubordination in the Corps either. Threaten me like that again, and I'll send an asset to deactivate you and reissue your husk to another agent."

My stomach growled as I slammed the empty refrigerator and searched my cabinets for something edible. All I found was half a loaf of moldy bread, three slimy black bananas, and a gallon of milk that could pass for cottage cheese. I'd only been back to my Hilo apartment twice since the accident, both times just long enough to do laundry and return to the summit. I had no food, and my plant hospice looked more like a plant graveyard.

The shriveled leaf of an orchid went from brown to yellow as my fingers grazed over the brittle surface. My gift pulsed down my arm like a heartbeat. The leaf turned green, and a new branch forked away from the stem. The nodule on its end grew to the size of a grape and popped open, transforming into a deep purple bloom that immediately wilted and dropped to the counter.

Without proper training, my gift would never be more than a pitiful party trick. What if healing Liam's cut had been a fluke? What if my ability hadn't evolved? What if Ziggy was just humoring me so I wouldn't throw her precious husk into the volcano and beg Pele for mercy? Not that it would do me any good. Like all the ancient gods of human history, Pele was long gone, fed to the Void. Ziggy was the only soul who could get me what I wanted now.

Still, repeating the trials would be risky. Those of us who made it through in one piece were given probationary assignments in the Corps. Those who failed were stripped of their husks and sent back to hell. I didn't know which was worse, being stuck in a monotonous support role with a traitorous gift that couldn't keep its syphons off my broody nemesis, or being sent back to Almega where my demons weren't just memories locked inside the tomb at my core.

I gathered all thirty-seven of my horticultural hospice victims and piled them on the kitchen table. If I went back to the Nursery to train as a healer, nothing was guaranteed. If I failed the trials, I'd be barred from the Corps forever. Gods, I needed to clear my head. I needed to run.

My heart lodged in my throat at a hard knock on my door. I closed my eyes and focused on Liam's energy. All six syphons pointed west like a compass, and I sighed. If in relief or disappointment, I didn't know. He was still sound asleep in his bed.

The knock, more insistent this time, came again. I glanced through the peephole at my neighbor, Mr. Ito's grandson, from the farmers market. Gods, what was his name? It'd been so long since that day, I couldn't remember. John? James?

A dry cottony sensation filled my mouth as I opened the door. "Hi... Jason?"

He stuffed his hands in his pockets and glanced around as if he didn't know where to look—my face, the cropped sports bra and running shorts I'd changed into, or the empty space above my head where my invisible syphons floated. He swallowed hard. "I... I tried to call first, but you didn't answer."

I didn't recall giving him my number.

"I lost my phone," I said. There was no point in replacing it now. Not if I planned on returning to the Nursery to train as a healer. "Was there something you needed?" I asked.

His eyes slid over my shoulder to the congregation of dead plants on my kitchen table. "I was heading to DaGrindz to pick up a to-go breakfast for my grandfather and saw your light on. I was wondering if you'd like to join me. Their breakfast menu is incredible, and I still owe you that cup of coffee and a tour of our greenhouse."

My stomach growled. "Gods, yes, I'm starving. Let me grab my bag and put on a shirt." The run could wait.

⁊

Jason hadn't exaggerated. The last thing I'd expected to find when we stepped into the unassuming café with its sunny yellow façade and a total of four dining tables was a twenty-page takeout menu.

An acrid tang laced my tongue as Jason drummed his fingers on the counter and waited for me to make a selection. "I don't know what I want. It all sounds so good." I flung out my arm and smacked a plate and mug out of the hands of a passing waitress. Coffee soaked through the front of her white shirt, and the plate hit the floor with a crack.

"Gods, I'm so sorry." I bent to pick up the broken pieces.

Honey, thick and sweet, choked my throat as she spoke. "It's fine. One more for the collection." She gestured to the wall behind the counter where dozens of repaired plates hung, their glued cracks painted over in bright colors. "Are you ready to order?"

"What do you recommend?"

"The special," she said with a smile that didn't reach her mahogany eyes.

"Great. I'll take that." She took the broken pieces from my outstretched hand and glanced at Jason.

"I'll have the same, and two macadamia nut lattes to go, please."

The waitress nodded and disappeared into the kitchen.

"What did I just order?" I asked Jason.

"Rice topped with a hamburger, fried egg, onions, and gravy."

"Ooh, that does sound good. I'll have to apologize to your grandfather for delaying his breakfast."

Jason tugged on his earlobe. "Can I make a confession?" he asked.

The cottony feeling returned to my mouth as Jason's energy rolled over me like a weighted blanket. My gift recoiled from the brief sensation.

"I used my grandfather as an excuse to ask you out."

"You needn't have bothered with the ruse. You had me at breakfast."

"Two macadamia nut lattes." The waitress set the drinks in front of me and handed Jason a plastic bag with our food.

I may have groaned as I sipped the steaming liquid. "Gods, I haven't had a good cup of coffee in weeks. The sludge they serve at the summit hotel is terrible. But this," I took another sip, "is divine."

"You work a lot of hours. You must love your job."

"Not particularly."

Jason's smooth brow folded into a scowl as he held the passenger door open for me.

"I just got lectured by my boss about my *lack of motivation*. I've been working twelve-hour shifts, seven days a week and literally passed out from exhaustion yesterday. I'm not sure how much more she expects from me."

"I totally get it. I'm on call twenty-four seven and have to drop whatever I'm doing when the boss calls. Sometimes it feels impossible to have a life of my own, but that's what I signed up for when I joined the family business."

"At least you're doing something you enjoy. I spend my nights locked in a windowless lab, staring at a computer screen. It's so tedious. It's not even the job I was trained for."

"Are you burned out or just bored?"

I held the coffee cup to my lips. "I don't know."

On the way to the nursery, Jason grilled me on the day-to-day logistics of my job as if he were trying to fathom how a person could dedicate so much time and energy to something they didn't enjoy. I didn't expect him to understand. He had a family legacy to care for, a passion to follow. All I had were orders.

That passion was written all over his face as he gave me an animated tour of his grandfather's greenhouse. Light danced across his obsidian eyes as he led me past tables covered with feathery ferns, spikey bromeliads, and wide-leafed philodendrons.

"The commercial production facility for our Forever Fresh preserved plants is in the next building."

A familiar astringent odor filled my nose as we entered the sterile warehouse behind the nursery. Rows of open top tanks eerily similar to the ones the Corps used to grow husks ran the length of the room. Each tank held a submerged rack of ghost-white specimens. Spectral versions of the lush plants growing in the greenhouse.

"These are the drying tanks where we leech the moisture from cuttings with an alcohol solution. The process preserves them without destroying the cellular integrity, so they retain their natural supple texture. If you look closely, you can see that the delicate veining in each leaf is intact."

I gathered my hair, leaned over the tank, and gasped. A pair of glassy black eyes stared back at me from between two stark-white palm fronds. "Is that a rat?"

Jason bent over my shoulder and peered into the tank with a sigh. His warm breath rolled over the back of my neck, sending a prickling sensation down my spine. "It sure is." He grabbed a net from the wall, fished out the poor creature and dumped it in a trash bin. "They fall in occasionally."

"Can't they swim?"

"The alcohol solution kills them almost instantly. We have to keep lids on the dye vats. The chemicals aren't as toxic, and the rodents end up thrashing around and destroying the entire batch." Jason gestured to a row of tanks filled with green goo.

"Once the plant husks are ready, we transfer them into the glycerin-based dye. The leaves soak up the solution and regain the appearance of living specimen."

"It seems like a lot of trouble to go through to turn a real plant into a dead plant that looks like a real plant," I said.

"The Forever Fresh line is our best seller. We ship them all over the world. I've found that people will pay a premium for the perception of perfection over reality."

"What's in there?" I asked, nodding to a vault at the back of the warehouse that looked to have been recently installed.

"That's where we hide all the bodies."

My armpits went sticky with sweat at the joke and the idea of anyone being trapped inside a room like that.

"Just kidding. It's where we keep the caustic chemicals." He transferred the bag containing our breakfasts to the opposite hand and gestured toward a side exit. "There's something else I want to show you."

The breath stalled in my lungs at the forest of lush foliage that greeted us as we stepped into a private conservatory behind the warehouse. Banana leaves and flowering trees stretched from floor to roof. Spanish moss hung from branches like delicate silver hair, and every nook and cranny was filled with blooming orchids. Some in pots, others clinging to bark, climbing trunks, or hanging from suspended beams, their bare roots dangling around us like naked vines. A sense of calm washed over me, wiping away everything else—the knot twisting in my stomach every time I thought about repeating the trials, and the constant clamor in my head that was Liam Riley. I was at peace for the first time in weeks.

"This place is incredible," I whispered as I slumped down on a bench next to Jason. "I can't even keep a houseplant alive without divine intervention."

"The arrow always strikes the eye," he said as he set the food out between us. "It means success follows intention. We are what we practice. My grandfather's mantra."

"Where *is* your grandfather?" I hadn't seen him, or another person, for that matter, since we arrived.

"Taking a nap at his desk, if I had to guess." Jason tugged at his earlobe again. "What's your favorite movie?" he asked, as if it were some sort of litmus test for the future of our friendship.

"*L'Éternal Retour,*" I said without hesitation before shoveling a forkful of rice and gravy into my mouth. I should have lied and gone with something released in my husk's official lifetime.

"Never heard of it."

"It's a 1943 French film. Tragic love story set in a castle by the sea." It was the last film I'd seen with my mother.

Jason grinned from ear to ear. "You get two bonus points for picking an oldie and one negative point for picking something I'll have to watch with subtitles." We ate and talked about his passion for vintage films, and for a brief moment, I forgot that I was a soul-sucking monster with a broken, traitorous gift.

"What are your plans for the rest of the weekend?" Jason asked when he walked me to my front door.

"I should probably go for a run after that breakfast," I said.

"Can I... take you to dinner tomorrow?"

Ziggy's advice floated through my head. *Enjoy your last few days in paradise.*

I bit back a smile. "Pick me up at seven."

# Chapter Nine

# LIAM

Sleep deprivation hangovers—all the pain and none of the pleasure of getting wrecked. A foul mood clung to me the same way volcanic fog clung to the grass on either side of my driveway. I inspected the skin on my forehead in the rearview mirror, pinching and pulling at the faint pink scar. Not bad, considering my bed looked like a damn crime scene. It didn't surprise me that Renae bolted. If she was like me, she wouldn't want to stick around and make excuses for her drug-induced stupor.

Something crunched under the clutch when I tried to start the engine. I picked up Renae's phone and ran my hand over the cracked glass. The lock screen lit up, displaying her notifications. One missed call from a local number and four texts from someone named Ziggy.

*Where are you?*

*You didn't come home last night.*

*Call me immediately.*

*We need to talk.*

My damn chest tightened as I chucked the phone into the seat next to me, refusing to let jealousy make me do something stupid like Googling local listings for someone named Ziggy. Her personal life was none of my damn business. That didn't stop me from hoping I'd find her thumbing it on the side of the road on my way into town. Or being a little disappointed and a lot worried when I didn't. It would take hours for a sober person to walk back to Hilo, longer for someone climbing their way out of a trank coma.

I tried not to imagine the packs of feral pigs that roamed the mountain. Those fat fuckers packed a nasty attitude. By the time I got to campus without a single glimpse of her, my stomach turned sour and I told myself she must have gotten a ride as I slipped her cell into my back pocket and headed to class.

I pushed through my lecture on 2-D kinematics, ending ten minutes early in search of naproxen and the dark refuge of my basement office to ease the pounding in my skull. No matter what I did, I couldn't get Renae's tortured fucking scream out of my head.

She needed serious help, and I was so *not* the best person for that. It had nothing to do with my lack of compassion for her insobriety and *everything* to do with me not hating how it felt to fall asleep with her in my arms. I needed to stay the hell away from her. My life was complicated enough without obsessing over a woman I couldn't have.

I rifled through my desk for a power bar.

"Lose something?"

My head jerked to the open doorway filled by Marcus Logan's wide-shouldered frame and gleaming bald head.

I held up a flattened peanut butter-flavored brick. "Just looking for lunch," I said as I peeled back the wrapper.

"How'd it go last night?"

A loaded question. "Not exactly what I expected, but I got some clear data, and I appreciate you working me into the schedule."

Logan cocked a brow. "Apparently, you made quite the impression."

*Fuck.*

"I'll be honest. I was kind of a dick last night. Whatever she says about me is true." I took a bite of the stale protein bar, waiting to be fired from my unpaid second job.

"She said you'll be an asset to the team."

I coughed, trying to dislodge the peanut butter lump from my throat. "You talked to her... this morning?"

"Just keep doing what you're doing and don't get sidetracked. I placed you under her supervision for a reason. You could stand to learn a few things from her."

Maybe Renae had decided not to throw me under the bus for the whole trying to kiss her thing after all. Or maybe she had, and Logan didn't give a shit, which I hoped wasn't the case because that would make me feel like even more of an asshole. How the fuck was I going to look her in the eye the next time I saw her?

"Go home, eat something more substantial than that garbage, and get some sleep. You look like shit." He shook his head as he walked away.

"Marcus, wait." I grabbed Renae's phone and followed him into the stairwell.

"Renae dropped this last night. Can you get it to her?"

He glanced at the phone in my hand with no intention of taking it.

"I won't see her anytime soon. But I'm sure you can manage. She lives in town. Cascade Palms complex, unit seventeen." He checked his watch. "You coming to the AA meeting today?"

"I have a shit ton of assignments to grade before my lab this afternoon. Maybe tomorrow."

He clapped his hand on my shoulder, and I flinched as his thoughts intruded my brain. *Nothing changes if nothing changes.* We both knew I had no intention of showing.

I went back to my office and logged in to the university's digital grading platform, knee bouncing. My eyes slid to Renae's phone every time it vibrated on the desk. Three more missed calls from this Ziggy person. I wanted to chuck the damn thing down the hall. Her boyfriend was either an impatient ass hat or there was some kind of emergency. Fuck it. I wasn't getting any work done anyway.

It took six minutes to get to her place. The narrow parking lot was a pain in the ass to maneuver with the truck. The only open spot had me wedged between a bubblegum blue hybrid and a half dead palm tree.

I leaned over the dash and stared up at the two-story complex. Logan had failed to mention whether Renae lived in unit 17A or 17B. Was it weird to show up unannounced? Not any weirder than sitting in my truck like a damn stalker. I didn't have a clue what to say to her. "You left your phone in my truck, and by the way, thanks for tranking yourself and dumping your shit in my lap."

I gritted my teeth and squeezed out of the truck. When I knocked on the first-floor apartment, a lanky kid opened the door.

"Sorry, man, I must have the wrong floor," I said, and glanced up the stairwell.

"Are you looking for Renae?" he asked.

"Yeah, she around?"

"She's out right now. Can I give her a message for you?"

"You're Ziggy?" She wasn't just seeing someone. She was living with someone. This fucking kid. I peered inside their apartment, expecting to see some sign of her—shoes by the door, candles, or fuzzy throw blankets, all the shit chicks liked, but the place was near empty. Barely looked lived in.

The kid flinched. "My name is Jason."

Ziggy must be her pet name for him. "Just tell her Liam stopped by to chat about last night. And to return this." I shoved down the jealous urge to say more and handed him her cell.

"Excellent. She thought she'd lost it. I'll give it to her as soon as she gets back from her run." He glanced up at the darkening sky and scowled. "Where did you say she left it?"

"I didn't." Fuck him. If he didn't know where his girlfriend slept last night, that was his damn problem.

I had a hard time imagining Renae with that squeaky clean kid as I jogged back to my truck. Were pretty boys her type? I didn't know shit about her life—except that she was deeply scarred, maybe even more screwed up and broken than I was. How many times had he held her as she screamed in the dark?

My phone vibrated on the dash as I hopped in the cab. A message from the dealership in Kona. My bike was ready to come home. I thought about the banked turns that led to the summit and the serious road ripping I needed to get out of my system before my next shift with Renae.

A guilty knot twisted in my stomach as I started the engine and headed to DaGrindz for a shot of caffeine and to check in with Monika. She'd backed off since the accident, waiting for me to get my head right.

Mons was leaning over the takeout counter on her elbows, inspecting a broken plate as if it were a piece of art.

"Another victim for your collection?" I nodded to the display of pieced together plates hanging on the wall behind her, all the cracks bulging with epoxy clay and painted over in bright colors.

Mons placed her newest project in a plastic bin of broken dishes and came around the counter to give me a quick hug. "It's called kintsugi, you asshole. Where the fuck have you been?"

"I know what it's called. Doesn't seem practical to spend all that time repairing shit that can never be used again."

"That's not the point. It's about seeing the beauty in imperfection and finding a new purpose for something broken." She gestured to her wall of frankensteined plates that had become the coffee shop's signature. "Why should I throw them out when I can turn them into something beautiful?"

I sat in my usual spot at the end of the counter while Mons put on her aloha smile for a couple who entered the café. As she took their to-go order, I rubbed the cord of scar tissue that ran down my forehead and wondered where I fit in her collection. On the wall of mended things or in the to-be-fixed bucket. I checked my phone. Still nothing from Renae.

"You look like hell," Monika said, brushing the hair away from my forehead when she returned.

"It's just a scratch. Doesn't even hurt." I rubbed the ridge of my brow where my face had split opened six hours earlier. No scab. Not even the hint of a bruise remained.

"You okay? You seem a little off."

"Is that my shirt?" I asked. She was wearing my only white button-down over her tank top and jeans. A huge brown stain painted across the chest.

"Sorry." She rolled her eyes. "Clumsy tourist knocked into me earlier. I'll wash it before I bring it back."

"Keep it. Looks better on you anyway. Can I get a double shot?"

She made my drink and handed it to me. "What are you doing later?"

"Sleeping," I said, trying not to picture Renae in my bed, her cheek pressed to my chest.

"You want company?" Monika wiped down the wand on the frothing machine and shot me a suggestive smile as she stroked it. If she came over, there was no scenario in which I'd be getting any rest.

Before the accident, I appreciated the hell out of her company at least once a week. "As tempting as that sounds, I didn't sleep much last night. I don't think I have the stamina to keep you entertained."

"Are you sure?"

"I've got a shit ton of grading to do before I crash."

She arched a skeptical brow. "Well, you better get a good night's sleep because I expect your undivided attention tomorrow."

"I can't tomorrow. Gotta go to Kona and pick up my bike."

"Oh my God, we talked about this right after you got out of the hospital when I drove you home. I've been planning it for weeks." Her face heated.

My jaw clenched. I had a vivid memory of the accident. The hours and days after, not so much. With the pain and frequent out-of-body hallucinations, I'd intentionally blocked Monika's constant jabbering about random shit. I'd fucking hallucinated Renae's presence on a daily basis, just like I had in the hospital, and every time I closed my eyes, I still saw the blood-red field. My ability to focus on anything else had been shit these last few weeks.

"Sorry, I have zero recollection of any such conversation."

She huffed a sigh. "I can't believe you forgot."

"Are you gonna remind me or are you gonna pout?"

Monika shot me a daggered glance. "You can be a real dick sometimes. You know that, right?"

I shrugged. Not like I could admit to being obsessed with thoughts of another woman. One who'd woken up in my bed. Mons and I weren't exclusive, but talking about other chicks with her just felt wrong.

She rolled her eyes as she tidied a stack of to-go cups. "You remember my brother Tyler?"

"The MMA fighter who threatened to kick my ass? Yeah, I remember." I'd only met him once, during a three-day beach crawl up the coast, and got the distinct impression that he didn't approve of his kid sister fucking around with someone seven years her senior.

"He invited you to spar at his gym. It was hardly a threat."

"Agree to disagree."

"He's been doing this community theater thing. Once a month, they reenact Hawaiian myths near the sacred grounds of Pu'uhonua O Hōnaunau. The show starts at sunset."

It didn't sound that terrible. "What's the catch?"

She scrunched up her face. "Tee and his friends are having a party at my parents' house before the performance."

"Goddammit, Mons." She was great, but she was one of those chicks who liked milestones, and meeting the parents was one box on her checklist toward a real relationship I'd never felt compelled to complete.

"Lee, please don't be mad. I wasn't trying to spring this on you, I promise. We talked about it. You agreed."

"It must have been the concussion talking because that doesn't sound like something I would ever agree to. I don't have anything against your family, Mons. I just don't want you to be disappointed." In my experience, family gatherings were cold and awkward at best, violent at worst, and I preferred to avoid situations guaranteed to test my sobriety.

"I'll be disappointed if I have to show up alone—again. You're going to Kona, anyway. What's the big deal? It's just a luau."

"Your brother wasn't too keen on his kid sister dating a haole the last time we met."

"Things are different now."

I scowled as I considered that statement.

"I'll pick up a dozen long johns and a few other sweets from the bakeshop. When you show up with pastries, they'll welcome you with open arms. I promise."

"I don't know, Mons. This new schedule is already killing me. Between teaching and working on my dissertation by day and pulling all-nighters at the summit, I need to front load on sleep this weekend."

She propped her hands on her hips and gave me that 'I'm not taking no for an answer' look. "I'll drive. You can sleep in the car."

There was no way to get out of this without cracking open a conversation about my fucked-up family dynamics or our yet to be defined relationship.

"What time do you wanna leave? I need to be at the dealership before three."

She gave me a quick peck on the cheek. "I'll pick you up after my morning shift. Oh, and you have to eat the poi. It's my aunty's special recipe. She puts all kinds of herbs and weird shit in it, but she's the family matriarch. If she takes a liking to you, you're in. So, just eat the poi, pretend to like it, and you'll be fine."

Something was off. I wasn't sure if it was me or my bike. Maybe we just needed a little time to get reacquainted. The stiff new forks and front assembly took some getting used to during the slow crawl following Monika back to her parents' place.

Neighborhood kids darted into the street, chasing a baseball down the hill, paying no mind to my bike as I swerved around them. I slammed on the brakes half a dozen times to avoid hitting the little demons. By the time we got to the house, my nerves were fried.

I pulled off my new helmet, and Monika combed her fingers through my hair before handing me the box of pastries she brought.

"You should carry these. If anyone asks, you got them from Hoa Hanau's."

The party spilled across half the block. Monika's brother was in the driveway, manning a rusted-out gas grill that'd been patched up with baking sheets and aluminum foil to turn it into a charcoal firebox.

"Makani," he bellowed, calling her by her Hawaiian name, "come give me one hug." Tyler wasn't much taller than Monika's five and a half feet. What he lacked in height, he made up for in sheer mass.

"Tee, you remember Liam." She yanked me forward.

He nodded at the pastry box in my hands. "What da kine you bring?"

"Long johns. I'm supposed to tell you I got them from Hoa Hanau's, but Monika bought them. I had absolutely nothing to do with it."

Mons punched my arm as her brother nodded in approval. "Your secret is safe with me, brah." He lifted the lid and pulled out two glazed donuts. "Long as you don't tell mommie I ate um before da lau lau." He winked at his sister as he crammed an entire donut in his mouth.

Tyler put down the barbecue tongs and clasped my arm. "You want something to drink? We got beer, soda, some water." He nodded to a large blue cooler on the ground behind him. "Help yourself."

The cooler was stocked with a local IPA, dark amber, nice and hoppy. The good stuff that would leave me with a decent buzz after two or three. I ground my will against the urge to pick one up just to feel the weight of it in my palm.

"Grab me a water too?" Monika made eye contact before giving me a nod. An affirmation that walked the line between being supportive and trying to run my recovery. She meant well.

I plucked two waters out of the ice and handed her one.

"You guys stay and grind. I gotta go get ready. Catch you after, yeah?" Tyler said.

Monika nodded, and he tugged on a strand of her mahogany hair before disappearing inside.

I chugged the water, trying to quell a different kind of thirst as we made our way to the backyard where Mons introduced me to her parents, cousins, neighbors, and then some. It wasn't as awkward as I'd imagined. No one stared at my scar or lectured me on what a disappointment I was. No one got drunk or flipped any tables.

It was... nice and strange. Like being dropped in a foreign country where you don't speak the language but could maybe learn.

Monika's aunt held court from a white plastic chair on a raised wooden deck in the middle of the yard. Half of her face hung limp like melted wax beneath her cataract clouded eye.

"Aunty Cici, this is Liam. He's a physics professor." Monika said, overselling it as we stepped onto the weathered wooden dais.

"I'm just a teaching assistant," I corrected.

"He's working on his PhD in astronomy," Monika said, jabbing me with her elbow.

The woman angled her face and gave me the once over with her good eye. "Tell me, child, what do you see when you look toward the heavens?"

"It's what you can't see that most interests me," I said. "I'm looking at inconsistencies in the invisible energy left over from the universe's conception—"

The woman's hands shot out, grasping my arm as the expression dropped from her half-paralyzed face.

My eyes flicked to Monika.

"She's having one of her visions," Monica whispered, cheeks flaming with embarrassment.

The woman's grip tightened. "The storm is inevitable, child. Be leery of the sharks it draws to shore. Your actions will determine whether they are friend or foe." The woman dropped my arm, and her previously animated expression returned.

"Here, Aunty, have some water."

"Thank you, Makani." She took a long sip before lifting her girth from the chair. "Now, if you'll excuse me, I must go prepare." She climbed off the deck and moved toward the house, bobbing like a buoy with the swell of each step.

"Am I supposed to know what that meant?" I asked once Monika's aunt was out of earshot.

Mons shuffled her feet in the grass. "When the time comes, it'll make sense. It's a gift. Two summers ago, she told me to be kind to a scarred stranger because they would save the life of someone I loved. A week later, I met this cocky white guy with a sexy scar getting his ass kicked by the storm surge at Pine Trees."

"As I recall, you were the one who dropped in on *my* wave. I bailed so you could have it and ended up with a wicked coral scrub." I shoved my hands in my pockets. "Do you... actually believe in these visions?" I asked, wondering what she'd make of the voices in my head. Would she see it as a gift or another crack to be glued and painted over?

Monika shrugged. "I know it's weird, but she's never been wrong."

The setting sun cast a golden glow over the stage as we took our seats on the wooden benches in the open-air amphitheater.

"I think you should stay out of the water for a while, that's all I'm saying," Monika said.

I tugged my head away as she reached up and tried to fuss with my hair. "Out of the question. I'm not gonna stop surfing just because your aunt had some sort of psychic premonition about sharks."

A drum cadence echoed through the amphitheater, cutting off Monika's retort as the spotlight fell on her aunt's face.

"Aloha, brothers and sisters. Mahalo for joining us for Voices of Hawaii, an evening of music and myth presented by the Kona Community Theater Corps."

Tyler and the other dancers moved across the stage in costume, acting out the ancient stories narrated by Monika's aunt. My eyes drooped with the heavy hypnotic rhythm and my mind drifted to Renae. I imagined her with that pretty boy, smiling and laughing as he opened the car door for her. My attention flickered between what was happening on stage and the scene playing out inside my head. One foot in each reality as they slid over one another like panes of glass.

"Our next tale of ill-fated lovers highlights the delicate balance between life and death, and it began here, on this hallowed ground." Her aunt's velvet voice echoed as the set changed.

Monika nudged my shoulder. "This one's my favorite," she whispered, "it's about demigod siblings, Hiku and Kawelu who... shit, Lee, your nose is bleeding."

My fingers met the wetness above my lip. I leaned forward aware of a faint metallic tang at the back of my throat as I pinched my nose shut.

Monika pulled out a plastic pack of tissues from her purse and shoved them toward me and I forced my attention to the stage. By the end of the play, my nose was dry.

"Are you sure you're all right?" Monika asked as we exited the amphitheater and strolled toward the moonlit beach.

"It's fine. Just a nosebleed. I spent half my childhood with a bloody washcloth pressed to my face." Either from my too-thin sinuses or one of the lessons my father liked to dish out with his fists.

"Well, I spent *my* childhood here. Aunty used to bring me to this beach all the time. She says the veil between the world of the living and dead is thinner here, easier to puncture. Told me if I concentrated hard enough on the energy pulsing around me, I could see and communicate with the spirits before they crossed through the barrier."

"So, your weird aunt brought you to a haunted beach to teach you how to talk to dead people? Not creepy at all." An icy hand slid across my shoulders, raising the hair on the back of my neck. I shook off the sensation and blamed it on the breeze rolling down from the mountains behind us.

"Yeah, all I ever got was chicken skin." She squinted and pointed at the open ocean. "There's a flat rock out past the jetty that sticks out at low tide. Tourists like to swim out and jump off, but you'll never see a local out there. Aunty says it's the secret entrance to the afterlife, the one Hiku used to rescue his true love, Kawelu." Her gaze swung back to mine. "What did you think of the play?"

"Your aunt has serious stage presence, but the whole incest thing in that last myth was fucking weird."

"Yeah, but if you look past that, the story of Kawelu and Hiku is kind of romantic."

"Come on, the guy goes off to sow his wild oats, and the chick offs herself because she can't take being alone. That's a horrible message, and then there's the nepotism. The father knows his son's a piece of shit, so he uses his god powers to fix everything so the dude can screw his zombie sister. None of that is even remotely romantic."

"How do you not see it? It's the ultimate love story. Hiku braved the dangers of the afterlife to save the woman he loved. It's about the unbreakable bond between two souls. Not even death could keep them apart."

"Sounds like a toxic relationship to me."

"You're an asshole." She spun abruptly and stomped off toward the parking lot.

When I caught up to her, Monika's eyes were wet with tears.

"What the hell, Mons? Why are you crying?"

She stared at the dark horizon, jaw clenched.

I brushed the hair away from her wet cheek. "Talk to me. What's going on? And don't tell me it's about the damn play. We've been friends long enough for me to know when you're lying."

"Oh my god, you're just making it worse." She swiped at her tears. "Don't you get it? I'm in love with you, Liam."

A knife twisted in my gut as I pulled her close. She was smart, beautiful, and everything I didn't deserve. It should have been easy to tell her what she wanted to hear. I just couldn't dislodge the words from my throat.

"I care about you too, Mons. You know that."

"Then show me." She stood on her tiptoes and kissed me as she unbuttoned my jeans. "Make love to me."

"Right here?" I glanced up the path toward the amphitheater, the lights still visible from the beach.

"Right here, right now," she said as she slipped her hand inside my boxers. And God help me, I leaned into her firm grip, letting her stroke me until I was rock hard. I pressed my forehead to hers as the pressure built into an aching need. When I closed my eyes, all I could see was Renae, wishing it was her delicate hand with those wicked talons clenched around my cock.

I groaned and grabbed Monika's wrist. "Mons, stop," I pleaded, pulling her hand away and zipped up my jeans. I was a piece of shit for letting it get this far. Her future was here, surrounded by family. With any luck, I'd finish my dissertation by the end of the year and start a full-time research position somewhere else, with an ocean between us. "You deserve someone who can give you everything." Someone who could give her their full devotion and attention.

"I don't want everything. I want you, Lee."

"No, you don't. You want someone you can fix. The parts of me that are damaged can't be glued back together and painted over in pretty colors like one of your fucking plates."

She flinched, and I immediately regretted what I'd said. Not the message, just the harsh delivery.

"I'm sorry. I just... you deserve to be with someone you don't have to piece back together or make excuses for. Someone who can live up to the standard you have in your head." I'd spent my entire life trying and failing to live up to someone else's impossible expectations. All it had gotten me was a nasty scar. "You deserve someone better, Mons. Someone who's deliriously in love with you."

"And you're not deliriously in love with me." A statement, not a question.

"I don't think I'm built that way." Aside from my brother, she was the closest thing I'd ever had to a best friend. I loved her. Just not the way she needed me to.

Her face twisted with pain as she sucked in a ragged breath. I tugged her to my chest, and damn if I didn't feel my own heart rip a little as she sobbed against my shoulder. The breeze kicked up around us, and we stood there a long time, clinging to one another like two wind-whipped palms in a storm.

Monika pulled herself free and took a step away, then another. Her words came out in one explosive shot to my gut. "I obviously want more from you than you're willing or able to give. I think it's time we go our separate ways. Don't call me. Don't text me, and please," she snorted back a sob, "*do not* come to the coffee shop. I never want to see you again." She turned on her heels and stomped back to the amphitheater. This time, I didn't follow. I just stood there with my heart in my throat, watching the best thing that had ever happened to me walk out of my life.

I'd been selfishly idling at this crossroads for a while, keeping her close but also holding her at arm's length where she'd be safe, where she couldn't see all the truly ugly shit at my core. The thing about crossroads is you have to commit. I'd spent too much time spinning my wheels and ended up getting blindsided by a fucking semi.

# Chapter Ten

# RENAE

AFTER AN HOUR OF online tutorials and several failed attempts to do something sexy with my mass of hair, I ended up with what could only be described as a flaming bird's nest on the top of my head. Messy braids twisted around each other like coppery snakes.

The outfit I'd thrown together wasn't much better—a pair of loose flirty pajama shorts that could pass as a skirt if you squinted just right and a cropped white tank top. It wasn't the blue dress, which I could have replaced, but I'd just have to give it up all over again when I returned to the Nursery and traded my current wardrobe for the Corps' white trainee uniform. This time, the four pointed eye emblazoned on the back would be green instead of black.

With every minute that ticked by, the likelihood of the recruiter showing up to assess me before my next summit shift with Liam diminished. It was only a matter of time before his scans of the Eridanus region revealed the thing I was there to keep hidden. The entrance to Almega. The only safe passage through the Void into the afterlife. If the recruiter didn't show up soon, I might have to go through with the lie I'd fed Ziggy. Seduce and distract and get close enough to pluck out more of his memories.

My traitorous gift fluttered beneath my skin at the thought. Physical distance and the glass embedded in my foot helped, but it was hard enough to ignore the tidal pull of his energy when we weren't in the same room, breathing the same air. Spending another night together in the cramped lab while his emotions and physical sensations pulsed through me would be a challenge.

I needed a release, something to take the edge off so my gift didn't take control and betray me. I bit back a smile as the squeaky stairs outside my apartment announced the arrival of my temporary distraction. I waited for Jason to knock before opening the door.

He wore a pair of pale green shorts and a white button-down with the sleeves rolled up to his elbows. Jason's too-strong cologne cloyed my nose. Top notes of bergamot and moss clashed with the astringent tang beneath, as if he'd bathed in the chemical solution that filled the tanks in his warehouse before spritzing aftershave all over his skin.

His eyes went straight to the nest on my head as my syphons hovered behind me.

"Too much?" I ran my hand over the braided monstrosity.

"It looks complicated." Jason reached up and tugged on his earlobe and Liam's words floated through my head. *Everyone has a tell.* "I... I like it. It suits you."

"Are those for me?" I asked, nodding to the bouquet of red ginger blooms in his hand.

He glanced at the flowers as if he'd forgotten he was holding them. "I know it's cliché, but I'm old-fashioned, and my grandfather said it's not a proper date without flowers. They're real, not preserved. You should put them in water."

"They're lovely. Tell your grandfather I said thank you."

Jason followed me into the kitchen, and I pulled a tall glass from the cabinet. I didn't have a vase or any of the other things humans collected during a life. Things that made it more difficult to move on.

"A guy came by looking for you yesterday. He said his name was Leon."

My pulse stumbled, and I almost dropped the glass. "Liam?"

"Yeah, maybe."

I forced my twitching fingers to relax as I attempted to fit the fat stems into the makeshift vase. "What did he want?"

"To return this." Jason set my missing cell phone on the counter. "I would have brought it by sooner, but I got stuck late at the nursery."

"Did he say anything else?" I asked, ignoring the traitorous flutter in my chest.

"No. He was kind of a jerk, though."

I loosened a breath and looked up from the lopsided arrangement. "Thank you for the flowers—and the phone. Shall we go?" I asked, ending the conversation about the man who hovered in my consciousness like a constant shadow. The awareness of him was so strong I thought I might glance back and see him standing there.

Jason held the car door open, and my shoulder grazed his outstretched arm as I squeezed past him into the passenger side. My gift recoiled as if determined to ruin my plans for what might be my last night in this husk. If the recruiter ever deigned to make an appearance.

The busy restaurant reminded me of a carousel, with its ruffled roof and shimmering gold and red trim. The two-story pagoda looked like a building out of time, yet still at home nestled between two towering hotels and a lush garden at the edge of Hilo Bay.

We found an empty spot on a low stone wall overlooking the koi pond while we waited for a table. Coins covered the bottom of the shallow pool. I dipped my fingers in the water as Jason explained how the hot-pot menu worked. My gift surged to my hand as if I'd touched someone, thousands of someones, all at once. All the forgotten wishes and secret desires lying dormant beneath the surface rushed through me in an onslaught of blurred visions and physical sensations. I grasped Jason's shoulder for stability with my free hand, my nails digging in as the world spiraled.

The spinning sensation ceased the moment I yanked my fingers from the water.

"Are you all right?" Jason asked.

I exhaled slowly, trying to settle the lingering nausea and too-light head. "It's just a little vertigo. It happens sometimes when my blood sugar drops. I'll be fine as soon as I eat something."

Jason's brow wrinkled as he resumed his menu recommendations, describing the appetizer special from a link on his phone—savory scallion pancakes and stuffed pork buns. It should have made my mouth water with anticipation. Instead, my stomach lurched.

I blocked out his voice and tried not to think about food. My gaze fell to the silver and copper coins asleep at the bottom of the pond. The ability to consume the traces of human energy left behind on inanimate objects was rare, even among reapers. Apparently, both of my gifts were evolving. What would the recruiter make of that? Gifts didn't just evolve on their own. It typically took multiple human lifetimes to build enough energy to level up. I'd only lived and died once, nowhere near long enough to build that kind of charge. I shoved down the only other explanation. One that revolved around a six-foot-two typhoon on a motorcycle.

"A penny for your thoughts?" Jason held up a shiny new quarter.

I held my breath as I took the coin, warmed from his pocket, and exhaled when nothing happened. No more nauseating visions.

"Do you believe in fate?" I asked.

"I believe in probable outcomes that can be surmised based on past events and individual and group behavior, but no, I don't believe in predetermined destinies."

A stifled squeak lodged in the back of my throat. Part laugh. Part grunt.

"You disagree?"

I ground the ball of my foot into the floor as Liam's energy surged to the forefront of my perception. "I'm not sure what I believe anymore. Do you remember what the fortune-teller said to me at the market?"

Jason's eyes narrowed. "Miss Cici says a lot of things. Whatever it was, I wouldn't take it to heart."

"She told me to be careful."

His brow furrowed. "I'm sure she says the same thing to every customer. It's her hook, to get you to pay for a full reading."

"She also said I should choose my steps carefully because the road would be covered in broken glass. I was so distracted by her strange prediction that I neglected to look both ways before crossing the street when I left the farmers market that day. I caused a traffic accident. A man almost died. Because of me." My mouth went dry with a thick cottony sensation as Jason's energy blanketed my senses.

"And now you're wondering if the prediction caused the accident or if the accident was meant to be and would have happened regardless?"

"Something like that."

"The future isn't divined by the words of old women. Our actions determine our fate, for better or worse. We choose our own destinies."

"Do we, though? How did you know you were meant to be a botanist?" I couldn't tell him about the Nūkiri—the three sentient entities who ruled over the worlds of the living and the dead with their divinations. "Did you choose it because you know in your heart it's what you're meant to do, or because the path was already laid out for you?"

Long lashes brushed his cheeks as he peered down at the water and scowled. "I've always wanted to teach. Make a difference by shaping young minds, steering the next generation toward science and tolerance and all the things we need more of in this world."

"Did your grandfather pressure you into the family business?"

Jason dipped his fingers in the water. "No. I forced him to take me on, because this is where I'm needed most." The taut muscles in his face shifted back into that aloof smile. "If you make a wish," he said, glancing up at me, "the owners guarantee it will come true, but I think there's a disclaimer around here somewhere about wishing for a full stomach."

There was only one wish in my heart, and it had nothing to do with my digestive track. I flipped the coin into the air. It bounced off a concrete statue, plunked into the water, and sank to the bottom, where it would sit, unfulfilled with all the others.

"There's something depressing about drowning your dreams in an algae-infested fishpond," I murmured.

"So, what did you wish for? A full stomach, or something less guaranteed?"

"If I told you, I'd be breaking the universal rule of wishing."

"Fair enough." Jason tossed his own coin into the pond. It landed flat on the surface, hovered for a moment, then tipped side to side and fluttered gracefully to the bottom.

A woman in a red tunic escorted us to our table, took our order, and proceeded to the bar, where she banged a massive gong. A ritual that was repeated after every order, sending a quake of unnerving vibrations rolling through the room. Despite the frequent clanging interruptions, I allowed myself to relax with Jason as we dropped vegetables and dumplings into the simmering hot pot between us on the table. We talked about the horticultural therapy program he wanted to start and our mutual affection for the French coffee press. The conversation was light and refreshing, and it required so little energy to exist in his presence. There were no emotional storms to navigate, no irrational desire to throw myself into his arms, just comfortable, safe companionship. As much as I hated to admit it, Ziggy had been right. I needed to fraternize with the locals, establish a human connection. I needed a friend.

Liam's mood shifted and demanded my attention. He'd been subdued for over an hour, and I assumed he was asleep. The sudden spike in intensity made it difficult to focus on anything Jason was saying. My face flushed, either from the steaming pot of broth in front of me or the low tightening sensation in my belly.

Apparently, Liam was having an *active* evening. I squeezed my legs together as a flame licked its way through my middle.

Jason pushed a piece of wilted bok choy around his plate with a pair of chopsticks. "I enjoy spending time with you, Renae," he said, looking up at me in a way that might have made my pulse quicken if it wasn't already pounding. "We have so much in common."

My hand pressed the underside of the table as I cursed Liam and the contaminating effect his energy had on my body. "Thank you for asking me to dinner. I can't remember the last conversation I had with anyone that didn't revolve around work."

"You must get pretty close to your coworkers, spending weeks together up at the summit."

I shrugged. "It's like any other job, I suppose. You click with some people more than others." I picked up my glass of ice water and gulped it down.

"Like the guy who had your phone?"

"Liam?" Wet heat throbbed through my groin.

"Are you okay?"

"Yup, fine. Why?" My voice squeaked as I squirmed in my seat.

"You just turned bright red at the mention of his name."

"Don't be ridiculous. It's just the steam." I stifled a groan. Gods, I needed to get out of there before I embarrassed myself in front of all these people. "If you'll excuse me, I need to visit the ladies' room."

As I locked the louvered stall door, Liam's mood shifted again. Vinegar frothed in my mouth and nose. Going in and out all the wrong ways. Whatever Liam was going through was more intense than usual and had my gift lashing against its leash. It pulled at my chest, straining toward wherever he was.

I pulled down the flowy gauze shorts, sat on the toilet, and relieved myself. I'd never be able to live a normal existence while bound to a raging storm. Sweat beaded along the nape of my neck and dampened my armpits. I stood and bore down on the balls of my feet. The heart pounding sensation lessened slightly, telling me the panic bubbling in my gut wasn't mine.

"Jason, I'm not feeling well," I said after returning to the table. "Can you please take me home?"

"Is it something you ate?" The cottony sensation returned in my mouth as Jason stood.

"Possibly." I needed one of Ziggy's blue pills. My frilly shorts didn't have pockets, and I didn't own a purse, just a wallet that doubled as a key chain. I dropped a handful of cash on the table and turned to leave, not waiting for him to object.

Ozone and the scent of soil tickled my nose as the sky opened and dropped a deluge of rain on my head. I paced the parking lot and balanced my weight over the balls of my feet in an attempt to shove Liam's presence to the edges of my awareness. How was I supposed to pass the recruiter's assessment with so much of Liam's energy contaminating my system?

Jason drove at a snail's pace through the sheets of rain, making the ten-minute ride take twice as long as it needed to. By the time we got back to our building, the storm hadn't slowed. Jason produced an umbrella and insisted on walking me to my door, despite my insistence that he needn't bother. I was already soaked and shivering.

"I'm sorry for ruining dinner," I said, my syphons squirming away from the firm hand pressed against the bare skin at the small of my back. There was no room for the visions that came with skin-to-skin contact, not while Liam filled every available ounce of my awareness.

"No, it's my fault. I should have checked those pork dumplings before you ate them all. I don't think we cooked them long enough. Do you need me to run out and get you anything? Crackers? Something carbonated?"

"Gods no. I can't handle any food right now. I just need to sleep it off. I'll call you tomorrow."

Alone, inside the confines of my apartment, I kicked off my sodden shoes, washed my face, brushed my teeth, scrubbed my bathtub—anything to distract me from the pressure tugging at my chest and the intense pull toward Liam. The longer I ignored it, the more my gift strained beneath my skin, making it difficult to take a deep breath. I needed air.

The scent of fish and rotting refuse hit me as I slid open the door to the balcony overlooking the alley behind my apartment. I pushed up onto the balls of my feet again. Sharp pain arced up my left leg as the glass dug deeper into my flesh, anchoring me in my own consciousness and pushing Liam's emotional turmoil to the periphery, where I peeled back the layers, trying to make sense of whatever he was going through.

There was a need at the center of it—one I was all too familiar with. The need to feel something, anything other than the regret sucking at your core. The kind of need that drives a person to do reckless things like running on lava or speeding around the island on wet roads in a storm. The bond between us tightened as I gave it a firm tug.

Liam was moving fast. Too fast to be driving anything other than that ridiculous motorcycle. If he wrecked, this time I wouldn't be there to save him. He could skid off the road and over a cliff in this weather. My traitorous gift tore from its leash and took control.

I cleared the railing and landed barefoot in the wet grass below. Rough pavement gave way to rocks, sticks, and mud as I ran west, then changed direction again and again, tracking his movement. I stopped to reorient myself each time he altered course. Why was he driving in circles? I closed my eyes and yanked on the cord between us. When it tugged back, his destination became clear. Home.

I dropped the human pace and headed south toward the volcano. Rain stung my face. Branches and vines snapped against my flesh. Welts and cuts healing as fast as they bit my skin. I burst through the tree line across from his driveway as the throaty hum of an engine reverberated through the dark. He was close. I sprinted toward his bungalow. I needed a place to hide until my gift was satisfied that he was safe.

Headlights cast a wide arc across the weedy grass as I ducked behind the back corner of his house. My chest heaved as I pressed myself against the splintered wood siding. Hair hung and dripping clumps around my face, the now ruined shorts and thin tank top clung to my body like wet toilet paper. Mud coated my legs and filled the space between my toes.

The engine died, and silence squeezed in around me. Each breath and thud of my heart too loud. I forced my body to relax and my gift relinquished control, leaving me lurking in the shadows like a stalker. I had to get out of there. My muscles coiled, readying to make a run for it.

"Who's there?" His deep voice echoed across the yard as a bolt of lightning split the sky. Surprise and something else flickered over his face as our eyes met.

It was too late to run.

Liam didn't say a word as he took in my disheveled appearance. He just shook his head and walked past me. I moved out of his way, unsure if I should follow or turn and bolt as he climbed the back steps, opened the door, and flicked on a light.

"Are you coming in or not?" His voice was flat, devoid of the conflicting emotions roiling inside him.

My lungs expelled the breath I hadn't realized I'd been holding, and I followed him, leaving muddy footprints in my wake.

Liam sloughed off his wet jacket and went straight to the fridge. He pulled out four bottles and raked two down against the countertop, popping off the caps and handing one to me.

"What are you doing here, Renae?"

"I don't know." It was the truth. I grasped the cold glass in my sweaty palm and took a sip. The potent ginger soda burned as it slid down my throat, and I coughed.

Liam leaned against the sink. "You can start by telling me how the hell you got here."

"I ran, mostly."

"You ran twenty-seven miles, with no shoes, in the middle of a thunderstorm?"

"I like to run."

He threw his head back and sucked down the entire bottle, his throat bobbing with each gulp in a way that made my gift thrum beneath my skin.

"So, you're on what? Coke *and* benzos then?" The hard edge of his voice scraped across my raw nerves. Liam turned and placed the empty bottle on the counter behind him. The muscle along his jaw pulsed.

"Am I supposed to know what that means?"

"What's your poison? What cocktail of drugs are you taking?"

"You think I'm on drugs?"

"Oh, I know you are." He crossed his arms, stretching the T-shirt taut across his biceps and chest. "I found the pills in your bag after you roofied yourself and passed out in my damn truck. You were high as hell the other night—all twitchy, pupils as big as frying pans when you gave me the grand tour of the telescope."

"I wasn't high." I lowered my gaze to the dark and light whorls in the wide planked wooden floor beneath my feet.

"Cut the crap, Renae. How often are you using?"

My gaze snapped back to his face. "I'm not taking any illegal substances. Not that it's any of your business. I... I have PTSD. My *therapist* prescribed the benzodiazepine to help settle my nerves." My fists clenched at my sides. Gods, why did I feel compelled to tell him that? Ziggy wasn't technically a therapist, but she had prescribed the pills to help mediate the panic attacks.

"You made it my business by passing out in my truck and then showing up on my doorstep in the middle of the night like a feral cat." His eyes grazed over my mud-streaked legs. "You still haven't explained why you're here, or why you're not wearing any damn shoes."

"I couldn't sleep, so I went for a walk. I took off without my shoes, without a plan or knowing where I was going, and ended up here." It was the truth. Sort of.

He uncrossed his arms and turned on the faucet before pulling a stock pot out of the cabinet and filling it with water. "We need to talk." His voice softened, sliding over me like a warm bath.

"Isn't that what we're doing?" I asked, glancing back at the door, wishing I'd run instead of following him into the house. Wishing my traitorous gift hadn't sought him out. Wishing it wasn't so difficult to peel my eyes away from the muscles flexing across his back as he lifted the pot of water from the sink.

"We need to talk about the other night." Liam threw a hand towel over his shoulder and set the pan on the two-burner stovetop.

Was he cooking? *Please, let it be pasta.* My now-empty stomach gurgled.

Liam leaned against the counter and faced me. His denim eyes darted to the rain-soaked tank top that clung to my breasts. He scowled and glanced away as a flicker of heat crawled across the cord between us.

I crossed my arms over my chest. "Did we get into an accident?"

"No."

"Why were we covered in blood?"

"Because I took a header into the coffee table trying to carry your comatose ass into the house."

"And you thought I needed help finding my way to your bed while I was unconscious?" My syphons shifted beneath my skin at the memory of waking up tangled in his limbs.

"What the hell else was I supposed to do with you?"

"I don't know; leave me out there until I woke up?"

Liam grunted and pushed away from the counter. He opened a cabinet and pulled out a container of sea salt. "Trust me, I was content to leave you out there drooling on yourself all night, but you started screaming like a fucking banshee." He ran a hand over his face. "You were freaking out, thrashing around, and talking in your sleep. I didn't plan to fall asleep in the bed with you. It just happened. I'm sorry if it made you uncomfortable."

My heart slammed against my ribs. "What did I say in my sleep?"

"I have no idea. Are all of your nightmares in French?"

The truth climbed out of my throat, like a snake shedding its skin. "Yes."

His energy tugged at the cord between us. "You don't remember any of it, do you?"

"I remember the nightmare."

"Do you want to talk about it?"

I'm not sure what compelled me to tell him the truth: knowing I might never see him again, or the contaminating effect of his energy pulsing through me and overcoming my better judgement, but I let the words drain from me like blood. "My family was killed when I was young." I grasped the back of a kitchen chair to keep my hands from trembling. "There was a fire. I dream about it sometimes."

"Shit, Renae. I'm sorry."

"It was a long time ago." No matter how much time or distance I put between present and past, the wound refused to scab over. The memories refused to remain buried in the tomb at my core.

Liam attended to the steaming pot of water on the stove. "Why do you hide the pills in a vitamin bottle?"

I couldn't bring myself to look at him. To let him see the things left unspoken on my face. "Because I spend weeks on end in a communal living environment at the summit lodge, and I don't want my coworkers or my boss to know I take tranquilizers to function like a normal human."

Warmth radiated at my back. He was behind me. "Normal is overrated," he said.

I twisted to face him as he pulled out a chair with his foot, holding the pot of steaming water with both hands, towels wrapped around each handle.

"Sit down." His low voice softened the abrupt command and sent my gift racing to comply.

Liam set the pan on the floor in front of me and proceeded to spread one of the towels over it and pressed it down into the water, covering the bottom and sides. "Just be careful. The metal might be hot."

I glanced at the bar of black soap floating in the water. "Excuse me?"

"You tracked red mud all over the floor, and I'm sure as hell not letting you in my truck and driving you back to town looking like you just crawled out of a damn grave."

"I'm perfectly capable of leaving the way I came."

"Not happening." Liam pulled out another chair and sat facing me. "Start scrubbing, chica, unless you'd like me to do it for you." Liam leaned forward and reached for the soap.

I ignored the chaotic flapping sensation in my chest and smacked his hand away before he could grab the bar. Near scalding water splashed onto the floor as I plunged my feet into the oversized pot. The mud caked between my toes loosened.

Cedar and salt infused steam warmed my face as I bent over and lathered the black bar between my palms.

"So, you're fluent in French, you like to run, and you have an aversion to shoes. Any other secrets you want to share?"

"None of those things are a secret." I massaged the tender tissue on the ball of my left foot, wincing as the glass embedded there pressed deeper.

"Did you live in France?"

"For a few years."

"What did you do between living in France and coming to Hawaii?"

I glanced up and found him studying me with the now familiar intensity that made my syphons ache with the need to taste him. "You want my entire life's story?"

"I'll settle for the abridged edition."

"I was sent to upstate New York to live with distant relatives, got my degree online, spent the last couple years working for a data firm." Not a complete lie.

I ran soap-slick hands over my calves. "I didn't say anything to Dr. Logan about the other night. Please don't tell him about the pills. I can't afford to have him question my ability to do my job."

"Logan would never hold something like that against you."

"I doubt he'd be keen to learn that his facility manager in charge of highly sensitive equipment relies on tranquilizers to get through most days." I scrubbed the last of the mud and straightened.

"You'd be surprised." His brow furrowed. "There's something you should know, Renae." Liam wrung the dry towel between his hands. "I'm an addict. Logan's my sponsor."

My leg twitched, sloshing more water onto the floor. I lived inside his head, experienced every swell and dip of his moods as if they were my own. How had I missed it?

Liam ran a hand through his damp curls, pulling them away from his face, exposing the scar that ran from his hairline to the bridge of his nose.

"How did you get the scar?" I asked.

"A souvenir from the last conversation I had with my father. I was twenty-one and shooting up daily at that point. I'd stolen money from my stepmother's purse, and he confronted me about it. We got into a fight, and he told me I wasn't his son, that I was the biggest failure of his life, and he was done waiting for me to live up to my potential. I lashed out and tried to tackle him. But he stepped out of the way, and I went headfirst through a sliding glass door. He never spoke to me again. Not even on his deathbed four years later when I tried to apologize."

I swallowed the bitter sensation that flooded my mouth. "I'm sorry."

"Don't be. It was honestly a relief, him being gone."

"About the souvenir, not your father." I knew all too well what it was like to live with a reminder of the past. At least my scars, the ones covering my hideous true form, were invisible to humans.

"How did you get clean?" I asked.

"Luck, and my brother Connor." He patted my right knee. "Give me your foot."

I obeyed and lifted my leg from the water as my syphons roved over him. My breath hitched as a calloused hand caught my ankle and brought it to his lap. Sweet milky heat laced my tongue, reminiscent of the creamed brandy my mother gave us when we had a chest cold. Gods, I wanted to drink in the flavor of him. He tasted of warmth and comfort—of home.

"My father had me arrested for assault that night, and I spent the worst seventy-two hours of my life detoxing in the LA county lockup. I would have died of dehydration if Connor hadn't bailed me out and driven me straight to the hospital."

Liam wrapped my leg with the towel. He made his way up my calf, applying light pressure as his grip tightened and loosened around me. My gift hummed beneath my skin, unable to settle with his hands so near my bare flesh.

"My father and stepmother had written me off by that point, but Connor never gave up on me." Liam reached into the water. He slid a wide palm along my calf, and lifted my left foot to his lap. I held my breath as heat pooled low in my belly. *Curse this man and his gentle touch.*

"My brother was in med school at the time. Cashed out part of his college fund and got me into a residential treatment program. I owe him my life—and close to thirty grand."

I gulped back the dry lump in my throat as Liam dried my foot with the towel.

"How long have you been sober?" I asked, ignoring the throb between my thighs.

"Seven years drug free. Sober going on three years." He worked his way up my calf, massaging me through the towel with muscular hands. All I could think about was how badly I wanted those hands to slide higher.

"Why are you telling me this?" I asked, my breath ragged.

Liam shrugged. "Because I get it. The struggle to keep up the façade. I wouldn't have gotten through that first year without help or the last few years without my sponsor. So, whatever you're going through, you're not alone. Whenever you need a safe place to crash, an open ear, I'm here."

"Or a seductive foot massage?"

His brow furrowed as he dropped my feet to the floor. "Fuck, I'm sorry. That wasn't my intention." He shoved his chair back and ran a hand through those amber curls again. "Look, I know my track record sucks, but I don't usually make a habit of touching women without being invited."

I leaned forward, and Liam's body went still as I ran my fingertips over his scar, down his nose, to his soft lips.

"And if you *were* invited?" *Gods, what was I doing?*

He closed his eyes, and his deep voice came out rough, strained. "I should take you home."

My gift flared beneath my skin. It wanted to close the loop, complete the connection. To consume Liam Riley in a way that had nothing to do with my growling stomach. This time, I willingly relinquished control as my syphons latched on to him.

"What if I don't want to go home?"

White-hot fire danced behind those denim eyes as they opened. "What are you suggesting?" His deep voice was like warm rain pooling over cracked earth, slipping between the crevices, wetting me from the inside.

"One night. No strings attached."

His gaze dropped to my mouth. "Does your boyfriend know you're here?"

"My what?"

"Look, your relationship with pretty boy isn't my business." Liam stood and grabbed his keys from a table by the door. "But I'm not into lies or keeping secrets, and no matter how you compartmentalize it, there are *always* strings attached. So, please, just let me take you home before we do something you'll regret."

My cheeks flared with the sting of rejection. "You don't even know me. How dare you presume to know what I would or wouldn't regret?"

"I know you're wound way too tight and came here looking for some kind of release. I also know I'm just screwed up enough to want to help you scratch that itch. But if we start this, there'll be no going back, and right now, you need a friend way the hell more than you need to be properly fucked."

"You don't know anything, Liam Riley." I stood and stomped toward the door.

He flashed me a cocky smile that made my insides blaze. "Agree to disagree on that one, chica."

# Chapter Eleven

# RENAE

Something hard bit into my hip. I rolled over and pulled the purple vibrator out from where it was wedged between my half-naked body and the bed. A soft tapping noise filtered through the apartment. I struggled to focus on anything past my sawdust dry mouth and the sucking pangs of my empty stomach.

Was there someone at the door? My gift leapt from my skin, expanded through the walls, and probed the space beyond. Not Liam. *Thank the gods.*

I bolted upright. The recruiter? I yanked on my bathrobe and did my best to smooth the knotted mess of braids as my heart galloped in my chest.

*Just breathe.* I bowed my head in deference as I opened the door. "Good morning."

"Morning?" Jason's voice pitched up with concern.

My head snapped up to where the sun hung too high in the sky. "What time is it?"

"A little after four p.m."

"What?" I darted to the kitchen and checked the clock. No wonder I was starving. I'd slept the entire day.

Jason hovered in the doorway. "I just got home from work and wanted to check on you. I came by yesterday, but you didn't answer."

"What do you mean yesterday? What day is it?"

"Monday."

I scrubbed my palms over my sleep-crusted eyes. How was I supposed to pass any kind of assessment if I couldn't even control my body's basic functions? What if the recruiter had come and gone while I slept?

Jason tugged his earlobe. "That food poisoning really did a number on you." He took a tentative step into my living room. "You must be starving. Why don't you let me make you dinner tonight?"

"I'm sorry, Jason, I'm still not feeling like myself." I doubted I'd ever feel like myself again. "I need to get ready for work," I groaned.

"No worries. I just wanted to make sure you were still alive." The smile on his heart-shaped lips didn't quite reach his eyes. "If you need anything, anything at all, don't hesitate to ask."

I pressed my cheek to the door after he left and watched him through the peephole. He lingered in the stairwell before retreating down the squeaky steps.

Is that what friendship looked like—checking up on someone when they're sick, offering to help without any ulterior motives? My stomach knotted with the realization that Liam was right. I could use a friend. One like Jason. What I did *not* need was the kind of friend who kept me up half the night draining the batteries in my vibrator. Fighting the urge to stay away from Liam was like fighting gravity, and it was exhausting. I needed to be more careful about maintaining my energy reserves. And I really needed to start setting the alarm app on my phone.

Three days sequestered at the summit without caffeine was not a good look for Ernie. His round face had turned sallow, accentuating the dark circles under his eyes. With all of my Liam-sized drama, I'd forgotten to switch Ernie's coffee back before I left for the weekend, and I wasn't looking forward to being stuck in the lab with him or his prickly mood.

"The network just crashed." Ernie shoved away from his desk. "We have a full schedule of obs tonight. We don't have time for this."

"Why don't you go make a fresh pot of coffee? I'll see if I can reboot the system from here."

He stood, then stopped in the doorway. "Would you like some?" Even caffeine deprivation couldn't dissolve his polite nature. He always asked, and I always said no. He didn't want to share any more than I wanted to drink the bitter sludge he made. But Liam would arrive within the hour, and ingesting a lousy cup of coffee or two was a necessary precaution.

"I'd love some if it's not too much trouble." Ernie's wide forehead furrowed as he pivoted and lumbered into the hall. I pulled up the spectrograph interface software and rewrote the temperature monitoring code so the cooling system would *appear* to be working. Letting the cameras run a little hot for a short time wouldn't damage the instrument. The heat, however, would be enough to corrupt the images and hide the smoking gun Liam was looking for.

Ernie returned with only one cup of coffee as I finished.

"No coffee for me?" I asked.

Ernie scratched his head. "Sorry I... I forgot. You can have this one. I'll go make another."

Guilt bubbled in my stomach. My manipulations had all but ruined the man's short-term memory. "That's all right. I can make my own. I need to do a manual reset on SpeX before we can reboot the system." I grabbed my radio off the charger. "Oh, and I'd like you to hand the reins over to the new guy tonight."

"Sure, let the unpaid intern have all the fun," Ernie grumbled.

Since my plan to seduce Liam had failed miserably, I needed a new approach. He'd be less likely to notice any issues with the hardware or corrupted data if I kept him distracted with the telescope controls. The new plan was to keep his hands occupied all night and to not think about how they would feel on my flesh. So far, I was failing miserably at that second part. And keeping my gift leashed was equally imperative if I had any chance of making it through the night without mortifying myself again.

"Give me a few minutes. I'll radio you when I'm done, and you can pull everything back online."

All warmth evaporated from the dome as I opened the shutter doors and stepped under the telescope's monstrous belly. SpeX, our primary spectrograph, hung beneath it like a blocky blue appendage. I unlocked the access panel and plugged in the network cable I'd disconnected earlier and wished I'd thought to bring my jacket. The first stars sparked against the dark sky as I rebooted the machine. My stomach did a foolish little flop as the throaty hum of an engine echoed across the barren summit.

Liam was early, and he was on the motorcycle. Aggressive energy pulsed through his system whenever he drove that awful contraption. I took a deep breath and hugged my arms around my body, hoping the spectrograph took its sweet time rebooting. I wasn't ready to face him yet. Not after offering myself to him on a silver platter and being summarily rejected.

The hairs on the back of my neck lifted as the room filled with static. I was no longer alone.

A sharp feminine voice cut through my mind. "Hello, reaper."

I bowed my head in deference. I'd expected the recruiter to show up in a husk, not as a shade. "May I see you?" I asked.

A shadow appeared on the catwalk and floated toward me, solidifying into the shape of a woman with too-heavy eyeliner, smeared red lipstick, and long black hair slicked back from her face. She wore an emerald silk gown that matched her eyes with a neckline that plunged to her navel, revealing near translucent skin stretched taut over a skeletal frame. Her ancient energy signature filled the cavernous room. A thin smile curled the corner of her mouth as she probed my mind, laying waste to the barriers and locked doors. I kept my syphons coiled as she waded through my subconscious.

"Shall we scrape away the char and see what you're made of, darling?" An icy hand slid across my shoulders as she circled around me. A sensation intentionally implanted in my head. As a deceptor, she could bend my mind to make me see, feel, and hear anything she desired. "Let's hope it's more than meets the eye," she said.

I squared my shoulders. "I'm ready to be assessed for admittance into the healer corps."

Her pale lips didn't move as laughter chimed through my head. "I'm not here to test you; I'm here to warn you." She pushed a life-size apparition of Liam toward me. I flinched as it passed through my body and dissipated.

A series of beeps sounded, indicating SpeX was back online. "I don't understand. What does *he* have to do with me becoming a healer?"

My skin prickled as another shadow appeared and moved toward us. It took all my strength to keep my gift leashed as the second shade settled into the form of an elderly woman with a profusion of metallic silver curls that floated around her head like a disco ball, sending sparkles dancing down her powder-blue pantsuit to the tops of her pristine white sneakers.

Her gentle voice chimed through my consciousness. "I am Marcella, and this is Cyrena. Apologies for the ambush, my dear, but we need to move fast. He's running out of time."

"Is this about his research? Because I have that under control. I can easily manipulate his data. And Liam, if needed." My stomach lurched, threatening to bring back the double order of spam musubi I'd eaten on my way to the summit.

"That's certainly not how it appeared last night," the one called Cyrena said.

"How long have you been watching me?"

She rolled her eyes. "We're not watching you, we're watching him. He's Anzillu."

The air sucked from my lungs. There were stories about the ancient abominations. Humans imbued with powerful gifts that had been stripped from other souls. Mutant soldiers created by the gods to fight against the Nūkiri in the All Souls War. "No," I said, my voice barely audible. "The Anzillu are extinct, banished into the Void, along with the old gods."

Cyrena's sharp voice pierced my skull. "Your limited intelligence is only half as disappointing as your lack of imagination."

The older woman, Marcella, stepped toward me, her metallic curls clinking softly against one another. "His mother, Amelia, was a Corps asset, like yourself. His father and his father's research partner were her marks. Do you understand now, child?"

I shuddered against the frigid air creeping in through the open telescope shutter two stories above. No, I didn't understand. Not at all.

"Liam was the brainchild of a geneticist named Issor Nella who believed he could push humanity into the next stage of evolution. He used Liam's father's fertility clinic as a front for his experiments. Amelia stole the Corps' modified DNA sequence data and traded it for the one thing she couldn't have. A child. One capable of wielding all seven sacred gifts. A living god."

My mouth went dry as I thought about the ocean of power at Liam's core. The same kind of power the Anzillu had been cursed with. Energy so powerful it destroyed the nervous systems and corrupted the minds of the unmodified human hosts it had been bestowed upon.

Marcella read the question floating though my head. "All tests indicated Liam was born utterly human, with no trace of the gifts they planted inside him. But his mother was an isolator. We believe she shielded his true potential during Issor Nella's initial assessment."

A weight settled in my chest. "How long have you been watching him?"

The deceptors exchanged a nod, as if they were having a silent conversation.

"Nella disappeared with Amelia and all the data shortly after Liam was born."

"What about Liam's father?"

"He couldn't replicate the experiment without Amelia's modified husk and womb, so he passed the child off as his own and—"

"Used Liam as bait," I said.

"Michael Riley was convinced Amelia would come back for the boy, and she would have, if she'd lived." Marcella's projection flickered. "We found her hiding among a fertility cult in South America. No sign of Issor Nella or their missing research data."

Cyrena smirked. "The zealots gave up mommy dearest without a fight."

"You executed his mother?" Gods, I couldn't breathe.

"We followed orders and deactivated her. She returned to Almega, where she was stripped of her memories and placed in a support role. She's lucky they didn't strip her of her power as well."

"For wanting a child?" Gods, I knew the Nūkiri could be severe in their punishments but stripping a soul of its identity? Memories are like threads woven into the tapestry of who we are. They gave our consciousness flesh and bone. You could remove a few and still remain intact. Remove them all and you're no longer you. Without her memory, she'd be nothing more than a spectral form, unrecognizable.

"There is no greater crime than disloyalty." Marcella's voice chimed through my head. "Best to not forget that, dear." The sweetness in her tone made it sound like a bit of friendly advice. The burn that laced my tongue told me it was a warning.

I paced the room, trying to catch my breath. "And now you're using him as bait to draw out the other scientist?"

Marcella looked to Cyrena, and I sensed something pass between them again before she continued. "Issor Nella will come for Liam when his abilities fully manifest."

"How much does Ziggy know?"

"The less she knows, the better," Cyrena said. "If you value your position in the Corps, you will not reveal any of what we've told you to your wet nurse. Liam is neither of interest nor a threat, as long as his powers remain dormant."

"Why are you telling me? What do I have to do with any of this?"

Marcella moved closer; her voice floated around me and inside me all at once. "His gifts are awakening. Cyrena sensed the change in his frequency three years ago when his father died. We needed to bond him to a reaper who could absorb the excess energy and halt the transition, so we assessed every new recruit at the Nursery until we found a compatible match. Cyrena ensured that you passed the trials and had you assigned here."

"That's impossible. Interference in the trials is forbidden." I clenched my sweat-slick palms.

"Don't fret, darling," Cyrena patted my shoulder. "Like you, the adjudicators were unaware of our presence or our manipulations. The same way you and Liam were unaware of them the day we brought you together with the accident."

I lost control of my syphons and they exploded from my back. "*You* caused the accident?" I asked through gritted teeth.

Cyrena's eyes slid over my shoulder to the soul-sucking appendages twisting behind me, and her lips curled into a coy smile. "Everything you've experienced since taking that husk has been part of our plan, reaper. Your trials. Your position at the summit. The accident. All of it bringing you closer to Liam so your gift would bond itself to him."

Both women flickered and disappeared as the radio clipped to my waist echoed Ernie's garbled voice across the room. I turned it off, and their ghostly forms reappeared in front of me.

I shuddered against the cold creeping through my body. "That doesn't make any sense. Why would you risk losing your only link to Nella, on the off chance that I would bring him back from the dead?"

"To invoke the Gi'dari bond. We've already covered that bit. Do try to keep up," Cyrena said.

My pulse thudded in my head as the room tilted. "No, no, no, no... that's not how it works." I backed away from them. "The bond is a choice. A gift given willingly. Not something that can be invoked against one's will."

Cyrena floated toward me. "Your romantic world view might be charming if it weren't so naïve. We don't choose who we give our bond to. Our gifts decide. We knew the ravenous reaper inside you wouldn't be able to resist gorging itself on the buffet of energy at Liam's core. All seven gifts sewn into a single soul. To taste the divine."

I curled forward and braced my hands on my knees. "I'm going to vomit." The Gi'dari could only be gifted once. An irrevocable bond giving the recipient full access to your gift, your body, your will.

A shiver crawled down my spine, and this time, it didn't come from Cyrena's vile touch. "No, I don't accept that." The words tumbled out, brittle and broken. "I cannot be stuck with him, not for an eternity."

Marcella flickered as the massive telescope moved into position above us. "No matter where you go or how many lives you endure, your gift will seek the part of your soul that resides within Liam. I have followed Cyrena through a hundred lifetimes. I've been her sibling, parent, friend, and lover, even her enemy, whatever the bond requires of me. I am hers to command." Marcella's eyes glistened as Cyrena stroked her like an obedient pet. My stomach revolted at the idea of being enslaved to Liam—to anyone—like that.

I stood and took a deep breath, willing the wetness from my eyes as I recalled how easily my gift bent to Liam's will. How it compelled me to seek him out and tell him things, things about my past that he had no business knowing. How I had zero control over the way my gift and my body responded to him.

"I'm assuming the bond isn't reciprocal. His gift hasn't chosen me."

Cyrena moved closer, circling around me like a vulture stalking its prey. "The Gi'dari bond can only be offered after a soul's primary gift had fully manifested. So far, only two have emerged. His primary gift may yet be dormant."

"Which gifts?" I ran through the seven sacred gifts: reaper, healer, telepath, forecaster, isolator, mimic, and deceptor. I hadn't seen evidence of any of them in Liam.

"He's a telepath. He can read thoughts. They come in broken bits when he's triggered by intense emotion," Marcella said.

"Well, that's a problem for me," I said. Liam felt everything with intensity. There were no flat roads in his emotional spectrum, just an endless landscape of peaks and valleys. "But it's hardly a reason to leash me to him for an eternity."

"On that, we are in agreement, child." Marcella's mirror-polished curls shimmered under the fluorescent lights. "It seems, however, that he is also a forecaster. Surely, you've noticed how his mood swings have been in line with recent weather events."

My stomach twisted into a knot as I considered the storms and heavy cloud cover that went hand in hand with Liam's darker moods. "Hardly concrete proof of anything."

Cyrena smirked. "Do you really think the Nūkiri would concern itself with such a trivial thing as proof? Despite our own personal interest in him as *bait,* as you so eloquently described it, we have orders to terminate if your reaper abilities are not up to the task and he becomes a threat to the human population." Bile pressed at the back of my throat. "We hope it doesn't come to that. The boy has immense potential." Cyrena tipped her head to the side, and her energy coiled around my neck like an icy rope. My skin froze and cracked. I told myself it wasn't real, even as my vision frosted over.

My syphons snapped forward and struck her spectrum with hollow talons, burrowing deep. Vinegar, thick and pungent frothed in my mouth and slid down my throat like spoiled wine as I gulped her energy and attempted to drain her.

Cyrena's projection didn't even flinch. A seductive smile curled her lips as she tilted her head back, letting me take my fill. Her voice hummed through my head as her energy churned in my stomach. "Someone likes to play rough. You should loosen that leash more often. It suits you." Blades of crystal-blue light erupted from her form, and my syphons fell away like severed limbs. Phantom pain cracked through me. "Best to practice sipping instead of slurping. We want you to drain the man, not kill him."

"You... you want me to feed on Liam?"

"It's not a request. You will remain close to him and syphon off his excess power to prevent his uncontrolled gift from manifesting and drawing attention. Do you understand your orders as we've explained them?"

"You want me to hide his emerging gifts from the Corps and buy you more time to complete *your* mission."

"Oh good. She has been paying attention." Cyrena's cold emerald eyes darted toward the hallway as awareness prickled through me.

I shooed their shades away. "He's coming."

Her sharp laugh left the sensation of brain freeze in its wake as she faded into the shadows of the room. "He won't perceive us unless we allow it."

My syphons stretched toward Liam as he strode through the door. I gave him my back and pretended to inspect SpeX's motherboard.

"Why do I get the distinct impression that you're avoiding me?" The heady sweetness of brandy and heavy cream bloomed in my mouth as my gift licked over him. Gods, he did taste divine.

"Don't flatter yourself." I grabbed a can of compressed air from the utility cart and used it to blow away imaginary dust from inside the housing before closing the access panel.

"Are you done yet?" he asked.

I made the mistake of glancing up at that cocky smile and cursed the way it made my insides go molten. "SpeX is up and running. We should be good to go for the rest of the night."

Liam stepped in front of me, blocking my retreat. "I meant are you done being pissed at me yet?"

"I don't have the bandwidth for this conversation right now." I planted both hands on his chest to push him out of my way.

He reached up and grabbed my wrists. "Jesus, Renae, you're fucking freezing. How long have you been in here?" Liam shrugged off his jacket and wrapped it around my shoulders. Gods, I wanted to lose myself in the scent of it. Salt and Cedar. My syphons burrowed deeper into him, filling me with his sweet milky spice. I wanted to drink it in until I was full up with it, with him.

"You're worse than a gluttonous cow," Cyrena said as she grasped my scalp with both hands and sank her ghostly fingers into my skull, piercing bone and tissue with excruciating force. "This should help you sip instead of slurp."

I gritted my teeth against the pain. "Don't touch me."

Liam took a step back, hands up in surrender.

Cyrena let go of my head, circling around us with a wicked glint in her emerald eyes.

# Chapter Twelve

Less than forty-eight hours after she'd shown up on my doorstep like a stray cat looking for shelter, we were back at square one.

"I can't do this. Not here; not right now." The way her eyes darted back and forth around the room, unable to look at me, said it all. She was pissed.

"How about we go to the break room where it's warm and we can talk?" Renae's eyes flared with that same liquid fire when she'd asked me to fuck her. If she asked me again, I would 100 percent take her up on the offer because I was *that* guy.

I'd been kicking myself all damn day for turning her down, for not taking her up on her offer to do exactly what I'd been thinking about since the day we met. It had twisted my gut all kinds of wrong to deliver her back to her apartment. *Their* apartment. I couldn't put my finger on it, but something was off about the pretty boy who shared her bed.

Renae's eyes landed on me for the first time since I entered the room. "I don't want to talk. I just want to do my job. So do me a favor and go back to the lab and get to work." She shrugged off my jacket and flung it at me. "Tell Ernie I need him to handle the remote astronomer interface while I check the server." Her face flashed crimson as she glared over my shoulder, too angry to even look at me.

There was a time when I'd used anger to push people away too. I wasn't about to let her talons scare me off. Not when all I could think about was letting her sharpen them on my back.

"Why are you smiling? This isn't funny."

I held up my hands and backed away. "Message received."

An hour later, Renae joined us in the lab, every trace of her fire locked behind a cool mask and a giant bowl of mochi-nori popcorn.

"Where have you been?" Ernie asked as she held out the bowl so he could scoop out a handful onto a piece of paper. "We're almost finished with the UVA observations."

"Great. I'll pull up the waiting room and see if the next team is ready to begin." Renae slid the bowl between our stations where we could both reach it.

We plodded through the observations with minimal conversation. Ernie and I took turns operating the equipment while Renae monitored the systems and interfaced with the remote astronomers, stopping constantly to scrawl on a notepad. She was cold, distant. Nothing like the beautiful mess that had shown up on my doorstep two nights before.

No. The Renae sitting in front of me was a completely different person. The hard shell of a woman hiding the real Renae—the one who'd crashed into my life and cried in my arms. That wild, untamed version of her was damn hard to forget.

She shot me an irritated glance. "Are you finished yet?"

"Just made the last pass over NGC 1300." I kept my tone light, determined to show her I could, in fact, keep it professional.

"Great, then we can finally get out of here." Renae flipped over the pad of paper she'd been taking notes on all night. "Go ahead and shut down."

"Are you interested in joining the team full time once you finish your PhD?" Ernie asked as he stretched in his chair, cracking his spine against the seat back.

"I'm hoping to get a faculty research position somewhere, but I wouldn't turn down an opportunity if it showed up on my doorstep again."

"We're not hiring." Renae got up and dropped her notes into the shredder. "You should apply at one of the new observatories in the Atacama Desert in Chile. I hear it's very dry there." She plastered a fake-ass smile on her face. "Ernie, can you give me a ride to the Lodge?"

"Sure. I'll wait for you in the parking lot."

"Thank you. I'll be out shortly." Renae didn't even glance in my direction as she returned to her computer.

As soon as I stepped outside, my phone vibrated in my pocket. I had four messages from my brother and zero bars. I held it in the air to search for a signal. It was unusual for Connor to call back-to-back, much less leave a message.

"Renae's right," Ernie said. "If you want to work on a cosmic microwave background team, the Atacama observatories are where you want to be. I'd be happy to look at your thesis before you have to defend it. Give you feedback. I'm sure Renae would as well."

"That would be great. I'll email you the files and come up early before my next shift. I'll even bring dinner for the three of us."

"What kind of dinner?" Ernie asked.

"Pizza and glazed donuts?"

Ernie nodded his approval. "I like plain cheese, no sauce and extra garlic, but only from Mako Mike's. And if you tell them to half bake it, we can meet at the lodge before work and throw it in the oven when you get here."

"Done." I smiled at his very specific pizza order and resumed my search for a cell signal.

Ernie stopped in front of the old Bronco parked next to my bike, the only two vehicles in the lot. "A little advice." He glanced back at the building. "You need to give up on that."

"Is it that obvious?" I asked.

He pointed to my phone. "The cell reception up here is terrible. And if you want to impress Renae, get her a large Hawaiian barbecue pizza with extra pineapple."

I slipped the phone inside my chest pocket, swung a leg over my bike, and watched him leave without Renae as if he'd forgotten or intentionally thrown me a bone. Ernie smiled and gave me the shaka sign before heading down the summit access road.

*Thank you, brother.* I returned the gesture as Renae stomped toward me across the gravel lot.

"Good thing I brought an extra helmet. Looks like I'm your ride again."

Her eyes locked on the narrow seat behind me. "How much did you pay him to leave without me?"

"You wound me, chica. Here I am offering you a ride like a perfect gentleman, and you automatically assume the worst."

"I *don't* like motorcycles."

"What'd they ever do to you?"

Renae rolled her eyes and headed toward the road, leaving a trail of frozen breath hanging in the frigid air behind her like little puffs of smoke.

I hopped off my bike and caught up with her. "Are you seriously walking? Tell me what you're so afraid of."

She spun on her heels in the gravel. "Death. I'm afraid of death. Are you happy now?"

I took a step closer and reached for her elbow. "I wouldn't let anything happen to you. You're safe with me, Renae."

"Well, maybe you're the one who's not safe with me. Maybe I'm the one who's dangerous. Did you ever consider that?"

"Pretty much every damn moment since the day we met."

"Whatever." She glanced over my shoulder in the direction of my bike. And damn, it looked like she was considering it.

"It's just a ride," I said. "Let me help you. That's what friends do."

"We are not friends." Renae stalked reluctantly toward my bike. "Give me the cursed helmet. You can drop me off at the lodge."

I threw my leg over the bike, stabilizing it as she climbed on in a huff. Renae settled herself as far back on the seat as she could without falling off and planted her hands square on my shoulders.

I flipped up my face shield and glanced back at her. "You need to scoot forward and wrap your arms around my chest. Otherwise, you'll wreck us before we get out of the parking lot."

Renae shook her head. "I'm more comfortable here."

"You are determined to be the death of me, woman." I reached behind me and tugged her to my back. Renae slid down the seat until her thighs cradled my hips and her helmet smacked into mine. I patted her thigh. "You ready back there?"

"Can we please just get this over with?"

"Not what I usually hear when a woman has her legs wrapped around me, but sure."

Her response, half growl and half curse, reverberated against my back as I flipped my face shield down and started the engine.

For someone who hated motorcycles, Renae was an instinctive rider, moving in sync with me without being told what to do. She tightened her grip around my chest, her head tucked against mine as we banked into the first hairpin turn, and I was acutely aware of every inch of her body against my backside. I desperately needed to adjust my jeans, but the road was slick with a fresh dusting of snow, and I couldn't risk taking my hands off the grips.

I could feel the rapid rise and fall of her chest. At least I wasn't the only one suffering. I followed the road behind the summit visitor center down to the lodge. When I turned off the bike, she didn't let go or try to get off right away.

I removed my helmet and twisted around to see if she was okay. "I believe this is your stop. Unless there's somewhere else you'd rather go."

"No. This... this is fine." Renae slid off the bike with one hand pressed to her stomach as if she had indigestion. "Thank you for the ride," she said and took off the helmet. She ran her fingers through her auburn hair, and it was all I could do not to reach for it.

"Look, about last night. I think I made—"

Renae let out an impressive belch and immediately covered her mouth.

"Oh, gods, excuse me. I... I don't know where that came from." The way her cheeks and neck flushed was sexy as hell, and I was thankful for the helmet sitting in my lap.

She scowled at something in the distance. "I proved I could do it. What more do you want from me?"

"Do you want me to make a list?" I asked, glancing around.

Renae's cold stare met mine. "Goodnight, Liam."

☙

I took a cold shower when I got back to the house and tried not to think about Renae and whatever game we were playing. A game with no rules, referees, or trophy at the end. She was right. Whatever the hell this was, it wasn't a friendship—more like mutually assured destruction.

I pulled a pair of sweats on over my damp skin and slumped onto the couch—unable to sleep in the bed that still smelled of her, even though I'd changed the sheets. My phone buzzed on the table. *Shit.* I'd forgotten all about the messages from Connor.

"Hey, Lee, call me back."

"Me again. Did you lose your fucking phone? Call me."

"Hey, Lee, call me as soon as you get this. I'm getting on a plane and heading your way in the morning for this conference. Please tell me you haven't forgotten. Text me as soon as you get this."

I had zero recollection of my brother even mentioning a trip to Hawaii. Fuck, my memory really was turning to shit. A sinking sensation took up residence in my gut as I listened to the rest of his messages.

"Okay. I'm starting to worry about you now. Just pick up the damn phone already. I texted you my flight info. I'm getting on the plane. You better be there to pick me up from the airport. You know I don't do rental cars."

"We just landed at LAX. I'm assuming you're still asleep. I land in Hilo at ten a.m. your time. See you soon, sunshine."

If his flight was on time, I'd be able to pick him up and spend some time with him before my afternoon class. I sent him a *fuck yeah* gif and stretched out on the couch.

I managed to sleep like the dead and still woke up exhausted, like every ounce of energy had been sucked out of me. After throwing back two energy drinks and leftover Thai takeout, I hauled ass to the airport and made it to the arrivals gate just in time to see Connor walk across the tarmac. He looked exactly like our fucking father. The same hard-cut jaw and dark hair graying slightly at the temples. Fortunately, that's where the similarities ended. Connor was only eight years my senior, but he'd been more of a father to me than the man who sired us.

"So, you are alive." He threw his arms around me like a doting parent. "I was beginning to worry," he said as he pulled away and grasped my shoulders. "I don't like it when I can't get ahold of you, Lee."

"I was working up at the summit last night; no service. What's up with the impromptu vacation? The last time we talked, I got the impression you were chained to the hospital."

He shot me a worried look. "I'm presenting at a convention in Honolulu. We talked about this weeks ago. I finagled a few extra days of leave in before and after the conference."

"Sorry, my short-term memory's been spotty since the accident."

"Did you go to your follow-up appointment with the neurologist?"

I didn't know why he bothered to ask. He knew I hadn't. "I feel fine."

Connor shook his head. "Do you remember me telling you that Patrick and I were thinking about getting married?" Connor held up his left hand and flashed a shiny black ring.

"Holy shit!" I punched his shoulder. "Why didn't you tell me?"

"I literally just did."

"What did Tamsyn have to say about that?"

"I had lunch with Mom on the layover at LAX. She's seriously tweaked about us denying her the joy of planning a wedding and threatened to throw us a surprise reception the next time we come home."

I cringed.

"Exactly. As if Patrick would let her plan *his* party." Connor handed me his carry-on as we approached the open-air baggage conveyor. "Patrick and I are meeting in Maui after the conference for a mini honeymoon. Even though it's already official, we decided to do the whole bachelor weekend thing with the two other most important people in our lives. PJ flew to Miami to see his sister, and I'm here."

My chest tightened as we collected his luggage and headed for the truck.

⁓

"So what sort of bachelor party antics did you have in mind?" I asked, stretching back in my chair as the server delivered our smoothies. Connor had picked a local joint specializing in all the organic, non-GMO vegan shit he loved.

"Are you going to be in trouble with your 'I don't want to put a label on it' girlfriend if I monopolize all your time for the next few days?"

"Monika and I don't talk anymore."

"What did you do?" Connor shot me a knowing glance as he pulled an alcohol wipe from his pocket and used it to sanitize his side of the table.

Besides ripping her heart out and stomping all over it like a degenerate asshole? "Not up for discussion," I said.

My brother raised his glass of thick green goo to mine. "To bad endings and new beginnings, then."

I choked down a sip of kale slime while he pounded the entire glass.

"How's your thesis coming along?" he asked. "You getting the research time you needed?"

"I don't really want to talk about that either."

"Jesus, Lee. Please tell me you didn't quit the PhD program." Connor's voice dropped an octave in a way that made him sound just like our fucking father.

"On the contrary. I should have everything I need to finish by the end of the semester. But you're never gonna believe this shit. You remember the chick I hit?" Connor nodded. "She's the night supervisor at the summit where I'm doing my observations."

"Awkward."

"You have no fucking idea." I hadn't planned on telling him about my less than professional obsession with Renae; it just poured out of me like diarrhea. The accident, that first night at the summit, her pretty boyfriend, and my inability to focus or think about anything else.

Connor cocked an eyebrow.

"What?"

"It was the same when I fell in love with Patrick," he said. "Like he sucked all the air out of the room when he walked into it, and all I could breathe was him."

"That's *not* what's happening." I chugged the rest of my green goo and slapped the glass down on the table. "It's just chemistry or pheromones or some shit. Something about her triggers the prehistoric part of my brain that wants to rip out the throat of anyone else who even looks at her. I spend half my time thinking about her and the other half trying not to. I've never been strung out over a woman before."

"When was the last time you went to a meeting?" He eyed me with our father's steel-gray eyes, and I was a kid again. No matter what I said or did, it was always wrong. But Connor wasn't anything like him. He'd always been there for me, letting me crash in his apartment when I was drunk or high. Fed me, took me to meetings, and made sure I had clean needles so I didn't catch anything. He'd seen me at my worst, and I couldn't blame him for not wanting to see me go there again.

"It's a legitimate question, Lee. How long has it been?"

"A few weeks."

Connor leaned back as the server placed a tofu lettuce wrap in front of him and a ridiculously real looking fake meat burger in front of me. "Can you find one this afternoon? I'll go with you."

"Look, I know you're worried the obsession might bleed over and become a problem, but it's not like that. I just can't stop thinking about her or counting the fucking seconds until I see her again, and I get this weird itch inside my brain telling me to go find her whenever we're apart."

"Repeat what you just said, but replace *her* with heroin and tell me again how it's not a problem."

"What are you presenting at this medical conference?" I asked as I grabbed a surfboard from the bed of my truck and handed it to Connor. I'd skipped out on my office hours to spend the afternoon with him.

"I'm hosting a Q&A panel about our initial research findings on the long-term outcome of patients who flat line and recover during surgery."

"Sounds thrilling," I said dryly.

"It's actually fascinating. We're looking at the five- and ten-year survival rates between patients who report having a near-death experience when they code and those who don't. The preliminary empirical evidence suggests the patients who report having an NDE score higher on all metrics associated with a positive long-term prognosis."

"And this is being funded by NYU?"

"A donor made a fifty-million-dollar gift to our new surgical center and got the green light on the study in return. It's his pet project."

"Who dumps that kind of cash on a pet project?"

"Allen Rossi, but don't repeat that. It's not public knowledge."

"The Argentinian gazillionaire who just petitioned the UN to purchase Antarctica?"

"The same." Connor pulled off his shirt and threw it in the back of the truck. He was way too fucking tan for a man who spent eighteen-hour days inside a hospital.

We picked our way down the switchback trail to the old mill beach, and I debated telling him about the trippy dream, the blood-red field, and the hallucinations of floating outside my body. Odds were good that he'd march my ass straight to the neurologist for a follow up.

"So, you're what, collecting anecdotal accounts from people who hallucinate going into the light and all that? Doesn't seem very scientific."

"The root of all science is collecting data and finding patterns. And we've found significant similarities in the individual accounts."

"Anyone ever report being pulled across a blood-red field or being struck by lightning?" My bare feet sank deep into coarse black sand as we stepped into the shadow of the old sugar mill that marked one of the best surf spots on the island.

"Vivid color is a common vector, as are reports of encounters with loved ones or beings of light. So far, all accounts have been classified as peaceful. No blood, fire, or brimstone, if that's what you're asking." I wasn't sure if what I'd experienced was a near death experience, or something else, and decided to keep it to myself.

Connor's jet lag finally kicked in after an hour of surfing. We packed it up, and I suggested we skip the NA meeting so he could crash, but he refused.

"Do they still serve free coffee?" he asked as we drove to the rec center.

I scoped out the circle of chairs set up on the middle of the basketball court and nodded to a few familiar faces. It wasn't my usual group, and I wasn't in the mood to share, but my brother was right. It was exactly where I needed to be. My shoulders relaxed as I thought about Renae and what it would be like to bring her here. I wanted to believe her about the blue pills, but my gut told me she was lying. The woman was hiding something. Something big.

I sipped the black sludge that passed as coffee and did my best to shove Renae from my brain. "What's your control?" I asked Connor as we took our seats along the back wall. "How do you prove your patients aren't all experiencing some sort of side effect caused by oxygen deprivation when they flat line?" I asked. "How do you know it's not all in their heads?"

"We've placed several physical markers in the surgery suite that can only be seen if you were, say, floating near the ceiling. Fifty-eight percent of patients who survive a code and report having an NDE have been able to describe the markers."

"No shit?" I grunted and downed the remainder of the bitter liquid.

"We're working on adding another control. One of Allen Rossi's companies in Argentina developed a device he calls the Kirlian Field Monitor. It uses optical and infrared cameras, magnetic and electrical field sensors, and radio frequencies to build a 3-D image of the otherwise invisible energy surrounding the human body. Unfortunately, it's malfunctioned every time we've had an opportunity to use it."

By the end of the meeting, I'd almost convinced myself that Renae wasn't a junkie and that my obsession with her wasn't a problem.

I dropped another log on the fire, sending a cloud of glowing ash into the air from the pit in my backyard. "I don't know, Connor. It sounds like you're crossing the line between science and metaphysics."

Orange light flickered across his face, giving his skin an oily glow. "The more we understand about our own physiology, the better we'll be at caring for it. You have to cross quite a few boundaries if you want to make seismic progress. You should know that better than anyone. Aren't you on a mission to prove we're connected to a parallel universe?"

I leaned back in the lawn chair, stretching my bare feet toward the flames. "That's different. Multiverse theory is based on mathematical probability, not subjective personal accounts."

"Whether we're talking about the extension of human consciousness beyond death or the existence of another world beyond the one we can see, we're doing the same work, trying to define the nature of reality outside our current observational limitations."

We'd have to agree to disagree on that one. "Speaking of limitations, you gonna clue me in on the rest of your bachelor bucket list? There's only so much trouble a sober alcoholic and a queer hipster can get into on this island."

Connor flashed a shit-eating grin. "Last time I visited, the weather didn't cooperate—"

"Absolutely not. There's no fucking way I'm going skydiving with you." Connor had been trying to get me to throw myself out of an airplane since I'd gotten sober. He begged me to go the last time he was here—after he'd already booked a non-refundable jump. Fortunately, mother nature sent in a typhoon and settled the issue. I wasn't afraid to push the limits on a bike or board, where I still had control. Hurtling myself to the ground from ten thousand feet with nothing but a piece of fabric strapped to my back was where I drew the line.

"As my unofficial best man, you're obligated to comply with any and all bachelor party requests. It's brother bond code."

"I'm good bonding right here on solid ground." I tipped back a bottle of non-alcoholic ginger beer, the kind with a satisfying bite that burned on its way down my throat.

"Come on, Lee, I'm doing this with or without you. It would mean the world to me if you were there. I've never asked you for anything; don't make me beg."

He grasped my forearm, and I saw the younger, less tan, less salt and pepper version of him who showed up in scrubs to bail me out of jail the night I took a header through a glass door. He accepted me at my best and at my worst, and no matter how dark shit got, he'd never run, never given up. I owed him my life and then some.

"Fine, but don't expect me to be all chipper about it."

The wind kicked up and blew embers from the firepit toward Connor. He coughed and fanned them away. "Wow, I didn't think you'd give in so easy. I think I need to meet this woman that has you turned inside out."

C HAPTER T HIRTEEN

# RENAE

I GRASPED THE BACK of the clear plastic chair across from Ziggy's desk. "Hypothetically, how would one sever oneself from a Gi'dari bond?"

Ziggy lifted my digital energy fingerprint from her display and suspended it in the space above her desk. "The Gi'dari bond is effectively irrevocable. The Void is the only entity that can destroy it."

I swallowed the cry that climbed up my throat. I'd never be rid of Liam Riley, not unless one of us was sacrificed to the Void—the dark space between worlds that fed on the souls thrown into it.

"Why do you ask?" Ziggy said.

Aside from doing her best to be a thorn in my shoe, Ziggy had never given me any reason to doubt where her loyalties lie. With the Corps. Always.

It was a risk to confess my growing list of infractions—killing and resurrecting what I assumed was a human without a direct order, lying to my handler, hiding my broken gift, getting duped into bonding myself to an Anzillu, and unwittingly cheating my way through the trials—but I needed advice.

Something about Cyrena and Marcella's story didn't add up. With the Corps' unlimited resources at their disposal, how had they not tracked down one missing scientist in twenty seven years? They were either lying, incompetent, or both, and I didn't trust them.

Maybe I hadn't earned my husk or right to be here, but I wasn't going to let two spectral assassins with questionable motives compromise my future in the Corps or drag me back to hell without a fight. I just hoped Ziggy's interest in maintaining her inventory of physical assets outweighed her strict adherence to protocol.

"I may have *accidentally* given up my bond," I said, surprised by the steadiness of my voice.

She didn't even look up as she scrolled through a report. "I'm sure you're mistaken. The Gi'dari isn't something you can accidentally give away. Besides, I'd know if you had. Your metrics would have spiked. Everything looks normal."

"What about the day of the accident?"

Her eyes flicked to mine. "What aren't you telling me?" she said in a voice that could freeze lava.

I sucked in a breath and spit out the admission that could get me kicked out of the Corps. "The driver died. I gave up my bond to resurrect him."

Ziggy's mouth opened, then closed like a goldfish. "Impossible. He... he wouldn't have been able to accept the bond without an activated gift, not while he's still—"

"Human? That's just it. He's not human. Not entirely. Not according to the deceptors I had the displeasure of meeting. He's Anzillu, and he's my new mark."

She knocked over her chair as she stood. "Details, now!" Ziggy slapped her palms on the glass desktop.

I recounted everything Liam's handlers had revealed about his parentage—the experiment, the missing geneticist, how they'd manipulated the accident to trigger the bond between us, how they'd murdered his mother and were using Liam as bait and waiting for Issor

Nella to make his next move. I left out the bits about cheating my way through the trials and how my gift responded to Liam as if he were the sun and I was starved for light.

Ziggy stood to her full height and smoothed her hands over her face. "If they've killed him once, they won't hesitate to do it again." Her voice was barely audible, as if she were speaking only to herself.

I slumped into the plastic chair. "That's the strangest part; they don't want to kill him. Not yet. They want me to siphon his excess energy and slow the manifestation of his gifts." I could still taste him on my tongue from the night before. Milky sweet spice that warmed my chest as it slid down my throat like brandy and cream. Gods, it was as intoxicating as the sensation of my thighs cradled around his hips during that ride.

"And?" Ziggy's clipped tone cut through the lingering haze of his energy inside me.

"And what?"

"Did it work?"

"I don't know. One of the deceptors had to zap my skull to keep me from draining him completely while he drove me home on that ridiculous motorcycle."

Her nostrils flared. "You fed on him while he was driving?"

"It was the only way I could get close enough without blowing my cover. Apparently, two of his seven gifts have awoken. He's a telepath, but he doesn't realize he can read me yet."

"And the other?"

"Forecaster."

Ziggy's lips twitched. "Is that all?"

"So far. They have something planned for him. Something big, and it has nothing to do with their orders from the Corps. I read it when my syphons struck one of his handlers and she allowed me to feed on her."

Ziggy's face went ashen. "Of all the impulsive... I cannot believe you attacked a deceptor. They've killed for far less. Yours isn't the only life you put at risk when you act impulsively. We need to be smart about this. Do not piss them off. The last thing I need is an internal audit if they decide to walk your husk off a cliff."

I bit back a smile. I knew I could trust Ziggy to prioritize her bottom line above all else. "Trust me, I won't be doing it again if I can help it. She tasted like sour wine."

Ziggy took a deep breath and righted her chair. She smoothed her charcoal skirt and pale blue blouse, collecting herself before pulling up the recording of our session and deleting it.

"What are you doing?"

"Protecting the innocent. The Corps has eyes everywhere. The less they know about your involvement in whatever the deceptors are doing, the better."

She moved from behind the desk, taking careful steps so her heels didn't snag in the thick carpet, and sat next to me. "If you want to survive this, there are a few things you need to understand. How much do you know about the All Souls War?"

I shrugged. "The same thing everyone knows. The gods fought each other and created armies of Anzillu to take out their rivals, devastating the planet in the process. The Nūkiri stepped in and banished all of them, the gods and the Anzillu, into the Void to protect the human population and the cycle of life, death, and resurrection."

"That's the version of history we've been taught, but it's not what happened. The original watchers were meant to be benevolent spirit guides dedicated to protecting human life and evolution. Civilization bloomed under their guidance. Until human fear and worship made them gods. It's a rare soul that can withstand the addiction of power, of having temples, sacrifices, and wars made in their honor.

"The early version of the Corps didn't have the same checks and balances we have today. The watchers reveled in their new roles and became hungry for more. More power. More sacrifice. More elaborate symbols of devotion. They fought for territory and control over the civilizations of men. The Nūkiri saw what was to come. Full cycle collapse and the annihilation of sentient life. They needed a solution. Something powerful enough to take on and defeat the self-proclaimed gods."

"Wait, are you saying the *Nūkiri* created the Anzillu?"

Ziggy nodded. "Human hosts possessed by seven souls. One for each of the sacred gifts. More powerful than any single entity. More powerful than any individual god."

I stood and moved to the window, looking out over the snow-covered grounds and the newest class of recruits jogging their engineered husks back to the compound in the morning light.

"Human brains aren't equipped to contain more than a single sentient energy," I said. "How could seven souls exist inside an unmodified husk at once?"

"They can't. Not inside an adult, anyway, not without destroying the host's neural pathways. The Anzillu were a short-term solution. Those possessed as children, while human brain plasticity was at its peak, survived the longest."

The tuna poke bowl I'd had for breakfast began to push its way back up. I pressed my hot face to the window, seeking the relief of cool glass against my skin, but the temperature hadn't yet been coded into the simulation.

Ziggy came to stand beside me. "They bonded you to him for a reason, and I doubt it has anything to do with syphoning his excess energy. If they wanted to suppress Liam's power, they would have asked the Corps to send them a more experienced reaper to keep him from becoming a threat. They would never have chosen a recruit who barely passed the trials."

"Are you suggesting they chose me because they think I'm incompetent?"

Ziggy's hand lifted to my shoulder, then dropped as if she'd reconsidered the gesture of comfort. "They may be using you as a pawn. If their plan backfires, they'll need a scapegoat, someone to take the blame for their failure. You can't trust anything they say or do until we know what their motives are."

I turned to face her. "You're not sending me back to the Nursery to train as a healer, are you?"

"There's too much at stake now for that, I'm afraid. You need to remain here and play their game. Stay close to Liam and keep him alive until we know what they're planning."

"You want me to spy on them?"

"I want you to do your job."

☙

The empty lounge at the lodge was a welcome sight after the cramped bus ride from Hilo to the summit's visitor center. It took every ounce of my energy to keep the syphons coiled around me, blocking the stifling press of bodies against mine.

Cyrena and Marcella hadn't made another appearance, and I still had an hour before I needed to make my trek to the summit. Cool air kissed my bare shoulders as I sloughed off my layers down to the sleeveless tank and massaged the knots in my neck. I groaned with relief as I toed off my hiking boots and flopped onto the distressed leather couch.

Gods, I longed to go back to a time when my biggest problem was avoiding a panic attack. Now, I was stuck between a man who owned a piece of my soul, the spectral assassins who may or may not want to kill him, and my handler who wanted me to play both sides.

I needed to reset my frayed nerves before my next shift with Liam and the angels of death that monitored his every move. I focused on relaxing different parts of my body, clenching and releasing my muscles one at a time from my feet to my face until my gift loosened and my back melted into the worn cushions.

The glorious scent of garlic and grease filled my nose as the couch shifted under someone else's weight.

"You look like you just sucked a lemon." His deep voice rolled over me like warm honey. My eyes flew open and darted around the room, scanning for his handlers before landing on Liam and the fitted white thermal that somehow intensified the blue of his eyes. I folded my legs under me, shrinking into the corner, and pressed my thumb into the ball of my left foot.

"Are you stalking me now?" I groaned.

"Ernie and I have a dinner date to discuss my thesis. I was hoping you'd join us." Liam nodded to the three pizza boxes he'd set on the table. "I got you your own pizza. Barbecue Hawaiian with extra pineapple from Mako Mike's."

"First of all, discussing work is a meeting, not a date, and second—" He cut me off before I had the chance to ask how he'd guessed my favorite pizza.

"You already have a boyfriend. I'm well aware. Not a fan."

I opened my mouth to correct him and paused. If assuming I was in a relationship with Jason kept Liam at arm's length, I didn't see the need to correct him. "Well, the feeling is mutual. Jason told me you were a dick to him the other day."

Liam scowled as he threw an arm over the back of the couch. I inched away from where the tips of his fingers grazed my shoulder, but not before his delicate yet possessive touch sent a flood of sensations through me—the migraine throbbing behind his right eye, the coiled tension in his muscles despite his relaxed posture.

My syphons unfurled and roved over his cheek, his chest, and his thighs. The decadent taste of him bloomed across my tongue as I drank him in and let it fill all the cracks and empty spaces.

"He's pretty, I'll give him that, but he isn't your type."

I took another drag of Liam's energy, pulling more of that sweet milky heat into my chest. "And I suppose you're going to tell me what my type is." I closed my eyes as his energy washed through me and my body went all warm and tingly.

Liam's fingers bit into my waist, holding me in place where I straddled him. "You tell me, chica. You're the one who climbed into my lap." His husky voice made my insides go hot.

My hands slid over his chest and shoulders and into those velvet curls, tilting his head up to mine. He wanted this—I wanted this.

Cyrena's voice cut through my perception. "Must I do everything?" she said as the sensation of ice water rushed over my skin.

I opened my eyes and blinked away the groggy feeding haze. I was still sitting on my side of the couch with my legs folded up beneath me, Liam's thumb tracing little circles on my shoulder from where his outstretched arm rested on the back of the couch.

*What just happened?*

Cyrena read the question in my mind. "It's the bond," she said, appearing on the couch between us. "When you feed on him, you take in his thoughts and desires, and they become yours. It strengthens the compulsion."

*Gods, is that what he's thinking about, me straddling and groping him?*

Her gaze fell to Liam's lap. "I believe you'll find he has a very active imagination."

"I can't do this," I said, unsure if I was talking to Liam or Cyrena or both. I shoved my feet into my boots and stood on wobbly legs.

He leaned forward and reached for me. "Renae, please. Don't run away. Tell me what's going through that head of yours, because I can't read your mind."

A hoarse laugh vibrated through my chest and fell apart like a rickety cart with loose wheels as I pulled on my fleece and my jacket.

"Where are you going?"

"To work. I can't be in the same room with you right now." I retrieved my backpack from the floor.

"Are you still pissed at me about the other night? For not fucking you? Is that what this is about?"

I sighed and slung the bag over my shoulder. "I'm not pissed at you, Liam. I'm angry at myself."

He stood and grabbed my elbow as I brushed past him. "Hey, I'm sorry. That came out all kinds of wrong. Let me feed you, and then we can chat about my thesis as soon as Ernie gets here."

"Oh, I think you already fed her, darling. Filled her right up," Cyrena said with a wicked smirk.

I glowered at her over Liam's shoulder.

"Fuck. You are pissed." Liam dropped my elbow and ran a hand through his hair. "I hate it when my brother is right. I'm in way over my head with you because I don't fucking care if you have a boyfriend or if giving in to temptation is bad for my sobriety. I want you, Renae." His voice rolled over me like the soft thunder of an approaching storm. "I want you to the point of distraction, and I regret turning down your proposition."

I pressed up on the ball of my left foot. The glass embedded there cut through tendon and flesh until it hit bone. "You told your brother about my proposition?"

Liam flinched. "He's visiting; it came up."

I dug my nails into my palm. "What else did you tell him? Did you tell Marcus too? How much damage control do I need to do?"

"I would never tell Logan about that, or any of the other stuff. No one else knows."

"Except your brother." I shoved past him and grabbed one of the pizzas on my way out the door.

Liam followed me through the summit's hotel lodge. "Why are you mad about this?"

How could I explain that the Corps had eyes everywhere? If they found out I'd told Liam even the most minute detail about my previous life, the deceptors and this incessant bond would be the least of my problems.

"Because I value my privacy, and you betrayed it." Icy wind cut across my eyes as we stepped outside.

"He's my brother; he doesn't count. Besides, he's only in town for one more day. It's not like he's gonna tell anyone. He's leaving tomorrow, right after he forces me to jump out of a plane with him."

Ash, dry and chalky, coated my throat. The flavor and texture of fear. My boots dug into the pavement so fast Liam crashed into the back of me. I pivoted on my heels to face him. "You can't be serious. Why would you agree to go skydiving if it scares you?" The tight control I held over my anger cracked. "Liam, you need to call him right now and tell him you changed your mind. I'm sure he'll understand." A fledgling forecaster with erratic mood swings and a fear of flying didn't belong anywhere near an airplane. Even a mild panic attack could mean disaster.

"Yeah, not happening."

Ziggy's advice lodged in my brain like a splinter. *Keep him alive.* Liam's forecasting ability was tied to his emotions. If his fear spiked while they were up there...

The sides of the pizza box buckled beneath my grip. "Liam, please don't do this."

"What the hell, Renae? You, of all people, don't get to stake a claim on anything I choose to do with my life or free time. You have some serious control issues to work out."

"You're right," I said, watching the wind whip snow across the ground the same way his anger scorched my tongue, the phantom capsaicin burning the inside of my mouth, making me sweat and causing my eyes to water. "It's just... so many things can go wrong. Any minor glitch at ten thousand feet can be catastrophic. Are you sure you want to do this?"

The corner of his mouth quirked up as he reached out to move a strand of hair away from my face. "Careful, chica, someone might interpret your concern for my well-being as affection."

I swatted his fingers away. "Impossible, since I don't even like you."

"Agree to disagree on that. Look, I did my research. The flight school has a stellar safety record. If you're really that concerned, why don't you just come with us and see for yourself?"

"Maybe I will." I pivoted and stomped off toward the trail leading to the summit with my dinner. "Enjoy your *date*."

# Chapter Fourteen

# RENAE

Seven blackened bananas stared back at me as I sipped my coffee and considered whether I had the mental concentration required to make bananas foster crepes. I ripped one off and palmed the firm shaft, assessing its length and width. The real question was whether I wanted to slice it up and flambé it or peel it open and devour it whole.

I'd hiked all the way home, hoping to burn Liam's energy out of my bloated system. It left me exhausted, empty, and hungry for more. He'd spent the entire shift trying to ignore me. I'd spent the entire shift trying to ignore his invisible companions.

The doorbell jolted me from my cursed thoughts and the man who inspired them.

"Perfect timing, Jason. I was just about to make breakfast. Do you like crepes?" I asked as I opened the door.

"Actually, I was hoping I could convince you to go to DaGrindz with me. I have a craving for their macadamia chocolate chip pancakes, and I hate gorging myself alone."

My stomach growled, and Jason's smile widened. "Is that a yes?"

"Let me grab my bag."

Twelve minutes later, we pulled into a parking spot along the back side of the farmers market.

"I just need to make a quick stop to see my grandfather before we eat," Jason said as he tugged on his ear.

"*Inside* the farmers market?"

"I... he forgot his glasses. Without them, he can barely tell a single from a ten. He'll squint and struggle to make change all day."

"I'll just wait in the car." While I didn't begrudge sweet Mr. Ito his unobstructed vision, I hadn't forgotten about the fortune-teller, and I was in no hurry to come face to face with her again.

"DaGrindz is on the opposite side of the market. We can walk there after I give these to Jiji." He picked up a pair of thick spectacles and dropped them in his shirt pocket and hopped out of the car.

My eyes landed on the shop across the street. "I'll meet you at the café. I need to pop into the hardware store for some batteries." Not a lie. I'd worn out my vibrator, and if I had any chance of resisting the persuasive effect of Liam's energy and the bond, I needed to replace them as soon as possible.

My mouth went dry as if stuffed with cotton as Jason's energy spread over me like a weighted blanket. The sensation vanished as quickly as it had come on. It wasn't the first time I'd experienced the heaviness in his presence, and if I didn't know better, I'd swear he was an isolator—a soul with the ability to lock down a person's senses and pull them under its influence. I shook off the sensation and let my syphons rove over Jason. Green tea, fresh and clean, wetted my tongue. I tasted no deceit or illusion, nothing to warrant the unease pricking at the back of my brain.

"The hardware store is closed on Wednesdays." He swallowed hard and nodded at the neon sign in the window.

Out of excuses, I reeled in my syphons and followed Jason into the market. We delivered the glasses to Mr. Ito, who sighed with relief as he pushed the square spectacles into place on the tip of his nose.

"You should be able to see the cash box better now," Jason said.

The older man tugged on his earlobe. They were so much alike they even shared the same nervous tick. Definitely human. "Sharp vision is more important when looking ahead than behind," Mr. Ito said.

"And when making change," Jason added as he reorganized his grandfather's money, straightening the bills and placing them in the correct order.

Mr. Ito dipped his head under the table, and his knotted yet nimble hands lifted a repurposed plastic takeout container. It held a leafy plant with spikey green fruit that resembled spiny strawberries.

"Would you please deliver this to Ms. Komahaya on your way to breakfast?" Jason took the odd plant, offering an arm to his grandfather as the old man lowered himself into a chair and bid us farewell.

We made our way toward the outer stalls, and my gift slithered beneath my skin, unable to settle as we neared the booth belonging to the woman with one good eye.

I spied a set of porta potties just past the exit, in the vacant lot across the street from the market. "Jason, I'll meet you at the café. I need to visit the restroom."

Jason glanced at the toilets. "Give the door a good kick and stand back before you open it. Rats like to nest in there."

"Rats?"

"Rats, mice, and the occasional gecko. It's the centipedes you want to watch out for. I don't recommend sitting down in there if you can help it. Centipedes love to hide in dark places, and they bite," he said as we approached the fortune-teller's booth.

"On second thought, I think I can wait."

The woman wore a warm smile as she talked to a well-groomed man with dark hair. Only the stricken half of her face was visible around his broad back.

I scanned the surrounding booths for a rack or display I might step behind to avoid her notice when I spotted a head of dirty-blond curls and a familiar brooding stance.

My stomach dropped. Liam leaned against one of the market's metal awning supports. He'd been so calm all morning; I'd assumed he was asleep. My gift hadn't picked up on the proximity of his energy. Maybe I'd been too focused on the fortune-teller to notice.

I grabbed Jason's arm and pulled him in the opposite direction. "She's busy. Maybe we should just go eat breakfast now and come back later with the plant." A bead of sweat ran down the flat valley between my breasts under the sports bra and loose tank I'd thrown on before heading out with Jason. I hadn't even bothered to brush my hair, which now hung in a lopsided knot on the top of my head. I looked like I'd just crawled out of bed.

"I don't want to carry this thing around all day," Jason said.

A prickle of recognition rippled along the cord connecting me to Liam. He straightened and turned toward me, as if drawn by a magnet.

The silent command in those denim eyes halted my retreat, pinning my feet to the ground. I really, really hated the bond.

"Jason, this is Liam."

"Nice to see you again," Jason said.

Liam slowly dragged his intense gaze away from me to Jason's outstretched hand. Jason's energy was an easy read, even for a beginner. I'd never needed to dive into the undercurrents of his spectrum. Everything was right there on the surface. Sweat dampened my armpits as Liam scrutinized my fake boyfriend. Gods, why hadn't I thought to put on deodorant. I glanced around for his handlers and froze when my gaze locked with a single dark eye.

Salt and metal popped in my mouth as I latched onto her spectrum. Something stung my tongue, and I yanked my gift back. It was more than

I'd gotten the first time. Either the fortune-teller's guard was down, or my ability to push through her defenses had gotten stronger.

"Connor, this is Renae," Liam said to the man standing in front of Cici's booth. Where Liam was all untamed curls, furrowed brow, and lazy stubble, his brother was sculpted stone, clean lines, and crisp cotton. Not a single one of his smooth dark hairs was out of place.

Connor's eyes shot to Liam and then back to me. "*The* Renae?"

Liam forced a throat clearing cough as I stepped in front of him to take Connor's manicured hand and braced for the rush of sensations.

Stillness and the strength of bedrock beneath me, a bright light in the dark, the tang of iron on my tongue, the somber weight of something warm and fleshy in my palm.

The corner of Connor's mouth quirked up as I dropped his hand. "I've heard *so much* about you," he said.

My face heated. I wanted to crawl under the nearest table and hide.

"I understand my brother invited you to go skydiving with us this afternoon."

"I hope it's not an imposition," I said, ignoring the grunt from Liam.

"Not in the least." Connor leaned in and gave me a conspiratorial smile. "I should probably thank you."

"For what?" I asked.

"For making my brother look forward to throwing himself out of an airplane."

Liam shot his brother a warning scowl.

"Renae, you didn't mention you were going skydiving." Jason's brow knit together. "Isn't that a bit risky?"

Connor ignored him and continued. "Lee needs all the moral support he can get. He's terrified."

The muscle along Liam's jaw ticked. "Anyone in their right mind would be terrified of plummeting to the ground with nothing but a bag full of nylon and rope strapped to their fucking back." The temperature dropped, and a gust blew through the tent as the shadow of a cloud settled over the market.

Cyrena took shape next to Liam. She let her long hair appear to be whipped by the wind, emphasizing the sudden forecast change. The deceptor certainly had a flair for the dramatic. I unfurled a single syphon and latched on to Liam's shoulder. My tongue crusted over with ash as I consumed the emotion rising to the surface. It was quickly replaced by the sweet milky heat at his core that made my chest burn and my head go woozy.

Cyrena reached for my skull. "That's more than enough. No need to be a glutton."

I snapped my gift back and stepped toward Liam, avoiding Cyrena's grasp and another one of her ice picks of pain. Liam's energy sloshed around inside me, and the ground beneath my feet shifted.

He gripped my bicep from behind, sliding his thumb softly, reassuringly, up and down my inner arm as the sun stabbed through the cotton batting clouds like a needle. It was all I could do not to lean back against him.

"Well done, though no one will ever accuse you of being graceful," Cyrena said. If she wasn't dead already, the compliment might have killed her. "Next time, try sipping instead of slurping like a dog."

Cici moved to the front of her booth, her one good eye sliding over each of us in turn, stopping on me, on the strong hand circling my arm. "I'd be happy to read your fortune, tell you if it's safe to fly today," she said as her gaze flicked behind me to Liam, who flinched and looked away.

This time, it wasn't the powdery residue of ash, gritty and bitter, that sucked all the moisture from my mouth. It was a sharp sting of vinegar. He released me, and I immediately missed the pressure of his possessive grip as I glanced between them. There was a history there. One that smacked of shame.

Connor stepped forward and took Cici's outstretched palm. "Sure, why not?"

The fortune-teller made a show of considering his manicured hand, turning it over to trace the lines on the underside. Her eye didn't go glassy as it had the morning of the accident when she'd warned of broken glass.

"No harm shall come to anyone who flies with the angel today." Cici patted Connor's hand and turned to Jason. "Is that my thornapple?" she asked, nodding to the plant cradled in the crook of his arm.

"Ah, jimson weed, if I'm not mistaken," Connor interjected. "You are aware this is toxic?"

"So are apple seeds," Jason said as he handed the pot to Cici.

"True, but this particular weed is one bad apple."

Cici regarded the plant with reverence. "Thornapple has many uses in the shamanistic arts."

"It'll also induce serious gastrointestinal distress, hallucinations, and loss of consciousness if ingested." Connor was serious now.

"It's a gift for my niece. Burning a leaf at bedtime can ease a heartache." The woman's monocular gaze landed on Liam.

"We should be going." I tugged Jason in the direction of the exit, eager to escape before the woman's attention fell on me. "We have a breakfast date to keep."

"And I still need to find a gift for my husband. See you this afternoon, Renae." Connor winked at me as he angled toward a ukulele vendor.

"*Enjoy your date,*" Liam whispered as he brushed past me and trailed after his brother. The vinegar sting in my mouth was replaced by his familiar milky sweet spice.

☙

A dozen people sat around weathered picnic tables, knees bobbing as they waited for their flight to be called. I entered the office—a rusted construction trailer near the end of its useful life—and asked Audrey to add my name to the sold-out flight roster. The advertised max of twelve bodies per run was more of a guideline, and Audrey always made room for me when I showed up without a reservation.

Skydiving had been the first of many tests during the trials. Pairs of recruits sent out with one parachute between them. Whoever made it to the ground without losing their husk moved on to the next round.

"I should've known you'd show up on the first clear day. You reconsider my job offer yet?" Garrett's vibrant orange hair was as vivid as his energy spectrum. He lived for one thing and one thing only—adrenaline. He ran the flight school and had been trying to convince me to sign on as an instructor since our first jump together several months ago.

"If I quit my day job, my boss will send someone to kill me."

Garrett laughed, but I wasn't kidding. Like the woman who gave birth to Liam, my life and my body were not my own. They belonged to the Corps. "Which plane are you running today, the PA or Nadine?"

"The PA, why?"

"Just curious." I forced the tension from my shoulders and hoped the fortune-teller's prediction proved accurate as I bypassed my personal locker and headed straight to the school's equipment closet to inspect the tandem rigs. Ten minutes later, I headed back to the lobby where Audrey was checking in Liam and his brother.

"I'm sorry, but we just filled the last seat. We don't have room for another tandem on the HALO flight."

The color drained from Liam's face. "What do you mean *HALO* flight?"

"It's okay, Audrey, I'm their third."

"You should have said you were with Renae. She's one of our pro members. She doesn't need a tandem instructor."

"Renae, what the hell is she talking about?" Liam asked through gritted teeth.

My gift shifted beneath my skin as I gave him an apologetic smile.

"Fuck this. I'm done with both of you right now." The cord between us went taut as Liam stormed out of the building. I took a step toward the door to ease the uncomfortable sucking sensation in my chest.

"Listen," Audrey said to Connor, "we won't take anyone up who doesn't want to jump, but he needs to decide now. There's no refund if he gets up there and chooses not to go through with it."

"Understood. I'll go talk to him." Connor stepped toward the door.

"Let me," I said.

Connor nodded and let me go. I glanced up at the sky as I crossed the grassy parking lot to where Liam paced next to his truck, keys in hand.

"It's not too late," I said. "You can walk away from this."

Liam pivoted toward me. "After all the shit you gave me last night, you never once thought to mention you've done this before?"

"Do you want to jump or not?"

Liam sighed, "This HALO thing. How high are we talking?"

"Twenty thousand feet."

He ran his hands through his curls. "How bad is it? Tell me the truth, not what you think I need to hear."

I squirmed under the intense scrutiny of those denim eyes. "It's cold and it's terrifying and it's the one thing in this world that makes me feel completely alive."

"I never would have pegged you for an adrenaline junkie."

"It's not about the adrenaline. It's knowing that, like the ground, death is rushing up to greet me, and I'm the one who gets to pull the rip cord. No one else. I get to choose whether I live or die."

We were both quiet for a moment.

"So you think I should do it?"

"Only you can make that decision. I'll support you either way."

"Jesus, the constant one-eighties with you are giving me whiplash. I swear, it's like you're two different people sometimes. I never know which Renae I'm gonna get. The carefully composed ice queen who can't stand to be in the same room with me, or the wild flame of a woman who screams in her sleep, shows up barefoot on my doorstep in the middle of the night, and has to jump out of an airplane just to feel alive. I'm pretty sure the real Renae lies somewhere in between. Where's that Renae? Because I'd like to have an honest conversation with her for once." The muscle along his jaw popped as he clenched his teeth.

My syphons strained beneath my skin, pressing toward Liam, itching for release. I struggled to hold them back and crossed my arms over my chest in an attempt to keep them leashed. "I'm right here, Liam, so ask whatever it is you need to ask."

"What's the deal with Jason? He didn't react like a boyfriend when he found out you were spending the afternoon with me." Curiosity crept along the cord between us until he was treading well within my energy field.

Marcella's melodic voice filled my head. "Careful, child, he's reading you quite clearly now. You can no longer lie to him any more than you can lie to yourself."

I had to give him something to keep him from digging deeper. "He's my neighbor. We're... friends."

Liam walked to the back of the truck and pressed his knuckles against the tailgate. "Why would you lie about that? About any of this?" He flung a hand back toward the jump school.

"I didn't lie to you. Not about that. You made an assumption, and it was just easier to let you believe it."

"Why does everything have to be so damn complicated with you?" Liam huffed a breath and leaned against the tailgate on his forearms. "I just want you to be honest with me."

Cyrena appeared and circled around him, trailing her thin fingers over his shoulder. "Poor man. Fancies himself in love with you and has no idea it's all a lie."

My eyes darted to the beautiful monster behind him.

"You heard me, darling. Let your squirming tentacles probe his system and taste the truth for yourself."

"I… can't." I couldn't let myself taste it, want it. I ground the ball of my left foot into the gravel and dirt, pushing the glass deeper into my flesh until the pain made my eyes water.

This thing he needed from me, to open myself up, to let him in fully, meant giving up control, giving up my last thread of free will, and it went against every instinct I had. He may be able to compel my actions through the bond, but I refused to be contaminated by his emotions. I couldn't allow myself to be completely consumed by him. If I was going to do this, open up to him, I needed a plan. One that would protect my autonomy, despite the bond.

I forced myself to take a step, then another, toward the rear of the truck, gripping the edge of the bed for support. "You're right. I haven't been completely honest with you, and you deserve the truth. No more secrets or lies, but now is not the time nor the place. Your brother is waiting for you to make a decision."

Liam reached for my hand and laced his fingers through mine. "I want to do this." The way he looked at me told me he wasn't just talking about skydiving anymore.

Connor eyed me warily as we walked back into the office hand in hand. Liam and I didn't speak—we just moved around one another in silence, the weight of a future conversation hanging between us. He deserved the truth. All of it.

I stayed close to him, keeping a hand on him at all times as I watched the sky. So far, the weather was holding.

"You guys stoked?" Garrett asked as we walked across the weedy grass runway toward the plane.

While the anticipation rendered Liam mute, it had the opposite effect on his brother.

"I'm even more excited than I was in tenth grade when Kyle Wilson offered to suck me off in his daddy's Miata. I've had a fondness for convertibles and wind in my hair ever since."

Connor's over the top comment broke the nervous tension pulsing through the group of first-time jumpers. There were six in total: Liam, his brother, a young couple on their honeymoon, and a mother-daughter duo crossing off an item on their bucket list. Everyone seemed content to let Connor's gregarious personality carry the conversation and set the mood, and I got the feeling that the man had never walked into a room and not been the center of attention. Tight anxious smiles transformed into relaxed grins, except for Liam, who remained stiff and stoic at my side.

"Wait until you see Renae fly. She's our resident daredevil. Her stunts are epic," Wes, one of the four instructors, said, throwing an arm over my shoulder.

A feral scowl sharpened the lines of Liam's face. The possessiveness that flashed across the cord between us should have annoyed me. Instead, it made my insides flutter. And *that* annoyed me. Gods, it terrified me.

"You've got to be fucking kidding me," Liam said, finally finding his voice.

I bit back a smile as Connor read the name painted in large blue scrolling script across the plane's fuselage. "Paradise Angel?" Connor clapped his brother on the back. "See Lee? The fortune-teller was right, nothing to worry about."

Garrett lined everyone up with their tandem partners in jumping order on the metal benches along the walls inside the plane. Connor with Wes, and Liam with Garrett would go last. There was no room for me on the bench, so I grabbed one of the frayed shoelace loops screwed to the ceiling and stood in the narrow aisle next to Liam.

The PA was an old, loud Cessna SuperVan, and once it took off, you had to shout or lean in close to someone's ear to be heard.

"We'll be in position above the drop zone in about twenty minutes," Garrett bellowed over the whine of the engine as the plane accelerated down the runway.

"This is where the magic happens," Wes yelled. Today's official hype master. Garrett always assigned someone to interject positive affirmations to maintain the mood. An effect lost on Liam.

He closed his eyes, exhaling slowly as the wheels left the earth with a momentary left to right wobble. All the other passengers hooted their excitement.

I rested my free hand on his shoulder. I didn't need to syphon him to soothe the sharp corners of his anxiety. Touch worked just as well.

When the plane banked in the direction of the drop zone, the shoelace I'd been gripping for stability tore from the ceiling. Liam grabbed my hips and yanked me toward him, causing our jump helmets to clack together as he settled me sideways across his lap. My face flamed, and I tried to stand.

Liam tightened his arms around me and rested his helmet against the side of mine. "Stay." Part desperate plea, part command that made my skin prickle with heat.

I took a measured breath and let my body relax against him. His breathing slowed, and his grip loosened around my waist. I tried not the think about what Cyrena said; how he might feel about me, or at least the woman he thought I was.

I shouldn't pry, and didn't want to know, didn't want his emotions contaminating mine. But as his thumb stroked the small of my back, I couldn't help myself. I let one of my syphons unfurl, wrap itself around him, and burrow deep.

As I probed, I pushed beneath the surface emotions, beneath the swirling and eddying currents, to his core. Love tasted different on everyone. It wasn't the flavor that set it apart; it was the texture. The way it felt in the mouth, fizzy and light. For the boy at the bus stop, it had been like sweet lemon-lime soda when his mother wrapped her arms around him. I'd tasted it on Cyrena as well—that sour over-fermented frothy champagne. Who she pined for, I didn't know.

I didn't find any effervescent fizz inside Liam. Instead, I found myself. The piece of my soul I'd sacrificed to save his life. It beat inside him like a second heart, my energy grounding all that raw, unrefined power. He didn't love me. He needed me. He needed the bond. I was his crutch.

Gods, Cyrena knew. She wanted me to explore. To see it for myself. It was her warning to be gentle with the man who couldn't tell the difference between love and need, and to be cautious of taunting the dormant power inside him. It was a reminder that I still had a choice, that I had control over his fate, and in turn, my own.

"Thank you," I whispered to the invisible soul hiding somewhere within the shadows around me.

Cyrena's voice swept through my consciousness like a brisk wind. "Don't let it go to your head. You're still a cow."

My belly shook with laughter.

"What's so funny?" Liam asked.

"Nothing, everything, this, us."

Liam tapped his ear and raised his voice. "I can't hear you."

I grabbed either side of his helmet, pulling his cheek to mine so I wouldn't have to yell. "We're almost there. When the door opens, the pressure inside the cabin will change. Your chest is going to feel too tight. Focus on taking deep, measured breaths. Once you're out there, you won't have a sense of how fast you're falling, unless you look back at the plane. So *don't* do that. Listen to Garrett and do what he says. I'll be right behind you."

Eighteen minutes into the flight, Garrett motioned for me to take up the position by the door and for the instructors to connect their tandem rigs. Wes, true to form, joked around and pretended to struggle with Connor's connection. Connor played along, but Liam was not amused.

The pilot signaled that we were ready to begin the exit procedure. I glanced back at Liam and gave him a nod before sliding the door open. The plane filled with a rush of frigid air that made my eyes burn. I pulled my goggles into place and blinked away the wetness as the first two groups exited the plane and plunged through cottony clouds. I rolled the door shut as we circled the drop zone.

Connor's face went ghostly pale as he and Wes moved into position in front of the door. I'd been so focused on Liam I'd forgotten about his full of bravado older brother. I unleashed my gift, lathing a syphon to his chest. The scent of ether clung to my nostrils and salt coated my tongue as I sucked out his anxiety before it had the chance to catch fire and turn to ash in my mouth. I gave Wes the go signal, and he pushed away from the plane. Connor screamed like a teenage girl as they dropped away.

Garrett said something to Liam, who crossed his arms over his chest and gripped his harness. As they stepped forward, the plane hit a sudden pocket of low pressure and dropped about twenty feet, knocking my teeth together.

My heart stopped as they lost their balance and started to tumble out of the plane. Ash filled my mouth and choked the air from my lungs as Garrett grasped the rail on either side of the door frame. I glanced at the pilot. He signaled Garrett to hold as he circled the plane around into a better position.

We banked, and my stomach deflated as I got a good view of the drop zone and the black cloud coalescing beneath us. I scanned the sky for Wes and Connor, my heart straining against the too-tight space behind my ribs. If Wes opened his chute anywhere near that front, they'd be in trouble, and I was too far behind to do anything about it.

My eyes landed on Wes' hot pink canopy, and I let loose the breath I'd been holding. They were moving in the opposite direction of the storm. I rolled the door shut against the violent wind that was battering the plane. The metal fuselage creaked and moaned in the turbulence, threatening to come apart at the seams.

Cyrena's voice filled my head as she appeared next to Liam. "You need to suck out his fear before it tears this plane apart."

I grasped Liam's harness, still attached to Garrett, and shoved them both against the wall. Our goggles bumped as I pressed my lips to Liam's. I didn't dare risk the fuzzy-headed haze that came from feeding on him. I needed to remain clearheaded until we were safe on the ground.

I released my syphons and probed his spectrum as I teased his mouth open. He groaned as he grabbed my hips, digging his fingers into the soft flesh and kissed me back with a hunger I wasn't prepared for. I unloaded everything I had into him, hoping it was enough to flood his system and dilute his fear. Liam took all I offered and more, possessing my mouth, the air in my lungs.

He took control of my gift, claiming me fully. My syphons burrowed deeper, drilling through the barrier at his core until it cracked and I went molten with need. Whether his or my own, I didn't know, and I didn't care. I wanted to consume him the same way he was consuming me. In a blaze as we both turned to ash.

Cyrena's ice talons clawed at my back and punctured my lungs, forcing me to drag my mouth away from Liam's and suck in a deep breath. "You gluttonous cow. That barrier is the only thing holding back his full power. You've just given him access to the one thing he needs to destroy it before we've gotten what we need. If you can't keep him stable and he becomes a threat, we'll have no choice. Do you even understand what you risked with that terrible kiss?"

"That definitely wasn't terrible," I mumbled into Liam's neck, still feeling a bit breathless.

He lifted my chin. White-hot fire danced behind those blue eyes. "Agree to disagree, chica. *That* was incredible."

Cyrena rolled her eyes. "When the time comes, do not get in my way. You've been warned." She vanished, but the cold, hollow feeling in my chest remained.

Garrett, still pressed between Liam and the wall, cleared his throat. "It was good for me too, if anyone was wondering. And it looks like the weather has cleared."

Liam released me with a wicked grin. A promise that sent a shiver down my spine.

The pilot gave the all clear, and I slid the door open. Liam didn't take his eyes off me as Garrett secured his head, tipped forward, and plummeted out of sight. I felt the bond snap in my chest as if we were connected by an invisible leash, one that pulled me out of the plane with them. In that moment, as the wind bit my cheeks and the ground rushed up to greet me, I knew, wherever he went, I'd have no choice but to follow.

# Chapter Fifteen

# LIAM

Crammed between my brother's larger-than-life personality and my long-ass legs, there wasn't much room for Renae between us in the cab of my truck. It was near impossible to ignore the press of her thigh against mine or the way her braid hung over her shoulder and tickled my bicep.

As usual, Connor carried the conversation. If he wasn't my brother, gay, and already married, I'd have been jealous of the way she paid rapt attention as he described his near-death experience research, hanging on every damn word that came out of his mouth. My brother, the heart surgeon, never failed to impress.

"How do you cope with the pressure of holding someone's fate in your hands? Of being responsible for whether they live or die?" Renae asked.

"The trick is not allowing your emotions to contaminate your mind. You have to set boundaries, separate yourself from the work, and just do your job."

Renae nodded as if he'd divulged something profound. She didn't speak again until I pulled into her complex.

I held the driver's side door open as she slid across the seat. "It was a pleasure meeting you, Connor. I'd love to hear more about your research someday."

"If you ever find yourself in New York, call me. I'd be happy to give you a tour of the hospital."

I slammed the door shut with a little more force than necessary.

"Are you seriously walking me to my front door?" Renae asked.

"After you." I gestured to the staircase and followed her to the second floor.

She fumbled in her bag for the key, and I leaned against the wall.

"Renae, I need to tell you something."

She froze, like an animal caught in a snare. "Please don't."

"You don't even know what I was going to say."

Renae sighed. "It's been a long day. I'm exhausted, and I don't have the energy for this conversation right now."

"Jesus fuck!" I pushed away from the door and ran a hand through my hair. "Why is everything a battle with you? I'm just trying to say thank you."

Her head whipped toward me. "For what?"

I grasped the doorframe on either side of her to keep from shaking her, or maybe to keep from pulling her into my arms and finishing what she started on the plane. I softened my voice. "For distracting me up there. I freaked out, and you just... you knew what to do."

"I've had enough panic attacks to recognize when someone's about to spiral. I'm glad it worked."

Oh, it definitely worked. It was getting harder and harder to see past my need for this woman. I cupped her cheek in my hand, tracing the curve of her bottom lip with my thumb. "Was that the only reason you kissed me? To distract me?"

"I didn't want any unfortunate incidents to ruin your brother's day. I really like him."

"I want you," I said, "and I think you want me too."

"It was *just* a kiss."

Renae gave up a breathy little gasp as I leaned down and brushed my lips over her ear. "Agree to disagree."

"I hate you," she said as she fisted my shirt and pulled me in.

My lips curled into a smile against that needy little mouth. I stepped away from her, walking backward toward the stairwell. "Rest up, chica, because I plan to take my time showing you all the ways I want you to hate me."

A door slammed behind me, followed by a muffled string of what sounded like French cuss words as I sailed down the steps.

Back in the truck, my brother didn't waste any time giving me shit about Renae.

"I get why you're into her. She's exactly your type," Connor said, rolling his eyes.

"Fuck you. I don't have a type."

"You *so* have a type. Intelligent, adventurous, strong willed. You're drawn to that combo like a moth to a flame. Doesn't she have a boyfriend?"

"She made that up. He's just a friend."

"I like her, I really do, but there are a lot of red flags—not the least of which is the obsession she's brought out in you. What do you even know about her?"

My knuckles went white from the death grip I had on the steering wheel. "I know that when I'm with her, I feel more like myself than I have my entire life."

"Lee, she lied to you. I thought that was one of your non-negotiables."

"I'm not having this conversation with you."

"See, that's what I'm worried about. You're sliding back into old patterns. Obsessive thoughts, getting defensive, refusing to have a serious conversation. I've seen you go down this road before, and it doesn't end well. Just think about what I said and ask yourself if pursuing this woman is worth the risk. That's all I'm saying."

# Chapter Sixteen

# RENAE

I slammed the door and stomped to the kitchen, where the carcasses of my plant hospice program still sat on the table. A glaring reminder that I would never be a healer. I'd never had control of a single choice I'd made since the day I'd died, and thanks to the bond, I never would again.

I swiped at the hot tears on my cheeks. How was I supposed to maintain mental and emotional boundaries when my gift and my body responded to Liam's physical presence without thought or reason? I'd had to clench my hands in my lap the entire way home to keep them from stroking the muscled length of his thigh. When he was that close, when there was no space between us, it was impossible to know whether the impulse had come from his mind or mine.

My fingers curled around the clay pot of a dead orchid as I lifted it above my head, ready to shatter it on the floor along with any illusions of choice I'd ever had, when my phone vibrated in my pocket. I slapped the plant down on the table with a crack.

It was a text from Ziggy. *Meeting. Now.*

I removed the neural-lace pods from their case and shoved them into my ears. The nano filaments tickled their way into place as I slumped into a chair at the table and waited for my consciousness to be transported into the virtual meeting space. The awareness of my apartment faded as her office took shape, with its panoramic view of the mountains surrounding the Nursery's training compound. Like her avatar, the thick carpet, glass desk, and window were all just part of the simulation.

Ziggy pulled up the local weather reports for Hilo and matched the time stamps between the storm front that appeared out of nowhere and the erratic readings from my tracker.

I braced for another lecture about taking too many risks. No more running on lava, no more skydiving. No more anything that could damage the husk I'd been assigned.

"Take a look at this." She brought up the undulating orb of black noodles representing my energy fingerprint and let it hover in the space above her desk. I watched as it flared, every strand going from inky black to a blinding white light that pulsed for a minute before blinking out.

*Liam.* I'd felt it when I kissed him and he took control of my gift, causing my body to go white hot with need.

"It's called the claiming," Ziggy explained. "It happens when the one you're bound to takes full possession of your gift. Bonded Gi'dari can wield and control tremendous amounts of energy when their gifts are combined. I encourage you to be cautious. Now that he's claimed you completely, the compulsory power he has over you will be stronger."

I thought about the moment on the plane when he'd asked me to stay on his lap and the night I'd fallen into an involuntary hibernation after he told me to get in his truck and get some rest. Both times, I'd complied without question.

I gouged my nails into my palms. "How am I supposed to protect myself or my cover when he can take whatever he wants?"

"The bond's subconscious compulsions can be managed as long as he doesn't give you a direct order. You may want to avoid physical contact for the time being."

My face heated. "That may be difficult," I said. "There's nothing subtle about the physical compulsions between us. My body and gift cleave to him like gravity every time I enter his orbit."

Ziggy cleared her throat. "I see." She glanced out the window and watched two forecasters who were sparring on top of the frozen lake, throwing ice and lightning at one another. "You're the most headstrong recruit I've ever met. You've found loopholes and ways to avoid my orders. I'm sure you'll think of something."

"What if I tell him everything?"

Her gray eyes flicked to mine. "Do I need to remind you that revealing your true identity to a human is grounds for immediate termination?"

"He's not human."

"And you think that will matter to the Nūkiri when his handlers place their failures on your shoulders? You need to follow protocol with this, Renae. Your loyalty must be unquestionable if it all goes sideways."

"I still don't understand what their plan is. If they're using him as bait, wouldn't they want his powers to manifest? If the missing geneticist hasn't come for Liam by now, the only way to draw him out would be to trigger—" I stood and paced the plush carpet. Gods, that was it. "I think they *want* Liam's gifts to manifest. That's why they bonded me to him. They think I'm incompetent. They want me to fail."

"I'm afraid you may be right," Ziggy said.

"What happens to him when they catch Issor Nella and Liam's no longer of use to them? What if I can't syphon enough energy away to keep him from becoming a real threat? He deserves to know the truth. To prepare for what's coming for him. He has a family, for gods' sakes. He deserves the chance to say goodbye to his brother, at least. I have to tell him."

Ziggy's eyes widened and then narrowed to piercing silver shards. Without tasting her, there was no way to know if the brief flash was anger at my insolence or something else.

"You will do no such thing. He doesn't understand the control he has over you. His ignorance is the last wall of protection you have against his will. Do not give him that power. Give him something else. Something he wants. Do whatever it takes to distract him and keep his emerging gifts in check. Once he becomes a threat, there won't be anything you can do to save him, or yourself."

Liam's words filled my head as I pulled the neural-lace pods from my ears. *I want you and I think you want me too.*

I could lie to myself, blame it on the bond or my traitorous gift, but I couldn't lie to him. Not anymore. I wanted Liam Riley in a way that made my insides go all hot and achy. Even now, when we were apart and the compulsory effect of the bond had dissipated, I still couldn't deny that I wanted to taste his dormant power—to feel the milky sweet heat of his energy as it slid down my throat or the decadence of his mouth pressed to mine. Gods, I'd wanted to ride the tidal pull of all that power as it rose inside him. Inside me.

I grabbed a pen and a block of sticky notes out of the kitchen junk drawer. Ziggy was right. I needed to find a way to give him something he wanted—something we both wanted—without giving up full control. I needed to seduce and distract while I waited for his handlers to make their next move.

# Chapter Seventeen

# LIAM

My knee bounced under the desk as I stared at my laptop in my stuffy basement office. A six-by-six concrete cave that Logan swore was not a toilet paper storage closet in a previous life, despite being sandwiched between the restroom and the stairwell.

I gave up trying to make any headway on my latest round of thesis edits and swiveled in my chair to brace my feet on the wall. My mind didn't have to drift far to land on Renae. She was there in the background every waking minute.

Connor's words stung like a bitch, but he was right. I was in way the hell over my head with her because it'd only been twenty-four hours since that kiss, and all I wanted—all I could think about—was getting another fix. I wanted to feel her body melt into mine again as she devoured me with that needy little mouth, and I didn't have to think hard to imagine what it might feel like to have those lips wrapped around my cock.

My phone vibrated on the desk. Probably Connor letting me know how his conference presentation had gone. I considered ignoring it, but he'd just keep texting until I responded.

I picked up the phone and dropped my feet to the floor.

It was a text from Renae. *We're on shift together tonight. Since you're not busy, I could use a ride to the summit.*

*What makes you think I'm not busy?*

Renae responded immediately, and I swear I could sense her eyes roll from across town. *If it's an inconvenience, I can find my own way.*

My chest swelled like a damn balloon as I imagined her scowling at her phone. *I'll pick you up in an hour.*

Two seconds later she added. *The truck. NO death machine. Please.*

Screw Connor and his "proceed with caution" and "what do you really know about her" crap. We were so doing this.

Out of curiosity, I typed her name into the search engine on my laptop. I didn't get a single hit matching the woman I knew. No social media profiles, LinkedIn page, or record of any kind on Renae Martin—unless she'd been moonlighting as a pediatrician in North Carolina for the last decade. I added the word France to the search window and still didn't get a damn hit on anything other than some disturbing photos of a World War II memorial. She wasn't even listed on the summit's staff directory. My name and extension were on there, and I wasn't even getting paid.

A knot formed in the pit of my stomach. I hated it when my brother was right. I didn't know shit about her.

Unanswered questions swirled through my head a half hour later as I climbed the steps to her apartment. She opened the door before I had the chance to knock.

Renae's eyes darted over my shoulder and scanned the parking lot as her voice popped into my head. *Gods, I hope he didn't bring that ridiculous contraption.*

"It's not a ridiculous contraption. It's a Buell 1125CR, built for performance on and off the road. But I brought the truck, as requested."

She stiffened. "Why would you say that?"

"Say what?"

"*Ridiculous contraption.* Why those exact words?"

"I was just repeating what you said."

"Liam, I didn't say anything."

Shit. I backpedaled. "Maybe I just know what you're going to say before you say it."

"What am I thinking right now?" She folded her arms across her chest.

I stepped closer and traced the neckline of her shirt, letting my fingers rest on her collarbone. I couldn't force the thoughts to come, and had no clue what she was thinking, but I hoped it was close to what I'd been thinking about all day, every day since the first time I'd laid eyes on her.

"You're hungry," I said.

She swatted my hand away and grabbed her bag. "I'm always hungry. Can we stop for tacos?"

I followed her down the steps toward the parking lot. "We can stop for anything you want, chica, if you tell me all about the mysterious Renae Martin. I couldn't find squat about you online."

She turned on her heel by my truck. "Are you Google-stalking me?"

"You're not exactly an open book."

"What do you want to know?"

"What's your favorite food? Why don't you have a car?"

"French toast, and because I'm conscious of my carbon footprint. Now hand me your keys. You're exhausted, and I don't want to end up in a ditch somewhere on Saddle Road."

She snatched the keys from my hand, and I didn't argue. I hadn't slept much in the last forty-eight hours, and I was happy to let her take the wheel.

We hit the drive-through, and after snarfing down six soft tacos all on her own, Renae talked non-stop all the way to the summit, but I didn't learn anything new about her. She blabbed on and on about the weather. Did I notice anything odd about the freak windstorm that kicked up during our jump? What were my thoughts about the unseasonal amounts of rain? Had I ever considered keeping a weather journal? All an attempt to avoid talking about the thing hanging in the air between us—that kiss and what came next.

When we got to the lab, she dove into work mode. We spent four tedious hours processing data from the active supernova in M83 before we got our first break.

"I'll be back in a few minutes. I need to check on SpeX, make sure it's not running too hot. If the research team from UNC logs on before I get back, entertain them for me?"

"On it." My eyes followed her round ass as it jiggled out of the room, and I tried not to think about how badly I wanted to bend her over a damn desk.

Renae's computer made a faint beeping noise. I checked the interface. No virtual team arrivals yet, so I clicked on a flashing icon at the bottom of her task bar. A "confirm batch deletion" prompt popped up. I opened the file and found fifteen images of the Eridanus quadrant, each showing a bright, deep space object I didn't recognize. I dropped into Renae's chair and did a few quick calculations. Seventeen billion. I redid the math and got the same result. It had to be a glitch. How could something be three billion years older than the known universe? Unless it didn't live in the known universe.

"What are you doing at my desk?" Renae snapped.

I jumped up and knocked her thermos of coffee onto the floor with a crack. "You scared the shit out of me. Come take a look at this."

She glanced at the screen. "How did you find that?"

"What do you think it is?" I asked.

"Another corrupted file. SpeX keeps overheating. We've had to scrap a lot of compromised data."

"How far back did you date it?"

"It doesn't matter. Like I said, it was a corrupted batch."

I handed her the notepad and pencil. "Show me yours, and I'll show you mine."

Renae deleted the files without even looking at them, then stood and placed her hands on my chest, running them up over my shoulders. "I can think of a few things I'd rather see than your red shift calculations."

I coiled a strand of her hair around my finger. "What will you show me in return?"

Renae reached into her pocket and pulled out a folded yellow sticky note. "I've been thinking about that," she said, "and I made you a list."

She yanked the note away as I reached for it.

"There are rules. We can do anything on the list. However, if you ask me to do something that isn't listed, you forfeit the other items. You will not make suggestions, requests, or demands. No exceptions. Just the list. Those are my terms."

"Can I at least see the list first?" I asked, unable to take my eyes off that damn scrap of paper as Renae started to tear it up.

I grabbed her wrist. "I accept."

She bit her bottom lip and slowly opened her palm.

# CHAPTER EIGHTEEN

# RENAE

LIAM SCRATCHED THE STUBBLE along his jaw as he read and reread the list. My stomach did a little flip when those denim eyes finally lifted and raked over me.

His brows knit together, deepening the scar that split his forehead like a seam, as if he'd been stitched together. In a way, I suppose he had. The seeds of all seven sacred gifts sewn into the fabric of one man. All that power thrumming through his veins. A power my gift ached to taste, consume, and serve. I'd erected my final boundary with the list. One I hoped would give us what we both wanted and keep me from losing myself entirely to the bond.

My heart flapped in my chest like a beast with feathered wings as I sat on my desk and let my syphons caress him, coaxing him closer. Hungry.

"There are four things on this list," Liam said.

"We can take a few off if that makes it easier for you." I reached for the sticky note.

Liam clutched it to his chest. "Not a damn chance." He spread my knees with his thigh and stepped between them. "I have a few questions."

"Then I suggest you choose your words wisely. I meant what I said before. No requests and no demands. That's the only way this can work."

He dipped his head and his breath ghosted over the shell of my ear. "Do we go in order, or can we skip ahead?" He slid his hands up the outside of my thighs to my hips, where they found their way under the edge of my blouse and the bare skin at my waist.

Gods, it was impossible to focus while his thumb traced idle circles on my ribcage. "We can go in any order you like."

His lips moved over my throat. Could he feel my pounding pulse?

"Is each item a one-time deal, or can I come back for seconds?"

"That depends on your performance," I said, unable to keep my pulse steady.

Liam gripped my backside and yanked me to the edge of the desk.

"Then I'll do my best to make sure you come so hard you forget your damn name." His lips grazed mine, and it was all I could do to turn away from his deliciously dirty mouth.

"Kissing isn't on the list," I said, my voice barely more than a rasp. My self-control was already starting to slip. If I allowed him to kiss me while I syphoned him, while his sweet, spicy heat filled me, I'd risk losing control of my gift and shattering what was left of my free will.

Liam started to protest, then caught himself, making a noise that was equal parts groan and growl.

I squirmed in his arms. "Let me go. They're watching."

He gripped my ass. "There's no one here. It's just you and me tonight."

"And the three visiting astronomers staring at my jiggly bits." I pushed at his immovable shoulders and nodded to the monitors on the wall behind him. One displayed the cocked heads of three researchers who'd just joined the call. The other was a closeup of Liam's palms splayed across my rear end.

He didn't move as my feet found the floor and the space between us evaporated.

"If anyone is going to get a good look at your fucking phenomenal jiggly bits tonight, it's gonna be me." He grabbed my hips and pulled me against the hard evidence of his desire, as if he didn't care who watched. As if Marcus wouldn't fire us both on the spot if the visiting astronomers filed a complaint.

I shoved him away, straightened my blouse, and thanked the gods for terrible lighting as I sat down. My cheeks weren't nearly as inflamed on camera as they felt. The three researchers kept their reactions in check for the most part. That didn't stop me from wishing my syphons could reach through the screen and suck the previous thirty seconds from their memories. The last thing I needed on top of trying to manage a living god, two murderous specters, and my handler was to get fired from my fake job.

Liam and I settled into a silent rhythm that was somehow louder than words as we worked. He operated the telescope while I tried to ignore the way his fingers kissed the keyboard with a delicate touch or the way he kept glancing at the folded yellow sticky note on his desk. Every time I made the mistake of looking up between calls, he pinned me with those electric eyes. A silent promise.

Heat pooled between my thighs as I anticipated which option he'd choose first. I shoved down the nervous knot in my stomach and did my best to charm the visiting astronomers, asking one enthusiastic question after another about their research. Anything to fill the shrinking space between now and the end of our shift.

Our current clients were researching a doomed binary star system. "We're mapping as many of the extra solar objects as we can before the stars collide. Especially ones that could potentially sustain subsurface life. The goal is to track what's left after the stars consume one another," one of the researchers explained.

"I can't imagine any of these planets surviving that kind of cataclysmic event," I said.

"There's one that has a chance. KTRI957 is approaching the farthest reaches of its elliptical trek around both stars. We believe it's covered by a thick shield of ice and has the potential to support subaquatic or subterranean life. There's a chance it could be ejected from its orbit by the shock wave and become a free-range planet. Theoretically, it could survive the ejection and remain stable for a time without a sun."

"*If* a planet capable of supporting subterranean life managed to escape the blast, everything on it is either close to extinction or has had their flesh melted from their bones in a fiery inferno. Getting burned alive is a fucking terrible way to go," Liam said.

A memory clawed its way out of the tomb at my core and made my stomach heave. "Excuse me," I said, pushing away from my desk as I tried to shove down the image of too many faces reduced to ash. The room was suddenly stifling. "I need some air."

"Shit, Renae. I'm so sorry. I didn't mean—" Liam stood and moved toward me.

"It's fine, I just... can you finish up here?" I sidestepped his outstretched arm. If I let him touch me, I'd break down and that was something I didn't do in front of people. I'd never let anyone see me cry. Not my family. Not Ziggy, certainly not Liam.

In the restroom, I soaked a wad of paper towels and pressed it to my burning ears and neck. Sweat slid down my spine. I unbuttoned the top half of my blouse and dabbed the wet wad over my chest, neck, and armpits. Why was the bathroom so hot? I considered running outside, lying down in the middle of the parking lot, and letting the night take me until the cold numbed my body and brain.

No. I needed someplace private. Somewhere I could ride the waves of the panic rippling through my body where cameras and nosy spectral assassins couldn't follow.

Cool air caressed my skin as I stepped into the dark server room that sat directly beneath the building's radio antennae, hoping the interference would be enough to keep Cyrena and Marcella away.

Hot tears stained my cheeks as I slid down the wall to the floor. My vision blurred as I stared at the twinkling lights shining through the perforated metal server racks. When I squinted my eyes, I could just make out the Global Operation Dynamics logo—an eye with four points. The Corps' insignia hiding in plain sight.

I wasn't sure how long I sat there letting the memories wash over me, giving the dead flesh and bone. This time, I didn't try to shove them back into the tomb. I let them trample me until I went numb and couldn't feel anything at all.

A soft knock pulled me from my stupor.

"Come in," I whispered.

Liam didn't say a word as he shut the door and lowered himself to the frigid concrete floor next to me. We sat shoulder to shoulder in the dark, his welcome heat radiating into my frozen body.

The tightness in my chest loosened as I shuddered a deep breath and leaned against him. He tipped his head back against the wall with a sigh, and we sat there for a long time under a comfortable blanket of silence.

Liam's breathing changed. I thought he'd fallen asleep until he took my hand and intertwined his fingers with mine. "I shouldn't have said that thing about the fire. I'm sorry."

"You're lucky to have Connor in your life," I said, directing the conversation away from my past.

"He's the only family I have."

"You're not close to your mother?" I asked, curious.

"You mean the woman who *pretended* to be my mother under duress until my father died and she no longer felt compelled to keep up the lie?"

I sat up and faced him.

"Apparently my birth mother was one of my father's patients who left me on his doorstep and disappeared without a trace. I tried to track her down after I got clean. Went through all my father's old files."

My heart kicked inside my chest. "What did you find?"

"Just a bunch of old medical records with her name and personal information redacted and a detailed pregnancy journal. Daily logs of what she ate, her blood sugar levels, and weird shit like the weather and entries with oddly specific details about places she'd traveled or maybe wanted to travel. I don't know. Like I said, it was weird."

"I'm sorry."

"Don't be. My father was a shit person who knocked up a patient and pawned his bastard child off on his wife. My real mother, whoever she is, escaped him, and I can't blame her for that choice."

"Do you still have the records?" If he still had the missing files, the ones she stole from the Corps, we could use them as leverage. We might be able to buy him clemency.

"My stepmother burned it all after my father died. I only have this."

Liam shifted so he could pull his wallet from his back pocket. He opened it and handed me a small photo. A side profile of a young woman with golden curls and vivid blue eyes, smiling at the infant cradled in her arms. Gods, he looked just like her. She wasn't just an incubator. She truly was his mother.

"You have her eyes," I said.

He shrugged as he took the photo and tucked it back into his wallet. Right behind the folded yellow sticky note with my handwriting, and gods help me, something in my chest cracked.

It was all I could do not to scream into the dark. For his future. For the past he knew nothing about and one I couldn't forget, no matter how hard I tried. For how terrified I was of whatever lived inside him and the part of me that wanted to let it swallow me whole.

"Is it weird to miss someone you've never met?" Liam asked.

I reached up and brushed an amber curl away from his face, letting my fingers trail over the scar. "I think it's beautiful."

He caught my wrist and pressed his cheek into my palm. "I think you're beautiful."

I rose to my knees and unbuttoned my blouse.

"What are you doing?"

"Asking you to keep your promise," I said as I stood.

"What promise?"

"I want you to make me forget my name."

Liam was on his feet before I could take my next breath. I wrapped my arms and legs and syphons around him as he lifted me. I resisted the urge to feed, to seek his mouth and suck in his sweet liquid fire. No matter how desperate I was for the crush of his lips against mine, I didn't trust myself not to give him everything. Gods knew I was close to letting him take it all, and then some.

His lips grazed over the curve of my throat as he walked me backward between the warm server stacks to the cold concrete wall.

I shivered as his calloused hands slid over my fevered skin, pushing my shirt off my shoulders until it dropped to the floor.

Liam pressed a knee between my thighs. "There's something you need to know before we do this, chica."

"Aren't we already doing this?"

"I want to wreck you in all the worst ways. The same way you've been slowly wrecking me since the day you stepped in front of my bike." A shiver spread across my flesh as he pulled the cups of my bra down and traced a fingertip over the curve of my breasts. "It's unreal how absolutely fucking perfect you are."

I ran my hands through his velvet curls. "No more talking." I fisted his hair and pulled his mouth to my chest as my syphons roved over him.

Rough stubble raked across my skin, teasing and toying with my senses as his lips trailed down my torso.

I toed off my boots as Liam peeled the leggings down my thighs until they were a puddle at my feet.

His hands trailed gently over my bare skin from my ankles to my waist where he pressed a kiss to the hollow of my hip. His denim eyes flicked to mine with amusement. "Pineapples?"

"What's wrong with pineapples?" I asked, glancing down to where he knelt before me, staring at the cartoon fruit dancing across my panties. "Pineapples have an enzyme that breaks down proteins in the stomach. It's the only food that consumes you while you eat it."

"I think I have a new favorite fruit." Liam traced the edge of the fabric from my hip to my inner thigh. "I want to hear you say it," he said.

"Say what?"

"Number two on the list. Tell me you want it."

My body prickled with heat as he pressed his lips to my stomach.

I lifted my bare foot from the floor and braced it against the warm metal cabinet behind him. "I want you to make me come with your mouth."

I sucked in a breath as he drew a line over the center of my damp panties. "Good, because I've wanted to taste you since the night you showed up on my doorstep."

"Liam, please." His sweet milky heat bloomed in my mouth, a decadent guilty pleasure as I drank him in and I knew, no matter how long I lived, I'd never be able to get enough to satisfy the growing hunger inside me.

He gripped the back of my knee and lifted it over his shoulder. I shuddered as he hooked a finger under the edge of my underwear and tugged it to the side. He parted my slick center with that finger and muttered an appreciative groan.

I clutched his curls as he did glorious, wicked things to me with his tongue until my body vibrated with need. Until I was convinced that this man and his mouth were the beginning and end of me.

A flame started in the soles of my feet and crept toward my center, and gods help me, I couldn't stay still. Liam braced a palm against my abdomen, pinning me to the wall. He used his thumb to rub methodical circles around my clit. When his tongue darted inside me, I came undone, and the orgasm ripped through me like lightning.

He didn't let up or give me a chance to catch my breath as he slipped a finger inside me, pumping slowly as I came down from the crest of one wave, only to rise on another.

I wanted to rip off his clothes and run my hands over his hot flesh, but he had me pinned against the wall, and all I could do was fist those velvet curls. I yanked his head back to get a better view of what he was doing down there. Our eyes locked and I couldn't look away.

"You don't need to be gentle with me," I whispered

"You're the sexiest woman I've ever met." Gods, I needed him deep inside me. All of him.

"I want you to come again for me, chica. Right now." His deep voice was a warm rain pooling over cracked earth, slipping between the crevices, wetting me from the inside.

He curled his fingers, and I broke. My gift exploded. All six syphons pierced his spectrum, holding him there, on his knees between my thighs. I grabbed the edge of the server stacks with both hands to keep from collapsing onto Liam as I shattered. His groan of satisfaction sent another pulse of pleasure through my core.

"Good girl." Liam scattered soft kisses along my inner thigh, still pumping his fingers slowly, letting me savor the sensation of him inside me as I came down a second time.

When I was confident that my wobbly legs could support my own weight again, I tugged him to his feet. He cupped my face in his hands and kissed my forehead. Gods, if I lived a thousand lives, all I ever wanted to feel was this man's hands on me. Possessive. Reverent.

"Tell me your name, chica. The one your mother gave you."

"What?" My heart strained against my ribs.

His lips curled. "Mission accomplished."

# Chapter Nineteen

# LIAM

Renae shoved me back against the warm server case and started unbuttoning my pants.

As much as I wanted every part of her on my cock, I wasn't about to press my luck and ask for anything in return. Chicks without boundaries didn't make lists, and I didn't want to lose any of the things she'd so generously offered to let me do for her.

I grasped her wrist. "That's not on the list."

"Don't you want me to touch you?"

There were a whole lot of things I wanted her to do to me, but that wasn't what this was about. "I want to play by your rules. The list is clearly about your pleasure, and your pleasure alone, and I'm more than happy to oblige."

She arched up on her toes and whispered in my ear. "Then take off your clothes and let me enjoy number four."

I didn't know what the fuck I'd done to deserve that gift, but I sure as shit wasn't going to tell her no a second time.

Renae stepped back and leaned against the concrete wall where she'd come unglued moments earlier and waited for me to obey her command. I pulled off my shirt and dropped it in the pile with her clothes. She bit her lip as I unbuttoned my jeans and pushed them down, along with my boxers, to my ankles.

Her whiskey eyes went straight to the dragon tattoo on my chest. I could swear I felt her gaze rove over me like multiple pairs of hands, leaving a warm tingling sensation in their wake before landing on my throbbing dick.

"Your body is exquisite," she said, "and gods help me, I want to devour you. But I don't trust myself yet, so I'm going to stand over here and watch. I want to see all that taut muscle tremble when you come undone."

I fisted my shaft and started stroking. If she kept talking like that, this was gonna be over real quick.

Renae played with her nipples with one hand and reached into her pineapple panties with the other. I could just make out the tuft of red hair peeking over the edge as she worked herself over. My groin tightened, and I had to back off the tip to keep from losing my load right then and there. This was about her, and I would never let myself finish before she did.

I braced my free arm against the perforated black metal cabinet, watching Renae fuck herself with her fingers as I pumped the base of my dick. The fan inside the server stack blew hot air over my face where her scent still lingered on my mouth. I groaned at the torturous sweetness of that scent, tasting her in my mind all over again.

Renae flung her arm out and slapped the wall as her body arched away from it. "Oh gods, I'm going to come again." She curled forward and slammed her hand on the cabinet next to mine as her body shuddered with release.

I adjusted my grip on my cock, wishing it was her cunt squeezing my shaft with those convulsions instead of my fist. Two strokes, and I was done.

"Fuck me." The pressure in my groin snapped, and it was all I could do to stay upright as I unloaded into my palm. I reached for my T-shirt to wipe off my hand, and Renae stopped me.

I let her peel my fingers back one by one, and holy fuck, I forgot to breathe as she dipped her pinky into my cum and proceeded to lick it. Renewed pressure built in my groin as my softening cock came back online, aching for the same attention she was giving that pinky with her tongue. I'd never been more jealous of a finger in all my life.

The need to claim her mouth was too much. I pulled her against me. My throbbing dick pressed into the soft flesh of her stomach. "I want to taste myself on that wicked little tongue of yours."

Her face went crimson as she shoved away from me and pulled on her clothes. "We agreed. That's *not* on the list."

Just like that. She was going to leave me standing there naked and alone in the middle of the fucking cold-ass server closet as if my entire world hadn't just tilted on its axis. I yanked my jeans up my legs, and something in my stomach twisted as she pulled on her boots and headed for the door.

Shit. I'd pushed too hard. "Hey, wait, I'm sorry. Don't go."

She froze as the door cracked open, letting in a beam of blinding fluorescent light from the hall.

"I need to go back to the lab and batch the data files."

Renae was shutting down again. I could feel her trying to push me out so she could reerect whatever boundary we'd stumbled past.

"Really? Because it feels like you're running away to avoid talking about what we just did."

"What's there to talk about? It was nice, but it doesn't change anything. I still have a job to do."

"Nice?" I ran a hand through my hair. "I just made you come three times in a row, and all you have to say is that it was *nice*?"

"What do you want me to say, Liam? That I don't know how to do this. That I don't know how to stop myself from getting lost in whatever this thing is between us?"

I stepped into the light and brushed a stray hair away from her flushed cheek. "I want you to tell me that we can keep doing this."

Renae crossed her arms over her chest. "Doing what? Arguing or getting each other off?"

"Being honest with each other. You showed me the real Renae tonight. The one you hide behind all those walls. I want to spend more time with *her*. If you'll let me."

Renae's eyes roved over the dragon on my chest. "I don't think you'll like the real me. What if, under this façade, I'm just a monster?"

I tipped her face up to mine. "Then show me your fangs and let me decide for myself before you shut me out."

"I don't have fangs."

"How disappointing," I said, tugging her toward me as she rolled her eyes. "Spend the day with me tomorrow. Let me take you surfing."

"Like a date?"

"If that's what you want."

"What if I don't know what I want?"

"Then we'll take it one day at a time."

"Fine, but you only made me come twice. The third time was all me."

⸎

"Maybe we should wait until there are fewer people around," Renae said, glancing at the black sand beach from her prone position on my yellow foamie. It was my oldest and most stable surfboard. Perfect for a beginner.

An offshore wind had Pohoiki pumping at peak conditions, packed with local kids and sunburned tourists playing in the first of three horseshoe shaped bays carved into the volcanic shoreline. Each one jutting farther out toward the reef.

I stood in chest-deep water next to her in second bay. The waves were rolling in like corduroy at about two feet. Small and consistent. I couldn't have asked for better conditions for her first time.

Renae gripped the rails. "How do you steer this thing? I almost hit that kid with the pink tube last time."

"It's called turning, and these are baby swells, chica. You don't need to steer. If you feel like you're gonna nail someone, just roll like I showed you. I'll push you in again. Paddle as hard as you can until you feel the momentum lift the back of the board, then try to stand up." I slapped her ass, not giving her any time to argue, and pushed her into the next wave. She popped up right away. Her stance was shit, but she powered through like a beast with those muscular thighs—thighs I wanted to bury myself in, repeatedly.

Renae snagged wave after wave all afternoon and only bit it hard a handful of times. She got pounded into the sand bar once and raked over the rocks twice. Each time, she came up ready for more, and it was sexy as hell. I grabbed the front of her surfboard and pulled it parallel to mine so we were facing each other, her thigh gliding against mine as we floated in the flats between swells.

"What are you staring at? Do I have seaweed on my face again?" Renae swiped at her cheek.

"No, I'm just having a hard time believing you've never done this before. You're a natural in the water. If I didn't know better, I'd say you were part octopus."

"Why would you say that?" She stiffened and leaned away from me.

"Your balance is incredible. The way you stick to the board, it's like you have invisible limbs."

"Would it bother you if I did?" Her voice wavered, half nervous squeak, half offended grunt.

I reached up and slid my thumb along the curve of her bottom lip. "Not as long as they were all on me."

Renae's tongue darted out and flicked the tip of my thumb. All I could think about was how she'd used that same tongue to lick her finger the night before.

"Be careful what you wish for," she said as her hand inched up my thigh, dangerously close to my hard cock, and damn, I wanted her to touch me, right there, in front of the whole fucking beach.

She nodded to third bay. "Take me out to the bigger waves, and I'll make every item on the list reciprocal."

My groin tightened as I scanned third bay. The swells were coming in at eight feet and climbing. I'd never seen the surf at Pohoiki close to maxing out like that.

"Look, I support your enthusiasm and I'm 100 percent down for what you just said, but you are nowhere near ready to take on anything that big. Those waves are pushing the limits of my abilities, and I've been surfing my entire life. Best case, you get pounded into the reef and spend the next week picking bits of coral out of your ass. Worst case—"

Renae was prone and paddling before I could tell her to stay put. Part of me admired her balls. The other part of me worried Connor might be right—that I was drawn to her the same way I was drawn to shit that wasn't good for me. *Like a moth to a fucking flame.*

I grabbed her leash and pulled her back toward me. "I'm serious, Renae. That's no place for a beginner. If you so much as think about going out there, I will drag your ass back to the beach. Do you understand?"

She glared at me with those whiskey eyes that burned through me like fire. "Don't you dare scold me. I am not a child."

"Then stop acting like one."

"I can take care of myself, and I know I can do it. Please, let me try."

I shielded my eyes from the sun and studied the incoming sets again. They were a mix of solid six-footers followed by heavier slabs. She might actually be able to hold her own on the smaller ones. "Stay here and let me check it out. If I think you can handle it, I'll come back and get you."

"Thank you."

I pulled the leash from my back pocket, snapped it into place, and paddled away from her. It was turning over fast, swells coming in at a ten second clip, and I didn't have to wait long for a ride. I dropped into an eight-footer and carved a hard-bottom turn, then rode the whitewash down the line. I glanced at Renae, who gave me a wicked smile that made my heart falter in my chest. Much to my surprise, she'd stayed put like I'd asked.

The swells continued to grow as I snagged two more damn near perfect runs. When conditions were good like that, it was easy to get overconfident. To forget that all that raw power could kill you as quickly as it could get you off. The surf was crashing heavy on the reef. It was no place for a stubborn chick with something to prove to herself. I glanced back to check on her.

*Fuck.*

She was sitting right where I'd left her, but she wasn't alone. Monika was straddled on top of her competition board, right next to Renae. My stomach twisted as they chatted and Mons ran her hand over the gouge she'd put in my yellow foamie when she dragged it across her roof racks that one time.

I didn't want to imagine what they were talking about. From the pinched look on Monika's face, I'd bet my left nut it wasn't the damn weather.

Renae was just starting to open up and trust me, being free with her body but cautious with everything else. What would she do when she found out I'd eviscerated the last woman who gave me access to her heart? Would she pull back to square one and try to keep things platonic and professional, or would she kick me out of her orbit entirely just as Monika had? Nausea churned in my stomach at the thought of losing her like that.

Renae whipped her head around and glared at me. Even from two hundred yards away, there was no mistaking the panicked look on her face. I should have told her about Monika from the beginning. I wasn't proud of the way I'd ended things with Mons, but I didn't intend for Renae to find out about it like this.

They looked at each other and then back at me in alarm. Monika gave me the signal to put my eyes on the horizon. I turned and rolled under my board to avoid getting nailed in the face by a set of fins as some kid skidded over me.

"Fucking haole!" he yelled, just before a twelve-foot wall of water unloaded on top of us.

I had a death grip on the rails of my board as my body twisted and rolled. The swells were coming in hard and fast, and it took all my energy to paddle out of the impact zone and back to the lineup.

Three massive humps raced toward us. They had to be twenty feet and growing. Someone yelled to pull the jet skis back, out of the bay, and the less experienced surfers started to scramble. I just sat there like a kook. Frozen. Everyone started paddling like mad to get to shore. They wouldn't make it, not at the speed those monster waves were clocking. I glanced back at Monika and Renae. Monika's eyes were transfixed on the incoming set. She had a gift for predicting exactly when and where a wave would break. She held up two fingers, which meant the waves were gonna break on the outer reef. It was closer than shore.

When I made eye contact with Renae, I got that creepy skin-crawl sensation that comes when weird shit's about to happen. Her voice floated across the water between us and exploded into my head.

*Liam, look at the trees!* She pointed toward the beach, where the shore huggers were scattering in search of higher ground. The trees were being whipped around by an onshore wind that had kicked up out of nowhere. The smaller waves had already turned to chop. I studied the approaching swells. They still looked solid. The kid that had nailed me earlier and I were sitting right in the middle of the impact zone. Once those massive waves stretched across the bay, there'd be no way for the skis to get in with the rescue sleds, and I certainly didn't feel like dragging this kid's carcass out of the wash.

"We don't have time to make it to shore before the first one hits. We need to swim straight out and try to get behind it before it breaks."

"Fuck that. I'm gonna ride it." He spat in the water and started digging hard toward the incoming swells.

My shoulders burned with fatigue as I followed, crossing the outer reef just as the slab tipped over. I shoved the nose of my board down, but I wasn't fast enough. The wave's momentum sucked me up like a backward waterfall into its mouth, then dropped me like a bomb. I tumbled head over ass as the weight of the massive wave drove me toward the reef. I tried not to panic. Where was my board? Where was the surface? Could I hold my breath long enough to get there? How long before the next wave hit?

I forced my body to go limp and roll with the current instead of fighting against it and braced for the inevitable coral scrub. My leg wrenched backward. Saltwater stung my eyes as I forced them open and searched for my board. It was twisting in the chaos above me, pulling me away from the reef. The pressure in my ears and chest eased as the wave rolled past. It was the moment I'd been waiting for.

I kicked as hard as I could and resisted the burning urge to inhale just long enough to break the surface. As soon as my head was out of the water, I heaved a desperate breath and a lungful of ocean as another monster wave collapsed on top of me and drove me back toward the reef. I coughed and choked, sucking in more liquid with each involuntary gasp. I kicked and fought against the current, trying to get back to the surface. A searing pain ripped through my chest as a sudden clamping sensation closed around my throat. My peripheral vision closed in, and the pain evaporated.

Renae's voice echoed in my head.

*Please, don't let go.*

They were the same words she said to me after that first night at the summit when she clung to me in her sleep. That was the moment I'd fallen in love with her, and I'd never get the chance to tell her.

As the darkness descended, it struck me as ironic that I'd also never be able to tell Connor what it was really like to die.

# Chapter Twenty

# RENAE

Liam's signal went dead.

"Come on, Lee. You got this. Please, God, let me see that fucking smug-ass smile one more time," the Hawaiian girl said, closing her eyes in prayer as the wave devoured Liam's body. I ripped the safety strap from my leg and dove off the surfboard.

As soon as my body was submerged, the connection came back, but it was fractured, bouncing all around me, and I couldn't quite pinpoint where he was. Chalk laced my tongue as I dropped all human pretenses and torpedoed myself toward the spot where he'd gone under.

A massive wave rocked my body as I reached the coral reef. It was impossible to see anything in the churning white foam it left in its wake. My heart sputtered in my chest as I scanned for his golden curls, his surfboard, any sign of him, until I could no longer ignore the burning sensation in my chest.

When my head popped above the surface, I lost his signal again. All this time, I'd been fighting the bond and had been surrounded by the one thing that could have dampened it. Water. I didn't know whether to laugh or scream. Neither would fill the aching hole in my chest.

I resisted the urge to gulp a quick breath and dive, desperate to get him back. Instead, I pulled air into my lungs in small, measured increments, stretching them past human capacity.

His signal returned as soon as I slipped beneath the surface, filling the void inside me. I didn't have time to consider what that meant. *Please, don't let go.* I tugged on the bond and repeated the plea over and over in my mind as I searched the reef for him.

A flash of green silk caught my eye. *Cyrena.*

I swam in the direction it had come from, toward the open ocean, as Liam's signal faded. Gods, he was dying. Air bubbled from my mouth as a cry ripped from my lungs. I kicked faster, following the flashes of green. If Cyrena was here, Liam had to be close.

Panic jolted through me as the last flicker of his energy went out.

Cyrena appeared, floating in front of me underwater without so much as a wet lock of hair. "You were too slow, you incompetent cow." Her voice stabbed my skull as I swam through her projection to where Liam's body swayed back and forth with the current, tethered to the surfboard like an anchor.

I shoved down my panic and wrapped my arms around him, kicking hard for the surface as my lungs burned and my throat tightened. I managed to get him onto the board and straddled it behind him, leaning forward to check for a pulse.

Nothing. The elastic cord between us stretched and pulled at my chest, threatening to rip out my insides as I screamed and pounded on his back. "No. You are not dead. Do you hear me? You are not allowed to die. Not like this."

An excruciating surge of electricity shot down my arms the same way it had after the accident when I restarted his heart. The day I'd given up my bond to save his life. Pain ripped through my chest as my own heart seized, but I didn't let go. I pushed everything I had into him. One way or another, we were leaving the bay together.

My body went limp, and I collapsed against him. Spent and delirious, I peeled my hands away from his back, taking the top layer of scorched flesh with me and re-checked his pulse.

Still nothing.

Hot tears slid down my cheeks as I realized how futile it was. I'd already given up my bond. I would give it up again if I could, if it meant keeping him here a little longer.

Cyrena materialized in front of his board, her skeletal fingers smoothing over his hair. The silver glint of a tear at the corner of her eye. I couldn't tell if her reaction was genuine or rehearsed. Why would she pretend to care?

"What have you done?" The words climbed up my raw throat.

"You're the one who caused this." She moved closer and my skin cracked like ice as her power coiled around me. "His swelling emotion for you brought those waves to shore. He's dead, and our plans for him are ruined because of your incompetence."

I stabbed her chest with all six of my syphons, latching on to her spectrum with barbed hooks. Cyrena fought and twisted and tried to free herself from my grasp. The acidic bite of champagne vinegar exploded in my mouth and turned my stomach sour. The visions hit me as I sucked her in. A cargo ship full of empty incubation tanks. A sea of ice and a barren artic coastline.

"What plans?" I hissed.

My syphons snapped back like frayed wires as Marcella's gentle voice filled my head. "Enough, child. He's coming back."

Liam coughed, vomiting saltwater and steam before sucking in a rattled breath. I checked his pulse again and thought my chest might split open at the steady beat beneath my fingertips.

"If we'd chosen a better reaper, one up to the task, which clearly, you are not, we could have been done with him by now." Cyrena gestured to the burn marks on Liam's back. "Bonding him to *you* was a mistake.

You're too stubborn, too resistant to the connection between you. He needs a more experienced reaper. We can't afford any more mishaps." Cyrena reached toward Liam and snapped her hand back when my syphons swept forward, building a protective cage around him.

"No, he's mine." The possessiveness of my own words surprised me. As did the realization that I would never allow another reaper's syphons near him. Not while I had breath in my lungs. "I can fix this. Let me train him. I can teach him to control his gift. I just need time."

Cyrena's voice danced through my head as the two specters collapsed into a single point of light before dissipating altogether. "You have seventy-two hours."

I scoured Liam's kitchen for a knife while he set the table, still clad in his swim trunks and a backward baseball hat. Among the mismatched silverware, cups, and plates, he had exactly four knives. Three large chef's knives stuck in a block on the counter and one small paring knife, which had likely never been used, given its sharp edge and resting place buried at the bottom of a drawer full of unopened plastic utensil packets.

My stomach twisted as I slipped it into my pocket. Ziggy forbade me from telling Liam the truth. She also told me I had a knack for finding ways around her orders.

The living god divvying up rice noodles, spring rolls, and avocado fries between two plates deserved the chance to participate in his own fate. Even if that meant blowing my cover and accepting the leash around my neck. One that was beginning to fit more comfortably than I was willing to admit.

Liam was a man of science. He'd need irrefutable proof. Something he could see with his own eyes. A small incision in the hollow at the base of my skull would allow me to dig out the bio tracker embedded beneath my skin. The filaments attached to it, which worked like the ones in my ear pods, would wriggle and hiss and try to burrow their way back into my flesh and reconnect to the neural-lace network woven into my brain. If that didn't convince him, seeing the wound close on its own would. If I could prove beyond a reasonable doubt that I wasn't entirely human, he might believe the other stuff. The things he couldn't see. And I needed him to believe.

"Liam, there's something I need to show you."

"Can it wait until after we eat? I'm starving." We'd spent six hours at the hospital after the incident at the beach. We didn't have any more time to waste.

"No. I'm afraid it can't."

"Hey, come here." Liam dropped the takeout container on the kitchen table and pulled me toward him. "You're shaking. What's going on?"

"How much do you remember—from the beach?" Gods, this would be so much easier if he remembered something, anything, about his second, brief visit to the afterlife. The blood-red harvest field. The nymphite swarms. The city of the dead rising in the distance behind its oil black gates.

"I thought I was going to die before I got a chance to tell you how I feel. Look, I know we said we'd do this one day at a time—"

My skin went tight as sweet ginger fizzed in my mouth. I pushed away from him as if I could put distance between myself and the pure emotion rising inside him. The one emotion that could irrevocably contaminate my system. "You experienced a trauma; everything you're feeling is heightened. We don't need to have this conversation right now." Thunder rolled in the distance. "You should eat something. You need to keep your blood sugar up. It's going to be a long night."

"Stop doing that."

"Doing what?" I asked.

"Trying to manage my fucking emotions."

I glanced out at the darkening sky and slipped the knife from my pocket as I backed out of arm's reach. "Okay."

The scar between his eyes deepened. "That's just it. I'm not okay. I've *never* been okay. I've been drowning my entire life. Held under by something I can't explain or escape. Being with you, it's like..." He yanked off the sun-faded hat and ran a hand through his unruly curls. "It's like I can finally breathe for the first time in my life." Ginger soda exploded on my tongue, the kind that made my eyes water as it fizzed in my nose and burned its way down my throat.

"I'm in love with you."

The confession crashed over me like a tidal wave, infecting my system until I had no idea where his feelings ended and mine began. The bond contaminated everything, and it was all too much.

"You don't even know me. Not the real me."

He crushed the baseball hat in his fist as lightning split the sky. "I know you're afraid of letting me in. Of what it would mean to allow someone else to own a piece of you. A piece that can be broken and abused and burned, and you're fucking terrified. Look me in the eye and tell me it's not the truth."

He was right. I was terrified. Terrified of how he would react to my real face—to the entity that lived beneath my engineered husk. "You want the truth, fine." I gritted my teeth and held the knife to my forearm and sliced deep from elbow to wrist.

"What the..." Liam bolted forward and clamped his hands around the wound. Blood seeped between his fingers, spilled over the edge of my arm, and pooled at his feet, slicking the floor.

"My name isn't Renae Martin."

# CHAPTER TWENTY-ONE

# LIAM

STATIC RIPPLED OVER MY skin, causing the hairs on the back of my neck to stand as I dragged Renae to the sink, looking for a towel, anything, to staunch the bleeding so I could call 911. She was right. I didn't know her at all. Who in their right mind fillets themselves open? Bile pressed at the back of my throat. *Fuck.* This was my fault. I'd pushed too far. I told her I loved her, and it sent her over the edge.

"You're gonna be okay. Do you hear me? Everything's going to be fine."

She raised her voice to talk over the wind and rain whipping at the roof the same way my heart was slamming against my ribs. "Liam, you can let go now." Renae placed her good hand on top of mine.

"And let you bleed out in my kitchen? I don't think so." Something tickled my palm where it gripped her flesh.

"Take a closer look." She pried my fingers away with surprising strength, and I watched as the gaping wound pulled together and sealed like something straight out of a sci-fi movie.

*My name isn't Renae Martin.*

I stumbled backward and slipped in the pool of blood. Her blood. "What are you?"

She washed her hands in the sink as if nothing out of the ordinary had just happened. "I don't even know where to start." Static crackled around us as lightning struck somewhere in the yard and shook the house. My eyes went to the angry pink skin on her forearm as she raised her palms and stepped toward me. Skin that had been gouged open minutes before. "I'll explain everything, I promise, but first, I need you to calm down before you blow the roof off the house."

"Stay right there," I said.

Renae froze as a sharp pain shot through my right eye and my vision blurred. The room erupted in a blinding rainbow of light. A shimmering black snake—no, not a snake, snakes had scales—a tentacle of some kind twisted around me, the open mouth at its end sucking and licking at my bare chest, leaving an iridescent residue in its wake. I shook my head. The hallucination evaporated, and I gripped the back of a kitchen chair to keep myself upright. Maybe I was the one losing it? I should have let them keep me in the hospital overnight.

"Liam, I think you should sit down."

"I think I'll stand, if it's all the same to you. Start talking."

"You're a forecaster," Renae said. "Your gift is tied to your subconscious emotions. You're angry with me, and you're scared. Gods, I can taste the ash on my tongue." She licked her lips and swallowed hard. "When your emotions spike, it creates an instant low pressure-vacuum around you. The surrounding air drops and fills the void. The sudden change creates a storm."

I followed her eyes to the ceiling as rain pounded against the metal roof. Was she shitting me? Had I heard her right?

"Liam, you created this storm, just like you created the one at the beach earlier today and the air turbulence during our jump."

I took a step toward her and studied her eyes. Her black pupils were huge, surrounded by a thin ring of gold. "Are you fucking high right now?" Only a coked-up addict would slice their damn arm open. But it didn't explain the whole instant healing thing.

"I need you to forget everything you think you know and just listen. I'm an asset for an organization that serves the Nūkiri, the three ancient souls who rule over the living world and the afterlife. An organization that would prefer to see you dead. Which is what we'll both be if you can't get your powers under control. Trust me, the afterlife is no place for an Anzillu and an Anzillu sympathizer. We'll be banished to the Void before we make it across the harvest field to the black gates of Almega."

I could hardly hear myself speak over the storm and the pounding pulse in my head. "The blood-red field."

"You remember. Thank the gods." Renae's body jerked as if she wanted to take a step but was glued to the floor. "We only have seventy-two hours to prove that you are not a threat to the human population and—"

"Is that what you are? An *an-zee-lou*?"

"I'm just a reaper. You're the Anzillu, Liam. A living, breathing god. The first in thousands of years. Potentially more powerful than the Nūkiri. That's why there's a price on your head and why you're being watched by two spectral assassins. The only reason you're still alive is because they need you for something. When you're no longer of use to them, they'll end you. And I... I can't let that happen." Her face pinched as if she were in pain, like she truly believed the nonsense she was spouting.

I tried to wrap my head around why an otherwise intelligent woman would make something like this up. My gut told me she was telling the truth, or what she believed to be the truth. But this was Renae. The woman who'd done nothing but lie to me since the day we'd met. *Fuck.*

"Do you know how delusional you sound right now? Gods, gifts, assassins..." I fisted my hair and paced the room, trying to decide who was more fucked in the head, her with her fantastical confession, or me for wanting to believe it.

"We only have three days to convince the Corps that you're useful. If we demonstrate that you can control and wield your gift, I may be able to convince my handler that you're a valuable asset. She has resources. She can protect you."

The front door blew open and slammed against the wall.

"You manipulative little cow." My stomach dropped as a familiar voice echoed through my head like soft wind chimes. The voice I'd heard so many times as a child, singing softly in my ear, blocking out the others. I glanced around for its owner, but there was only me, Renae, and the blood on the floor.

I followed Renae's eyes to the rain and debris blowing through the open door. "You promised me three days," she said.

The hair on the back of my neck lifted. Why was Renae having a conversation with the voice in my head?

"That was before you decided to betray us. I should have known you'd sell him out to that handler of yours."

"I have the situation under control," Renae said through gritted teeth.

"Clearly," the first voice said, drawing the word out.

"He deserves to know. To participate in his own fate," Renae said.

"Who are you talking to?" A crawling sensation erupted along my spine. Shadows from every corner of the room drifted across the floor and coalesced into a woman with long black hair.

"Hello, Liam," the voice inside my head said, only this time it came from a lipstick smeared mouth. Yeah, I was definitely the one losing it.

Renae stepped in front of me, using her body like a shield. She winced when I grabbed her arm and jerked her back, her newly healed flesh smooth beneath my fingertips.

"Stay behind me, Renae."

"They won't hurt me, but if they try to kill you again, I will end them."

"We are not here to hurt anyone." A second voice crept through my brain, brittle and laced with age. I followed Renae's gaze as a person-sized shadow solidified into a woman wearing a blue leisure suit, with tissue paper skin and metallic silver hair that reminded me of tinsel, the way it shined and threw light around the room.

"I'll make no such promise." The younger woman glared at Renae, her voice sliding over me in the same way her green dress trailed along the floor behind her with a hiss. I could see through her, straight out the front door.

I pulled Renae closer as thunder cracked overhead. "Please tell me you're seeing this."

"It's all right, Liam." Her whiskey eyes were dilated with fear, betraying the absolute calmness of her voice. "I won't let them take you."

"What the fuck are they?"

"We've been called many things. Ghosts, angels... demons," the one in the green dress said.

"They're deceptors," Renae said flatly. "The one in green is called Cyrena; the one with silver hair is Marcella, and they shouldn't be here. They promised me three days."

"Our agreement stands. However, your pathetic plan to out yourself was in desperate need of an intervention, so we thought we'd offer our assistance," the one called Cyrena said as another crack of thunder shook the house.

"You mean you didn't trust me."

"Semantics, darling."

"Let's back the hallucination train up for just a second," I said, still gripping Renae's arm. For her protection or mine, I didn't know. "Did you say they tried to kill me?"

"They did kill you. Twice. I brought you back both times."

I let go of her arm and grasped my skull as my head spun like a carnival ride. Renae prowled behind me like a guard dog ready to attack.

"We didn't kill him the second time," Marcella, the older woman, continued, "his euphoria brought those waves to shore. He lost control of them when his mood shifted. Fortunately, he was the only person harmed. Cyrena would not have led you to him or allowed you to bring him back if that were not the case."

Renae pressed her back to my chest as Cyrena floated closer and disappeared. "Liam, stay close. She can project anything she wants into your mind."

I wrapped an arm around Renae's waist, pulling her against me and slowly backed toward the wall. I froze as an icy hand slid over my shoulder and down my arm.

"How cute. She protects you. You protect her. It would be endearing if she hadn't revealed her little scheme. Run to Mommy and ask for help. As if that bureaucratic babysitter could protect either of you. Whatever power you think your handler has; you are mistaken."

Renae's body went rigid. "What did you expect me to do? You bound me to him against my will. I had no one else to turn to for help."

"I don't understand why you're so desperate to break the bond. Your gift chose him. We just made sure you were both in the right place at the right time to make it happen. You should be thanking me, you ungrateful cow."

I let my arms drop. "What bond?"

"Renae gave up a piece of her soul to save your life. Once accepted, the Gi'dari bond cannot be undone or given back. It cannot be broken by time or distance or even death. She is bound to serve you for eternity the way I am bound to Cyrena," Marcella said.

"Like a soulmate?" I grunted and glanced at Renae. She wrapped her arms around her middle as if she could hold herself in as she toed at the pool of blood on the floor. "Wait. You can't be serious. Look at me."

Her wet eyes snapped to mine. "Stop. Telling. Me. What. To. Do."

"Devotee is a more accurate description," Cyrena said as she moved closer to the other woman. "Marcella gave me a precious gift when she bound her soul to mine. A piece of her will forever live inside me, giving me access to and influence over her actions and her gift. Through our lifetimes together, we have been friends, siblings, lovers." She caressed the older woman's metallic hair as if she were stroking a pet. "It's the intense pull you feel toward one another." Cyrena paused, eyes flicking to Renae. "No matter how hard you try to resist or how many lives you live, she will be compelled to serve you, and you, my glorious creature, won't be able to resist the urge to claim her."

My gut cramped as I looked at Renae. She rocked up and down on the ball of her left foot like she wanted to bolt, to be anywhere but here, and it clicked. The list and the lies. The walls she kept erecting between us. *Fuck.* She was trying to protect herself from becoming a brainwashed soul slave like Marcella. Protecting herself from me. "You didn't choose this?"

"Does it matter?" Renae asked.

"Of course, it matters." I took a step toward her and she backed away.

"The bond is more instinct than choice," Marcella said. "Renae invoked the Gi'dari when she sacrificed a piece of her soul to resurrect you after the motorcycle accident. You solidified the bond when you chose to accept her gift instead of death."

Thunder shook the house again. "You're telling me I died and was resurrected, and as a result, Renae is stuck with me for eternity, and I have... some kind of mutant power?"

Green silk hissed along the floor as Cyrena circled me like a cat toying with a mouse. "Renae didn't give you your powers, darling. The man you knew as your father did. Well, he and his research partner. You weren't his bastard child. You were their experiment. An attempt to create a living god, a soul imbued with all seven sacred gifts. Reaper. Healer. Forecaster. Mimic. Isolator. Deceptor. Telepath."

Ozone filled my nose as a prickly static coursed through my veins and my palms heated.

"So far, the only gifts that have manifested are the ones you inherited from the woman who bore you."

My hand went to my pocket, but I was still wearing swim shorts. My wallet was on the table by the door, getting soaked. I hugged the wall and rounded the room, giving the two assassins a wide berth as I shut the door against the storm and palmed my wallet. The leather would dry, but the photo... I pulled out the picture of my mother. The edges rippled with damp, and the ink from Renae's note had bled onto the back, but it was otherwise intact. My chest loosened as I stared at the stranger's face. A face that had my eyes.

"Did she know what they were doing to her?" I asked.

"Your mother was an asset like me," Renae said, keeping her voice intentionally gentle as she followed my movement around the room, positioning herself between the ghosts and me. "She worked for the Corps. The geneticists who created you were her marks."

I backed away from her, from all of them, until my ass collided with the kitchen sink.

"Until she went rogue and stole DNA modification blueprints from the Corps in exchange for the chance to have a human child. She was a willing participant in your father's research," Marcella added.

My stomach threatened to unload my dinner all over the floor. "Are you saying that my mother wasn't human, that you're... not human?" She fucking felt human that night in the server closet.

"My husk is what we call post-sapien, genetically altered flesh and blood and bone grown in a lab with a few cybernetic enhancements. But my true form is more like theirs." She turned to Marcella. "Show him."

"Are you sure, child? Some things cannot be unseen."

Renae nodded and squared her shoulders.

I grasped the counter behind me. She was right. I needed to fucking sit down.

When Renae lifted her eyes, I came face to face with the demon who'd yanked me away from the blood-red field and black gates of hell. Her entire body was charred to a crisp like a damn burnt marshmallow. The only recognizably human part of her was a pair of haunting gray eyes.

"This is what I am without the engineered façade."

"Our shades take the shape of our last human body at the moment of death," Cyrena said, gesturing to her ghostly, gaunt form. "This is what a steady diet of champagne and cocaine looks like. And that," she gestured to Marcella's silver hair, "is what happens when you have a heart attack on Halloween."

Renae sat at the table, folding up like a child, legs crossed beneath her in the wooden chair.

"How old were you when you died in the fire with your family?"

"Sixteen, and it wasn't just my family. My entire village died on June 10, 1944. They massacred the entire town."

The one with silver hair moved closer to Renae and placed a supportive hand on her shoulder. Marcella dropped the projection, and Renae looked like herself again.

History wasn't my strong suit, but 1944 was during WWII, when the Nazis occupied France. "Were you bombed?" I asked.

"No, our village was somewhat isolated from the conflict. The war was just something adults talked about in hushed voices. It wasn't real to me, not until that day."

"What happened?"

Renae took a deep breath and picked at the hem of her shorts. "It was the week before my father's birthday. Maman wanted to make something special for him. We'd been saving ration coupons to buy sugar. She knew I was excited by the promise of something sweet and she let me walk with her and my sisters into town that morning, even though I slowed them down." Renae wiped a tear from her cheek.

"It's all right, dear." Marcella squeezed Renae's shoulder. "There's no need to unearth the past."

Renae's eyes met mine. "No, I don't want there to be any more secrets between us. Liam, I need you to understand why I'm here. But if I go on, it will change things between us."

Cyrena snorted. "I think it's safe to say we're well past that point, darling."

The emaciated ghost was right. I crossed my arms and stared at the floor, unable to look at Renae without seeing her charcoaled corpse.

"Marcella, can you project my memory onto the television screen?" Renae asked.

"I can do better than that, dear."

Children's laughter bubbled through the room as the walls of my bungalow fell away. We stood in the middle of a bustling town as Renae's memory played out around us. Sun warmed my face, and a faint scent of vinegar and yeast hung in the air.

A slender woman in a pastel yellow dress clutched a brick of sugar to her chest as she helped a teenage girl with crutches and leg braces navigate the cobbled sidewalk. A net bag of pears hung from the girl's wrist. Her two younger sisters skipped ahead, singing and giggling, a floppy blue bow bouncing on the top of the littlest one's head.

The floor of my bungalow rumbled beneath my feet as a regiment of SS soldiers rolled into the village on the backs of open trucks and motorcycles.

Renae's mother called out in French, and I understood every word. "Claudine, quick, bring your sister." She took the bag of pears from the teenage girl and dragged her down a side street, crutches clattering against the stone where they fell. The younger ones followed, hand in hand, as they ducked into an alley and huddled behind a cluster of empty wine barrels.

The throaty pop of a dual cylinder engine crept down the side street toward the alley.

Renae's sisters whimpered to their mother. The youngest, not more then five or six years old, pointed at the forgotten brick of sugar lying on its back in the middle of the road. "Maman, you dropped the sugar."

"Shh... be like quiet mice, my darlings." The woman pulled the little girls tighter to her chest as Renae stood and hobbled into the street. "Hélène, stop!"

She ignored her mother's panicked command and stooped to pick up the sugar.

The engine noise stopped abruptly and two soldiers approached, shouting at her in German. Renae glanced at her mother and sisters as the soldiers stalked forward, guns pointed at her head.

One of the soldiers dragged the woman and two girls from their hiding place. The first soldier shouted as Renae's mother pleaded with them and tried to show them a handful of papers. The second knocked the crumpled documents from her hands and ground them into the dirt with the heel of his boot.

"Shut your mouth and start walking," he commanded in broken French as he herded them out of the alley and across the town square to a church full of women and crying children. Hundreds of bodies pressed together like fucking sardines.

The stench of incense and sweat packed my nose. I flinched as gunshots cracked off in the distance.

More soldiers came in with metal cans, dousing gasoline on the walls, women, and children before wiring boxes of explosives near the entrance and barricading the door from the outside.

I glanced at Renae, still sitting trance-like in the wooden chair at my kitchen table. Tears streamed from her closed eyes. I wanted to tell her to stop, that I didn't need to see any more.

Marcella's voice filled my head. "Let her finish. It may help bring her closure."

I nodded to the apparition and watched reluctantly as Renae's mother shoved her children under a pew. An explosion sucked the air from my lungs and the church erupted into chaos. Smoke and fire climbed the walls. Shrill screams pierced my brain. The same kind of scream that woke me the night Renae passed out in my truck.

This was her nightmare.

I blinked back the wetness pooling at the corner of my eyes and turned away from the scene unfolding in the middle of my living room. No matter where I looked, the projection followed. Even when I closed my eyes, I couldn't escape it. Was that how it was for Renae? Her mind held hostage by these memories for decades.

My skin crawled as the mass of bodies moved through me and pressed back toward the church's altar. Mothers attempted to shove small children through a high, broken window. Shots came from outside, picking off anyone who attempted to escape before their feet hit the ground.

The scent of scorched flesh made my stomach roll. I turned and hurled into the kitchen sink as Renae's sisters choked and coughed on the floor behind me.

Her mother's soft voice floated through my head. "Don't be afraid, my doves. It's time to sleep." She bunched up her skirt and held it firmly over the older girl's mouth and nose, hugging the protesting child tight to her chest. She nodded for Renae to do the same to her youngest sister.

"No, I... I can't. I won't." Renae tried to scoot away, but there was nowhere to go.

Her mother spoke through clenched teeth, the whites of her eyes now an aggravated red. Tears slid down her cheek as the older girl twitched in her arms. "You've always been stronger than your sisters. Stronger than the pain." Black smoke crept into the space between them. "You must be strong for them now. It is a kindness to spare Lucienne from the flames."

Renae untied the blue fabric from her sister's hair and bunched it into a ball. Pudgy fingers dug at Renae's hand as she pressed the fabric to the little girl's face.

"That's enough," I said. "No more." I pinched the bridge of my nose again, putting pressure on the inside corners of my eyes, trying to block the vivid replay. An icy hand slid down my arm as the scene evaporated toward the ceiling like smoke.

"Are you all right?" Cyrena asked.

"They burned her alive, and you're asking *me* if I'm all right?" I jerked away from her. "I hope those fucking Nazis are rotting in hell."

"The difference between heaven and hell is a matter of perspective," Marcella said, her voice echoing through the now-empty room. "The afterlife is a bit of both."

My spine stiffened, and I glanced at Renae. "The red field?" I asked.

"The harvest fields are the entry points to Almega."

"And all those Nazis are just hanging out in the afterlife with the innocent people they slaughtered?"

"The Nūkiri banished the unrepentant souls to the Void. The rest were offered a choice between banishment or redemption. Most chose redemption," Cyrena said.

"Redemption? You can't be serious."

"Redemption is not an acquittal. It's a sentence. Their memories and gifts are stripped. Everything that makes them who they are gets siphoned away before they are released."

"So, the innocent are damned, and the guilty get a clean slate? That's fucked up."

"The victims have always carried the burden and responsibility of knowledge. It's the only way to prevent history from repeating itself."

"And now you understand why I couldn't stay there," Renae said, hugging her knees to her chest. "Why I joined the Corps."

"To make the world a better place?" I grunted.

"To escape. The harvest is a giant party. The dead feed on the influx of energy from new arrivals. Everyone reminisces about their death as if it's a badge of honor. Those who've experienced the most gruesome and painful ends are given exalted status. You saw my shade. Everyone expected me to recount and relive what I'd been through for their macabre entertainment." Her gaze fell to the floor. "No one should be forced to endure something like that over and over again. It's cruel."

Silence settled over the room. Renae looked so damn human sitting there with her chin propped on her knee. She certainly felt human when we... when I... *fuck*, when I had my fingers and tongue inside her. "How did you become this?" I gestured to her body.

"Our husks are grown at the Nursery. Before the Corps developed the cloning technology, assets had to possess human hosts."

"Like a parasite."

"Unmodified human husks can't contain more than one sentient entity for long without breaking down. Once a host was used up, assets jumped into another body and masqueraded around in a new skin. It was a barbaric practice." Renae shuddered. "Our engineered forms are more durable."

I eyed her forearm. All traces of her earlier wound were gone. "Durable enough to survive a head on collision with a motorcycle?"

She nodded.

"How bad was it?"

"I have a high pain tolerance."

"Just fucking tell me, Renae."

"The impact fractured my pelvis."

I closed my eyes as the realization of what the accident had cost her sunk in. "Why don't I remember any of that?"

"I snuck into your room at the hospital and altered your memory of the accident."

"You fucked with my head?" Thunder rumbled above us, and my stomach dipped as all the holes in my memory suddenly made sense.

"It was a necessary precaution. I couldn't have a human asking questions about my miraculous recovery."

"Is that your gift? Being a memory thief?"

"I'm a reaper. I can syphon and manipulate memories and emotions."

"She can also suck the soul out of your body, darling," Cyrena said. "Best not get too close to her pretty lips. Renae has an insatiable appetite."

My eyes landed on Renae's mouth. That's why she wouldn't kiss me. I took a deep breath and tried to slow the collision of evidence and disbelief happening inside my head. My brain told me I was experiencing a post-drowning oxygen-deprived psychosis, that none of this was real.

My gut, however, knew differently.

"So, the three of you are what, some sort of supernatural recruitment team? Join or die. Is that the pitch?" I turned on the faucet and cleaned out the sink before rinsing the sourness from my mouth.

Marcella and Cyrena shared an affirmative glance.

Renae's bare feet slapped the floor as she bolted upright from the chair. "We are definitely *not* a team. These two are using you as bait to catch your father's research partner, and I'm just trying to figure out how to avoid losing my job and being deactivated. I only have three days to teach you how to control your gift and convince the Corps to take you on as an asset. It's our only way out of this mess. I will not go back to that sensory-deprived hell. Not for you. Not for them. Not for anyone."

Finally. The real Renae. Connor was right. I didn't know *this* woman at all.

"No more secrets, no more lies. That's the deal, right?"

Renae gave me a curt nod.

"Do you regret it? Saving my life and invoking the bond?"

Something ripped inside me as her answer filled my head. Loud and fucking clear.

"Yes."

"Then why are you helping me?" I asked.

"Because it's my job and because I can't walk away from you." Her whiskey eyes flared. "The bond won't let me."

# Chapter Twenty-Two

# LIAM

Rain soaked the back of my shirt as I stepped outside and leaned against the deck railing. The garbage and recycling bins were on their sides. Trash and branches littered the grass.

Renae descended the steps and started cleaning up like nothing out of the ordinary had happened and my entire world hadn't just been knocked sideways. As if she wasn't some kind of undead mutant cyborg.

"You said Cyrena orchestrated the accident. How?"

She picked up a soggy pizza box and placed it in the trash can. "Deceptors can project anything they want into your cerebral cortex. They can make you see, feel, and hear anything they like. She can walk you in front of a bus, and there's nothing you can do to stop it."

"What else can she do?" I asked as I joined her in the yard.

"She's the best telepath I've ever met. You won't be able to keep her out of your head. Don't underestimate her, Liam. If she decides to take you out, you'll never see it coming."

I righted the upside-down recycling bin. "How am I supposed to defend myself against an invisible assassin who's already killed me once?"

"You can't," Renae said, walking toward me with an armful of empty bottles. "Your only option is to play their game and remain as useful as possible without becoming a liability."

"A liability to them or to you?" I had no idea whose side Renae was on, theirs, mine, or her own. All three. None. Did she even know? "Wouldn't want you to have to do something you regret, like resurrecting me from the dead."

Glass clattered into the blue bin, and she spun toward me. "Liam, I don't regret resurrecting you; I regret failing to suppress your power. I regret ruining any chance you had of living a normal human life. If I hadn't let myself become distracted by..." her eyes grazed over the dragon tattoo on my chest, "the bond, we could have avoided all this."

"You mean *you* could have avoided telling me the truth." Thunder rumbled overhead.

Renae crossed her arms. "Instead of arguing with me over a moot point, we should be practicing. You only have three days to learn how to control your forecasting gift."

I threw my hand toward the sky. "Great. Am I supposed to instinctively know how to stop the damn rain?" A sheet of lightning illuminated the black clouds above us.

"Before you can control any gift, you need to learn how to ground yourself. It's the first thing they teach new recruits at the Nursery. If I can help you find an anchor, you should be able to use it to control your gift, or at least stop it from putting your life in danger again."

"Okay. So how do I ground myself?"

"You need to choose an anchor. For some, it's a phrase or a prayer; for others it's an image. It can be anything, really, as long as it carries emotional weight."

"What's your anchor?"

Renae winced as she rocked up onto the balls of her feet the way she did when she was impatient or frustrated or trying to concentrate. "Focus all your energy on reading my thoughts and let the bond amplify what you hear."

My gaze drifted from her whiskey eyes to where her teeth bit into her swollen bottom lip as I waited for something to happen. "This is ridiculous. I can't read your mind on demand."

She held out her hand. "Physical contact may help." A sharp pain shot across the arch of my foot when our fingers brushed.

"Shit, something just bit me." I kicked off my flip-flop and searched the ground for a centipede.

"It's not a bug, Liam." The pain evaporated as soon as I dropped her hand. "It's my anchor. Half a dozen shards of glass I embedded in the bottom of my left foot."

"Why the fuck would you do that?"

"Before the accident, I could ground myself by biting the inside of my lip or pinching my arm, but it wasn't enough, and I was desperate to sever the connection at first."

My chest tightened at the realization that the woman I loved had mutilated herself to escape me.

"We need to find you an anchor."

"Well, I'm sure as hell not letting you shove glass in my feet."

Renae scowled. "I would never do that to you." Rain-damp lashes brushed her cheeks as she nodded at my hand. "Try pinching yourself or biting your tongue. A little pain goes a long way."

I bit down hard. Nothing happened. "This is absurd," I mumbled.

"You're not taking this seriously." Renae groaned and pulled my bloody kitchen knife out of her pocket.

I held up my hands and backed away not sure if I could wrestle it from her before she cut me.

"Close your eyes and focus."

"No fucking way I'm closing my eyes while you're holding a knife, chica."

She heaved a sigh and wrapped her fingers around the blade.

"Renae—" I lunged forward, and my vision exploded with light as if a flash bang had detonated in front of me. I tried to shield my eyes, but the light was coming from everywhere—as if the entire electromagnetic spectrum was assaulting my retinas. Pain pinched behind my right eye. I rubbed it away as the blinding sensation slowly dissipated and an entirely different vision came into focus.

My head reeled as my brain struggled to process what my eyes were soaking in. Everything pulsed with energy. The trees and grass were a hazy purple, and my gravel driveway glowed like magma. Orange radio waves rippled from the cell tower half a mile down the road. The night sky was backlit with brilliant color. Even the brightest stars were mere red specks against a boiling sea of blues and greens. I'd dropped plenty of acid when I was using, but the resulting hallucinations had nothing on this psychedelic disassociation.

I waved my hands in the air. White-hot tendrils of static crackled around them, and no matter what I did, I couldn't shake it off. Just like those damn bugs in the red field, it was under my skin. A part of me.

When my eyes landed on Renae, the air left my lungs.

A golden corona looped around her. She dipped her chin to her chest as the light condensed into tendril-like flares that curled away from her back and solidified into six iridescent black appendages with barbed hooks at the end of their open mouths.

She was the most terrifying thing I'd ever seen, and I couldn't look away.

"You... have tentacles."

"They're called syphons. Eyes down here." Renae snapped her fingers, dragging my attention away from the mouths of those suckers, each as wide as my palm, back to the blade in her hand.

"Drop the knife, Renae." A rope of electricity shot from my palm. It snapped around her wrist and coiled up her arm, tightening until she released the blade. I raised my hand and tugged the glowing filament toward me and Renae stumbled forward.

"Now we're getting somewhere," she said, voice tight. "Try leashing the clouds. If you can control your aim, you should be able—"

"They're watching me," I said, staring at her extra limbs. They tracked my movements as if they were ready to strike.

"Liam, I need you to focus on the electrical storm before my hand starts to heal and we lose your enhanced forecaster vision."

"And do what, exactly?"

"I don't know," she growled.

I flinched at the pain in my palm as she gouged her talon-like nails into the bloody wound.

"Why aren't you healing as quickly as before?"

"Because I'm hungry." Renae's syphons twitched, and I took two steps back. "At the Nursery, forecasters talked about pushing their energy into things to either leash or lash them. Please just try to do something before my pain dissipates and we lose the anchor."

I rolled my neck and tried to push the electrical current away from my body toward the sky. A ropey beam arced over the cloud like a searchlight.

"Did they mention how to lasso water vapor with a flaccid flashlight?"

The energy around her flared. "We're running out of time." Her syphons struck toward me. I toppled onto my ass, and the technicolor vision vanished.

Renae pinched the bridge of her nose. "I'm sorry. I just... I don't know anything about being a forecaster."

"That makes two of us." I stood and brushed the mud from my shorts.

She flexed her palm and scowled at her newly healed skin. Her eyes searched the ground as her thought pinged in my head. *Where's the knife?* She turned and spotted it in the grass behind her.

I lunged forward, grabbed her around the middle and hauled her back against my chest before she could stoop to pick it up.

Renae squirmed in my arms, her round rear end grinding against my crotch. "Let. Me. Go." The salt and sweat scent of her skin engulfed me as I tightened my grip, crushing her breasts with my forearm, immobilizing her before my dick betrayed me.

"Is it true? What they said about the compulsory effect of the bond?"

Renae went still as stone. I had my answer.

I shifted my hips away from her backside and barely managed to rasp out the command. "Don't even think about cutting yourself ever again, chica. I can find my own damn anchor."

# CHAPTER TWENTY-THREE

# RENAE

Lightning split the sky as Liam shoved me away from him. His anger exploded like a capsaicin bomb in my mouth, burning my tongue, the inside of my nose, and my eyes. Anger wasn't the only thing I tasted. Fear chalked my throat, and the bitter bite of regret soured my stomach. His emotions had been spiraling for the last two hours, and he had every right to be upset. His entire life had been a lie.

"The storm is getting worse, Liam. We should go inside or at least move to the covered deck, where it's safe."

"Go wherever you like, chica. I'm gonna take my new powers for a test drive. The sooner I get this weatherman thing under control, the sooner I can get back to my life." Liam raised his hands to the sky.

My hair stood as lightning forked overhead. The boom that followed shook the ground and made my ears pop. Liam laughed as if his sanity had finally snapped.

"You're going to get yourself killed."

"What do you care? I'm just a job to you. Just like I was to my father. At least cocaine barbie and disco grandma were honest about using me as a goddamned pawn." Another bolt of lightning struck somewhere nearby. I couldn't tell if it was getting closer or moving farther away.

"Who's the waste of flesh now, old man?" Liam knocked his fist against the dragon on his chest. "While your useless corpse is rotting in the ground, I'm a fucking god."

I grabbed his arm and tugged him toward the house. "Liam, please, I won't be able to resurrect you if we both get hit by lightning."

His denim eyes flashed silver in the fading light. "Go inside."

"No," Pins and needles prickled through my feet as they moved of their own accord. I fought each unwilling step. The sensation climbed my calves the same way it had in my previous life whenever I pushed my broken body too far and refused to accept the limits of my affliction. The more I resisted the compulsion to move, the more painful it became.

I stomped up the steps and into the house, slamming the screen door behind me.

"There's no need to throw a tantrum like a petulant child." Cyrena's voice filled my head as she appeared beside me.

"The storm could kill him." I gestured to Liam, who was pacing a muddy path in the grass behind his truck.

"He's already dying."

"What?" The numbness in my limbs evaporated, replaced by a petrified stillness. I didn't dare breathe or blink.

"His transition began long before he met you. There was never anything you could do to stop it."

"Yet you forced me into the bond." I clenched my fists at my sides. "Why?"

"To buy him time. His telepathy gift was the first to emerge, and like your useless healing ability, the frequency is far too low to be of any consequence." I bit down on my tongue. Arguing with Cyrena wouldn't help Liam. "His forecasting ability, however, ranks at the top of the scale. It's only a matter of time before he suffers the same detrimental side effects as the original Anzillu."

My ribs were suddenly too tight. "What are you saying? Is he sick?"

"Not yet. Not as far as we can tell." Cyrena's projection flickered. "I knew an Anzillu in my first life. He was possessed at age seven. He had an aneurysm at thirteen, but his mind was gone long before that. Watching someone you love slowly lose cognitive function is a torture I would not wish on anyone. Even a cow like you." If Cyrena had known an Anzillu, that meant her soul was over three thousand years old. "Marcella and I would rather not see Liam suffer any more than is necessary."

"Suffer? You orchestrated an accident to kill him."

"He was going to die anyway without a Gi'dari. We bought him time by bonding him to a reaper. You must continue to syphon him and keep his energy below the debilitating frequency."

"I need more than three days to train him. Give me three months." Three years might not be enough.

"I'm afraid that's not possible. If he's not stable when I report back to my handler, they'll accelerate the timeline and come after him. Trust me when I say that is not in anyone's best interest at the moment."

An uncomfortable ache gripped my stomach as I watched Liam through the screen door. He clutched the tailgate of his truck, head down, rain-soaked curls plastered to his face and neck. The taut muscles along his back bunched with tension.

"How will I know when I've drained him below the threshold and taken enough?"

"That's the beauty of the bond. Your gift knows what he needs. You must feed until it no longer craves him. Your hunger will only be satiated when his power is depleted and he's safe."

My skin tightened. I'd only come close to being satisfied once. In the server closet. Even then, the desire to drink him in was barely diminished. Gods help me, this man was like a decadent dessert. Too tempting to abstain, too sinfully rich to take in all at once without losing my self-control.

"You need to stop fighting the connection and start learning to navigate it. He told you to come inside. He didn't say you had to stay."

I took a tentative step onto the porch. When the pins and needles sensation didn't return, I descended the creaking wooden stairs and crossed the yard, my bare feet squelching in the oversaturated grass until I stood beside him.

"You're not just a job to me," I said. It was the only confession I could offer to the man who'd possessed my soul.

Heavy arms circled around me, crushing me to his chest. My nose and cheek squished against his salty flesh.

"I know." His deep voice rumbled through me, knocking loose the moorings holding up the walls I'd carefully erected.

"It's been a long day. I think we could both use a break," I managed to mumble.

"Agreed."

"You have a lot of volatile energy pulsing through your system right now. I... I could help with that." My gift shifted beneath my skin as I forced a little space between us, as much as his tight grip would allow.

"What are you suggesting?" His voice dropped an octave as his hands slid to my hips, holding me in place.

I traced the scar between his eyes and then down to his parted lips as my syphons unfurled. I caressed his unshaven jaw, recalling the glorious burn the rough stubble had left on my thighs. My thumb grazed over his parted lips.

"Renae." Liam sighed my name as if it were a plea for mercy, and it made my insides go molten. We'd blown past so many boundaries; what was one more for the sake of keeping him alive?

"I don't think you should be alone tonight."

# CHAPTER TWENTY-FOUR

# LIAM

"I'm sorry, you want to do what?" I asked through the bathroom door, hoping I'd misheard her.

Renae stepped out, wrapped in a towel. "It'll be easier to control your forecasting gift if you allow me to syphon your excess energy," she repeated calmly, squeezing the water from her auburn hair as if she hadn't just asked to feed on me like some kind of tentacled vampire. Not exactly what I'd had in mind when she said she wanted to spend the night.

I handed her a clean pair of boxers and my faded UH hoodie, giving her my back as she got dressed. "When you say you're a reaper, are we talking like the grim reaper?"

"That old ghast? Gods, don't ever invite him to a party. He'll suck the life out of the entire room."

"Wait, are you serious?" I glanced over my shoulder, and all the blood left my brain at the sight of her tugging the boxers over her perfect fucking ass.

Renae shot me a sideways glance. "It was a joke. The grim reaper is a fourteenth century urban legend created by the Corps to cover up the truth. We help the dead transition into the afterlife. We're rarely contracted to hunt down and eliminate a soul." She tossed her wet hair over her shoulder. "You won't feel a thing while I syphon you, I promise. We can sit and talk. You can even sleep if you like."

My eyes flicked to the empty space behind her where those inky black appendages had hovered earlier. "Have you ever... you know, sucked out a soul?"

"Every Corps trainee must pass a set of trials before being assigned a probationary assignment. Consuming a soul was my final test."

"When you say consumed..." My throat went dry.

Her face pinched. "It was either mine or theirs and I didn't want to die, so I followed orders and did what I had to do to survive. I'm no better than the monsters who burned me alive."

My gut twisted with disgust. Not because she'd sucked out someone's soul in self-defense. That I could stomach. What I couldn't stomach was the knowledge that she'd been forced into a fucking test where her only options were to kill or be killed. My palms went white hot as I imagined wrapping my fingers around the throats of anyone who tried to hurt her.

"You have nothing to fear from me, Liam."

That was the ironic bit. I wasn't afraid of her. Not her charred corpse or those snake-like appendages. The only thing about her that gave me pause was her ability to fuck with my head.

"How many times have you hacked my brain to manipulate my memories and emotions?"

She brushed past me and dropped into a kitchen chair. "I didn't have a choice. It was my job."

I scrubbed my hands over my face, wondering if anything that had happened between us had been real. "Answer the question."

She winced as if I'd hit a nerve. "I didn't make you fall in love with me, if that's what you're asking. Gods, this would be so much easier if you hadn't."

"Easier for whom?"

"I'm constantly aware of your emotions and... inclinations." A flush crept into her cheeks. "You don't know what it's like to feel as if you've lost control of your body, your ability to trust your own mind."

"I do, actually." I crossed to the kitchen and pulled bacon and a wedge of parmesan cheese from the fridge. I didn't know how the feeding thing worked, but I sure as hell didn't want her starting on me with an empty stomach. "You know you're talking to an addict, chica. Lack of self-control is a hell I'm well acquainted with."

"I know." Her voice softened.

"No, you don't." I grabbed a stock pot from under the sink and filled it with water. "I started hearing the voices when I was ten. Thought I was, you know... fucked in the head or haunted by demons or some shit until I figured out what was happening." My knuckles went white where they gripped the pot handles. "My old man was cold and cruel to my face. The stuff he didn't say was worse. I used drugs and alcohol to quiet the intrusive thoughts. I would have given anything to be able to tune it out any other way."

I don't know why I told her. I'd never told anyone before. Not even Connor.

Renae wiped a tear from her cheek.

Fuck. I didn't want her sympathy. I just wanted her to know I understood what it was like to be enslaved to something you had no control over. The fact that I was that thing for her made my skin crawl. I grabbed a frying pan and started chopping the bacon.

"Can I help?" Renae asked.

I nodded toward the fridge. "Grab the eggs and parsley." I watched as she hopped up and crossed the room. The oversized hoodie hid the boxers and grazed the backs of her thighs in a way that sent my imagination to all the wrong places. I forced my attention back to the cutting board. "What other mutant powers should I expect from the bag of tricks my asshole father planted inside me?"

Her shoulder grazed mine, and I froze as she reached across the counter and pulled a knife from the block. "Your primary gift seems to be forecasting, which makes sense, as it was directly inherited from your mother. She must have also been a telepath." The way Renae chopped the parsley in haphazard pieces and zero precision made me smile. "That makes two so far. I'm hoping none of the others manifest. The energy scales needed to wield so many at once would be enormous, more than your brain can handle without a neural-lace mesh."

"Where do I get one of those?" I asked as I washed my hands, trying hard not to imagine what kind of surgery or modifications it might take.

She put the knife down. "You can't. The brain and body need to be grown around the mesh in a specialized tank at the Nursery."

"So, I'm riding bareback with this shit. Great." I ripped open a box of pasta and dumped it into the boiling water.

"All the more reason to find an anchor and learn control. Healers, like telepaths, operate at a low frequency. If the healing gift emerges, you won't be in any more danger than you are now." Renae propped a hip against the counter. "I'm technically a healer, but the gift barely registers."

"You resurrected me from the dead. Twice. I'd say that registers pretty damn high."

"That only works on you. Benefits of the bond." Renae's shoulders slumped. "I can't even keep a houseplant alive. Deceptors, like Cyrena and Marcella, and isolators operate in the mid-range, while forecasters, reapers, and mimics run at an extremely high frequency. Which is why I need to feed on you. My engineered husk can handle your excess power. Yours can't, not without irrevocable damage. Like I said before, you won't feel a thing."

I glanced at her as I pushed the bacon around in the pan. Fuck, I wanted to feel it. "What's an isolator?"

"Isolators can protect themselves and anyone within close proximity from external influence. They can also exert their will over you while you're under their net. Be careful who you allow to shield you."

"What about mimics?" I asked as I handed her the parmesan.

"They can split their consciousness between multiple physical forms. Not very practical in the field. They can't get far from their doppelgangers," her eyes darted to mine, "but they're fun at parties and in bed." She wasn't joking this time.

Thunder roared in my head as I imagined that scenario—Renae sandwiched between two of me. The thought made me angry and instantly hard all at once. I couldn't stomach seeing her with anyone else, but having a second body to protect and pleasure her jumped straight to the top of my mutant wish list. "What about flying and teleportation?"

Renae rolled her eyes. "Technically, forecasters can fly by manipulating air currents, but it's forbidden outside the confines of the Nursery's training center. It tends to blow their human cover. There are two other gifts, but travelers are pretty much extinct, and oracles might as well be. The Nūkiri are the only three oracles in existence. They're older than the banished gods, and some say they were here long before humans evolved, that they seeded our developing species with the sacred gifts."

My brain came to a screeching halt. "Are you implying that human evolution was spurred by a trio of ancient ghosts who can predict the future?"

Renae's brow furrowed. "The Nūkiri don't predict the future. They know the future and they take steps to either assure or change it as they see fit, and they do not abide dissent. Anyone who works against their agenda is sacrificed to the Void."

The stove hissed as the pasta boiled over. "Shit." I yanked it off the burner and searched my cabinets for the strainer. "What's the Void?"

"The membrane between worlds. There's only one safe passage through to the other side. Souls who attempt to cross elsewhere are ensnared and devoured."

Question after question ran through my head, but I was already well past the load of information I could process in a single day. Renae seemed to get that and busied herself braiding her damp hair and opening two glass bottles of ginger beer while I finished making dinner.

Watching her eat was like watching porn. The way she licked her lips as her eyes fluttered shut. The little moans she made with each bite. Would she make the same sounds when she fed on me?

I cleared my throat. "This feeding thing, how does it work?"

She pushed her plate aside. "It's easier if we're in physical contact. We can hold hands and do it here," her eyes flicked to the bed, "or we can lie down. It makes me a bit woozy, and it may leave you a little drowsy."

I palmed one of the metal bottle caps as I stood and held out my hand. "Come on." My pulse pounded in my veins as I led her to the bed.

"Now what?" I asked when we were on our sides facing each other.

"Just try to relax. I'll do everything. Are you ready?"

The jagged edge of the bottle cap cut into my palm. White light flashed, and my vision changed. I was so fucking ready.

Golden light looped around us as three black tentacles uncurled behind her. I reached up and let one coil up my arm. She was wrong about one thing. I could 100 hundred percent feel it caressing me. A warm tingling sensation rolled over my skin. Every nerve in my body was focused on where it licked me. I caught my breath as its barbed mouth pierced my palm and began sucking something out of me with deep pulls. It was disturbing and hot as fuck.

Renae grabbed my wrist as the syphon released my hand. "Let me do the touching. I won't be able to focus if you keep trying to pet me."

"Sorry, I just—"

"Give me the bottle cap."

"I want to watch."

"Liam, please. It will be easier for me if you don't. This is clearly turning you on. Gods, I can taste it." She closed her eyes and exhaled slowly, as if she couldn't stomach the flavor.

I released the bottle cap and the enhanced vision dissipated.

"Tell me about your tattoo," Renae said. "Why the dragon?"

"Would you be disappointed if I told you I picked it out of a book?"

"Did you?" Renae pushed an unruly curl away from my face.

I tucked my hands in my armpits to keep them from reaching for her. "We had this picture book of fairytale creatures as kids, unicorns and mermaids and shit like that. I used to have nightmares about the dragon eating me alive, so Connor made up these ridiculous stories where I was the dragon, and instead of eating people, I ate clover and went on adventures with a goat named Sir Stallion." I rolled onto my back and opened the nightstand drawer. "When I went into treatment, he gave me the book and told me not to let anyone else define who I was or what I could do."

My stomach twisted as I handed the book to Renae and watched as her talon-tipped fingers traced the green beast on the cover. The same one that was tattooed across my chest. I'd stopped letting other people tell me who I was a long time ago. Now I could barely wrap my head around who or what that could be. My father created me to be a living god. Cyrena and Marcella were using me as a pawn in a game I didn't understand, and Renae wanted me to be her career ladder. I yawned as she flipped through the pages. What the fuck did I want?

I woke up to a round ass pressed against my hips. Her breathy little snores did weird things to my chest, making my lungs expand like balloons.

It felt like I was floating weightless above the ground and in danger of drifting away if I let go.

My arms tightened around Renae as I inhaled the scent of my shampoo in her hair. Everything had changed in the span of twenty-four hours. And yet nothing had changed. Not for me. For her, it was the bond. For me, it was more. So much more. The only thing that made sense was her right here, curled up against me.

I didn't understand how the bond thing worked, but the whole soul slave thing made my stomach revolt. She'd mutilated her feet, stolen my memories, and lied about a fake boyfriend to keep me at arm's length, and now she was in my bed, and I had a sinking suspicion it wasn't by choice. Not entirely.

The worst part was that I knew if there was a way to release her, to break the connection between us, I wouldn't. The bond was the only thing keeping her in my orbit.

As much as I wanted to feel that sweet ass wiggle against my raging cock, I shifted my hips away, slipped out of bed, and took a shower. Renae didn't deserve any more compulsory suggestions from my overactive libido. It didn't take long to ease the aching need in my balls imagining her wet cunt squeezing around me instead of my soapy fist. I leaned against the wall, waiting for my pulse to settle and my dick to soften before toweling off and pulling on a pair of jeans and a T-shirt over my damp skin.

Every good intention I had flew out the fucking window when I stepped out of the bathroom and saw her standing barefoot in my kitchen wearing the oversized hoodie I'd let her borrow the night before. Most of her hair had escaped the messy braid and hung around her face as she clutched a steaming mug.

"I made coffee," she said.

Need ripped through me as Renae twisted and grabbed another mug from the counter and handed it to me. I would do anything to keep her here, like this. Always.

"You don't have any more eggs, and it looks like we ate all the pasta. Give me a minute to change back into my bathing suit and shorts and we can run to the store. You should increase your calorie intake. It will help with the post-training burnout, and I can ask my handler about getting you a supplement pack designed for forecasters."

I set the coffee down and glanced at the clock on the microwave behind her as I shoved my feet into a pair of flipflops. "I have class in an hour. I'll just grab a power bar from one of the vending machines on campus."

"You have the rest of the week off," Renae said. "I cleared your schedule with Marcus so we can train."

Static prickled over my skin. "You what?"

Renae nodded to my phone sitting facedown on the table. "Relax. I texted him on your behalf. He thinks you have the plague."

I grabbed the phone and my backpack and headed out the door before I lost my shit. Fuck, I needed to get away from her and clear my goddamned head.

She slapped her mug against the counter and chased after me. "Where are you going?"

"To work." I swung a leg over the seat of my bike. If I blew off a week of class, Logan would fire me and prove that my father was right. That I was a failure who couldn't hold down a job and who'd never amount to anything.

"Liam, we need to train."

"You're not the only one with boundaries and career goals, chica. Don't ever interfere with my job again." I pulled on my helmet. "The keys to the truck are on the hook by the door. Go home. We can train tonight when it gets dark." I didn't have neighbors, but trying to emulate

Thor, God of Thunder in my front yard during daylight hours seemed like a bad idea.

"I have a shift at the summit tonight." Renae grabbed my handlebars.

Was she shitting me? So, my job was expendable, but hers wasn't? "What do you even do at the summit?"

Renae's eyes darted over my shoulder. She released my bike and backed away. "You're right. We shouldn't train during the day. Meet me at my apartment at midnight."

&

I wrote the lecture topic on the board as my second class flopped into their seats. First Law of Thermodynamics: Problems in Solid Phase.

"Today, we'll explore the reverse relationship between pressure and heat capacity and how it seems to contradict with theory. If you turn to page 397, you'll find the chapter summary and the formulas needed to reconcile this contradiction. We will pick up where we left off last week with problems eleven b through f. You have thirty-five minutes, and you may work in small groups."

I walked between desks, checking their calculations, all too aware of the entity that had been watching me from the back corner all morning. Her silver hair caught the light, reflecting it on the walls like a prism. Why she chose to show herself, I didn't know, so I did the same thing I had as a kid with the voices. I ignored her. The next time I glanced at the back of the room, she was gone.

While my students worked, my mind drifted to Renae and her cagey reaction when I asked what she did at the summit. I imagined her sitting in the lab, in a pair of jeans and my UH hoodie, scrolling through data, reaching out for her coffee, and the way her forehead wrinkled in annoyance when she tipped back the empty mug. The scene at the summit superimposed itself over my cramped classroom as Renae stood and walked through the first row of desks as if they didn't exist. She did a double take as she brushed past me, and I could swear I caught a whiff of my shampoo.

A static shock pulsed up my arm as someone touched me, and the lab at the summit evaporated. "Sorry, Professor Riley," one of my students said. "Your nose... it's bleeding."

I brought my fingers to my face and caught a handful of blood. "Shit." I leaned forward, pinching the nostrils together.

"Here." The girl handed me a tissue.

"We're gonna end early today and pick up here next time. Bring your completed calculations to class on Monday." Pain throbbed behind my right eye as I trudged to the bathroom to clean myself up.

☙

My knee bounced under my desk an hour later as I attempted to revise my thesis. It was the one normal thing left in my life—a life that was careening off a cliff. Aside from staying sober, getting my PhD was the one goal I'd ever set for myself. Not finishing wasn't an option. Especially when I was this close. I was only missing a few key pieces of data to complete the calculations.

After an infuriating hour of searching the IRTF database for the files, I gave up and called the university's astronomy center. They transferred me to someone in IT who gave me the number to a server farm in upstate New York that managed our backups.

"Global Operation Dynamics information technology support services, can you hold please?" a young woman's voice said on the other end of the line.

"No, I can't hold. I've been waiting for a live person for ten minutes. I'm calling from the astronomy department at the University of Hawaii. We manage the NASA infrared telescope on Mauna Kea. I need to talk to someone about missing files from our recent observations. I'm in a bind here and need to get my hands on a copy of the raw data."

"Hold please." The line clicked several times before the elevator music started.

Another woman picked up a few seconds later. "Do you have the batch IDs and dates?"

I gave her the numbers and waited while she checked.

"I'm sorry. It looks like the files were corrupted. Fortunately, they were quarantined and deleted at the source before they could corrupt the entire data set."

A sinking sensation settled in my stomach as I recalled the anomaly that had popped up on Renae's computer. The one she swore was a corrupted file and promptly deleted before gifting me a sticky note of sexual distractions.

"Does the record show who posted the batches?"

"I'm afraid I cannot give you that information."

After I hung up, I pulled up the remote access link and logged in to the summit's server. I opened several files at random from each batch in question. They were all tagged with the same user ID.

What the fuck? It was a palindrome. The number was the same whether you read it backward or forward. Which was a weird coincidence since all of the University issued user IDs were randomly generated. The probability of randomly generating a twelve-digit palindrome was one in a million. Not fucking likely.

I flipped over a quiz from the stack of vector equations I still needed to grade and wrote out the number again and again. When I dropped the second half of the mirrored sequence, it looked like a date. 06-10-44.

She might as well have signed the files with her damn name.

June 10, 1944, was the day Renae said she'd died. My chest tightened as everything that had happened in the last forty-eight hours—fuck, the last two months—congealed. She'd been cagey about her role at the summit. Now I knew why. Was that her plan from the beginning? To manipulate me with smoking hot succubus routine and keep me close enough to sabotage my work? The pressure headache behind my right eye pounded, and I chased two extra-strength Motrin with the last swallow of a Red Bull left over from my lunch, wishing it was something stronger.

☙

I grabbed two bottles of ginger soda and hoisted myself onto the porch roof from the railing. The first stars were just beginning to pop against the twilight sky, and my brain throbbed with questions. Questions I needed Renae to answer face to face, where I could force her to tell me the truth.

My truck sat in the driveway. Right where she'd left it. She probably walked all the way home out of spite. I smiled and knocked back one of the bottles, imagining her stomping down the road barefoot in my boxers and hoodie. Stubborn and sexy as all hell.

I pressed the sharp edge of the bottle cap into my palm and focused on the pain. A flash exploded in front of my eyes as my vision shifted. I reclined against the roof, clutching the metal tighter in my fist. As the white light faded, the world came into focus in a kaleidoscope of color. The trees, the grass, the water molecules in the air. Everything pulsed with a heartbeat-like energy. It shouldn't be possible to see anything outside the visible spectrum. NASA spent billions on telescopes to get images like this, and all I needed to do was clutch a goddamn bottle cap. It was fucking surreal. The forecaster sight made my head spin like being four shots into a killer buzz.

The Eridanus constellation glowed like a beacon. A web of luminescent filaments stretched across the sky toward a funnel-shaped vortex at its base. I sat up and steadied myself on my elbows. "What the hell is that?"

Marcella appeared next to me, her tinsel hair clinking in the breeze. She had the same looping flares as Renae swirling around her, only hers were a pale purple instead of gold. "We call it the river of souls." She waved a hand toward the sky. "Every one of those specks of light is a soul making its way to the afterlife."

"They're coming from everywhere, not just Earth."

Marcella patted my knee. "Dear boy, did you think we were alone?"

"No, but..." My stomach did several roller-coaster drops between fear and excitement. Based on the amount of light spreading across the cosmos, we were most definitely not alone. A chill ran down my spine as every alien invasion movie I'd ever seen flashed through my brain.

"Is that what Renae does at the summit? Hide evidence of alien life?" The balloon inside my chest expanded. If she wasn't targeting my research specifically, there was a chance this thing between us wasn't a complete lie.

"You'll have to ask her, I'm afraid."

"Do all the alien ghosts communicate on the other side?" Now there was a sentence I never thought would fall from my mouth.

Cyrena raised a brow. "Only the Nūkiri have contact with the others. Even then, it is limited."

If the other species were anything like humans, territorial and self-absorbed, that was probably a good call. "How do you communicate without a body?"

"Almega is inhabited by a non-sentient species of insects. They're like living nanobots and are attracted to our energy. They colonize around it, forming a symbiotic psychic relationship that allows us to build the facsimile of a corporeal form. They have no touch or taste organs, but they have a visual and auditory awareness that we're able to harness."

"Not having a real physical body must have its perks. No more pain, illness, or addiction."

"It takes some time to get used to. Imagine not being able to feel the weight of a lover's arms around you, the texture of grass beneath your feet, or the softness of a kiss. The absence of sensation is a hard thing to live with, for reapers and deceptors especially. Our gifts are less effective with so few senses to manipulate."

I thought about the way Renae engrossed herself in every physical experience, surfing, skydiving, eating—getting off. It was as if she wanted to savor everything while she had the chance. The lists and the lies and the glass embedded in her foot made more sense. They kept her from becoming a slave to her own sensations.

"How long have you been bound to Cyrena?"

"Nearly a millennium."

"So there really is no escape?" I flicked the bottle cap across the metal roof. It skittered into the gutter as I shook off my enhanced vision.

"My relationship with Cyrena is one of respect and deep affection. She has never taken advantage of our imbalance. Even if she wanted to reciprocate the bond, she couldn't."

"Is that possible, to reciprocate the bond?"

"Your gift must choose her, but it can only do so when you are willing to give up your life and your soul."

"I'm willing to do both right now," I said.

"Your life is not the heart beating in your chest nor the air circulating in your lungs, child. It is the people and things you hold dear, your research, your sobriety, your brother. Are you willing to give them up if she were to ask it?"

Marcella read the answer in my mind. "Then the bond cannot be reciprocated. The Gi'dari can only be gifted once. Cyrena gave hers to another—long before we met. She lost him to the Void during the All Souls War between the gods and the Nūkiri. You remind her of him."

"At least you both had a choice. Renae didn't have that luxury. What did she give up when she saved me?"

"The thing she values most. Her freedom."

The glass bottle in my hand started to melt as my body went hot with anger. I dropped it and it rolled off the roof and landed in the dirt with a dull thud. "Please tell me that was a forecasting thing." I inspected my glowing palm. There were no signs of damage, despite the intense burning sensation.

Marcella's eyes crinkled with a smile. "I see the feeding was successful. One night with Renae, and you're already less volatile."

I couldn't read her thoughts exactly, but my gut told me she was hiding something. "If I'm such a risk, why are you trying to keep me alive? And don't feed me the bullshit you sold Renae. I don't believe for one second that you're trying to lure out some wayward scientist. What's your agenda?"

The old woman patted my knee. "Fret not, my boy, all will be revealed in time. Unlike Renae, Cyrena and I do not answer to the Corps. Our orders come from a higher authority, and they are curious to see what you are capable of."

At the moment, I wasn't capable of much beyond being a danger to myself and the woman I was in love with. "Does she know?"

"She does not. And if you care for her, you will keep it that way."

"What if I don't want to play your games?"

"We are here to ensure that you do. It would be a shame if anything happened to the girl."

My hand burned white hot as I reached for the specter's throat. "If you ever threaten her again—"

Marcella dissipated as my glowing fingers passed through her form. Her tinny voice echoed through my head. "You're almost ready, child."

I pulled the second bottle of ginger beer from my pocket and hurled it across the yard, where it shattered with an explosive pop against a tree.

Their agenda didn't matter. The only thing that mattered was mastering my fucking mutant powers. It was the only way to protect Renae.

⁓

"You wanna elaborate on why we're sneaking into the national park in the middle of the night?" I asked as I hopped out of the truck and tossed our empty pizza boxes in the bed. Renae was still wearing my UH hoodie and a pair of jeans.

Her eyes darted down the closed access road and then up at the overcast sky before landing on me. "No witnesses."

I ducked under the barricade and followed her past at least six signs warning of active volcanic activity as we picked our way along a jagged path toward the ocean. Renae had convinced my supernatural entourage to back off so she could help me focus while we trained, which was going to be damn near impossible with all the questions drilling through my head. Who the fuck did Cyrena and Marcella work for? What did they want with me? What did it have to do with Renae and the Nūkiri?

"I can taste your curiosity. Go ahead and ask your questions."

My groin tightened at the memory of her tasting me. "What does curiosity taste like?" I asked.

"Chlorine. Now ask me what's really on your mind."

The real question, the one burning a hole in the back of my brain, lodged in my throat and stayed there. "How many others are there like you?" I asked instead.

Renae glanced over her shoulder, and I felt a tug at my chest. The momentary heart failure I got every time I imagined her syphons sucking and probing me. Feeding on me. Part of me longed for that touch, the part of me that was pressing hard against my fly. The other part of me worried how much she could read by feeding on me. If she could taste the weight of what Marcella had told me.

Renae picked her way down the rocky path toward the sea cliffs, her steps sure, as if she could see in the dark. Fuck. Could she see in the dark?

"We have agents embedded in every government, bio tech, space, environmental, and disease control agency across the planet. All trying to keep humans from orchestrating their own extinction."

"I'm still trying to wrap my head around it. The physics alone of what I can do—"

Renae caught my arm as my flip-flops slipped on a patch of wet rock, every nerve in my body hyper aware of her firm grip on my elbow.

"Sorry." She dropped her hand and flexed her fingers. "You're asking the wrong questions. The how doesn't matter."

"Okay, why? Why would the dead give two shits about what happens to the living? What's in it for you?"

"Our souls aren't immortal. Without the constant influx of energy generated by the cycle of life, death, and rebirth, our sentient forms would cease to exist. When the human population eventually obliterates itself, our souls will slowly wither until we dissipate completely."

"Why stay hidden? Why isn't the Corps using forecasters to generate wind and hydroelectric power? You could do so much more if you weren't bogged down by the bureaucratic bullshit of keeping your existence hidden from the rest of us."

Renae guided me around a deep fissure. "Watch your step."

"Thanks."

"The sum of human history can be boiled down to two driving forces. Greed and corruption. It's programmed into our DNA."

I couldn't argue with her on that.

"Post-human sentients are prone to the same inclinations. Being dead doesn't change our base instincts. The bureaucracy and secrecy established by the Corps are the only things keeping assets from going rogue and seeking their own glory, like the old gods. The system has worked for thousands of years. Why would we change it?"

I hadn't spent much time considering what the afterlife might be like, or if there was one for that matter. A supernatural bureaucracy was the last thing I fucking expected.

"There's nothing altruistic or enlightened about life in Almega. It's the same tainted power dynamic, only on Earth the currency is money. In Almega, the currency is energy. It's bartered and sold like a life-sustaining drug."

"Great." I massaged my forehead, trying to relieve the tension headache building behind my right eye.

Renae stuffed her hands into her pockets. "I promised you the truth."

I kept my eyes on the slick slope beneath my feet and finally asked the question itching at the back of my brain. "What do you really do at the summit?"

"That conversation can wait," Renae said. "We're here."

The path spit us out onto a narrow ledge overlooking the base of Kilauea, where the ocean hissed against the slow crawl of lava oozing over the edge of the cliff.

"What now? Do I need to get angry and Hulk out?"

"I want to try something different," she said.

The balloons in my lungs strained against my ribs as she inched closer. Renae took my hand and lifted it to her throat, holding it in place with her own.

"What are you doing?" I focused on her thoughts, but they flitted through her head too fast for me to track, flashes of things that blew her little sticky note list out of the damn water. Things that rivaled even my depraved imagination. Was she intentionally trying to distract me, knowing I'd try to read her mind?

"I want you to use me as your anchor." She tightened her grip, forcing my fingers to bite into her neck.

"I'm not going to hurt you." My voice came out all kinds of strained, but I didn't let go or loosen my grip. What the fuck was wrong with me?

"The bond gives you access to my gifts." She swallowed hard, and heat flashed through me at the roll of her throat against my palm. "On the plane, when I kissed you, you took control of my syphons and latched them on to me. This time, I want you to latch them on to the cloud." Her eyes flicked to the heavy black mass creeping across the moon.

"Are you asking me to inflict pain on you so I can use it as an anchor?"

"I'm asking you to claim me. Use my gift to stabilize yours."

"I won't hurt you," I repeated, unsure of who I was trying to convince.

"I trust you." Renae reached up and slid a reassuring hand over my shoulder.

That made one of us. I didn't trust myself, and I certainly didn't trust the primal urge rising inside me. The urge to take what she offered. Renae took a step forward, and I tightened my grip. Whether to stop her from advancing or to pull her closer, I wasn't sure.

"Liam, please." The words came out tight, constrained by my grip on her throat. "We're running out of time. I don't know how to train you to be a forecaster, but I can give you my gift. If this works, we'll prove to the Corps that you're an asset worth protecting."

I stroked her pulsing carotid with my thumb, and her thoughts finally slowed enough for me to grasp as they filtered through my head. *He thinks I'm a monster.*

"Is this what you really want?"

"Oh my gods, just shut up and kiss me already." Renae fisted my shirt and pressed her lips to mine. Not with the frenzied urgency like before on the plane. This time, she seduced me with slow strokes of her tongue, and I didn't care that she'd been toying with my emotions, scrambling my memories, sabotaging my research, and manipulating me from day one. In that moment, all I knew was need. Need to close the loop, complete the connection, and possess her completely.

I gripped her braid with my free hand and yanked her head back, giving me better access to her mouth as my power, no longer a flaccid beam of light, slipped down her throat and swelled at the thought of filling every crevice inside her.

Renae's pulse sputtered beneath my fingers. I wrapped my free arm around her, cleaving her body to mine. Her hands snaked through my hair as my energy inflated the undulating appendages at her back, filling the syphons as they grew and stretched toward the sky.

My energy pooled inside her like liquid lightning, and I realized the bond didn't just make her a slave. It made her a fucking conduit.

A deep moan climbed her throat, but I held her mouth to mine, unwilling to break the connection or relinquish control. I needed more. She arched against me as I pierced the cloud with her syphons. Hunger flared inside me, but there wasn't anything there to feed on. It wasn't alive. Not like the seductive warm body pressed against me.

*Gods help me, I've wanted to feel you inside me like this since that first night at the summit. Liam, I want you to fuck me.* Her voice spread through my head, and my energy exploded through her and into the cloud, obliterating it. Renae convulsed against me as the mutual orgasm spread through my groin and spilled into my damn pants.

Renae clung to me as I kissed the bruised flesh on her neck where my fingers had been moments before. "Did you just ask me to fuck you, or did I just imagine that?"

She reached up and traced my scar. "You didn't imagine anything. I'm tired of fighting this, Liam. I left an amended list in your glove box."

I kissed her forehead and thanked the damn gods.

Renae's eyes darted over my shoulder as someone clapped behind me.

"Bravo, darlings. Incredible teamwork, though I've never seen the claiming done quite that way."

Renae glared at Cyrena. "We still have thirty-six hours."

The woman's form floated toward us, blocking the only safe path away from the narrow cliff. I glanced between the spectral assassin and the eighty-foot drop to the glowing lava below. She had us cornered.

"By all means, keep practicing. I do so enjoy watching, especially now that it's gotten interesting."

Renae laced her fingers through mine. "She's right. We need to keep practicing until it's second nature. Until you can control my syphons without ravishing me in the process." Renae swiped at the sweat beading up on her brow.

"Now, where's the fun in that?" Cyrena pouted.

"No," I said, my voice barely audible beneath the thunder pounding in my head at the thought of energy fucking Renae again in front of a live audience. Heat flared in my hand. The scent of burning flesh struck my nose, and Renae yanked her charred and blistered palm away from mine. "Shit, I'm sorry. Are you okay?"

Renae flinched when I reached for her, my palm still glowing white hot. "It's fine." Her eyes flicked to Cyrena as if some unspoken conversation passed between them.

The specter floated around us like a predator stalking its prey. I angled my body between them. She'd have to go through me first. No way I was letting her get close to Renae.

"You were supposed to find him an anchor," Cyrena said, the sudden softness in her voice at odds with the way she glared at Renae.

"I am his anchor," Renae said.

"You won't always be here to channel his power. He needs to learn to control it on his own." An unnatural fog climbed over the edge of the cliff and crept toward us.

I shoved Renae toward the path. "We need to get to safer ground."

Renae stumbled over the rocks as I glanced over my shoulder, scanning for the spectral assassin. She was gone. Her soft chuckle clogged my ears like water, muting everything else. When it cleared, the world was eerily silent. Waves no longer crashed against the cliff. The lava ceased its hissing. The crunch of Renae's footsteps halted.

"Liam." I froze at the tremor in her voice.

Time slowed, and I was acutely aware of three things.

The bony arms wrapped around Renae's body, holding her hostage.

The river of molten rock beneath the edge of the cliff where they stood.

The white-hot lightning wreathing my wrists.

"Agree to disagree, darling," Cyrena said. "*Fear* is his anchor."

"Let her go." My vision changed like before. This time there was no flash of light and I didn't need pain to force the shift. I just willed it to happen.

Renae let out a choked cry as Cyrena floated backward over the lava, dragging Renae with her until their feet dangled above a fiery grave.

Cyrena clicked her tongue. "Tick tock, darling. I can only hold my corporeal form for a short time, and it would be a shame to watch her pretty little husk burn."

My heart climbed up my throat. Each erratic beat making it difficult to think, to breathe. "What do you want from me?"

"I want you to embrace your fear. Sink into it the same way this one sinks into her pain and uses it to anchor her gift. Tell us, what are you most afraid of?"

Renae's voice filled my head. *Tell her the truth. That you're afraid your father was right. That you're worthless and unworthy of the gifts he gave you. That your mother knew it too, and that's why she abandoned you. Tell her you're afraid your life isn't worth the sacrifice I was forced to make for you.*

"No." I shook my head as the words cut through me like a blade.

"Gods, spare me the melodramatic angst." Cyrena flung an arm through the air. Renae slipped in her grip.

I held up my hands, as if I could stop her from falling. "Cyrena, please, don't let her go! I'll do whatever you want."

Cyrena stroked a flickering hand over Renae's cheek. The specter was losing control of her form.

"It's quite natural to feel attached to your bonded Gi'dari. That kind of pure devotion is like a drug." Cyrena's eyes rolled back in her head as she sniffed Renae's hair. "That's why I chose her for you. I knew you wouldn't be able to resist her fire in your veins. Time to prove yourself, darling."

Renae's scream cleaved the air as Cyrena evaporated. I didn't have time to think. Wind whipped around me as I lifted from the ground and shot forward in jerky thrusts. I tumbled over the edge of the cliff and reached for Renae. But I wasn't fast or coordinated enough to catch her. I heard a splash, and my brain tried to reconcile the sound with what I'd seen—Renae's body splashing into a river of molten rock. Lava was denser than water. It didn't splash. Not like that.

*Cyrena can make you feel, see, and hear anything she desires.* I held my breath as I plunged into the cold ocean beneath the cliff and realized there was no lava. It was all in my head. The entire scene had been a deception. Fucking Cyrena. She'd projected it into my brain.

Pitch-black liquid pressed in around me like a watery grave. I kicked hard for the surface. I had to find Renae. I yanked on the bond like before. The connection went taut, and I focused on the water around her, pulling it with me as a swell rose beneath us, dragging the weight of the ocean up the cliff. Against gravity; against the tide. Against myself.

Renae sputtered and coughed as the wave crashed over the rocky ledge. I let go of the enormous weight bearing down on me and grabbed the back of her waterlogged hoodie with both hands. The ocean retreated with a thundering boom that reverberated in my chest. Renae swatted at my hand as I brushed a slimy chunk of kelp from her temple.

Cyrena appeared next to us. "Well done. Now do it again. This time, we'll forgo the theatrics. I don't think our little actress enjoyed playing the damsel in distress."

My eyes slid to Renae, who was wringing the water from her clothes. "What the hell is she talking about?"

"I've been trying to get you to choose an anchor for two days, Liam. Cyrena's right. I won't always be here to direct your power. We can't be together twenty-four seven. You have goals you want to achieve, and I have a job I can't walk away from. The charade was the only way to convince you that you can control it on your own. You don't need me, or anyone else to wield your gift."

I took a step back. "The two of you planned this... together?"

Cyrena smirked at Renae. "Tell Liam the first thing they teach you in the Corps."

"Keep your enemies close."

I glared at Renae. "Who's fucking side are you on?"

"How can you even ask me that? I've sacrificed everything for you. My freedom, my future in the Corps."

"You've done nothing but lie and manipulate me from day one." She'd distracted me with lies and lists and the promise of even more, and I'd fallen for it hook, line, and sinker. I fisted my hair. "Was any of it real? Don't fucking lie to me."

"What do you want me to say? Yes, I've manipulated and lied to you. You're my mark and my Gi'dari. I'm beholden to you and to the Corps, and navigating that line is tearing me apart at the seams. But I won't apologize for the deception or for trying to protect you, Liam. What has or hasn't been real between us is irrelevant. The only thing that matters is keeping you alive."

Cyrena stepped between us. "I think we could all use a little separation. Liam's proven he's more than capable of controlling his power. We can continue training when he's ready."

I glanced between them. Cyrena was right, we both needed space to breathe. "You said before that the bond wouldn't allow you to walk away from me, but you're wrong. I can give you what you want. I can give you your freedom."

"Liam, please, don't do this."

"Renae, I want you to stay the hell away from me. Don't come within compulsion range of me again."

# CHAPTER TWENTY-FIVE

# LIAM

A SWARM OF BUZZING insects took flight, expelling gold dust as I crossed the red field. Three stony figures stood at the edge of a clearing, their heads bent in prayer.

My gait slowed. I wasn't supposed to be here. Their stark marble faces swiveled toward me as I backed away.

Cyrena's voice cut through the fog in my head. "You've always had a vivid imagination, even as a boy." She stepped between two of the stone figures, her green dress catching in the crimson grass as she circled around them. I watched as she reached up and gouged out their eyes, one by one. Tears of blood oozed down the white stone.

"The Nūkiri can't see you. Marcella is an isolator. She's been cloaking your energy from their sight." Cyrena nodded to the middle of the field. "I believe what you're looking for is there."

I stepped around the hollow-eyed statues. My kitchen table sat at the center of the clearing, an altar for the recently unearthed coffin sitting on top of it.

"Is that supposed to be for me?" I asked.

"You tell me. This is your dream, darling. I'm just along for the ride." She trailed a bony finger through the clumps of wet mud on the lid. "From the looks of it, I'd say it belongs to someone long dead."

Something sharp tugged at my chest as I pulled at the splintered wood, attempting to pry it open with my bare hands. It gave way, crashing to the ground as thunder rolled in the distance. Renae's lifeless body lay in a bed of crimson vines.

"No, no, no!" I reached in and tried to pull her out of the box. The vines coiled around her, slithering into her ears, out of her mouth and nose.

"Don't just stand there. Help me!"

"It's only a dream." An icy hand grasped my shoulder as a jolt of pain ran down my arm. "Liam, she's not here."

When I glanced down, my hands had gone white hot and Renae's body was charred beyond recognition.

The ground shook as lightning struck the marble statues. They cracked and disintegrated into ash. A gust of wind scattered their remains across the field like a blanket of snow as my heart seized in my chest.

&

I bolted awake in a cold sweat and reached for my phone. It rang in my hand before I could dial her number. Renae.

"You're talking to me now?" she asked. "I didn't expect you to answer. You've been ignoring my calls for a week." The tightness in my chest eased at the sound of her voice.

"Where are you?" It came out more demand than question.

"At work. You ordered me to stay away from you five days ago, remember? Where else am I supposed to go?" Her voice softened. "Is everything okay? Your anxiety just spiked."

"It was just a dream." I let out a ragged breath.

Renae exhaled through the phone. "Thank the gods. That means the storm that rolled over the summit was just a coincidence. If you didn't answer, I was about to borrow Ernie's Jeep and drive down there."

"I don't need a babysitter anymore. Your little stunt worked. I can control it now."

"You need to keep training."

I swung my feet to the wood floor and padded to the fridge. "Agree to disagree."

"Liam, I'm serious."

"So am I. Marcella and Cyrena are satisfied that I'm no longer a threat, and I have zero interest in joining your soul army. End of discussion."

I could swear I heard her curse in her head from across the island.

"Controlling your gift takes more energy than wielding it. Your metabolism must be in overdrive by now. You need to eat constantly to avoid burnout."

I stared at the fresh stack of blue-lidded plastic containers that filled the refrigerator. "We need to talk about boundaries. You can't keep breaking into my house when I'm at work and stocking my fridge."

"Order me to stop, and I will."

My chest tightened again and I grabbed two of the plastic containers. I didn't want her to stop. I liked knowing she'd been in my space while I was gone. The room temperature dropped thirty degrees as I crossed the kitchen. Chicken skin broke out on my arms as my vision blurred, and I saw the telescope rising behind my couch. It was like looking at a cross processed photo, two shots overlapping the same frame. "Are you outside?" I asked.

"It's the only place I could get a signal. Why?"

This bond thing got weirder by the day. "I think I can see what you're seeing. Are you looking at the dome?"

"Yes, what am I looking at now?"

I refocused my vision, but all I saw was the eerie snow-covered field from my dream. "I got nothing, just a bunch of snow."

"Liam, it's been snowing up here for hours; ten inches so far. They're talking about closing the access road. Ernie and I may have to sleep in the lab."

"Shit. It snowed in my dream." I put Renae on speaker phone, pulled up the weather app, and watched the storm tracker replay. Radar showed it forming directly over my house and spreading out in a cone, encompassing the summit and northern half of the island. "Fuck. I don't think the storm was a coincidence."

"Okay, wait for me there. I'm going to get Ernie's keys."

"Stay where you are. I already told you, I don't need a damn babysitter."

"You have every right to be angry with me, Liam. But you can't avoid me forever. I'll need to syphon your energy soon."

After the incident at the volcano, I begged Logan to switch my schedule so I didn't have to work any shifts with Renae. I didn't explain why, and he didn't ask.

"If I wanted to avoid you, I wouldn't have answered the phone at two in the morning."

"Forcing me to keep my distance isn't the answer. I can't protect you if you keep pushing me away." My stomach twisted at the plea in her voice. "I don't know what game Cyrena and Marcella are playing, but I don't trust them."

Neither did I, and that was why I needed Renae to stay the hell away from me, and from them. "I'm exhausted. Can we argue about this later?" I asked.

"Are you going to pick up the phone later?"

After I hung up, I devoured the chicken and rice she'd left for me, along with the contents of every single blue container in my refrigerator, hoping my intestines could keep up with my new appetite. I couldn't tell if the twisting sensation in my gut was indigestion or something else.

The only thing I was sure of was that the timing of my dream and the snowstorm weren't a coincidence. The forecasting thing took constant concentration and was hard enough to control while I was awake. How was I supposed to avoid bombarding the island with inclement weather every time I took a damn nap?

Since staying awake twenty-four seven wasn't an option, I needed to find a way to stop dreaming. The idea of popping pills and drugging myself into oblivion didn't sit well, but it was looking like the only viable solution.

Once an abomination, always an abomination. My father's words pricked at the back of my brain. Had he been referring to my addiction or his failed experiment? Or both?

Marcella materialized at my table. "Renae's right. You need more training."

"I don't want to see her." We both knew that was a lie.

"Fortunately, Cyrena's the only one you'll need for this particular lesson. She can project herself into your dreams, and she can teach you how to remain lucid and in control, even in sleep."

"I'm open to any option that doesn't turn me into a pill-popping junkie." I probed the old woman, and my gut told me there was more. "What's the catch?"

"You'll need to trust her while she's inside your head, or it won't work. She's been a frequent passenger in your dreams your entire life. You have nothing to fear from her in that space. You are in full control."

A chill ran down my spine at the thought of where my depraved dreams typically went. "Fine. Like I said. I'll try anything."

"Very well then. We'll begin as soon as you fall asleep." Marcella vanished. Not gone. Just invisible. My constant fucking companion. I couldn't take a dump or rub one out in the shower without wondering if they were watching. Fortunately, they'd been willing to give me space whenever I asked for a few minutes of privacy in the bathroom.

Falling asleep, however, was damn near impossible. I kept imagining them hovering next to the bed like two spectral stalkers. I tossed and turned until exhaustion finally won.

A strip of LED lights pulsed along the ceiling as I pushed the wheelchair through the sterile halls, searching for an exit. My unconscious patient's arm flopped over the side and dragged the ground. When I circled around him, I came face to face with my doppelganger.

The hiss of silk over smooth tile slithered through my brain, causing the hairs to raise on the back of my neck. Cyrena's green dress trailed behind her like a shimmering green tail. The harsh light made her hollow cheeks, smeared lipstick, and smudged mascara appear more sickly than menacing.

"Trust me, darling, this look was all the rage in 1981." She brushed past me, lifting my doppelganger's hand. A tingling sensation crawled across my palm.

"What are you doing?" I asked.

"Helping you break the wall between your conscious and subconscious mind. Let's play a game, shall we?" She crouched in front of my patient and pushed the hospital gown up his thighs.

"Stop."

Cyrena pouted as she climbed into his lap. "You're going to have to try harder than that, handsome." She leaned forward and whispered in his ear, and her voice filled my head. "It's just a dream. Nothing that happens here is real. We can do anything you like, as often as you like." She fisted his hair with her bony hand and yanked his head back. My neck prickled where her tongue licked the column of his throat.

I closed my eyes against the disgusting sensation. "And we can stop anytime you want, but you'll need to push past the haze and bring your conscious mind in here with you."

The inside of my lip throbbed as I bit down hard and focused on the pain. When I opened my eyes, I was the one sitting under her frail body in the wheelchair.

"You always were a quick learner. Let's play another round, shall we? Would you prefer me like this?" She brought my hands to her hips as she transformed into Monika, and the scent of coconut filled my nose as she started unbuttoning her coffee-stained shirt.

"What? No."

"Pity. I enjoyed playing her in your dreams." Even her voice sounded like Mons, deep and sultry. "Though I suppose this one will do." She phased into Renae, auburn hair spilling over her naked shoulders and full breasts. Six undulating syphons rose from her back and roved over me, up my arms and down my torso to the throbbing bulge tenting my hospital gown. "I'll let you do all the things she won't." I moaned as one of Renae's syphons coiled around my cock the way it had so many times in my dreams. But the woman on my lap wasn't Renae.

I gathered the air around me and shoved her off my lap with a violent gust as I stood, disgusted with myself for letting the monstrous impostor touch me like that. For wanting to let her continue. Cyrena laughed as she sprawled on the floor thirty feet away, her body bending the wrong way as she returned to her true form.

Lightning wreathed my wrists. I let it extend and wrap around her long neck. "How many times have you fucked me in here with someone else's body?"

"You've been practicing." She smiled as she tipped her had back and let me tighten the noose.

"How many times, Cyrena?"

"I haven't been counting, darling."

I released her and positioned the wheelchair between us, grasping it for support as nausea ripped through me. "You're a goddamn succubus."

She reached up and fingered the burn marks on her throat. "That title belongs to your Gi'dari. Though I believe she prefers the term reaper. Succubus is so fourteenth century."

"I don't care what you call it. I still feel fucking violated."

"Everything we've ever done has been consensual. You are in complete control here. I'm just along for the ride."

"You're seriously twisted. What about Marcella?"

"You are not her type, darling."

"That's not what I meant."

Cyrena's sneer faltered for a brief second as she rose. "Your connection to Renae is new. As you transition through your lives together, you'll come to understand true commitment has nothing to do with sex or even love. It's about honor. Marcella honors me with her devotion, and I honor her by treating her as an equal partner and never taking advantage of the bond's compulsory imbalance. I allow her the space she needs to make her own decisions. I've never forced her to stay, and I would never dishonor her by commanding her away. That's what's real. The things we do in here," she gestured to the sterile ceiling and walls, "are only in your head. Now, conjure up an exit and take us somewhere less depressing. This dreadful place reminds me of the Nursery."

Something tugged at my sternum. Renae. I bolted through the maze of hallways, led by the pull in my chest. It tightened each time I turned in the wrong direction and loosened when I followed the right path, which ended abruptly in front of a steel door large enough to drive a dump truck through.

"Bravo, darling. You found the exit." Cyrena's long black hair whipped in the breeze as I manipulated the air current to slide the door open. A rush of frigid wind blew into the hall.

"Not an exit," I said as I strode into a tunnel lined with ice.

My breath crystalized in front of my face as we descended deeper into what had to be the base of a mountain. The corridor opened into a massive cavern that stretched farther than I could see. The frosted walls and ceiling glittered like stars, reflecting the lights pulsing from thousands of vertical twin tanks.

The set closest to us lit up as I ran my hand over the glass, revealing the forms of identical boys in their early teens. I passed row after row of lifeless humanoid bodies in every stage of growth, suspended in amniotic sleep.

Another set of tanks lit as Cyrena touched them. "You'll be an excellent deceptor when the ability manifests. Your commitment to detail is impressive."

I stalked up and down, row after row, until the ache in my chest eased in front of an unlit tank. "I don't understand. How can it be empty?"

"Because she's not here, Liam. It's just a dream, remember?" The adjacent tank lit as Cyrena leaned against it.

Renae's red hair floated around her face. Her eyes popped open when I knocked on the glass, but they were all wrong. Milky white, lifeless.

I ran my hands over metal and glass, looking for a seam or release valve.

"The tanks open from the inside." Cyrena pointed to a handle on the lid above Renae's head.

"I'm gonna get you out of there, chica." Her empty eyes stared straight ahead.

Cyrena grasped my shoulders as I glanced around for something I could use to smash the glass.

"Liam, that isn't Renae. It's a dream. Look around; you've created a replica of the Nursery from her memory. When did she show you this?"

"I've never seen this place before."

"You must have. You wouldn't have been able to recreate it, unless—"

Hundreds of egg-shaped auras came into focus, solidifying into men and women, all wearing the same stark white uniform with different colored symbols on their backs.

Cyrena spun in a circle, eyes wide. "You're not dreaming, darling, you're a traveler." She gripped my arm as if she needed to steady herself.

"What the hell is a traveler?"

"An extremely rare gift. A gift the original Anzillu never had. Even the gods didn't possess the ability to separate their consciousness and travel away from their physical form without dying. Aside from you, I've only met two others. One was your mother."

"That explains the out-of-body experiences I've been having since the accident."

"This has happened before?"

I shrugged as a man with a tablet approached Renae's pod. His brow furrowed as he studied her glassy eyes. He hit something on the screen, and the tank hummed in response. Renae's muscles twitched, and her eyes closed.

Concern flashed across Cyrena's pinched face. "Liam, how many times have you left your body?"

"I don't know. Half a dozen." I peered over the man's shoulder and read the screen on his tablet.

Husk 061044440160*02. Neural Lace Status: inactive.

Muscle Activity Error 719. Corrective shock successful, 12.3 volts.

A message popped up. Run Primary Husk Diagnostics? He tapped on the screen, and a photo of Renae in a white uniform appeared, along with a scrolling list of reports I had no idea how to read. He tapped a map icon and zoomed in on a real-time satellite image of the summit covered in snow. A pulsing green arrow hovered over the corner of the building that housed the lab. The man clicked on a tab in the sidebar menu and opened CCTV footage from inside the room, where Renae sat at her computer eating a pink frosted donut.

My stomach dropped. Were there cameras in the server room? "Why would they spy on their own operatives?"

"The Corps has layer upon layer of oversight. Like any bureaucracy, it's their greatest strength and weakness. Amelia, your mother, knew how to hack their system. She manipulated loopholes and blind spots to steal the Corps' DNA database and cloning tank blueprints." A smile curled her thin lips. "She was one of the Corps' best hackers. The missing files were never recovered."

Cyrena's body went eerily still as her eyes glazed over. She reached up and placed her hands on either side of my head. "Time to go, darling."

A sharp pain shot through my skull, and I fell backward to the stone floor.

☙

"What that hell?" Blood gushed from my nose as I sat up and crammed the bed sheet against my face.

Marcella's form flickered next to my nightstand. "You were bleeding, and I couldn't wake you, so I asked Cyrena to pull you out of the dream."

"He wasn't sleeping, he was traveling." The two women exchanged a dark look.

"What aren't you telling me?"

Marcella sighed and sat on the edge of my mattress. "Traveling takes a tremendous toll. Every time you cleave yourself away from your body, it leaves a scar, fine cracks in your energy spectrum. There are only so many fissures your consciousness can withstand before it shatters. That's why so few travelers remain."

"Great, another gift that can kill me."

They both stared at my bloody face.

"It's just a nosebleed. I haven't had one since..." Last week, in class, when I hallucinated seeing Renae at the summit. And at the play, with

Monika, when I was daydreaming about Renae. Only it hadn't felt like a dream. It felt like I was there with her, listening to her conversation with that pretty boy neighbor of hers. The same way I'd eavesdropped on her conversation with the cop, and at the hospital the day we met.

The room tilted sideways as I stood. "I need to talk to Renae."

"Liam, you can't tell her," Marcella said. "Renae may be bonded to you, but she belongs to the Corps. If they find out you're a traveler, they'll execute you, wipe your memories, and force you into service just like they did with your mother."

"And ruin the game the two of you are playing at?" I glanced back and forth between them. "Who do you really work for?"

Marcella looked to Cyrena, who folded her twig-like arms, refusing to say any more. I shook my head and stumbled toward the bathroom.

"Where are you going?" Cyrena asked.

"To take a dump and a shower," I lied. "I'd appreciate a little privacy, if it's not too much to ask."

Steam filled the room as I leaned against the back of the toilet, still fully clothed. It was the only way to keep my nosy entourage away. I let my mind drift to Renae. To the way her naked body melted against mine the night she let me help her forget her name and how she'd wrapped my fingers around her throat and asked me to claim her. My imagination went to all kinds of depraved places until I felt a familiar tug at my sternum. I let it pull me away from my body the same way it had so many times before.

An office with floor-to-ceiling windows overlooking a partially frozen lake materialized around me. A middle-aged woman with gray eyes sat behind an oversized glass desk, pinching the bridge of her nose. Renae sat with her back to me, her hair pulled into a tight braid. She was wearing the same white uniform as the people I'd seen in the Nursery, a black star with an eye at the center emblazoned on her back.

"I thought you had the situation under control," the older woman said.

My bare feet made soft impressions in the thick carpet as I crept around Renae. She had some sort of device in her ears. Like a pair of oversized AirPods.

"Anyone could have called from that extension," Renae said in the same cool tone she used when she lied. "The Global Operation Dynamics logo and help line is literally plastered to the side of the server."

The woman rapped her manicured nails on the glass. "I understand you have a connection, but he's also your mark. Is his research going to be a problem?"

"I'll take care of it."

"You may have to go back to your original tactics. Seduce and distract. If he keeps poking around, I won't be able to deflect the Corps from looking in his direction."

"I understand." Renae pulled the device from her ear and disappeared.

Her handler tapped something on the desktop. The windows and walls and carpet disappeared, replaced by a sterile white room. The glass desk was the only thing that remained. She glanced over her shoulder before loading a new simulation. The cell-like room took the shape of a small library lined with books and boxes of files. She stood and fished through one of the cardboard boxes and pulled out a photo. I circled behind her, and the room began to fade as I lost my hold on the location.

"We'll be together again soon, my sweet child."

My stomach dropped as my eyes landed on the picture of a young woman with golden curls smiling at the infant clutched in her arms. The same photo I carried in my wallet.

# Chapter Twenty-Six

# RENAE

I sat on the stiff hotel mattress and tucked the neural-lace pods back in their case. At some point, I was going to have to tell Ziggy that Liam refused to see me and that he had no intention of joining the Corps or giving up on his research. I couldn't blame him for wanting to cling to a normal life. Especially after everything I'd put him through.

My phone vibrated on the nightstand. Butterflies took flight in my chest when I glanced at the message notification. The acid that bloomed on my tongue told me Liam wasn't over his anger at me for orchestrating the deception on the volcano, but at least he was texting me again.

*We need to talk about the missing files.*

My first instinct was to type back something sarcastic or even flirty to lighten his heavy mood, but we were well past all that now. It was better to be direct.

*You can still use the data sets to do your calculations. The missing files will only increase your margin of error by a fraction. Logan won't dock you points for that. He may not even notice.*

Liam responded immediately. *I'm not talking about my dissertation.*

I winced at the sudden bitterness in my mouth as a bone-weary exhaustion that was all mine swept through me. The time away from him had helped me redefine where he ended and I began. I was grateful for the reprieve, but the truth was, I missed him. I missed his snarky comments and deep voice. I missed the way his denim eyes followed my every move when we were in the same room. Gods, I missed the ability to sleep soundly, knowing he was safe curled up next to me. I'd barely slept since the the night he sent me away.

*How long have you known?*

*You'll need to be more specific*, I replied.

*About my mother.*

I toed off my boots. Cyrena must have told him how his mother had been killed. *I'm sorry you had to find out that way. No one deserves to be hunted down and exterminated like that. I wanted to kill Cyrena myself when she told me. She likes to play games. Don't let her goad you into a reaction.*

Capsaicin bloomed on my tongue as I waited for him to respond.

*What the hell does Cyrena have to do with my mother?*

My mouth went dry. *We should be having this conversation in person.*

When he didn't reply, I put the phone down and grabbed a bottle of water from the mini fridge to wash the heat from my tongue.

"Agreed."

I dropped the bottle on the floor and nearly jumped out of my skin at the sound of his voice. "Gods, you scared me." He wasn't wearing a jacket or shoes.

"Tell me the truth. How long have you known, Renae?"

"What are you talking about?"

"The very not-dead woman in the glass office overlooking a frozen lake you just fucking met with."

"I... I don't understand."

"That night in the server room, I told you about my mother, and you didn't once think I might want to know that she's alive and that you fucking work for her?"

Cold sweat broke out across my skin as I bore down on the ball of my left foot. "I don't know where you got your information, but the woman in the glass office is not your mother. Her name is Ziggy. She's my handler."

A yellow sticky note fluttered to the floor as Liam pulled the photo of his mother out of his wallet. "I watched her after you left. She had this same photo hidden in a box of files. I think it may be the missing data she stole from the Corps. She's hiding it in some kind of virtual reality program."

I backed up until my calves hit the bed. Ziggy's office was in upstate New York. My heart skidded to a stop. There was only one way he could have seen it. "You're a traveler."

"Why does everyone keep saying it like that?"

"Like what?"

"Like it's a death sentence."

"Because it is." I dropped to the bed and caught a whiff of my sweaty armpits as I reached up and loosened my too-tight braid.

The mattress dipped under Liam's weight as he eased down next to me, keeping his distance. I probably smelled atrocious. I hadn't washed my hair in a week. Could travelers smell?

"Are you sure?" I asked. "That she's your mother?" She was my handler, but I knew absolutely nothing about her or her life outside of the virtual meeting space. I'd never met her in person. Her office could be anywhere. She could be anyone.

Liam rubbed his sternum and studied me with an intensity that used to put me on edge. Now it just felt... warm. "I'm sure," he said.

A ginger-infused fizz bubbled on my tongue as Liam brushed a stray hair away from my face. "What's she like?"

"Annoying, brutally honest, and good at pushing my buttons." I shook my head at the realization. "Gods, you are related."

The scar on his brow deepened. "I want to talk to her."

"You can't." How could I say it without tainting the obvious love he had for the mother he'd never met? The emotion was so powerful its effervescence was burning the inside of my nose and making my eyes water. The Corps had to be watching her. How had she retained her memories? How had she managed to hide, all this time, in plain sight? Did Cyrena and Marcella know? Was that why they were keeping Liam alive? To draw her out? Would they try to execute her again? Would they do the same to Liam once he'd served his purpose?

My breath came in short gasps as hot tears threatened to spill down my cheeks.

Liam scooted closer and wrapped his arm around my shoulders. He pressed his lips to the top of my head and inhaled. "You still smell like my shampoo."

"Cedar and salt," I said, leaning into him.

"What's going on in your head, chica? I'm having trouble following your thoughts."

"Ziggy hasn't made contact with you for a reason. Cyrena and Marcella hunted her down and executed her, but they never recovered the missing data she stole. They could be using us to draw her out. If you go to her again, it will destroy whatever safety net she's built around herself." I angled toward him so that we were face to face. "We need to protect her, Liam. Aside from you, she's the only person I trust."

"You're right. There's just one problem. I can't keep Cyrena out of my head. They're with me twenty-four seven. She's even been inserting herself into my damn dreams." Liam flinched, and a sudden shot of bile pressed at the back of my throat.

"I can help with that, but you're not going to like it." Letting me feed on him was one thing. Allowing me to rearrange and remove his memories was another. I'd tasted the disgust when he'd asked me about my gift and the soul I'd consumed. I'd told him the truth, and he would never see me as anything other than what I was. A soul-sucking monster.

Liam reached forward and cupped my face in his hands. "Stop that line of thinking right now, chica. We're all fucking monsters. We can't change the festering piles of shit in our past that made us this way. Don't let anyone else dictate who you are. Only we get to choose what kind of monster we become. You could have chosen to walk away the day I hit you. You could have let me die. Even though you regret it, you gave up a piece of yourself to save me, and I don't deserve it. I don't deserve you."

"I..." The words got trapped in the ginger-laced fizz bubbling up in my chest and my throat and my nose.

His thumbs swept over my cheeks, wiping away the tears. "Tell me what we need to do to protect my mother from the deceptors."

"There's a technique Ziggy taught me to help mitigate my panic attacks by burying an unpleasant memory inside a tomb of sorts. I'll need to use my syphons to pluck out your memory of her and inject it into a different one. You won't lose any continuity or nuance, and anyone reading you from the outside will only see the surface thought."

"Hiding in plain sight?"

"Exactly. You should pick a boring memory as the tomb, one that Cyrena will skim over and never have the desire to dig into, but it needs to be something that wouldn't seem out of place if she catches you thinking about it frequently. Something mundane like your favorite song lyrics."

"I've got one. Just do it."

"Are you sure?" My stomach twisted. "I've never actually done it to anyone other than myself."

Liam grasped my hands. "I trust you."

I squared my shoulders and unfurled my syphons. Liam groaned when they struck his chest and began to burrow. Could he feel them? "I need you to focus on the memory you want to use as a cover." Red wine, oaky with notes of cherries and chocolate, bloomed on my tongue, decadent and warm and oddly familiar. "Are you sure you want to use this one?" I asked. "It tastes... significant."

"Trust me, chica, Cyrena won't look here."

I nodded and let the delicate filaments inside my syphons emerge and lick through his consciousness, tasting every thread until I found what I was looking for—the sweet and sour tang that tainted every thought he had about his mother. I extracted them gently and deposited them deep inside the rich memory he'd chosen.

Liam's eyes tracked my syphons as I reeled them in with a yawn. "What was your cover memory?" I asked.

He picked up a strand of my hair and slowly wound it around his fingers. "The way you tasted when I went down on you."

Heat crept up my neck as I brought my hands to my face. "Oh my gods."

"It's the one constant thought in my head and the last place Cyrena will ever look."

He stood and picked up the yellow sticky note from the floor and handed it to me. "I believe this belongs to you. I won't take advantage of the bond again. I promise."

"That list was a gift, as was the amended one I left in your glove box last week."

"You've already given me enough."

While I appreciated his chivalry, it was egregiously misplaced. "Maybe I want something from you." I stood and ran my hands over his muscled chest. He felt solid and warm beneath my palms. How was that even possible? "I made the lists of my own free will and volition. My choices. Promise me you'll remember that the next time we see each other in the flesh." I grabbed my towel and toiletry bag off the dresser. "Now if you'll excuse me, I haven't taken a shower or slept in five days."

# Chapter Twenty-Seven

# LIAM

My hands shook as I opened the glove box and pulled out the hot-pink sticky note.

*Dear Liam,*

*I trust you with my heart, my soul, and my body. I want to sleep beside you and wake up in your arms. I want you to kiss me, always, and I really, really want you to fuck me in every depraved and delicious way you can imagine.*

*XO, Renae*

This woman was definitely gonna be the death of me. I was a stubborn asshole for refusing to read the note earlier. She'd been waiting patiently for a week for me to get my damn head straight, and there was no way in hell I was going to make her wait until the next time I saw her in the flesh to honor her choices.

A cloud of steam engulfed me as I went ghost mode and passed through the door into the hotel bathroom. Unlike bursting a cloud, holding back the tide, or trying to direct a lightning strike, the traveling thing took zero effort. All I had to do was think about Renae, and I was with her. The only part that took concentration was phasing from ghost mode back into a physical form once I got there. Something I 100 percent planned to work on as I stared at her naked perfection through the clear plastic shower curtain.

Soapy water trickled down her stomach and into the tuft of soft curls between her thighs. I wanted to spread them apart and make her squirm with my tongue.

Renae's hands slid down her belly as she propped her left foot on the edge of the tub and cupped her pussy. She arched her back and let out a breathy little groan as two of her fingers disappeared in the folds.

I felt my dick harden and thanked whatever broken law of physics allowed my body to shift into solid form.

Water soaked through my T-shirt and jeans as I pushed back the curtain and stepped into the shower with her.

Renae backed up to make room for me. "I was wondering if you were planning to join me or if you preferred to watch."

"How'd you know I was here?"

She took my hand and placed it between her breasts. Above her sternum. "Because I can feel you. Right here."

In that moment I knew there wasn't anything I wouldn't give up to reciprocate the bond. My life. My career. My family. My freedom. She'd entrusted me with her heart and I wouldn't do anything to dishonor that, including contaminating her head with any more declarations of love. She'd already given me more than I deserved.

Renae toyed with the sleeve of my T-shirt and scowled. "You're overdressed."

I peeled it off and let it drop to the floor with a wet slap.

"How do you get the clothes to travel with you? They're inanimate objects; they shouldn't be able to—"

"Do you really want to hear my theory on quantum anomalies right now?" I asked.

Renae reached up and traced the scar on my forehead. Her fingers ghosted over my face. They fluttered along my jaw, down my neck and chest, leaving a trail of chicken skin in their wake. "Kiss me."

I threaded my fingers through her hair and swept my tongue over those red-wine lips, coaxing them open. When she let me in, it was all I could do not to let my energy pour down her throat and take control.

My groin throbbed as she fumbled with the button on my jeans.

"I need these gone. Now." Renae groaned and tugged at my pants.

I didn't waste any time shoving them down my thighs and barely managed to get one leg free when she pushed me against the wall and wrapped her fingers around me. She stroked slow, intensifying the deep ache in my balls. Her eyes lifted to mine as the silent thought sounded in my head, telling me exactly what she wanted.

Words lodged in my throat, and all I could do was nod. Every muscle in my body tightened as she crouched and took me into her mouth.

I watched the woman on her knees in front of me, giving me everything so I wouldn't have to take it. But I *wanted* to take it, all of it, because I was the worst kind of monster. I would never order her away from me again. Even if I could release her from the bond, I wouldn't. I would never, ever, let this woman go. She was mine.

I grasped the back of her head, holding it firm as I fucked her mouth. Her nails bit into my ass, refusing to release me when I tried to pull out. She forced my cock deeper, and holy fuck, her tight throat spasmed around my tip like she was trying to swallow me whole. I almost lost my load right then and there.

Renae might be able to come back-to-back, but I'd need time to recover. If I let her keep going, this was gonna be over way too soon and I wanted, *needed*, to be in her cunt and feel it clench around me when I came.

I forced a deep breath and pulled out as I shook off the nagging pain behind my right eye.

Renae rose with a wicked smile and wrapped her arms around my neck. "Too much?" she teased.

I growled as I took her mouth, tasting myself on her tongue as my fingers found their way to the slick slit between her thighs. "Never."

Renae bit my lip, and my vision shifted with a flash of white light.

The complaint died on my lips as a translucent shimmer rippled over her skin like summer heat hugging pavement. Her energy looped around us in golden bands as her ravenous syphons twitched behind her.

I pushed the wet hair over her shoulder and kissed her neck. "You're beautiful," I whispered.

Her syphons swept forward and curled around my arms and legs, licking and sucking at my skin, leaving a tingling sensation that made the hair on the back of my neck stand.

No way in hell I was letting her have all the fun. I cupped her breast, testing its weight in my palm as I traced little circles around her nipple. Her flesh puckered under my touch. I dipped my head and teased the pink bud, rolling it gently between my teeth as I palmed her cunt.

Renae rocked her pelvis, grinding against my hand. I dragged two fingers through her folds, pulling the wetness up to her engorged clit. Her syphons slid over my back as I repeated the motion, increasing the gentle pressure with each stroke.

"Gods, yes, just like that," she said. A syphon slithered between my legs from behind. Heat radiated through my groin as the snake-like appendage licked me from ass to shaft before coiling around my cock, squeezing and sucking in a way that had me wound tight with need.

My mouth found hers again, and she shuddered a breath as I pumped two fingers inside her. "Chica, please tell me you have condoms." I had no idea how the traveling thing worked, but I wasn't taking any chances.

"You can't get me pregnant. I don't have the necessary equipment. Oh gods, don't stop. She rocked her hips, chasing my retreating hand."

My lips traced the shell of her ear as I fingered her deep. "Tell me what you want."

"Liam, please—"

"I need you to say it."

"I want you to fuck me."

Renae hooked her legs around my waist as I lifted her against the shower wall. Every thought left my brain as she sank onto me and let out a breathy moan. The need to claim her, to make her forget she was anything other than mine, took control. She arched against me as I buried myself in her velvet cunt. My vision blurred as my bathroom came into view. I didn't want to risk dropping her if I lost my hold on the location. I carried her to the counter and focused on the feel of her around me, refusing to let go or break the connection until we were both spent.

Renae gripped the back of my neck with one hand and the edge of the counter with the other as I slid out slowly until only the tip of my glistening cock pressed at her entrance. I dragged myself through her folds and rubbed her clit with my dick.

"Liam, please, I'm so close. I need you inside me."

I forced myself to go slow, letting her stretch around me. She threw her head back and lifted her hips, taking me even deeper. My fingers worked the swollen bundle of nerves between her thighs as our bodies sought a steady rhythm. I watched her syphons retract in the mirror and vanish beneath her skin, and I swear I could feel them sucking me off inside her.

"Oh, gods." Renae clenched around me as she came. My vision blurred and I picked up the rhythm—faster and harder—as our hips slapped together. Static crept over my scalp. Something snapped behind my right eye as I came, and the darkness swallowed me whole.

# CHAPTER TWENTY-EIGHT
# RENAE

A SUCCESSION OF LOUD taps knocked inside my head.

"Is everything okay in there?" Ernie asked.

My fingers grazed the gaping wound at the back of my scalp and came away tinged with blood. Cold overspray from the shower soaked the floor.

Another hurried rap on the door. "Renae? I heard a scream. Are you all right?" Ernie asked.

The room wobbled as I peeled myself off the cold tile. A crimson pool marked the spot where my head had been. I must have slipped. Why couldn't I remember?

I grasped the edge of the counter and hoisted myself up. "There was a... a centipede," I said. "Everything's fine." Everything was not fine. Not fine at all.

I wiped the condensation off the mirror and twisted to inspect the split flesh on the back of my skull. Why wasn't it healing? A black blob in the shower caught my eye.

Not a blob. Clothes. Liam's clothes.

My stomach dropped as the memory crashed over me like a tidal wave. A hollow sensation sucked at my chest, as if something had been ripped from my core. An empty space where the bond had once been.

"No, no, no. This can't be happening." I fumbled with my leggings, dragging them up my damp legs, and barely had the tank top over my torso as I shoved the door open.

Ernie stepped aside. "Jeez, how big was that centipede?"

My heart seized as I followed his gaze to the carnage on the bathroom floor. I'd been too caught up in my own physical need to consider the danger of allowing Liam to use his new gift for... for what? Gods, what had I done? I needed to get to him. I needed to know if he was still alive.

I rubbed the raw ache beneath my sternum as if I could stitch up the hole left by the absence of Liam's presence. "I'm sorry, I need to go." The walls pressed in around me as I ran down the hall.

*Deep breath. Hold. Exhale.* I repeated the mantra until I was alone in my room. I held my breath as I called Liam's cell.

It rang several times before clicking over to voicemail. I threw my phone on the bed, pulled on my boots and a coat, and climbed out the window, landing with a muffled thud in the snow. The rising sun painted the horizon in pinks and purples, casting deep blue shadows across the stark white landscape. Shadows that could have easily hidden me if I moved between them.

I ran straight down the mountain instead.

Witnesses didn't matter.

Blowing my cover didn't matter.

Liam was the only thing that mattered.

I tripped over invisible rocks and potholes under the white powder. The snowy road eventually gave way to a sheet of black ice as I ran at an inhuman pace. I fell half a dozen times, ripping through the knees of my thin leggings and my flesh. Twisted ankles and torn ligaments would heal. The hole in my chest...

Faster—I had to go faster. My lungs burned and threatened to peel away with each breath. Friction rubbed my thighs raw. I didn't relent until my feet finally bit into loose gravel and ate up the length of his driveway. The sight of his truck sent a dry flutter through my chest like dusty moths locked inside a too-small box. Was he here? Without the bond, I couldn't be sure.

My voice cracked as I broke through the front door, nearly taking it off the hinges. "Liam?"

Marcella appeared near the bathroom. "In here."

The air evaporated from my lungs as I stepped through her staticky form. Cyrena hovered over Liam's naked corpse like a vulture. Dried blood crusted his nose and lip.

She didn't waste a moment to acknowledge my presence. Her long, bony fingers roved over his face and head and chest, as if scanning for any sign of life, as if she were checking to make sure he was dead.

I stabbed her with my syphons. "I'm going to desiccate you until your soul turns to ash in my mouth."

A sudden stinging pain wrapped around me, dropping me to my knees, paralyzing my gift, as Marcella's voice filled my head. "Release her, child. Cyrena is not to blame for this. We warned Liam about the consequences of traveling, the permanent damage it can inflict. Liam has always been headstrong, impulsive."

"And too obsessed with you to heed our warning. He couldn't resist the urge to see you. If this is anyone's fault, it's yours. You knew the risks. You should have sent him away."

My stomach roiled as I thrashed against the truth and the invisible net searing my skin. She was right. This was all my fault. If I hadn't reminded Liam of the letter I'd left in his truck, he wouldn't have used his gift to return to the summit. But I'd wanted him to return. Desperately. And now he was gone. The tears rolling down my cheeks had nothing to do with the excruciating pain of Marcella's isolation net.

Cyrena's icy voice cut through my skull. "He's not dead. Not yet."

Marcella loosened her psychic grip on my body. "I'm going to release you. Slowly. And you are going to retract your suckers from Cyrena. Are we in agreement, child?"

I nodded, and the pain slowly unraveled as she retracted her gift. My fingers pressed to Liam's throat. I didn't dare breathe until I felt a faint pulse tick beneath his clammy flesh.

Cyrena leaned back, letting me attempt to read him. To search his energy as she'd been doing. Only there was no energy left to read. Not a single thread. Just the barely perceptible rise and fall of his bare chest.

Energy poured down my arms into his body. Not in a desperate, searing rush like it had after the accident or at the beach. This time, it pulsed like a heartbeat. His heartbeat. I focused on the soft cadence as images formed in my mind. Muscles and tendons and bone defined themselves. Everything seemed normal enough, but I wasn't a doctor.

"Do you even know what you're doing?" Cyrena hissed.

I ignored her and kept searching. When Liam vanished from my bathroom at the lodge, I'd felt a sharp pain behind my right eye. I pried his eyelids open one at a time. His left pupil constricted under the bright light. His right stared back at me blankly. A cold black marble circled by a thin blue halo.

My fingertips spread around his scalp. I pulsed my stunted healing gift through layers of bone and tissue and crept along the spiderweb of veins inside his brain. I scanned the area behind his right eye and found what looked like a ruptured vessel and pool of dark blood.

I couldn't fix this. Not without the bond. Not without causing more damage. I pulled out my phone and dialed 911 with trembling hands.

Everything that happened from that moment forward felt as though I were watching it from a mile away, keenly aware of only the hollow sensation spreading from my chest. Untethered, my body and mind became weightless in the storm spinning around me. The emergency operator's steady voice on the other end of the line was the only thing keeping me anchored in the nightmare.

Numbness crept through me as I watched the medevac team strap Liam to a stretcher and wheel him out the front door, two flickering forms trailing behind him like a pair of spectral guardians.

Silence smothered the empty bungalow. My thoughts rattled inside my empty head, too loud. Kona was a three-hour drive. The truck would need gas, but I'd left my wallet—everything—at the lodge. My hands and feet moved of their own accord. I dumped out the contents of his backpack and stuffed his wallet and cell phone into the pockets of my jacket before bolting out the door.

Sickly sweet fumes tickled the hairs in my nose as I pumped the gas. The same nauseating scent that preceded the end of my first life. It had been there too when I knelt beside Liam's body sprawled in the street the day we met. The scent that plagued my dreams. I heaved over and vomited the contents of my stomach onto the pavement next to his rear tire.

Back on the road, I pulled out Liam's phone. My hand shook as it rang against my ear. Once. Twice. Three times.

"Hey, Lee, it's not a great time. Can I call you later?"

"Connor, it's Renae." My voice came out raw, jagged.

"What's wrong? Where's Liam?"

"They took him to the Kona Trauma Center. In a helicopter. I... I think he had an aneurysm."

"Shit. Where?"

"In the bathroom." My wet eyes squinted against the too-bright sun.

"No, where in his body, Renae? Heart, brain, abdomen?"

The phone slipped from my sweaty palm and landed in my lap. "Sorry, in his head."

"Were you with him?"

"Yes, I mean, sort of."

"Renae, I need you to tell me what happened."

"I don't know. One minute he was fine and then he grasped his head and collapsed." My stomach rolled again, threatening to heave.

"Was he conscious when they took him?"

"No."

"Fuck." He rattled off more questions I couldn't answer.

"Connor, how bad is it? Will he recover from this?"

"I'm going to call the hospital. Keep his phone close. I'll be there as soon as I can."

Connor hung up and I cranked up the radio, filling the empty space with noise to keep my mind from spiraling. Was Liam still alive? What was I willing to do if he wasn't?

After ninety minutes with no word from Connor, I called again. Another man answered.

"Hi, Renae, it's Patrick. Connor's getting our tickets transferred. We should be there this afternoon." The gentle timber of his deep voice draped over me like a blanket.

"From New York?" I asked.

"No, we're still in Maui. We were supposed to fly home today."

"Right, I forgot. I'm sorry I ruined your honeymoon."

"Oh honey, don't you dare apologize. None of this is your fault."

*Agree to disagree.* I choked back a sob as Liam's words ghosted through my head, and I couldn't stop the hot tears from spilling down my cheeks.

"Okay, I'm gonna hand you off to Connor. Hang in there."

Connor's matter-of-fact tone was unintentionally abrasive. Salt to Patrick's honey. "Are you driving?"

"Yes."

"Pull over and let me know when you've stopped."

"Connor, just tell me." My knuckles blanched as I gripped the steering wheel as if it could keep me from coming apart at the seams.

"Not until you pull over."

I swerved off the road and screeched to a halt. "I'm stopped."

"You were right. Lee had an aneurysm in his right prefrontal cortex. The good news is that it seems to have clotted on its own, which is a miracle in itself."

"And the bad news?"

"His intracranial pressure is dangerously high. They're prepping him for surgery now. They're going to put in a drain to evacuate the excess fluid. It should relieve the swelling and hopefully reduce the extent of long-term brain damage."

My heart climbed into my throat. "What kind of brain damage?"

"We won't know until he wakes up, but you need to prepare yourself, Renae. He may have serious visual and cognitive impairments."

My breath hitched as I stepped into Liam's room in the ICU. An oxygen mask covered his mouth and nose, and his body was strapped to the bed like a prisoner. His sun-kissed curls were gone. Shaved to accommodate the orange tube stapled to his scalp. It curved down behind his ear and connected to a bag hanging from a hook beneath his bed.

I did my best not to look at the tube coming out of his brain or the bag of bloody fluid and concentrated instead on the rise and fall of his chest. I placed my palm on Liam's stubbled cheek. His skin still felt clammy, unfamiliar.

A nurse in dark blue scrubs stepped into the room, and the numbness that had settled into my body began to crack with questions I was too afraid to voice.

"I'm Danny, I'll be looking after Liam today."

"Why is he in restraints?" The words came out garbled, like water slipping over rocks.

"It's just a precaution until the drain is removed. We can't risk him trying to get up or pulling out the tube when he wakes up."

"When will that be?" I asked, surprised by the sudden steadiness of my voice that belied my wobbling legs.

The nurse glanced at his watch. "The anesthesia should be worn off by now. His intracranial pressure is coming down, but we won't know the extent of his coma until the neurologist makes an assessment."

"Coma?" I grasped the bed rail to keep from wavering.

"It's not uncommon considering—"

"No. There has to be something you can give him to wake him up. He has to come back. I need you to wake him up right now."

Chamomile laced my tongue as the nurse's lips pursed in a sympathetic smile. "I'm afraid there's no alternative to the healing effects of time. Liam's brain needs to reboot, so to speak. You don't want to rush that process."

"You people put men on the moon and created computers that fit in your pocket, for gods sakes. You're telling me you can't wake an unconscious man? There has to be something you can do." My armpits went damp as heat crept up my neck and set my ears on fire.

"I understand your frustration," the nurse said, his voice softening. "Waiting is the hardest part. The best thing you can do for him right now is to remain hopeful and patient." He glanced at his watch again. "I'm afraid I have to ask you to leave the room for a few minutes. The doctor will be coming through on rounds shortly. There's a café downstairs. The coffee is terrible, but the food is decent. The next few days may be difficult. Don't forget to take care of yourself."

Marcella appeared next to me, her hand on my shoulder. A warm weariness spread through me as her voice filled my head. "He's right. You look like you haven't eaten or slept in days."

"Gods, that's it. When was the last time Liam ate anything?" I asked Marcella.

The nurse flipped through Liam's chart. "We don't have that information."

"Breakfast, eighteen hours ago," Marcella replied.

I took a step closer to the nurse. "Liam has a hyper metabolism. He needs a constant intake of nutrition. You need to put him on a feeding tube immediately."

"I... I didn't see that in his chart. I'll mention it to his attending physician, but they usually prefer to wait and see how much he improves over a twenty-four-hour period before ordering an NG tube."

I latched on to the nurse with my gift. "I'm not going anywhere until you feed him." The syphons burrowed deeper, searching for the right thread to tug. My mouth went paper dry as the man's emotions played across my tongue. There. A faint yeasty flavor coated the inside of my mouth as I teased out his confidence. "If you suggest it to the doctor; you might save his life."

The nurse squared his shoulders. "I need you to step out of the room so I can call the doctor in to discuss it."

"If he wakes up, I want to be notified immediately." My eyes landed on Marcella, and her chin dipped in agreement.

I wandered out of the ICU begrudgingly in search of caffeine. The term café was a generous descriptor for what I found—a windowless room with four small tables, a refrigerated vending machine, and an instant coffee dispenser with a handwritten sign taped over the front that read *Outta Order, E Kala Mai*.

The hollow ache in my chest had expanded to my stomach. Anything I put in it was likely to be rejected and sent back up, but Marcella was right. I needed to force myself to eat something if I wanted to avoid an involuntary hibernation. I swiped Liam's credit card through the reader and made my selection—cellophane wrapped sandwich triangles and a yogurt cup. A message scrolled across the pin pad screen. *Declined. Insert cash to complete purchase.*

Something inside me cracked. My hands grasped the edges of the refrigerated case, rocking it back and forth. Yogurt cups and sandwiches jumped from their coiled nests and plummeted to the bottom.

A scream tore at my throat. The metal edges of the case crumpled under my grip. Glass cracked as I thrashed and pounded and yelled until snot choked off my voice and I coughed myself blue. I slumped forward.

Silent sobs stole the air from my lungs. What if he couldn't control his gift when he woke up? What if I couldn't repair the bond? What if he didn't wake up? What if I never got the chance to tell him I loved him?

I collapsed against the vending machine, pressing my cheek against the barrier that separated me from everything I couldn't have.

Cyrena appeared next to me. "Are you done having an emotional breakdown over egg salad and strawberry yogurt?"

"I can't feel the bond." I sniffled and rolled my forehead against the cracked glass.

"I know."

"The Gi'dari is supposed to be irrevocable. How could it be severed by a coma?"

"There's only one force strong enough to sever a bond. Liam isn't in a coma. He's in the Void."

# Chapter Twenty-Nine

# RENAE

A SINGLE TEXT TIED up the loose ends of my life.

*Protocol 8.*

It was done. In a matter of hours, Renae Martin would no longer exist. I stole a scalpel from the hospital and removed my tracker. The filaments hissed as I crushed it against Liam's dash before driving back to Hilo.

How much Ziggy knew about what had happened to him or where he was, I didn't know. I couldn't risk telling her. Not when there was a better than good chance that she'd try to stop me from deactivating my husk.

Cyrena followed my every movement at a distance. She'd given up trying to convince me that my plan was doomed to fail. Still, she maintained her spectral projection, reminding me of her constant presence. To intimidate me? For moral support? To see if I'd truly go through with it? Her motives no longer concerned me.

The old souls told stories about the spirits held captive and tortured by the sentient life-form that occupied the space between worlds. The Void was an energy, a place, and weblike structure so large that its gravity literally held the multiverse together. Like a carnivorous plant, it fed on whatever happened to be drawn into its snare. Tethered to neither the world of the living nor the dead, travelers could exist in both places at once, making them susceptible to being sucked in and devoured.

There were two problems with all those stories. If escaping the Void was impossible, where did the tales originate? And if the Nūkiri could puncture the barrier to send a soul in, there had to be a way to pull someone out. At least, that's what I told myself. I knew it was a thin, frayed line of reasoning, but it was the thread of hope to which I clung as I poured a gallon of milk into the sink. The heavy liquid left a slimy residue on the metal where it spiraled the drain.

"What's your plan?" Cyrena asked. She opened and closed a phantom hand around an apple, as if she were testing its firm flesh.

I dragged the already too-full garbage bag across the floor to the island. "I'm going to use Liam's gift as leverage. When the Nūkiri find out that he's one of the last travelers, they'll have a vested interest in acquiring him."

"Yes, I'm sure they'll be positively giddy to erase their four-thousand-year-old Anzillu eradication edict to retrieve him."

My stomach twisted into knots. "That's why you're going to go with me to act as my witness. You're an ancient soul. You've known other Anzillu. You need to tell them he's not like the ones who came before, that he's not an abomination. They'll listen to you."

"They were innocent children. What was done to them was the abomination. Even if the Nūkiri agree to see you, there will be no trial, no opportunity to argue your case. When you place your hand on their Eye, they will know your every thought, action, and deed. You cannot hide anything from them, no matter how deeply you've buried it." The green silk of her gown shifted as she twisted toward me. "My first child was chosen as an Anzillu. He served them dutifully, and when he was no longer of use, I watched them feed him to the Void. Trust me, you do not want them to read me. It will not help your case."

"I'm sorry," I said as I blinked away the wetness pooling at the corners of my eyes.

"The punishment for begging for my son's life was a two-thousand-year inscription in the Corps. Imagine what they'll do to you. An irreverent deserter who's abandoned her post. There is no greater offense than disloyalty. They'll send you straight into the Void."

I bit back a smile. "I'm counting on it."

The overloaded garbage bag tore as I dragged it down the steps.

A long shadow fell over me as I collected the slimy contents.

"Bit of a mess you've gotten yourself into," Jason said.

"I'm busy right now, Jason." I didn't intend for the words to snap from my lips like a fly swatter, but I didn't have the time or the patience for a filter.

He crouched down and stilled my hands. "Let me help you." Warmth pulsed up my arm the same way it had when I used my healing gift on Liam.

I pulled away from him and stumbled back on my haunches. "What are you?"

He tugged on his ear, just like his grandfather. "There is nothing as visible as that which we try our best to hide," he said in Mr. Ito's gentle, withered voice.

"You're a mimic." While a traveler could occupy two temporal places, a mimic could occupy two, or more, physical bodies at the same time.

"I'm also an isolator and a healer. I really thought I'd blown my cover that night you got sick at dinner when I tried to alleviate your ailment. But you weren't sick at all, were you?"

"Who do you work for?"

"The same as you. Ziggy is livid, by the way."

*We have eyes everywhere.* That's what Ziggy had said. I scrambled to my feet and backed away as Jason stuffed the last piece of trash into the bag and tied a knot in the hole.

"I've already initiated my exit plan. You can't stop me from returning to Almega."

He dropped the bag on the sidewalk and stepped toward me. "She didn't send me to stop you; she sent me to help you. What's your plan? Please tell me it isn't skydiving. There's nothing I hate more than reclaiming a liquified husk for the Corps."

I glanced up at my living room window, willing Cyrena to wonder what was taking so long. I needed to stall. Jason may have lied and pretended to be my friend, but I wasn't going to drag him into this with me, or risk implicating Ziggy in my betrayal of the Corps.

"There's too much time to back out and pull the ripcord when you jump," I said as I scanned his smooth calves, assessing whether I could outrun him and get to the volcano first.

My muscles coiled, ready to bolt as I compressed my energy into an explosive charge and tore across the parking lot.

The rapid slap of feet speeding across pavement sounded behind me. I cut across the grass and slipped in a patch of red mud. A firm arm circled around my waist. My feet lifted from the ground as we spun around.

"She said you'd try to run."

"I thought we were friends."

"We are. That's why I'm going to help you peel off this husk without destroying it."

"And how exactly do you plan to do that without a stasis tank?"

"What makes you think I don't have a tank? How do you think I cloned the old man's body?"

ॐ

Jason ushered me past rows of feathery ferns, spikey palms, and wide leafed philodendrons.

"The tank is in the warehouse, in the refrigerated storage room. I had it installed after I acquired Mr. Ito."

"Acquired?" My stomach rolled. Before the Corps developed the cloning technology, watchers were forced to possess humans. To steal their bodies and masquerade in their skin. My heart clenched for the sweet old man.

"I don't take my hosts without consent. Mr. Ito has stage four lung cancer. I offered to remove his disease in exchange for the brief use of his body. When I'm done with it, he'll be able to return to his life, cancer free."

At least he'd given Mr. Ito a choice.

I cringed as we entered the room of ghost-white ferns suspended in chemical drying tanks. "Please tell me I'm not going to be bleached like one of these."

"It's a process," Jason said. "I don't have access to the Nursery's inventory of proprietary chemicals to create the amniotic stasis fluid, so I found a workaround." His eyes traveled from my head to my feet. "You won't bleach out completely, but your new death shade will be pale."

It couldn't be any worse than the charred appearance I'd been stuck with the last time I died.

"The tank is through here." Jason gestured to the concrete block structure at the back of the room.

"How does this work?" I asked, more than a little nervous.

"It will feel like you're drowning, just like the quickening when you woke in your husk at the Nursery, before you climbed out of the tank," he explained. "Once you've detached from your body, I'll need at least a month to prepare it for reanimation. If there's anything you'd like to change about your hair, skin, or eye color, tell me now."

"Don't bother. I won't be coming back," I said.

Jason unlocked the door, and I followed him into the refrigerated room.

# Chapter Thirty

# LIAM

The cobbled streets all looked the damn same. I stumbled down alleys and around corners searching for a place to hide from the storm. The village was a fucking ghost town. Not another living soul in sight.

I ducked inside a stone church. The arched red door groaned on rusted hinges as I shoved it open with my shoulder and stepped into the darkness.

The place smelled like an old campfire. Something snapped under my foot, like a dry twig, as my eyes adjusted to the dim light. Not a twig. Bones.

I found them. The entire damn town, buried under a pile of ash.

A shudder ran down my spine. Renae's body was here somewhere, beneath the charred remains.

The scene she'd shown me of her last day played through my head over and over. Women and children screaming. I staggered back through the door and bolted from the church. From the hell that she'd endured.

Fuck the Corps and their bureaucratic bullshit. Anyone willing to hide in the shadows while innocent people were slaughtered needed to be held accountable. My pulse thudded in my ears as my feet pounded against the ground.

Static crackled over my skin as my fury ballooned around me in a ball of electricity. I wanted to punch the sun. Let shit go supernova and wipe the scar of what happened here from my memory.

The ball of energy exploded, sending lightning out in every direction, shaking the ground and the surrounding buildings until they crumbled. My hands went white hot as I dropped to my knees and dug my fingertips into the pavement, crushing it in my fists until it turned to sand.

A tonsil-busting scream escaped my throat, and the heat radiating from my palms cooled, rendering the grit in my clenched fists into rough lumps of glass.

Stillness swept over me as I exhaled. It was just a dream. I forced my mind to conjure a different place, somewhere serene where I wouldn't accidentally unleash a storm on the outside world as I slept.

I focused on the sound of waves crashing, the heat of the sun on my skin, and the briny scent of the ocean. When I opened my eyes, I was staring out at a white sand beach. One identical blue swell after another rolled in with unnatural consistency, like a screen saver on a repeat loop.

I scanned the beach for Cyrena, wondering what shape she'd take for our next lucid dream training session. There was no sign of my personal dream demon. My bungalow, however, was tucked in the shade at the edge of a stand of tall palm trees.

My stomach rumbled as I hauled my ass off the ground and headed for the house. The fridge was stocked with Renae's blue containers stacked neatly next to a case of beer. My old favorite IPA, golden, light on the hops with a malty caramel finish. I could almost taste it.

I pulled out the six-pack, cracked them all open and dumped them down the fucking drain. The temptation to guzzle an imaginary beer left an anxious knot in my gut. The worst part of dream drinking was waking up with the urge to do it for real.

Even in my dreams, one drink was too many and still never enough. One was a tease. It was as if my subconscious was intentionally toying with me. Hungry? A fridge full of food appeared. Thirsty? A case of beer materialized.

I roamed through the house, wondering what surprise I'd find next. Cyrena in another Monika skin suit? Renae's body trapped in another damn coffin? My bike was MIA, but my father's red tool chest sat on the back porch. My heart raced. I hadn't seen that damn thing in over a decade. It was as shiny and unblemished as the day my stepmother gifted it to him. An attempt to get him to take up home repair projects instead of day drinking at the LA country club every day after he retired.

My stepmother never grasped his disdain for broken things. He had rolled the red tool chest into the garage and never touched the damn thing again. I kept my stash tucked under the rubber liner in the third drawer. Part of me got off on the thrill of watching him walk past it every day without a clue. Part of me hoped someday he'd actually care enough to stop and look.

My skin itched with anticipation as I opened the narrow drawer and lifted the false bottom. Fuck my fickle brain. A box of syringes, a tarnished spoon, and a baggie of white powder stared back at me.

"Fuck, fuck, fuck!" I tore at my hair.

I paced the deck and forced my racing heart back into a steady rhythm. "This shit isn't real." It sure the hell looked real. I reached out and picked up the baggie, testing the weight. Enough to get me through a day, two maybe. I pumped the brakes on that line of thinking, walked to the bathroom, and flushed the heroine to hell.

Back on the porch, I shoved the tool cabinet off the deck. The metal whined and clattered as it thumped down the steps and landed on its face in the sand. The sun sank into the ocean as I dug a deep hole and buried the chest with my bare hands.

I crawled into bed, coated in a layer of sweat and sand, and waited for the sun to wake me from the god-awful nightmare.

The next day, I woke with a wicked headache and a dry mouth. I stumbled into the bathroom, thankful that my ghostly entourage had the courtesy to remain hidden while I took my morning shit.

My truck could handle the snow, and I planned to haul ass up to the summit as soon as they opened the access road. I needed to see Renae.

We still had to have a conversation about my thesis and how the hell I was supposed to move forward. My hypothesis was correct; the Eridanus Supervoid was an umbilical connection to another universe. But the all-knowing Oz organization Renae and my mother worked for would never allow the truth to trickle down to mere mortals. Still, the idea of faking data and publishing a lie sat like rancid meat in my gut.

I threw back three extra-strength naproxen and went to the fridge for a Red Bull to chase it down. Another six pack of the IPA sat there, next to Renae's blue containers. Not this shit again. Glass rattled as I slammed the fridge shut and walked outside. To my own private beach and the wall of water that rose like a prison wall just offshore.

Still dreaming.

Every surfboard I'd ever owned was propped against the wooden siding. I pulled off my shirt, grabbed the closest board, and walked toward the ocean, hoping a good coral scrub would drag me out of this damn nightmare.

I paddled out to the reef. When the first swell rose beneath me, I intentionally bailed and let it drive me into the sharp coral. A spike of excruciating pain shot through my shoulder and neck as my collarbone snapped, and I sucked in a lungful of saltwater.

I woke up in my bed, gasping for air in the dark.

My shoulder ached as I ran my hands over my body. No broken bones. I had on a pair of loose joggers instead of board shorts. *Finally.*

I flicked the light switch next to my bed. No power. A knot formed in my gut. I ransacked the house looking for my phone. I needed to check the weather. To see how much damage I'd caused in my sleep. Where was my fucking phone? Had I left it in the truck? I went outside.

A shiny red tool cabinet sat in the middle of the deck.

"Fuck!" A bolt of lightning split the sky and struck the metal box, knocking it fifty feet back into the trees, where it melted into a gnarled and glowing heap. Static crackled around my wrists. It licked up my forearms as I ran toward the surf. I flicked my arms, trying to shake off the charge. White-hot electricity slammed into the ground left and right, liquifying the sand to molten glass.

I fell to my knees and plunged my burning hands into the surf. The saltwater boiled and popped as steam rose around me. Where the hell was Cyrena? Why couldn't I wake up from this fucking dream? Was this some kind of test?

The last thing I remembered was making love to Renae, wishing I could give her more. More than just my heart and my body. I wanted to reciprocate the bond. I'd been willing to give up everything, my life, my job, my fucking PhD—even Connor—to make it happen. Was this my price?

I wasn't dreaming, and I sure as hell wasn't in the afterlife. There was no crimson field or golden gnats swarming around me. I was in some kind of hell—one tailored to my worst fears. One where Renae didn't exist.

I walked to the house and used a knife to carve three lines into the top of my kitchen table. One for each day I'd been there. Three marks became seven, then thirty. I eventually covered the entire table and moved on to the walls. As the weeks turned into months I became increasingly desperate for a way out.

I devoted my days to testing the boundaries of the prison I was trapped in. Every time I tried to cross the island to the other side, I ended up right where I started. I tried paddling out past the churning wall of water, only to be pounded by one crushing wave after another. It was like the island didn't want me to leave.

Foul moods and violent storms became my constant companions. I embraced them. Taught myself how to control wind and rain and lightning until I could target marks with accuracy. I leveled trees and melted the red tool cabinet every day. No matter how many times I destroyed the chest or flushed the baggie of heroin down the drain, the island brought them back.

After three years, seven months, and twenty-eight days, I stopped carving lines and accepted the only form of escape the island offered.

# CHAPTER THIRTY-ONE
# RENAE

PALE WASN'T A STRONG enough word to describe my new shade. My auburn hair had gone stark white, my skin ghostly, and my pointed nails were translucent. Nymphites took flight, expelling a cloud of iridescent gold excrement as I sat up and squeezed the alcohol solution from my braid. More of the symbiotic micro insects took their place, replicating my appearance at the moment of death.

*Great.* I flicked my ghostly hands, sending more nymphite dust into the air that now shimmered around me in the half light of Almega's perennial sunset. Never day and never night.

The body assembled by the insects didn't take as long to get used to this time. There were others in the field. Some sitting; some standing. Some stumbling toward the oil-black city in the distance. There would be no one there to celebrate my return. Deserters didn't get welcome-home parties. They were taken into custody upon arrival. The Corps would either send an isolator to escort me directly to the Nūkiri or a reaper to eliminate me before I made it past the gates. I needed to find my own way to the Eye, the monstrous monolith at the center of Almega.

The dark outer walls of the lower city held seven sets of black gates. Harvest fields stretched out in every direction, surrounding the ancient dwelling place of the long-dead gods and giving it the appearance of a dark fortress floating on a sea of blood. The clamor that arose from behind the walls was part euphoric celebration, part bustling market. Each new arrival brought a wealth of energy with them into the afterlife. Energy that could keep a soul alive for centuries if it wasn't spent on useless distractions.

I scanned for an alternate entrance as I moved quickly through the chest-high crimson grass, avoiding the attention of the reapers who patrolled the harvest and herded new arrivals toward the gates and throngs of hungry souls waiting to greet them. I slipped into one of the carefully disguised service tunnels that led away from the fields.

Darkness swallowed me as I followed the gentle curve of the outer wall. The nymphites that made up the cells of my new corporeal form buzzed as a child's effervescent laughter floated toward me. "Welcome home, Renae."

Emotions were muted in Almega without the physical feedback of the human body. Still, if I'd had any tears to shed, they may have streamed down my face at the sight of my little sister.

Like every other soul in Almega, Lucy still wore the face of her most recent death. She looked just as I remembered, cherub cheeks and cropped brown hair held back by a wide blue satin band. The ribbon I'd used to smother her. I would have recognized her energy signature even without the familiar face.

"Why are you sneaking through the reaper tunnels?" she asked in French. She'd lived dozens of lives before we were sisters, and I knew better than to take her appearance for granted. As an isolator, her gift allowed her to place a psychic hold over me. To protect. To capture.

Time moved at a different rate in the afterlife. A single day on Earth passed in the blink of an eye. What had been three years of training for me on Earth had been a matter of weeks for my family. Not long enough for me to be missed. Lucy's presence at the exact moment of my arrival wasn't a coincidence.

"Looking for you, little bug," I teased warily, keeping my syphons coiled. Without the sensation of taste, I wasn't able to glean her emotions or intent. When I'd left, Lucy had just taken a position with the Sacred Guard—the personal security force of the Nūkiri.

She propped her hands on her hips, inspecting my assembled form. "I told them you wouldn't come through the arena. Too many souls crammed into one place."

"Can we get this over with?" I didn't have time for pleasantries. "Take me to the Nūkiri."

She led me through the harvest district's open-air market, where energy was exchanged as currency and entrepreneurial souls hocked their services. Forecasters took up space on every corner, shaping small lumps of metal into intricate moving objects; birds with matriculated wings, mechanical cats that purred, and dogs with wagging tails. They sold comfort items to the newly deceased, taking energy as payment.

The crowded streets were home to the fading forms of nearly depleted souls begging for scraps of energy to keep them from flickering out. I let my fingers trail across their upturned palms as we passed, coating their hands with enough static to get them through the day.

"Please don't encourage them," Lucy said. "They'll just spend it in the undercity and come back tomorrow begging for more."

"And I would gladly give it." The distractions of the undercity were the only things that made the afterlife bearable for some souls. I'd spent more then my fair share of time there before joining the Corps.

Lucy glanced up at me with a conspiratorial grin. "You must have done something very naughty, considering the bounty on your head."

"I killed a man, brought him back to life—twice—gave him my Gi'dari, helped a pair of deceptors hide the fact that he's Anzillu, lied to my handler, and deserted my position with the Corps."

Lucy stopped abruptly, and pulled me into a narrow alley between the buttressed limbs of two buildings. The intricately carved arches, like everything else in Almega, had been shaped by forecasters wielding lightning to melt and reform the massive metallic trees that covered the planet. The entire city had been honed from a stand of them. Deep red leaves sprouted from the black walls and roofs, covering everything in blood ivy. A living city for the dead.

"The Anzillu are extinct," Lucy said in a hushed tone.

"I don't have time to explain. Please, Lucy, just take me to the Nūkiri."

Her net tightened around me, bending me down to her level so she could read me. Her control was complete. I couldn't stop her from probing my memory. When she finished, she kissed my forehead, a kiss I couldn't feel, and whispered, "I'm so sorry."

"Will they agree to send me into the Void?"

Her round face pinched. "They may agree to send you, but even if it were possible to return, they would never allow it. Especially now. There are already too many threats to their power."

"What kind of threats?" The Nūkiri's control had been absolute since the All Souls War. What had changed in the short time I'd been gone?

"Come, we should not keep them waiting."

The shops and buildings along the sides of each street grew as we got farther away from the fields. Forecaster firms advertised the ability to erect buildings in a single day. Healer corporations promised to grow and deliver a stand of trees for any size job. Grand theaters and concert halls run by troupes of famous deceptors glittered in the fading light.

There were other services to be found as well, if one dared to descend into the catacombs of the undercity. Private projection clubs that specialized in the phantom physical pleasures—taste, smell, touch. Isolators selling psychic influence and protection against it. Reapers who could eliminate unwanted memories or unwanted enemies. All for a price.

As we ascended to the upper city, the architecture and energy changed from fevered commerce to hushed reverence. While the lower part of Almega was shaped from the dark metallic tree trunks, all iridescent blues and blacks, the upper city had been formed from the sacred roots in pearlescent pinks and white. The Eye a dark pupil at its center. A monolith atop a massive ziggurat and the operational headquarters for the Corps.

Palatial dwellings that rivaled the palaces and pyramids of kings perched along the rise that led to the Eye. Each estate was home to an ancient soul group. Lineages of power that could trace their history back to the origins of human sentience.

Lucy shook her head at the crackle of idle energy that permeated the very air. We climbed polished steps for what seemed like hours before we got to the base of the spire. Another staircase spiraled up the center of the Eye—the steps so smooth I could see my ghost-white reflection in the mirror-polished surface.

Lucy nudged me forward with her gift. The interior walls of the spire were carved with murals representing the entirety of human history. I stopped a third of the way into our ascent and ran my hand over a depiction of the All Souls War and detailed faces of thousands of Anzillu children, many who looked as young as Lucy. Their hollowed-out eyes followed me as we continued our climb.

An unadorned door greeted us at the top and opened on invisible hinges, allowing us entry into an antechamber where we waited with dozens of other souls for an audience with the Nūkiri. Cyrena was not among them. I refused to let her absence destabilize my already wavering confidence.

We may have waited minutes or hours. It may have well been an eternity. The transition had warped my sense of time. When they called me to testify, Lucy led me into the witness chamber.

"Keep your head down. Do not look at them and do not speak unless invited to do so." Lucy released her isolation net and stepped back into the antechamber.

"You're not coming with me?"

The doors slammed between us before she could respond.

I kept my gaze on the four pointed star etched into the polished metal beneath my feet. Forms shifted above me, casting monstrous shadows across the floor. I didn't dare lift my eyes. Terrified of what I might find.

The center of the star on the floor ratcheted open. Three sets of translucent glass hands holding a white-hot ball of light rose from the hole as the Nūkiri spoke as one.

"Place your hands on the eye, child of Almega."

I squinted and reached toward the light. Electricity wrapped around my wrists and pulled my palms flat against the surface. The Nūkiri's collective conscious immediately took control of my mind as they drained me. Within a matter of seconds, they'd absorbed every bit of residual energy I'd carried with me when I crossed over. They knew what it was that I asked of them. When they released me, the glowing eye retracted, and I collapsed on the floor.

"Denied." Their unanimous decision echoed off the walls as the doors opened behind me.

"What?" I released my syphons and glared up at the gallery. At the three ancient souls who controlled the worlds of the living and the dead and the future of humanity from their glowing alabaster thrones.

Words froze on my lips as I stared, mouth agape at their elongated faces and wide-set yellow eyes with slitted pupils. Their lips curled back as they hissed, revealing razor-sharp teeth. Holy gods. Whatever the Nūkiri were, it wasn't human.

Lucy's net clamped down around me, and my chin snapped to my chest. "Do not say another word. Let us go before they decide to suck what little energy remains from your soul."

"No." I lashed against her psychic net. "They have to send me in to the Void. I *have* to find him. Lucy, let me go. I need to make them understand."

"You are the one who doesn't understand. Their decision is final, Renae. Be thankful they didn't strip your memories or your gift. Very few have laid eyes on the Nūkiri and left with their souls intact. You dishonor them by questioning their judgment."

My sister grabbed my forearm and tore me away from the room and away from my last hope of ever seeing Liam again.

"Lucy stop. I *need* to get into the Void. You have to take me back." I knew it was impossible, but I couldn't walk away willingly, not while I still had the strength to fight.

"Hush!" My sister snapped her fingers and tightened her control, cutting off my ability to speak or look anywhere other than my pale feet as we descended the polished steps.

She didn't release her hold over me until we were in the courtyard of our family compound along the western edge of the lower city. Red-leafed vines grew out of the walls and hung over the garden walls.

"Maman will want to see you. I should go let her know you're here."

"I don't want to see her. I don't want to see anyone. Not yet." I sat on the ledge of a small reflecting pool and let my hand drag through the bubbling silver liquid. Whether it was cool or warm, I couldn't tell.

Lucy sat next to me, her eyes focused on the swirling ripples created by my fingers. "How long do you plan to stay?"

"That is an excellent question." Green silk floated over the ground as Cyrena emerged from the shadows and grimaced at my appearance. "Virginal is not your color, darling. I liked you better crispy."

"Where have you been?"

"In the undercity."

"Every second Liam spends in the Void brings him closer to true death and you chose to spend half the day chasing your pleasure?" The nymphites holding my form together began to shift.

"You wasted precious time going to the Nūkiri. There are other ways to get into the Void." Cyrena turned and smiled sweetly at Lucy. "What kind of access do you have to the Astral's arena?"

Her hair bounced as she shook her head. "No. Even if I were willing to take you to the Astrals, they wouldn't help you without a direct order from the Nūkiri."

"But you *can* get us inside the arena?"

My sister stood, stretching her tiny frame taller as she glared up at Cyrena. "Even if I could get you inside, I wouldn't. The Astrals are guarded by a legion of reapers, and I'm not interested in having my soul sucked out of existence for the privilege of helping my sister commit suicide."

"Lucienne, please. I sacrificed myself for you once, saved you from the pain of being burned alive. I beg you, do this for me. Save me the pain of living an eternity without him."

She closed her eyes, shaking her head. "It will never work. You'd need a small army and a traveler. Good luck finding one and coercing them into committing treason."

"I believe I can help with that." Cyrena opened the courtyard gate.

A cloaked figure stepped through the archway of twisted vines. Deep cracks cut through the oddly familiar form leaving voids where the nymphites couldn't take hold—fault lines that might cleave apart at any moment. A traveler.

The woman pushed her hood back, slowly revealing a head of mousy brown hair and tired gray eyes.

I nearly toppled into the reflecting pool as I stood.

"Hello Renae," Ziggy said. "It's a pleasure to finally meet you face to face."

"I don't understand. How are you here?"

"As a traveler, I can project my consciousness a great distance from my body to any physical location."

"Can you get inside the Void?"

I swayed on my feet as she shook her head. "The Void isn't a physical place. It's an energy field. Travelers are the only souls who can reset the coordinates of an Astral. If you get me close enough to touch one, I can disrupt the field and create a fissure. All you have to do is walk through."

I focused on her cracked face and had no idea how she was holding all the pieces together. "Can you do it without shattering?" I asked. Liam had just found his mother. He'd never forgive me for letting her sacrifice herself for him.

"I'm not as fragile as I look," Ziggy said. "Still, we may only get a split second to send you through. Cyrena will need to create a diversion, and we'll need an isolator."

We all looked at Lucy.

"I can get you in," Lucy said, eyes shifting to mine. "But this makes us even. We should go now, while the deployment arena is dormant."

# CHAPTER THIRTY-TWO

# RENAE

"You said the arena would be dormant," I glared at my sister as we watched thousands of souls stream into the Astrals' arena.

"This may work in our favor," Cyrena said as she moved toward the throng of souls.

"How could this possibly help us?" I asked. "There are hundreds of reapers and isolators on guard and only four of us. We won't be able to fight our way in, or out."

"It's easier to disappear in a crowd," Ziggy said.

Cyrena looked at me. "Tell the brat to extend her net over the rest of us, and I'll make sure the guards only see what they expect to see."

Lucy plastered a sweet smile on her round face. "Call me a brat again and I'll fold your spine in ways it's not meant to bend."

"Such violent words from such an angelic little mouth. How delightful." Cyrena shot me an exasperated look. "The family resemblance is absolutely uncanny."

"Deployments are done in batches to one location at a time. It's easier on the Astral," Lucy said, ignoring Cyrena's snark. "We need to know which nursery they're going to. You'll be asked to confirm your destination when you enter the temple. The guards know me. Wait here while I find out." Lucy's short hair bobbed behind her as she skipped up the incline toward a group of reapers. She said something to them, and they laughed, but they didn't look in our direction. Lucy curtsied and trotted back to our group.

"They're headed to the Moscow nursery."

Ziggy's mouth pressed into a thin line the same way it did every time I'd attempted to sell her a half truth during our sessions. I glanced back at the guards. Two of the reapers Lucy had spoken to watched over the throng of souls with casual disinterest. The other two were moving with purpose toward the south gate.

"They said we should enter through the south gate," Lucy added.

I grabbed her arm and tugged her toward the north wall. "They lied." Lucy spent her days fetching souls for the Nūkiri, but she'd never been in the Corps, never seen any of the nurseries. "There's no way a single facility can handle an influx of this many souls at once." There had only been two hundred of us in my deployment to the New York compound. It was the largest training facility in the Corps. "Tell them you're going to New York."

Lucy scowled but didn't argue. "If anything happens," she whispered, "stay close to me. My net has a short range."

We shuffled forward with the crowd.

The guard smirked, looking down at Lucy as she stepped up to the gate, the rest of us invisible behind Cyrena's projection. "Destination and designation," he asked.

Lucy squared her shoulders. "New York. Isolator."

"Dais 187."

Lucy's net cinched around us as the guard waved her through the gate. We followed behind onto the mezzanine. The rounded interior dome and balcony levels were held up by sinuous columns that retained the branch-like appearance of the massive tree the building had been honed from. Black vines covered in blood-red leaves twisted around every archway.

The temple floor held rows of raised pyramid-like platforms. An undulating bioluminescent sphere large enough for a horse to walk through without ducking its head hovered above each dais. Light pulsed through the gelatinous globes as soul after soul stepped through and disappeared.

There was an urgency in the deployment. The ritual preparations had been suspended, and the lines moved at an unnerving pace. My gaze floated over the arena. Six guards, three reapers, and three isolators circled the base of each Astral platform. Dozens more roamed the floor and mezzanine.

"We need to approach carefully," Ziggy said. "I've never seen this much security for a single deployment."

Our turn came quickly. Lucy's protective energy spread over me as I climbed the dais behind Ziggy. Shouts drew my attention to the south gate above us. The missing guards Lucy had spoken to were pointing in our direction.

I glared at my sister. "What have you done?"

"Entering the Void is a suicide mission, Renae."

"It's my choice," I said.

Lucy dropped her protective net. "One I cannot honor."

Cyrena's thin lips curled back in a feral snarl as she stepped toward my sister. "Conniving little brat."

"You need to go now, Renae." Ziggy thrust her hands into the Astral's rippling form. A storm flashed across its surface as the Astral fought the psychic intrusion. "I won't be able to hold the position for long."

Cyrena and my sister turned to face the reapers bolting up the steep steps. "Go, you gluttonous cow. I've got your back."

Guards on the mezzanine shouted to others on the floor, and the arena erupted in chaos. I didn't want to contemplate what might happen once I was gone. The three of them could take care of themselves—at least, that's what I told myself. I couldn't allow any room for their fates in my conscience where it might eat away at my resolve. Finding Liam was the only thing that mattered.

"Hurry up," Ziggy said. "I'm losing the connection." Electricity arced from Ziggy's body and clamped on to the orb.

A violent gust of wind swept me from the dais. I landed on the steps and swiveled in the direction it had come from. A forecaster ran toward us. The lightning wreathing his wrists shot out and pierced Cyrena's chest.

She dropped to her knees, and I unleashed my ravenous gift. The forecaster stopped in his tracks as my syphons struck. His body floated apart, hissing bugs taking flight and expelling gold dust as I consumed his soul without a second thought.

I helped Cyrena to her feet as her colony of nymphites closed the gaping hole in her chest. "Are you all right?"

"Glorious." The corner of her mouth twitched up, the closest she'd ever gotten to a smile. "Violence looks good on you, reaper."

"Don't test me, deceptor. I just obliterated a man's soul to save you."

"Does that mean we're friends now, darling?"

"Renae, you need to go through before I lose the connection," Ziggy yelled from the dais. "And before your sister loses her hold on the guards."

Lucy stood at the top of the platform, arms flung wide. I followed her gaze to the steps below me and the faces of six frozen guards.

"Are you with us or against us, brat?" Cyrena asked.

"I'm only here to protect Renae."

The crowd scattered as a legion of reapers and forecasters rushed toward us from every corner of the arena. Lightning shot past the dais, striking the one behind us, thanks to Cyrena's altered projection of our position. Arches and columns melted as hastily thrown attacks landed around us.

The Astral convulsed as I approached. "What's wrong with it?" I asked.

Ziggy glanced at the motionless guards below. "One of the guards froze the Astral and its coordinates before Lucy's net snapped into place."

"What does that mean?"

"It means you need to get ready to jump."

My ears rung as the air split and Ziggy sent a bolt of lightning into the orb, cracking the surface. A torrent of black fluid sprayed from the fissure, showering me in a thick oily substance.

"*Now!*" Ziggy screamed as she tackled my sister off the dais.

A protective dome snapped into place above me, trapping me alone with the Astral. The orb cleaved apart and fluid exploded toward me, slamming me against the boundary of Lucy's net before sucking me into the Void.

# CHAPTER THIRTY-THREE

# LIAM

SOBRIETY WAS A DAILY fucking battle between my will and the island that wasn't really an island. Most days, the island won.

I still had no idea where I was—hell, purgatory, a prisoner in my own mind.

All I knew for sure was that I was alone. I hadn't seen or spoken to a single living thing in the decade that thinned my hair and leeched the color from my beard. On the hard days, the ones that had me convincing myself that giving in to the itch couldn't possibly make the situation worse, I stayed away from the house and that damn red cabinet. On the harder days, I gave in and let the island have its way with me.

I hadn't been in the house in over a month. My longest stint without using, but the itch was strong. I melted sand into molten glass, and erected thick walls between myself and temptation before focusing on my latest project. A life-sized sculpture of Renae. The details blurred over the years and it got harder and harder to recall the exact shape of her face.

The old ache tugged at my chest as I finished melting and reforming the slope of her nose. I still needed to brace the six syphons so they wouldn't break away from her back under their own weight again.

I rubbed at my sternum as the pull at my chest grew, a cruel phantom ache I hadn't felt in a long time. Just when I thought the island had given up finding new ways to torture me, it had to remind me of what I'd lost. The one temptation it knew I couldn't resist. Lightning forked from the darkening sky, shattering wall after wall of glass as I let the sensation tug me down the beach toward relief.

Toward Renae.

Fuck, I could feel Renae. I scooped up a handful of sand in my fist and ran like hell toward that feeling. The grains melted and reformed into a sharp blade that sliced through my palm. My vision shifted, and I stumbled to a stop. A comet barreled straight for the beach, leaving a fiery trail of energy in its wake.

It was either a goddamned miracle or the island had finally decided to take me out dinosaur style. The latter, if I had to guess. I knew better than to trust anything this place offered up freely. Especially when it was the one thing I wanted, had longed for, day in and day out for ten years. I backed up as if a few extra steps would save me from the impact.

The shock wave blew me back onto my ass. Sand and globs of some kind of black fluid rained down on top of me. I deflected the larger chunks with a brisk wind as I scrambled to my feet and peered into the crater.

Renae lay at the center of the pit, curled in the fetal position and covered in oil. I slid down the side, sending a landslide of sand over her. Hallucination or not, I needed to see her face, hear her voice, feel the warmth of her skin.

I dug her out and pulled her into my arms as I pleaded with the island. *Please let her be real.*

Renae stirred in my arms as I climbed out of the pit.

"Liam?"

"I've got you, chica."

Her eyes fluttered open, and she gave me a half smile. "I found you. Even without the bond, I found you." A tear carved a path down her sand encrusted cheek. "Promise me you won't ever leave me like that again."

I tightened my grip around her body. There was no fucking way I'd let anyone or anything separate me from this woman ever again. "I promise." The words came out like gravel, my voice strained from lack of use.

Renae's head lolled against my chest. "You taste like home," she whispered, her breath cascading across my bare skin as her syphons coiled around me, stirring a need a decade in the making. "I love you, Liam. I'm sorry I didn't tell you before."

She shuddered a breath and went limp in my arms.

# Chapter Thirty-Four

# RENAE

Sawdust filled my mouth as I stretched beneath sheets that smelled of salt and cedar. The same scent that had accompanied the soothing voice and warm gods-blessed body I'd felt pressed to my back as I'd tried and failed to crawl out of the involuntary hibernation.

*Liam.* My heart thudded in my chest as I bolted upright. I was in his bungalow. In Hawaii.

This was wrong. This was all wrong. I needed to find Liam. Blankets tangled around my feet as I lurched from the bed and collapsed.

An arm circled around my waist and held me upright. "Slow down, chica. You've been asleep for two weeks. You nearly killed yourself trying to crash my personal purgatory."

I leaned back against him. "Gods, please tell me this isn't a dream, that I'm really here," I whispered.

"In the flesh."

I twisted in his arms and caught my breath. The lines around his denim eyes had deepened. His curls were equal parts silver and gold, and the scruff on his face was pure white. My knees buckled. "How long have you been in here?"

He scooped me up and sat on the bed with me in his lap. "I stopped counting for a while." Liam nodded to a wall covered in hash marks. "Best guess, close to ten years."

I reached up and traced the scar on his forehead. "I'm so sorry. I got here as soon as I could."

Liam caressed one of my syphons with the back of his hand as I wrapped them around him. The sensation set off a spiral of heat inside me. He groaned as my gift licked his hand and coiled up his arm to his chest, where it burrowed into his core. My mouth exploded with the sweet milky fire that was his essence. He closed his eyes and held me there as I tasted the veins of power thrumming inside him. Three fully evolved gifts. There were others there too, still dormant. How much power would it take to get us out of here? To get back to our lives, our families, the souls who'd sacrificed everything to send me here. To give us this.

"This place is a living hell, Renae. You shouldn't have come." He rested his forehead against my shoulder with a sigh. "You should have left me in that coma and gone on with your life instead of sacrificing yourself to the Void."

"How do you know about the coma?"

"I haven't been able to breathe since you got here for fear that you'll disappear. I read your mind while you slept. I needed to know if it was you, if you were real or just another hallucination sent to taunt me." He tightened his arms around me.

"You read me... while I was asleep?"

"I get that I crossed a line, I just—"

"Stop." I cupped his face in my hands. "You are my heart and my soul. I ripped a hole in hell to find you, so don't you dare tell me I shouldn't be here. You are my home, Liam. I love you, and wherever you are is where I belong. Promise me you'll never force me away from you again."

"I promise." The salt of his tears graced my tongue as our lips met and the hollow sensation in my chest filled.

❧

"You still hungry?" Liam asked as I eyed the pile of empty plastic containers on the glass table. He'd insisted on eating outside. Said the house did strange things, and he couldn't stand being in it any more than necessary. The man practically lived outdoors if the deep tone of his skin and the assortment of glass furniture were any indication—tables, chairs, a weight bench, something that looked like it might be a bed.

Liam had done his best to clean me up while I was unconscious, but I was in desperate need of a shower. "Does the bathroom work?" I asked.

"Another reason the house freaks me out. None of it should work, but it does."

After scrubbing the oily residue from my hair, skin, and under my nails, I put on the T-shirt and sweats Liam left out for me. Gods, it felt good to be clean. Hot water, a private beach, an endless supply of food—being stuck here for an eternity with Liam didn't seem all that bad. But we didn't have an eternity. The Void had aged him. It would eventually suck the life from us both.

The sun had set by the time I dragged myself out of the bathroom. Liam was waiting for me on the deck. Static caged within glowing glass balls lit a path into the rain forest behind his house.

"What's this?" I asked.

He shrugged. "I thought we could sleep outside tonight." He reached for my hand, and I felt his power pulse through me as our fingers intertwined.

The path ended in a fern grotto. More shimmering balls hung among the trees and vines and lush, feathery foliage. A glass bed sat at the center of the clearing. He'd somehow managed to encase an electrical storm inside it. Blue and purple lightning forked beneath the surface, illuminating dark clouds. He'd even brought out pillows and blankets from the house.

"You did all this while I was in the shower?"

The corners of his mouth quirked up in that lazy, confident grin that made my insides go molten. "You were in there a while."

"It's incredible."

"I have something else for you." Liam pulled something from his pocket and sank down on one knee.

*Oh gods.*

"I can't give you much, but I can give you this." He took my hand and placed a folded yellow square in my palm.

My vision went watery. "How do you still have this?"

"Just read it." He watched me with intense focus as I unfolded the sticky note.

*My heart, body, and soul are yours to command. I give you my Gi'dari.*

My chest cleaved as I dropped to my knees in front of him. His gift had finally chosen to reciprocate the bond. I'd felt it latch onto me and pull me toward him the moment I entered the Void.

"I love you," he said. White hot tendrils of light curled around us as he traced my bottom lip with his thumb.

My hands wove through his velvet curls, and I let my syphons unfurl as I kissed him. Static crackled over our skin and in the air. Sweet milky heat poured into me. His energy warmed my chest and continued to curl lower until it settled into a throbbing ache and an overwhelming *need* to claim him.

Another flavor bloomed on my tongue, something rich and smokey that licked its way through Liam. The taste of our energies fused in a mutual, irrevocable bond.

I nipped at his lip with my teeth as my nails dug into his back. "You're mine," I said.

"Make your demands, chica."

My eyes slid to the beautiful bed he'd made for us. "I want you to make love to me on a storm beneath the stars."

Our clothes found their way to the ground, and I wrapped my legs around him as he carried me to the glass altar.

We'd figure out what came next tomorrow. Right now, we deserved this. To give ourselves over to one another completely. Gods knew we might not get another chance. No matter what happened, no matter what fresh hell fate threw at us. We had this. We had each other. And it was more than enough.

# READ MORE

J. Ember Hintz writes fantasy and paranormal romance because the real world has too many monsters and not enough magic. Follow her author life shenanigans by joining her No Damsels Newsletter and receive exclusive bonus content, ARC and Street Team invitations, and MORE!

For more stories about women fighting for agency in a dark world and the morally gray men who burn for them, check out her other works.

### Dark Eden Series
Garden of Echoes and Ash
Scars of Seduction and Sacrifice

### Masquerade of Bones Series
Last of Her Kind  (Series Prequel May 2025)
Masquerade of Bones
Book Two (Spring 2026)
Dagmara and Gideon's Story (Holiday Novella Fall 2026)
Book Three (Spring 2027)

9 781958 602959